UNTIL I DIE AGAIN

TINA WAINSCOTT

UNTIL I DIE AGAIN

*Golden Heart Award Winner from Romance
Writers of America*

CHAPTER 1

Seventy-five miles per hour. Chris Copestakes shifted her eyes from the speedometer to the narrow portion of her face in the rear-view mirror. Worried brown eyes stared back. She watched the road ahead, her fingers gripping the worn steering wheel tighter than necessary. Her gaze shifted to the map scrawled on the scrap of paper. She shouldn't be meeting her boyfriend, Alan, at some strange address. Instead, she should be going straight to the police. Couldn't the flat tire have been an omen against going? Shifting on the cracked vinyl seat, she found it hard to get comfortable—her uneasiness of mind manifesting itself in the physical.

Would her life with Alan become shattered pieces of a sinister lie? She already knew the answer. There was no denying what she had just discovered. Alan—handsome, charming, and full of secrets. He was her one voyage into murky waters, and now she was drowning. He had begged for the chance to prove his innocence. What kind of proof would he have? Could there be some plausible explanation for it all?

The change in the sound of the tires brought her

back to present. Not another flat tire, she hoped. She swallowed hard, her fingers gripping the wheel. No, the Crystal Bridge. That irrational fear of driving over bridges returned full force. She laughed aloud, trying to force the building tension away. Hah! A fear of bridges and born and raised in Colorado.

She slowed down and stared straight ahead, careful not to look at the deep pit of rock that dropped hundreds of feet on either side. Her throat was suddenly dry, and her heart beat a little faster.

Rapid movement in the rear-view mirror caught her attention, a black semi zooming up behind her. Too fast, she thought as her stomach clenched. *It's too early for drunk drivers to be out. Just wait ten more seconds, and then you can be on your way. Don't you dare pass me on this bridge!*

In seconds, its huge chrome grill filled the mirror. She jumped at the blast of a horn but didn't go faster. Her gaze kept shifting between the thin strip of road ahead and the truck in the mirror. With a squealing of tires, the rig swerved around her, roaring up beside her car. Her GTO rocked in the heavy current of air as the semi revved its engine and started rumbling past.

Chris's fingers froze on the wheel, holding the car steady. *Damn you, impatient jerk! You'll get us both killed.*

Determined to file a complaint against the driver, she shot a glance at the truck for identification. Two painted elf shoes caught her attention a fractured second before the truck slammed into her sideways.

The resounding thunderclap ripped through the car. *Oh my God, oh my God.* She jerked the wheel to the left. Disbelief turned to panic—the trailer was blocking her. Metal grated against metal. She couldn't swallow or breathe. Grinding breaks. Shattering glass. She smashed through the guard railing. Then a whooshing sound as she dropped down, down. Silence before the scream tore from her, releasing the terror inside. The world turned black as she mercifully fell unconscious an instant before impact.

***

"We're losing her," a controlled voice called out. "Come on, come on!" another voice urged.

Chris looked around at the icy whiteness of the room, at the doctors and nurses rushing frantically to retrieve instruments from various tables. She tried to listen to their quick, efficient dialog over the roaring noise. *What is happening? Where am I?*

No one looked at her or gave the slightest clue that they had heard, too busy doing whatever it was they were doing.

A long steady beep pierced the air, and the orderly chaos halted. With defeated faces, they moved slowly away, and Chris now saw the body below her, a tangled mass of blood and torn flesh, legs twisted into bizarre angles. *No. Not me.*

The person on the table had no recognizable features. The face was so swollen, it barely looked human.

"I was amazed she made it here alive in the first place," a voice softly said.

"She must have had one heck of a will to live," another voice uttered. "Call it."

"Time of death: 4:35."

Panic gripped her as some of the orderlies left the room. *What about me? You can't just leave me here! I'm still alive. Can't you see me?*

No one looked at her, no one heard. She tried to move toward the floor, toward the body on the operating table...and then she screamed, a hollow sound that faded the second it left her throat. That twisted flesh was her! She was dead. The *body* she occupied now was misty, like a cloud. She struggled to move toward her physical body. *I have to get back! I have to talk to Alan. He may have done something horrible, and I have to tell someone. I have to tell my sisters what happened.* She knew no way to accomplish it.

Panic subsided, turning to regret. *I haven't done anything with my life yet. I haven't finished school so I can help rejuvenate the state forests; I haven't really and truly loved a man; I never got married and had a baby. I never told my sisters how much I love them.*

How much time passed, she had no clue. Time didn't exist in this place. Floating just below the white ceiling tiles, she watched a young woman unhooking the IVs, trying not to look at Chris's body as she did so. Chris wasn't afraid to look at her body. Even as she saw her mortal wounds, she felt no pain. *That body is not me; I am here, floating above it. That was a shell, but this, this is my soul.*

A man walked in the room and covered her body with a white sheet. When he opened the doors and wheeled her out, heart-rending sobs poured in from the waiting area. Her mother and sisters. She knew their voices, felt their grief. Getting the hang of moving around in her disembodied state, she moved toward the wall, wondering if she could go through it.

At that moment, a dazzling light filled the room and pulled her gently into its warm embrace. She turned toward the source and found that the light did not blind her. With the light came a sense of overwhelming peace and love. God.

He spoke to her, not in words she could hear but thoughts. *You are not ready to die?*

Her own voice was the same, not spoken, yet heard. *There are things I need to do. Things I want to do. But I will come with you.*

Your willingness is appreciated, child, but it is not your time yet.

Even with the light, she could clearly see the room below. She looked at the space her body had once occupied. *But my body is broken. How will I live in it?*

You will not. You have a new task.

I will do whatever you wish. What is my task?

Find his heart.

Before she could ask what He meant, she fell backward as a blanket of darkness wrapped around her. Gone was the freedom of her spiritual body; she felt blood pumping through her veins again, the rhythm of her heartbeat, and dull pain. Then the deepest, darkest sleep she had ever experienced claimed her.

***

Jamie DiBarto's wife was *not* dying beyond those doors. He paced in the hospital waiting room, glancing every two minutes toward the operating room doors. He refused to believe the paramedics' mutterings about a brain hemorrhage and coma. The feeling that he'd had riding with her in the ambulance...Jamie shook his head.

He wanted to attribute it to the shock and panic of her collapse, the fear that built in him as he watched the blood drain from her face. Yet the feeling still lingered, the feeling, knowledge almost, that she was gone. While he had held her hand in the ambulance, he could feel her soul—her essence—slip from her body. He ignored it, yet afterward the body that lie in front of him seemed empty.

He shook his head again, refusing to believe it. She was alive, her heart was beating, her lungs breathing. By machine, but she was alive, dammit. It seemed like hours since some stone-faced entity told him the doctor would be out soon. He was almost glad that his mother and Hallie's mother wouldn't be arriving for another few hours. He wanted to take the news alone.

"Mr. DiBarto?" a soft male voice asked.

Jamie jumped at the sound of his name. "Yes, that's me. How is she?"

The dark-haired man held out his hand, and Jamie grabbed it as a drowning man might clutch at a rope. The doctor's healthy, California glow looked out of place in a hospital filled with sickness.

"My name is Doctor Barrett Hughes. I'd like to talk to you in private. Please follow me."

In private. Those words made Jamie feel cold all over. It wasn't good news. The doctor gave you good news right there in the waiting area. They gave you bad news in private.

Jamie followed the doctor down another corridor to a closet-sized room with a large window that let sunlight filter in. There was a tiny desk, and chairs for up to five people to receive bad news at the same time. He chose the one farthest from the desk, as if that could put distance between him and the words on the papers Dr. Hughes held so tightly in his hand. Instead of sitting behind the desk, the doctor took the seat next to Jamie.

"I'm afraid the news isn't good. We can't be hopeful about your wife's condition."

Jamie's throat tightened, and he couldn't swallow. He suddenly felt warm, then cold as a chill possessed him.

The doctor continued. "Hallie suffered a massive intracerebral hemorrhage near her brain stem. She had a stroke. Right now, she's in a coma."

The ocean roared in his ears. The room spun around, leaving him disoriented and clutching the arms of his chair. Suddenly he wasn't feeling so brave about taking the news alone.

Jamie found his voice. "It sounds...bad. But she's going to be all right, isn't she?"

Dr. Hughes's dark eyes were blank, his mouth a grim line. "Your wife had one of the most serious kinds of stroke. Of the many patients I have seen with this massive a CVA, that is, cardiovascular accident, most don't live long. It's usually fatal, perhaps within an hour, a day. It's hard to determine."

Jamie stood up, his balance precarious. "There must be something you can do. You're a doctor. All this instrumentation, these gadgets and machinery...there has to be something that will save her."

Dr. Hughes touched Jamie's arm in a silent request for him to sit again. "We have on staff one of the best neurosurgeons in the country. His judgment is that surgery is useless. And possibly dangerous at this point. The worst of the bleeding is already over."

Jamie sat staring into space, feeling cold turn into the heat of despair and anger. He thought of that warmth, soon to be absent from Hallie's body. Finally, he tuned into the present and asked, "She's going to die?"

"Yes."

Jamie's heart turned to stone.

The doctor rested his chin on steepled fingers. "Most people go through a whole range of emotions while the realization process takes hold. Give yourself time to accept each one."

"It sounds so damned clinical."

Dr. Hughes smiled faintly. "I'm sorry if it seems that way. Comes with the territory."

"Can I see her?"

"Of course. And I would suggest you call her family and let them know that there isn't much time."

"Her mother is on the way now. No one has any idea where her father is. That's all the family she has." Jamie's voice sounded flat, as if it came from a cardboard box.

"Follow me to ICU then."

He couldn't believe he was walking down the sterile corridors of the hospital to say what might be his final words to his wife. Their marriage had shattered long ago, but the thought of her dying still ripped him apart.

Dying. Hallie dying.

Hallie lay in a glassed-in room, a fragile creature in a protected environment. Jamie stood alone by the door for a few minutes, sustaining a hope that perhaps this was the wrong woman. As long as he didn't see her face, there was the smallest chance that Dr. Hughes had gotten Hallie mixed up with this dying woman. But soon he was drawn to her side, and the limp hand he held was definitely Hallie's.

His mind tried unsuccessfully to erase the tubes

from her mouth and nose, the IV stuck in her arm. The respirator issued a soft, wheezing sound every time it gave her a life-sustaining puff of air. He couldn't understand the green scribbles on a nearby monitor but was thankful that something was happening.

Life flowed under the serene exterior, but where was her soul? Right there, he told himself, still locked inside her body. He squeezed her hand hard, as if by holding on, he could keep her from slipping away. He envisioned himself in a tug of war with Death. Of course, Death would win. Jamie had to keep reminding himself of that; it hadn't sunk in that she would actually die.

He had heard that people in comas could sometimes hear the sounds around them. So, he would talk to her then and try to pull her back. Starting from the first time he'd ever seen her, he told her how stunning she'd looked in that sparkling blue dress.

Throughout the night, in between the times when her mother spent time alone with her, Jamie went back and forth between forgiving her for the heartbreak she'd caused, and asking her why she had betrayed him. How he wished he would have asked her before. Now he might never know why she wouldn't fully open herself up to him, or give her heart to him.

***

Chris swam up from the depths to consciousness, lured by a man's voice. She didn't have the strength to open her eyes or respond, but slowly her mind began to recognize his words and put them into logical order.

"You actually died last night. You were gone and then you came back to life. That has to mean something. Dammit, it has to mean that you're going to come out of this coma."

I'm here, Alan. Or is it Dad? Then she realized what he had just said. She had died and come back. She had gotten her second chance! Only vaguely did the memory of her twisted body return. She felt no pain, only a spear of panic as she wondered what her life would be like now. It didn't matter, she was alive! She clenched her fists, testing.

"You moved again." He took her hand in his, and his warmth felt good on her chilled skin. "Oh, Hallie," he said, drawing it out into a sigh. "Dr. Hughes keeps reminding me that it's not unusual for people in deep comas to move or twitch. He calls it posturing or something like that. But I can't help wondering if you're trying to tell me you're in there.

"So many times..." He took a deep breath, and his voice sounded more strained when he continued. "So many times in the last two years I wanted to rip that wedding ring off your finger. I couldn't, God help me, I just couldn't do it. Now that it's not there, it seems strange. The hospital sent all your jewelry home with me." He forced a laugh. "You'd be hollering how naked you feel without it."

Wedding ring? Chris groped for memories of her life. Alan. They were dating, but not married. She slowly opened her eyes, focusing in on her surroundings. The machines didn't surprise her; she had expected that. But the man did. His arms were outstretched on the wall opposite her, his head was pressed against the glass. His breath made a circle of fog in front of him.

He was not Alan, nor her father. She could only see him at an angle from the back, but she already knew she had never seen him before. His straight blond hair tapered down the back of his neck. His wrinkled shirt and jeans outlined a lean, muscular body.

When he started to turn around, her eyelids fell shut under the weight of fatigue. Why was he in her room, talking to her like this? She needed more time to figure it out.

It took little effort for Chris to keep perfectly still. He came close and gently rubbed one hand, then the other. When he laid her hand down, she had to quell a desire to reach for him.

"I guess I should tell you that Mick is not on the list of people allowed to visit you. Maybe you'd be mad at me for that. I don't know. As soon as he heard, he came right here. Then he blew up in the lobby when he was refused admittance. Family only. Color me old-fashioned, but I don't think it's right, your lover being in here."

Chris could hear his shoes scrape the floor as he paced next to her bed. Her *lover*, Mick? Now she was sure this man had the wrong room. She wanted to open her eyes and tell him he'd made a terrible mistake, tell him how crazy it was, his thinking she was his wife. But all she could do was listen.

"And I know about your plans to take off with Mick. I found the plane tickets when I grabbed your suitcase after the stroke. Even you couldn't lie your way out of two one-way tickets to France with both your names on them." He laughed softly. "Don't worry, I'm not going to hold that against you now. Hell, I'm even gracious enough to wish you all the happiness in the world."

This is crazy! I've got to tell him he's made a mistake. How can he think I'm his wife? Just when she started drowning in a sea of confusion, she got a reprieve.

17

After a whoosh sound, Chris could hear a vast array of noises from the hallway: a distant conversation, a doctor being paged. A feminine voice said, "Excuse me, Mr. DiBarto. You're going to have to leave for a little while. You can come back in about an hour."

The door quietly closed, leaving the drone of machines to press down on her. After a few minutes, Chris forced her eyes open, looking everywhere around the vacated room. She moved her hand again, and smiled to feel it there. And she smiled just because she could. Then she realized there were tubes in her nose and mouth, and one started to cause a strangling sensation in her throat.

When her hand reached up over her mouth, she jerked her head around, ready to encounter the owner of the graceful fingers with long bright-pink nails. She had never worn nail polish, nor had nails long enough to paint. She stared at the hand that hovered shakily over her face, and moved a finger. One long finger moved. Then another moved at her will.

The hand moved lower, and pulled the tape away before pulling the tube from her throat. The slight gagging sensation was followed by the wonderful feeling of taking a breath on her own. She could breathe! Next came the tubes in her nose. But the hand still looked foreign to her.

Chris tried to remember what had put her there. An accident. Yes, she could hear the distant memory of crunching metal, screams. Her screams. It hurt to think of anything else. She had to get up, to see herself and make sure she was whole. Her arms felt weak, but she pushed herself up a few inches at a time. The room started to spin, and she closed her eyes and held fast.

Finally, it passed, and she tried to still the waves of nausea pulsing through her stomach.

Once she felt stable again, she held her breath and looked down. The blankets had slid down to her waist, and she pushed them to the floor—and stared. Not at herself, not the straight, boyish figure and skinny legs. Something was wrong, terribly wrong! This was not her body!

She moved legs that seemed twice as long as her own, shapely legs with small feet and painted toenails to match those fingers. They moved in unison with her thoughts. Her arms moved at will, and her eyes widened. Her chest was not the barely-a-B she was used to seeing, but much more than that! Beneath her hospital gown, voluptuous breasts rose each time she inhaled. Her hands moved to her head, desperately wanting to feel the kinky curls she had hated all her life. She pulled a handful of long dark-blond hair in front of her face.

Panic twisted her heart, and dazed confusion rushed through her blood. Or was it her blood? Nothing else was hers! No, it had to be a horrible, distorted nightmare.

The picture filled her mind, this time vividly. Her twisted body, the blood, oh, the blood. But there was so much more than that. She remembered floating above her body, feeling detached from it. The clear, bright light telling her that it wasn't her time yet. He'd said something about a new task. She had been given another chance as...Chris's gaze fell to the plastic band on her wrist: *H. DiBarto*. She was in another woman's body!

"Hallie! You're awake."

The man who had been talking to her earlier rushed

to her side, followed by a tall woman in her fifties. Chris looked at them blankly, the reality of her situation crashing in over her.

"Hallie, it's Jamie, your husband. This is your mother. Are you all right?" Then he shook his head, smiling. "You're okay. I knew you'd come back."

Jamie leaned over and hugged her, followed by a crushing hug from the woman who was supposed to be her mother. The woman touched Chris's face, hair and arms, as if to assure herself she was really seeing her daughter and not an apparition.

Chris tried to talk, but nothing came out. Finally, a sound croaked from her throat. "Why am I in here?" She gestured to all the equipment around her.

Her mother leaned forward and gripped her hand. Chris wasn't sure whose hand was shaking, but their clutched hands quivered. "You had a brain hemorrhage, sweetheart."

Chris's weight pulled her back to a prone position. All the while, she kept staring at Jamie, keeping her focus on one person to keep her mind from exploding into a thousand directions.

His face was finely sculptured, and his eyes were the lightest shade of blue she had ever seen. He had one of those regal noses seen in advertisements for cologne and blue jeans. He must have been staring at her with the same disbelief that filled her face. Then he smiled, and the whole room seemed to light up. Maybe she was in Heaven after all, and he was an angel.

The illusion of Heaven was disrupted when a nurse pushed her way in after looking through the large glass window. Everything happened quickly after that. She called the doctor in, ushered Jamie and her *mother* out of the room, and put her through a battery of embarrassing and lengthy tests. All the while, the doctor kept asking her questions.

"What's your name?"

"Hallie..." She stole a glance at her bracelet. "Di-Barto."

"How old are you? Where were you born?"

The questions kept coming, and she didn't know the answers to most of them. At least the answers that belonged to the body she was in. Her own life was clear and the memories vivid up until the day she'd died. She squeezed her eyes shut. *Who am I now?*

"Are you all right?" asked one of the nurses.

Chris shook her head. No, she wasn't all right. She would never be all right again.

***

Jamie, his mother, and Hallie's mother all gathered in the closet-sized room with Dr. Hughes. The bad-news room. He tried to keep telling himself that Hallie was all right now, but another dark thought kept pressing into his mind, spurred on by the memory of that blank look on Hallie's face: brain damage. What would he do if she never recovered mentally?

Dr. Hughes looked at his paperwork, then set it down on the desk with a short sigh. "I have been a doctor for fifteen years, and all I can tell you about Hallie's recovery is that it is a miracle. I have never seen someone in so deep a coma awaken so suddenly. Her movements are purposeful, hand and eye coordination much better than anyone could ever expect."

"She'll be okay?" Hallie's mother asked, nervously fingering the frosted hair piled on top of her head.

"Well, Mrs. Parker..."

"Please," she interrupted, placing a hand on Dr. Hughes's sleeve. "Call me Velvet."

Jamie always cringed at the mention of her mother's name, Velvet. Her real name was Hedda, but she kept the stage name she used when she had been an exotic dancer years ago.

Dr. Hughes leaned back in the brown vinyl chair. "We've run tests, numbers of them. There isn't a trace of the hemorrhage or any damage. Physically, she's perfect."

Jamie pushed out the words, "And mentally?"

Dr. Hughes tilted his head. "That's what we're not too sure about. Both long and short-term memory are impaired. She seems to know little other than her name, and the nurse saw her peek at her name band for that. With the kind of recovery she made, it's going to be hard to predict her progress. In normal cases it could take up to two years for her memory to return, and even then, some of it may never return."

Velvet's face registered shock. "You mean she might always look at me with that nothing look on her face?"

"I'm not saying that at all. But you may have to fill in the blank spaces for her."

Jamie leaned forward. "Will she be the same? I mean, her personality and all?"

"Yes, in time she will become basically the same person she was. She will, of course, be different in some ways. This kind of experience changes a person. She'll probably appreciate life a lot more."

"Hah!" Velvet's deep, harsh laugh seemed to ricochet off the walls. "She already did." When she noticed Jamie's right eye narrow, her smile died.

Dr. Hughes cleared his throat, perhaps in an attempt to clear the air of tension. "I would like to keep her here for a few days, just for observation. Then she's free to go home, although she should stay near the hospital for a few weeks."

A sick feeling churned in Jamie's stomach. "Do you think she'll have another stroke?"

"No, not at all. The last CAT scan we did came out completely clear." He shook his head and looked away for a moment, as if still stunned. "It might be a good idea, though, to keep her nearby in case of complications. This isn't an average case, so it's hard to foresee any problems that might occur."

Jamie turned to his mother, squeezing her hand in question, trying to read those beautiful icy blue eyes of hers for an answer. As usual, they revealed nothing, but the slightest nod of her head confirmed it.

"She'll recuperate at my mother's home in Los Almeda," Jamie announced.

Velvet spoke up. "I don't think that's appropriate, considering the circumstances. She should—"

"She's staying with us. You don't have the time, nor the room, to house her comfortably." She also didn't have the wits, but he wasn't going to get into that. "Besides, she'll be closer to the hospital. When she's up to it, she can do whatever she pleases."

Dr. Hughes stood, holding his clipboard against his chest. "Good. We've moved her to a regular room, 425. You can go in to see her now if you'd like."

***

After hours of being treated like a lab specimen, Chris was escorted to her new room. The end result...

No one had a medical explanation for her miraculous recovery, except that it *was* a miracle, as one doctor had whispered reverently. Oh, how she wanted to tell someone about her experience, about the love and peace, and the light.

As soon as the nurse tucked her into her crisp, cold sheets and left her alone, Chris shoved out of bed and studied herself again. It still wasn't her body. Her hands moved up to her face, touching her cheeks, following the lines of her bones. What did she look like now? She had to find out.

After a wary glance toward the door, she climbed out of bed and walked stiffly to the bathroom. She felt the hesitation of meeting someone new. *Being afraid is silly. It's still you, Chris.*

For the first time, she was able to do more than snatch a vague reflection off the face of some monitor. A deep breath served to inject a few ounces of bravery into her, and she stepped up to the mirror and stared. A stranger stared back. She touched the mirror, just to make sure it wasn't a window into her neighbor's bathroom. A long slender hand moved with her to touch the glass.

Chris moved back, taking in the stranger's reflection. Blond hair hung limply around her face, looking flat and oily. Her nose was petite, her lips shapely, not too large, not too small. Her eyes were a deep blue, set just a little too far apart. And her body...Chris shook her head. Pulling the thin cotton gown tight from the back, her curves showed through. What was she going to do with a body like that?

"What are you doing out of bed?" A concerned male voice rocked her out of her thoughts, and she whirled around. The man was definitely not a nurse, dressed in a red shirt and black jeans. He walked right into the bathroom with her and hugged her fiercely before pulling her back to bed. "Leave it to you, Hallie, to come back from the brink of death and be worried about how you look. Don't you know you're beautiful, no matter what? Come back and lie down, dear."

Chris had been about to object to this stranger's forwardness when his familiarity indicated he was someone else she was supposed to know. *Oh, boy.* She followed him to her bed and let him tuck her back under the sheets. His hair hung in strands around his face, and beneath thick glasses, she saw worry and strain grow into love. He knelt on one knee beside her bed and took her hand in his, planting a long wet kiss on it.

"I would have been here sooner, but that damn husb —" He shook his head. "It doesn't matter. I'm here now, you're here." He squeezed her hand, and his brown eyes grew shiny with tears. "I thought I'd lost you. My heart would have shriveled up like a pea without you."

"To match your brain?" Jamie's flat voice asked from the doorway.

The man stood, still gripping Chris's hand. She wanted to pull free but was too mesmerized by the fire in Jamie's eyes to move.

Jamie stepped forward, power in his strides. "Who let you in here, Mick?"

"You can't restrict her visitors anymore, James. Besides, she needs me." Mick tilted his head up, as if daring Jamie to challenge him.

Jamie's gaze flicked to her, then back to Mick. His slight smile was a bit crooked. "How can she need you if she doesn't know who you are?"

Mick's panicked expression heightened when he looked at her. He leaned closer and stared into her eyes. "You know me, darling, don't you?"

Fatigue was beginning to shroud her, and she wanted nothing more than to close her eyes and not answer any more questions. But she couldn't ignore the earnest face hovering in front of hers. "You...you're Mick, Hall —" She'd started to say *Hallie's lover*, as if talking about someone else's life. It was, in a sense. Jamie's expression bit into her, though, his obvious disappointment in her remembrance of Mick. Actually, she'd only deduced his identity.

Mick grinned triumphantly. "When she's released, I'm taking her home with me."

Jamie's voice returned to the flatness it had earlier, and his eyes narrowed. "As long as I'm her husband, she's my responsibility. At least until she gets better."

Mick's face reddened. "Hallie's a grown woman. She can do what she wants." He turned to her and asked, "Do you want me to take care of you?"

"She can stay with me, too," Hallie's mother added from her place behind Jamie. "Who do you want to stay with, darling?"

Chris looked at the faces around her as they waited for her response. Mick appeared as though his life hung on the balance of her answer. Honestly, he gave her the creeps. Velvet didn't inspire much confidence in her caretaking skills. Jamie looked resolute, despite offering a choice. She looked at each face, not sure where they fit into Hallie's life. Her gaze drew back to Jamie. "I want to stay with you."

Mick dropped her hand and took a step back. Velvet crossed her arms over her large chest and pursed her lips. But Jamie looked the most surprised of all. She left them all and slipped into a haven of darkness.

**

Sometime later, Jamie's voice pulled Chris from sleep again, much like the day she had come out of her coma. This time another male voice spoke with him, in soft, hushed tones. It sounded like Dr. Hughes's voice. "Have you given any thought to our earlier conversation?"

"You mean what to do with her if she's...brain-damaged?"

Chris strained to hear their whispers coming from the far side of the room. She kept perfectly still, holding her breath.

"Right now, all we know for sure is that she's lost a good deal of her memory. Her friends and family can deal with that. But if she experiences lapses in logic and reality, or starts having seizures, it may be too much to handle. Remember, thinking about it won't make it happen. It's better to be prepared."

"I know that." After a pause, Jamie said, "What about the Sharp Rehabilitation Center in Sacramento? You said that was the best in the area."

"Absolutely. They'll work with her, take care of her as long as she needs it. She'd make friends there. And maybe some of their advanced methods would help her to eventually become independent again."

"But we don't know that she has any damage, right?"

"There seems to be no indication yet. But keep an eye out for unusual behavior in the next few weeks. If she..."

Dr. Hughes's voice drifted out into the hallway and

was swallowed in hall noise as the door opened, then closed. Her eyes snapped open. *The Sharp Rehabilitation Center? A mental hospital?* What would they think if she told them that her real name was Chris Copestakes from Colorado, that she had died, and God had given her a second chance in Hallie's body? Would that be considered a lapse in logic? They would surely think she was brain damaged. Or just plain crazy. Then off to the Sharp Rehabilitation Center they would send her, just like her Uncle Tom.

She had vivid memories of Tom, playing tag with her and her sisters in the yard, helping in the kitchen during the holidays. He hadn't acted crazy, but her mom had confided that he was manic depressive. He had an episode that put him in a mental hospital.

Her mother visited him every Saturday afternoon. She told Chris that if she didn't go, he would cry out for his sister at the top of his lungs, pounding on the walls until the orderlies restrained him. Chris went with her mother one time, for support. And curiosity.

The sprawling one-story building had smelled like a hospital, sterile with the faint odor of decay and urine. What struck Chris the hardest was the absence of hope in everyone's eyes. Nurses and doctors looked as much like zombies as the patients did, bringing the gown-clad man who had once been a baseball player into the visitor's room with mechanical efficiency.

The sight of him had horrified her: not the Tom she remembered but a shell of the man, vacant eyes, fits of irritability over nothing. She had stared at his fingers, covered with spots of red flesh where he continually picked at the cuticles. He had chewed his nails to the bloody quick.

It was the medication, her mother had said, trying in vain to get it changed to something better.

Chris shut the memory away, as she had done so many times during her life. She would not go to a mental hospital.

CHAPTER 2

C hris's stay at the hospital was finally behind her; four miles behind her, to be exact. Los Almeda sprawled lazily among the hills and valleys of Southern California. Chris immersed herself in the scenery, trying to absorb the life that pulsed everywhere around her. Everything had a new vibrancy, a new meaning to her. Where did each tree fit into the scheme of life? What of the creatures that depended on that tree to live? There were so many things to think about now, so many different ways of looking at everything around her. She watched the wild shadows dance across Jamie's face as they passed a park with towering eucalyptus trees.

The town looked as if it had been plucked from Mexico and cleaned up for the wealthy, with its picturesque red tile roofs and adobe-style shopping centers. Flowers bloomed everywhere, and palm trees swayed on their ridiculously tall, skinny trunks in the afternoon breezes.

As they headed inland, the town quickly turned rural, and shopping centers turned into country clubs and nurseries. Sprawling homes were perched on hillsides to catch a glimpse of the ocean, and she felt even more out of place from her middle-class, small-town origins.

She had seen little of the cast of characters in her new life during her last three days at the hospital. The Sharp Rehabilitation Center plagued her thoughts. Now she had a chance to prove that her mind was intact, if in the wrong body. Jamie had picked her up at the hospital that morning, but a glimpse of Mick lurking near the lobby had sent an eerie panic pulsing through her. After the scene in her room that day with Jamie and Mick, she was glad Jamie hadn't spotted him. Now she occasionally glanced back to check for suspicious cars.

"Mick's not back there," Jamie said in a matter-of-fact way.

Chris looked at him with widened eyes. "You saw him at the hospital?"

Jamie stared ahead. "Did you?"

"Only in the lobby. He looked like he was hiding."

"He was spying on you. He likes to do that."

She tried to still the shudder that ran through her. "Why?"

His shrug was pronounced, perhaps not as casual as he might have intended. "I never could figure out the guy. Or your attraction to him."

She looked at his profile, at the blond bristles that covered his chin and jaw, the faint darkness beneath his eyes for lack of sleep. Even so, he was far better looking than Mick could ever be.

"You're not angry about...the affair?" She didn't want to claim it as her own by saying *my affair*.

"We all make our choices. Sometimes they're not the right ones, but we have to live with them."

Was he talking about Hallie's choice to cheat or his choice to marry her? The short conversation left tension in the confined space of the car. Chris wasn't sure what else to say. Exactly where these two men fit into her life wasn't clear yet. In fact, where *she* fit into her life wasn't clear.

They drove farther up into hills spotted with brown and green sagebrush in bloom, white stalks reaching for the sky. Red tile roofs dotted the hills to the south, and huge boulders created bald spots on the mountains to the north and east. The wavy, beige strip snaking horizontally along the side of one of the mountains caught her eye. She had heard about the flumes that brought water to cities with none of their own.

Jamie drove between two wrought-iron gates and onto a zigzagging drive. Through the haze, she could see the deep blue of the ocean in the distance. The grounds that stretched out on either side looked like a golf course, with rolling hills, ponds and perfectly manicured grass. The house itself was magnificent, a fortress of the rich. It was set off from the other homes in the distance by its charcoal tile roof. She closed her mouth and tried to hide her awestruck expression.

When they pulled into the circular drive, one of the massive front doors opened, and a tall man with a thin build stepped outside. He was dressed like one of those butlers she'd seen in old movies. She realized that he actually was a butler when he walked over and opened her door before Jamie could get around the car.

"Good to see you feeling better, Mrs. DiBarto," he said in a dull voice, no smile to indicate he felt the least bit glad to see her alive.

Jamie helped her out of the car, and she stood a little

shakily in the sunshine. The butler pulled a couple of suitcases out of the trunk and walked inside. A short blond woman in her early fifties passed him on the way out. She issued some instructions to the butler, then continued walking toward them. The woman's face glowed with a smile as she reached up and bussed Jamie on his cheek.

Chris could see some resemblance between them, and guessed her to be his mother. She looked like the perfect Italian mother, warm and loving. It made her ache for her own parents, still alive and mourning her death. When the woman turned to her, that warmth froze over, and her steel blue eyes were colder than Jamie's when he'd walked in and seen Mick at the hospital.

Jamie turned his mother toward Chris. "Do you remember her?"

To pretend to remember, or to pretend to have amnesia? The more she *remembered*, the more she would appear normal, recovered.

Chris smiled. "Your mother," she guessed in a confident tone. When she saw that she was correct, she asked, "Did I call you *Mom*?"

If someone like Jamie's mother could snort, that is what Chris would have called the sound. "No, you called me Theresa."

"I see."

"You're feeling much better, no? I told my son you could recuperate here for a few weeks. It could be even less time before you're on your way, maybe?"

Chris didn't know how to react. She had never done anything to this woman; the question was, what had Hallie done? "I—I don't know." She turned to Jamie.

He looked at his mother, a silent demand for peace in his eyes. "As long as necessary."

She touched his hand, her small blue eyes issuing a stern warning that Chris didn't understand. Then Theresa waved them inside as she walked toward the open door. Chris glanced at Jamie, but his gaze was aimed straight ahead. She had never felt so lost in her life.

***

Jamie knew that bringing Hallie here was not going to be easy. He wasn't even sure why he had been so adamant about it. Mick would have probably been attentive. He seemed almost obsessed with her. Velvet was her mother, and that had to count for something. Then there were her dozens of friends in San Diego and Los Angeles. Of course, they were too busy partying or being self-involved to care for someone else. So, Mick would have been the obvious choice. He had been anyway.

There was something, though, something about the way she had looked at Jamie in the hospital. And, given the choice, she had chosen to let him take care of her.

They followed Theresa up the winding staircase to the second floor. Solomon had already put the luggage on a bench in the second master bedroom.

"James, we're going to have dinner around six o'clock," Theresa said. "You look exhausted. Why don't you rest before then?"

Jamie smiled. Mothers never stopped mothering. Just the mention of looking exhausted made him yawn. "I probably will."

He found Hallie just standing there, looking at the room as if she'd never seen it before. Usually she darted directly to the bathroom and, amid complaints about the long flight, immersed herself in a bubble bath and long beauty routine. How much memory had she lost?

He looked at the bed, then at the chest of drawers and armoire. "I'm going to sleep in the room on the other side of the balcony, considering..." No need to state the obvious.

She sat down on the bed and looked up at him, seeming more like an innocent girl than the woman he knew so well.

"Considering what?"

He walked closer, leaning against one of the wooden bed posts. "Considering what happened before your collapse."

Uncertainty lingered in her eyes. "What was I doing when I had the hemorrhage?"

"You were asking me for a divorce."

Hallie's face paled. "Oh." Her voice sounded so small. "What did you say?"

His upper lip twitched involuntarily. "I said, '*Absolutely*.' I had my reasons for letting our marriage go just as I once had reasons for holding on."

Jamie studied her reaction. He didn't think she could get much paler, but she did. She seemed to be bracing herself on the bed. "What were the reasons you wanted to hang on?"

"They don't matter now."

She chewed her bottom lip, looking up at him with a wide-eyed expression. "And you said *go*, just like that?"

He pressed his forehead against the post. He didn't want to get into the painful discussion they had that day. Obviously, she didn't remember it. The doctor had warned that people with brain damage usually didn't remember events just prior to the incident.

"We had an argument after I walked in on a phone conversation you were having with Mick. I told you that something had to be done about the farce we called a marriage, and you stormed out. I followed you to get some answers and that's when you asked for a divorce. Then you got one of your awful headaches, only it was worse than usual. You said you couldn't feel your arm and then you collapsed."

Hallie shook her head. "There's a lot I don't remember."

"Do you remember me?"

She nodded, but he sensed a trace of hesitancy. Was it raw alarm he saw in her eyes? He had a sudden desire to sit down beside her and hold her. He tightened his grip on the post, as if to keep a strong wind from blowing him toward her. She was vulnerable now, and the rare state was touching the outer edges of a heart long frozen. It would pass. Soon her memory would return, and with it her old self. By then she would be living in France.

"How do you feel?" he asked, noticing the color slowly returning to her cheeks.

"I couldn't begin to tell you. I don't even know myself."

He nodded. "Rest for a while. I'll come by around dinner time to get you."

When the door clicked shut, he leaned against it. Maybe it had been a mistake to bring her back here. Right now, she was delicate, weak. He had never seen her that way before, and it had the most curious effect on him. But it was his duty, as her husband, to take care of her. Once she was back on her feet, he would set her free.

***

Chris sat on the bed, her knees pulled up to her chest. Jamie had left a few minutes ago, but his presence still lingered like good aftershave. The drapes were drawn, but the grim darkness seeped inside her. Hallie had left her a mess to deal with. A wrecked marriage, an affair with a man Chris had absolutely no interest in.

She knew only two things at this point: she could not tell anyone that she was someone else in Hallie's body, or Sharp Rehabilitation Center would be the next stop. Therefore, she would have to pretend to be Hallie, to actually be the woman. That was why she lied when Jamie asked her if she remembered him. Her memory loss would seem plausible, but she was going to have to assume Hallie's life in full. To do that, she would have to find out more about the woman.

She got up, pushed apart the lace drapes and walked to the nearby mirror. It startled her every time she looked at her reflection, still expecting the tomboyish girl with kinky brown hair and brown eyes.

She was no longer tired, just curious. Her quest was to find out more about the woman she was. She had two weeks, more or less, and then she was on her own. Jamie could go on with his life, and Mick would have to forget about their trip to France.

Chris opened the suitcases on the bench. Everything had been thrown in haphazardly. Everything, except the collection of perfume bottles that were wrapped in hand towels. She pulled out linen shorts, silk shirts, and jewelry, jewelry, jewelry. The makeup kit filled the entire carry case. She found the two tickets to France.

And two tickets to the San Diego Opera. She had never been to an opera before. If the former Hallie had liked it, then she would have to give it a try. She tossed the opera tickets on the long dresser next to the line of perfume bottles.

In the armoire were suits, dresses, and shoes. Obviously, they went to fancy parties when they stayed in Los Almeda. She touched the tuxedo, picturing Jamie stepping out of a white limousine, his wide shoulders filling the jacket, the black of it setting off his blond hair.

Shaking the thought from her mind, she turned and was caught short by a photograph on the wall: Hallie and Jamie on their wedding day. She no longer had to imagine what Jamie might look like in that tux. Hallie had been gorgeous, glowing. Jamie looked handsome and happy. The date, inscribed on a gold plate, was three years before. They had been in love then. What had happened?

The small plastic bag with the hospital label on it caught her eye. It contained even more jewelry, what Hallie had been wearing the day she collapsed. She laid out the necklaces, watch, earrings, Hallie's wedding ring. A large perfect diamond surrounded by a swirl of smaller diamonds. She slipped it on her hand and let the strange feeling of suddenly being a married woman wash over her.

Chris walked out onto the balcony, breathing in the fresh, slightly salty air. The distant mountains looked majestic and hazy in the distance. She would enjoy living in California, she decided. Still, the mountains reminded her of home in Colorado. A tidal wave of homesickness washed over her as she remembered her parents, her three sisters, her friends, her dogs.

Alan. There was a pang of a different sort when she thought of him. She had been so in love with him, and so unsure where she stood.

A faint knock drew her back into the room. When she opened the door and realized it wasn't Jamie, a spike of disappointment poked at her. It was the solemn face of the butler.

"Ma'am, you have a visitor. A Mrs. Mellondorf."

Chris's expression went blank. "Oh. Okay, send her up."

The butler's eyebrows rose, making his face seem even longer. "Ma'am, we don't invite guests into the bedrooms. You may receive her in the living room where she waits for you."

"Oh. Right. I'll be down in a minute."

He turned and walked away. With a panicky feeling, she realized that she had no idea where the living room was. Catching up to the butler, she sheepishly asked, "Can you show me where the living room is? I'm afraid I can't remember."

"Certainly."

He continued walking, and she fell into step behind him, imitating the stiff way he lifted each leg straight up before moving it forward. When her stifled giggle reached his elongated ears, he turned around. The grin disappeared, and she looked back at him as if she had no idea why he was staring at her. *Boy, did I need that laugh.* She followed him down the winding staircase, and just to the right of the entrance, he pointed to a closed door.

"Thank you," she said.

As her hand closed over the doorknob, she took a deep breath. Another person to deal with. She hoped this one was friendlier than the other three occupants in the house.

"H-a-a-l-l-i-e!" the woman squealed out, then leaped at her before Chris could even get a good look.

Chris hugged her back, her face lost in a mass of curly red hair somewhat like her own had been. Finally, the woman moved back, a warm smile on her face.

"Let me see you! I was so worried! But you look great, well, as great as you can look without makeup or your hair styled, which is pretty great. I hate you." The woman stopped to catch her breath, then said, "Why are you looking at me like that? You're mad at me because I didn't come visit you at the hospital, right?" She plopped down on the blue velvet sofa. "I wanted to, I really did, but Stan was in a pissy mood all week just because I took off with some friends to the Baja and didn't give him a month's notice! You know how he is, such an old fuddy-duddy when it comes to my having fun with my friends. Anyway, if I told him I'd be leaving again to visit a friend in the hospital, you know he'd never believe me."

Chris smiled, grabbing onto a tiny thread in the conversation and going with it. "Yeah, your dad can be a bummer sometimes."

Now it was the woman's turn to look blank. "My dad? I'm talking about *Stan*. My husband, Stan. Hallie, are you all right?"

"I've lost some of my memory from the stroke. I don't remember you."

The woman's mouth dropped into an open-mouthed pout. "You don't remember your best friend, Joya? We grew up together."

Chris touched her hand. "Joya, I don't remember anyone. It's kind of like starting over."

Joya's brown eyes widened. "You didn't remember Jamie? Or Mick?" she added in a low voice.

Chris shook her head. "I even had to ask the butler where the living room was."

Joya leaned her head back and hooted. "I'll bet he loved that! Considering how much he likes you, I mean."

"I got the impression he wasn't too friendly, but I thought butlers were supposed to act like that. They do in the movies."

Joya gave her an odd look. "How come you remember butlers in movies, but you don't remember Solomon?"

Chris shrugged. "Good question. So, why doesn't he like me?"

"Well, the way you told it, and I wouldn't know firsthand since I wasn't invited, but you got drunk at a party Theresa threw here and propositioned him. Then you started to strip off his clothes to a jaunty tune. It sounded hilarious! I guess neither he nor your mother-in-law were too happy about it. Or Jamie," she added. "Then again, he's no fun at all."

Chris reddened at the thought. That man was cold toward her because she'd embarrassed him in front of Theresa's friends and acquaintances. And *she* didn't even do it! Chris would never do such a thing. She hardly drank at all.

"Aw, don't sweat it," Joya said with a flip of her hand. "He's only a servant."

"Yes, but he's a person, too."

Joya laughed again, then sobered. "You're serious? Oh, get with it. Ever since you were ten years old, you liked picking on people. It's no time to stop now."

Chris forced a laugh. She wasn't too sure she liked Joya, but at least she was the first friendly person she'd met. Besides Mick, of course, who was too friendly.

"You'd be surprised how dying and coming back can change a person," Chris said. "I hope we can still be friends."

"Friends? We're more like sisters." Then her expression became serious for the first time. "I really was worried about you, hon. Did you say *dying* and coming back?"

"Yes, I did die. I got a second chance."

Joya reached out and touched her arm. "You actually came back from the dead? I can't believe it. Remember when we were kids and watched that old movie your mother loved *Heaven Can Wait*? How neat we thought that was, that you could get a second chance. Hallie, you got that chance! Look, it gives me chills!"

Chris got chills, too, but not because of her second chance. Hallie didn't get another chance. At least not that she knew of.

"I've decided to make the most of my life now that I've got it."

Joya leaned forward, as if sharing a secret. "Are you still going to run off with Mick? I blame myself for introducing you to that guy. If I hadn't dragged you to La Moustache that night, you would never have met him. It was bad enough you only being able to visit for a week once every two months, but now you're going to be too far away to visit!"

"I'm not going to France. Joya, I don't know where these people fit into my life anymore. I don't know Mick."

Joya pushed out her bottom lip. "Aw, I'm sorry, honey. I keep forgetting. It's just that I can't believe you don't remember that much. You look, well, you look fine. A little tired maybe, but otherwise, just like your old self."

Chris warmed under her friend's sympathetic gaze. "You're going to have to bear with me until my memory...until things are back to normal." Which would be never.

When a clock somewhere in the room chimed six bells, Chris remembered dinner. "I've got to get ready for dinner. Thanks for coming by, and call me soon."

Joya gave her a hug and an air kiss on each cheek. "Take care, hon. I will call, I promise. We'll get together when you're up to it."

Her friend stood and tugged her suede mini skirt over her hips, her gold bangles jingling with every movement. Chris wondered how Joya could do anything with nails that long. Heck, even going to the bathroom could be a dangerous proposition. Chris had found that out right away and filed hers down.

"It sure was nice mee—seeing you again, Joya."

"Yeah, you too, hon. If you need anything, anything at all, call me. You know, of course, that you can stay at my place if you need to."

"Thanks, I'll remember that."

Joya strode out of the room, turning and sending her another air kiss before leaving. Chris headed toward the door, pausing only briefly when she glimpsed the blond hair in the mirror. She didn't know if she would ever get used to looking the way she did. When she walked out of the living room and started for the staircase, a voice stopped her.

"I see you're catching up with old friends."

She turned to see Jamie leaning against the wet bar. He was clean-shaven, wearing a crisp white shirt and a casual jacket. The crystal chandelier above spun fiery highlights in his blond hair. He looked *debonair*, a word she had never used before to describe any man she had known. The tired look was gone from his features, but something in his eyes made them icy cold, lending an edge to his remark.

Chris smiled nervously. "I don't remember her. She seems...nice."

His smile showed no trace of warmth. "Don't let that fool you. But I'm sure everything will come back soon enough. It sure sounded like you two were laughing it up as usual."

Her eyes narrowed, and the tone of his voice chilled her. Looking at the close proximity of the wet bar to the living room doors, she asked, "Were you eavesdropping?"

He shrugged without a trace of shame. "Old habits are hard to break."

What had she gotten herself into here? She felt as if she had walked into the middle of a movie. She had no lines, no idea what had happened up to that point. *Give me my script so I'll know my part!*

"I guess I'd better get upstairs and change." Nodding toward the dining room across the way, she added, "It looks like dinner's almost ready." A uniformed woman was setting the table and pouring water into crystal glasses. Without giving him much chance to respond, she padded up the stairs to her room.

From Jamie's attire, she guessed dinners at Theresa's to be formal affairs. She was not a formal person. In fact, the last time she had dressed up was for prom six years earlier. That made her think of something else. How old was Hallie anyway? Something else to add to the list of things to find out.

All she could find in her search through the armoire and closet were slinky dresses she'd be too embarrassed to try on for fun, much less wear to dinner with her mother-in-law and the stranger who was her husband. The things Hallie had packed were even worse. Finally, she settled for a light-blue, calf-length dress with spaghetti straps and thin material that clung to her new figure. It barely covered the top of her chest, but it was already quarter past six, and she didn't want to cause any more of a fuss than she apparently had before. As a last-minute addition, she threw a shawl over her shoulders.

When she walked into the dining room, Jamie and Theresa were already seated and in deep discussion. They stopped abruptly when they heard her approach. Theresa nodded toward the chair across from Jamie, and Chris took her seat.

"You look nice tonight," Jamie said, although his expression lacked the appreciation that might usually go with the compliment. "Back to normal, except for the shawl."

Theresa made a *humph* sound under her breath. Chris felt more than self-conscious about her dress, but smiled. Should she dump the shawl or wrap it more tightly around her?

"Thank you, Jamie. I didn't get a chance to tell you how handsome you looked when we met in the foyer earlier."

"I see your internal clock is still set for arriving late,"

Theresa said.

She had successfully interfered with her compliment and made her feel like an ill-mannered child with one simple comment.

"Mom," Jamie murmured in admonition.

As Chris started working on the salad in front of her, a uniformed woman began taking away the other two salad plates. When she approached her, Chris let her take her plate too. A few minutes later, a bowl of thick spaghetti was set in front of her. Her stomach growled, and she futilely bit her lip to calm it. In her family, something like that was funny, and everyone teased and laughed about it. Here she felt as if she had committed a travesty.

As soon as she finished her spaghetti, another plate was put in front of her, this time a pork chop and vegetables sautéed in olive oil. Her stomach was already tied up in knots, and the rich smell of the oil made her appetite flee. She ignored Jamie's occasional glances in her direction as she pushed her food around on the plate.

"Are you all right?" he asked after a while.

Theresa clanked her fork on her plate. "She never ate much. At least not in my home."

Chris wanted to kick her under the table, but that was out of the question. The little Italian spitfire made it obvious how she felt about her son's wife.

Chris looked across the table at Jamie. "No, I'm feeling a bit tired. I think I'll go up to my room." As she rose, she remembered her manners and turned to Theresa. "Excuse me, please."

Theresa waved her away as if dismissing a servant, then returned to eating. Jamie, however, surprised her by standing. "I'll walk you up."

Chris had to keep the look of shock from her face. One minute he was treating her like a dog, the next, like someone he cared about.

"Go ahead and eat. I'll be fine."

"I insist."

He was at her side, leading her out of the dining room by her elbow. Theresa's reproving look didn't escape Chris's notice and probably wasn't intended to be subtle.

When they reached the top of the stairs, she turned to him. "Thank you for walking me up."

"I didn't want you to get dizzy and fall down the stairs."

"That was thoughtful of you." His touch on her elbow felt warm on her skin. "Do you have any videos here? Of me? Us? Maybe they'll jog some memories."

His expression was strange, almost melancholy. "There are a couple in the conservatory. I'll get them."

He returned a few minutes later, handing her two DVDs. "This is all I could find."

She glanced at the labels on the two cases: *Jamie and Hallie's Wedding* and *Summer Parties/Misc.* "Is there a DVD player nearby?"

He walked down a darkened hallway, passed the room he slept in, and turned on a light. She followed him into what appeared to be another living room, only smaller. He gave her quick instructions on operating the television and player. When he turned from the television, his expression was serious.

"I may not always be the first to admit when I'm wrong." As if he expected her to reply, he quickly added, "Or the last. But maybe it was a mistake you coming here."

She felt panic creep like heat up her neck. "What do you mean?" What had she done?

"My mother, of course. I knew you could relax here, and still be close to your friends. I figured with you being frail and recovering, Mom would be more understanding. But you're far from frail, and she's far from understanding."

His smile warmed the chill in her heart, but she wasn't sure what he was getting at. "You want me to leave?"

"Hallie, when I saw you in the hospital, come back to life after dying, you looked so vulnerable. Despite everything we've been through these past two years, it's my duty, as your husband, to take care of you. To protect you." His hand subconsciously moved up over his heart. "When you chose to stay with me, I figured you were helping me to save face in front of Mick. I appreciate that, but your heart is with someone else, and I realize it's not fair to keep you to your decision."

Her grip on the DVDs tightened. Mental pictures of Mick kneeling by her bedside, love dripping from his eyes; of Velvet, the stranger who was her mother; of Joya. Jamie, sometimes icy, sometimes something else. Jamie, who considered it his duty to take care of her, as if she were an illegitimate child! Anger mixed with her frustration, and she fought the tears that threatened to overflow.

"Do you want me to leave?"

"It's not what *I* want, it's what *you* want."

She swallowed hard and squared her shoulders. "If you want me to leave, just say it." She had no idea where she would go if he did say the word, but she wasn't going to stay where she wasn't welcome.

He seemed to weigh his words carefully. "Tell me what you want to do."

"I want to stay."

Something warm sparkled in his eyes, if only for an instant. "You're free to stay as long as you need to. All I ask is that you not bring Mick here. Not into my mother's house."

"That won't be a problem." The more she thought about him, the more he gave her the creeps.

"Let's get you to bed," he said. "You look tired."

The bedroom looked cozy and romantic with the lace draped over the four posts on the bed. The antique brass light filled the room with a warm, peach glow.

"If you need anything, I'll be downstairs for a while, then on the other side of the balcony." He hesitated for a moment, then closed the door.

She sat down on the bed, realizing the room had lost its romantic feel now that Jamie had left. At least she was comfortable here, if not in the rest of the house. With tile and marble floors, high ceilings, and dark wood everywhere, the place seemed more like a castle than a home. Beautiful but untouchable. Like Jamie himself.

She only needed a couple of weeks to get on her feet emotionally. To figure out who she was and where she wanted to go. Jamie would be all right. He had told her that earlier, hadn't he?

After searching through every drawer for a nightgown, she finally found a deep blue peignoir with the tags still attached. She slipped it on, imagining it was her old body in the silky gown and robe. Long t-shirts were bedtime fare for her, sometimes with teddy bears or kittens on them. The cuter, the better. Not fancy, sexy things. She didn't need anything fancy to impress her family and dogs. She found herself drifting over to the mirror above the dresser, again startled to find someone else staring back. Would she ever get used to that?

CHAPTER 3

Nightmares about bridges haunted her sleep: crashing metal, shattering glass and screams. Chris bolted upright, hand to pounding heart, as the echoes of words drifted away from her.

Find his heart.

That was all she could grasp as wakefulness found her and yanked her up from the depths. Then that was gone, too.

She rolled to the side of the bed and stretched down to—nothing. Then she remembered, and reality left her cold and chilled. She was Hallie. Her furry friends weren't lying on the floor next to her bed. Her Shetland sheepdogs weren't there to give her comfort by their presence alone, weren't there to offer their warmth or accept a hug. She stared into the darkness.

"Phoenix, my buddy. Where are you? Shelby, Tubby?"

The strange sound of her voice, softer, more refined than her old one, echoed in the room. Pulling her knees up to her chest, she huddled in a ball, trying to remember her other life as Chris. Just a week before, she had sat at a much-used dining table with her parents and three sisters, Paula, Charlene, and little Bernice. The Shelties were lying at her feet, pretending not to beg. Mom had been talking to Chris's sister Paula:

"You gotta eat more than that if you're supporting a little one in your belly!"

"Mom, how can I eat much when I know I'm just gonna throw it up again?" Paula had rubbed her belly.

Bernice made ralphing noises until her mother silenced them with a look.

"Isn't normal, you getting sick at five months. I only got sick for the first two months with all four of you. What does Dr. Roy say about it?"

Paula cocked her head as she always did when Mom worried too much. "He said everyone is different and that we shouldn't worry."

Mom tilted her curly head up indignantly. "I'll worry all I want. You're carrying my first grandbaby."

Paula's husband, Kerry, leaned over and put an arm around his mother-in-law. "Mom, do you think I'd let our girl wait one minute before going to the doctor if I thought something was wrong?"

"Don't worry about Paullywog," Chris had chimed in. "She's in good hands with all of us breathing down her neck."

Chris didn't realize she was crying until a teardrop splattered on her knee. Her mouth was so tightly stretched into a grimace that she couldn't make it go away. She wanted to go home. *Home.* That thought released a sluice of tears that froze up her nose as her whole body shook with sobs. Sheesh, the last thing she needed was Jamie to hear her crying.

The thought of going home had occurred to her, maybe a thousand times. But how could she tell her family and Alan that she was actually Chris in a different body? What would it do to her father's fragile heart? He would think someone was playing a cruel trick on them, and when she disclosed details that only she would know, he might be so overwhelmed his heart would give out. She could never forgive herself for that. Besides, it wouldn't be the same, not with her family or friends.

Then there was her mission, from He who gave her a second chance. *Find his heart.*

She followed the soft orange glow of the nightlight to the bathroom, purposely avoiding the mirror for two reasons: the disconcerting feeling every time she saw a stranger looking back, and that this time the stranger would have puffy red eyes and tear streaks down her cheeks. She blew her nose and washed her face. The two DVDs caught her eye.

Peering out into the dark hallway, she listened for any sounds in the deep night. Jamie's bedroom door was ajar, and she studied the slit of black to see if he might be standing there. She could make out no distinct shape. No doubt, he was lying there in blissful sleep, unaware that a stranger slept across the balcony from him.

When she reached the living room, she turned on the lights. To her chagrin, there was no door to close. She turned the volume knob way down. She chose the wedding DVD first.

She turned off the lights, sat on the floor, and leaned against the burgundy leather chair. She studied every move Hallie made, the way she laughed and talked, the way she walked, or more like sauntered across the room. Chris realized then that she still walked in her old style, casual with a slight bounce. *That's because you still see yourself the way you used to look.* The reason she was always startled at the mirror's image.

Weddings always made her cry, and this one was no exception. It was hard to relate herself to the woman in the video. Hallie was in control, confident, and sexy. Even in a white wedding dress and on the arm of the most handsome man there, the other men in the video gawked at her. Chris was sure she'd never received one single look like the ones those men were giving Hallie. No, she was an average girl, nowhere near glamorous.

Although her goal was to study Hallie, her gaze kept drifting to Jamie. She had never seen a more debonair, charming man in her life. *Debonair.* There was that word again. Oh, did it fit. In his black tuxedo, setting off his light hair and vivid blue eyes, he could easily be a movie star. Those finely chiseled features, high cheekbones, and sensual lips. And his crooked smile. She caught herself grinning every time he did. He was the kind of guy she had had crushes on in high school, the ones who treated her like a little sister or one of the guys. Being a tomboy did have its drawbacks. Those guys always went for girls who looked like Hallie.

Their reception was held in a huge formal banquet room with crystal sconces and chandeliers. The party itself was nothing near formal and stuffy. Jamie whispered in Hallie's ear during their dance, and she blushed before nibbling his chin in response. Then, for the camera, she winked and pinched his buttocks, which elicited a wiggle from him.

During the toast, her glass of champagne splashed over the side of her glass and down to her elbow. Jamie ran his tongue down the length of her arm, licking off all traces of the champagne. He made the most of the garter removal, moving to the jaunty tune and pulling the garter back up her leg just when he had it to her ankle.

Chris found herself laughing, feeling jealous and wistful all at the same time. It was the kind of wedding she'd always wanted. She tried to picture her old self and Alan having such a wedding, but the image refused to form. Instead, she saw herself and Jamie. This Jamie on the video seemed a different man than the one she had just met. His blue eyes sparkled with love and laughter, as did Hallie's. Something had gone terribly wrong with their marriage, despite the promising start.

Chris wiped her eyes when the video ended with a beautiful sunset shot over the pool, silhouetting the newlyweds in an embrace. Leaning over to the player, she put in the next disk, hoping it would give her more clues to Hallie's personality, and why their marriage had fallen apart.

That DVD was a mixture of different events. In one section, Jamie ushered a blindfolded Hallie along a stone pathway that led around a lovely one-story brick house. When he removed the silk handkerchief, her bright blue eyes widened at the sight of a red Porsche in the driveway, a huge blue bow on top. With a squeal, she hugged Jamie, then leaped into the car.

The date at the bottom of the screen moved closer to present, and slowly Chris could see a change in Hallie. A year previous, there was an extravagant party on what looked like Theresa's lawn. Jamie walked in the garden gate with Hallie on his arm, but minutes later she was off visiting with friends, mostly males. That brilliant blue in his eyes in the earlier sections was a distant memory by then. Chris watched carefully, only getting glimpses now and then of Jamie or Hallie in the background. Never together.

There were a couple of larger parties on the DVD, and Chris watched Hallie flirt and get drunk. She watched Jamie's eyes grow dimmer, and his face grow older. It was almost like seeing two entirely different couples. She felt sad for them, for the death of their marriage. And she felt sad for herself. She had always held the strong belief that her first marriage would be her only. She would be a divorced woman before she'd ever really fallen in love and married.

***

Jamie leaned against the doorframe just outside the living room, watching Hallie sitting in a pool of light cast by the television. He noticed that she wore the blue peignoir he had given her a year ago. The one she had never worn before.

She had watched their wedding video and had even cried. He'd seen her wipe her eyes and sniffle. Then she'd watched the second DVD, her shoulders slumping as the scenes grew more dismal. At least it looked that way; maybe he was projecting his own feelings onto her actions. Would the videos spark a memory or two in her mind? Would they swiftly return her to her former self?

The sooner the better. Her staying there was a big mistake, and now she didn't want to leave. She hadn't taken the hint, in any case. What had possessed him to insist on her staying with him? He should have turned her over to Mick when he had the chance. But she was here, and he was watching her like some voyeur.

He had never seen her sit on the floor. In fact, she used to comment that people who sat on floors must see themselves as dogs. Yet, there she was, like a dog on the floor. He turned to go, but found himself drawn back again. There was something different about her since her stroke. She looked the same, but something in the way she moved had changed. Her voice was different, too, as well as the way she said things.

He realized there *was* something different about her looks, although he thought it might be his imagination. Now that he had watched the videos, he knew what it was: her eyes. They were a deeper blue now, as if she had borrowed some blue from the clouds on her halted trip to the pearly gates.

The fact that she was wearing her wedding ring had not slipped his notice either. During dinner, the diamonds had glittered every time she moved. He wanted to ask her why she still wore it, but for some reason he didn't want to hear her answer.

Hallie stopped the video and started to get to her feet. He scooted out of the doorway and back down the hall to his room. He didn't want her catching him there. He felt foolish enough. In a couple of weeks, he would return home, and she would run off to France with Mick. His life would be free of pain and disappointment. *Free* because he would never again let himself love any woman the way he'd loved Hallie. What a fool he'd been. But he had learned. Yes, he had learned well.

***

It was nearly eleven o'clock before Chris woke the next morning. The late summer sky was blue and bright, and she sat up and stretched, adding a yawn for good measure. Then she remembered once again where she was. Mornings were hardest. She awoke thinking her death and new life were all just a bizarre dream, only to be jolted by reality.

The only good thing about her new life, she mused as she looked in the bathroom mirror, was that her hair looked a lot better in the mornings. No more brown afro that had to be tamed into a thousand ringlets.

The only pair of shorts she could find in her suitcases that sufficiently covered her buttocks were so tight she could barely squeeze into them and still breathe. An off-the-shoulder peasant top covered the most skin. Even without any makeup, the woman in the mirror was a knockout. Okay, another plus for the new life.

Jamie's door was open, and she could see no sign of movement within. With just the slightest trepidation, she ventured down the winding staircase in hopes of running into him before she encountered his mother. The house was quiet, like a museum.

She walked behind the stairs and into the great room. The smell of lemon oil drifted through the air, reminding her of days when she and her sisters would pick slips of paper out of a jar to see what job would be theirs that weekend. Chris hated polishing duty, because afterward she smelled like oily lemons all day.

A woman dressed in drab brown looked up, startled by Chris's entrance.

"Good morning, Mrs. DiBarto," the young woman said quietly.

Chris felt strange being addressed so reverently by someone who was probably in her own social class.

"Hi, what's your name?"

"Elena."

"Well, good morning, Elena. Have you seen Jamie?"

"He's out back." The woman returned to her task of polishing the dark wood.

"Nice work."

The woman looked surprised as she stopped mid-wipe and stared up at her. "Thank you."

When Chris walked out back, she found herself on a terrace that spiraled down to the deck below. The sound of splashing water drew her attention to Jamie, furiously swimming laps in a huge rectangular pool. Sunshine glinted off the waves and spun his wet blond hair into gold. She watched him and wondered if he'd get mad when he saw her there. She didn't care. If the tension between them was a string, she could add it to a guitar. Yet she couldn't take her eyes off him, his lithe, tan body gliding through the water, the way his long muscular legs pushed him from the wall and back into stride.

Something else, perhaps, to add to the list of good things in her new life? She shook her head. Definitely not. In her twenty-three years of life as Chris, she didn't have a lot of experience with men, but she knew a defensive barrier when she saw one. She saw his every time he looked at her. Not that she could blame him. His wife had mistreated him, taken him for granted. Worse yet, he had once loved her so very much.

Chris couldn't even dare to hope her someday husband would look at her the way Jamie had looked at his bride. Maybe someone would be able to penetrate the insurmountable fortress he'd built around his heart; his wife could not be that person.

Something strange clutched her insides for a moment, and her fingers tightened on the railing. When she had thought about the fortress around his heart... there it was again, that odd, squeezing feeling. She dropped her head and closed her eyes, a bright light filling her eyelids.

"Hallie! Are you all right?"

Jamie's voice pulled her from whatever spell had gripped her, and she snapped her head up. The pool was empty. A hand touched her, and she whirled around to find him at her side, concern-filled eyes that matched the sky.

"What's wrong?"

"I'm fine. Just a little..." She tried to find a word to describe what she'd been feeling. "Strange," was all she could come up with.

"Here, sit down."

His touch made her arm tingle as he led her to a wooden chaise lounge. She couldn't keep the tiny grin from showing at the fact that he was creating a puddle around his feet. She glanced down to hide her eyes from him until she could pull herself together. The blond hairs on his legs were plastered against his skin. Part of what made her smile was his gallant effort at coming to her aid, racing up the stairs to the rescue.

"What's so funny?" The concern in his eyes was transforming to something close to a smile.

"You're dripping wet, and your hair's sticking out." A giggle escaped her lips, but it was the tickling feeling in her stomach as he leaned close that made her feel giddy.

"You're something else, and I truly mean that." He shook his head, a lopsided grin on his face. "One minute I think you're fainting and the next, you're grinning. At me."

He was crouched beside her, and for a moment, they just stared at each other. To her surprise, she realized her heart was hammering away inside her. *How crazy,* she thought. They looked at each other for the longest time, their smiles fading as the moment became serious. His eyes searched hers for a moment, and her gaze dropped to his mouth as she thought about leaning forward and touching her lips to his.

Jamie squeezed his eyes shut and stood, running his long fingers through his wet hair to smooth it back. He looked intently out over the property, then back at her from a safe distance.

"Have you had any of those awful headaches since the stroke?"

Chris shook her head, aware of her blond hair swinging in the corners of her eyes. "No, I've been fine. I feel like my old self again."

The hardening in his expression was barely noticeable, yet she had seen it just the same. She had studied his face as much as Hallie's last night. She knew every inch, every line and feature.

He walked over to the railing and leaned against it, putting more distance between them. His voice took on that flat tone she had heard before.

"I'm glad to hear that."

Her words slipped out before she could hold them back. "Would you have been happier if I'd become an invalid? Maybe you would have preferred that I die to pay for my sins?"

Fire lit his eyes as they met hers, and he stood up straight to face her. "Yeah, you're definitely sounding like your old self again. I don't love you anymore, but I don't want you dead or an invalid. The faster you return to full health, the better. Then my husbandly duty is over, and you can go your own way."

The strain of the last few days culminated in a blast of her temper. "Oh, I'm sorry. I thought you were doing this out of the kindness of your heart. But I can see you don't have one." Instantly, the strange feeling returned, and with it regret.

He flinched at her words but bit back, "Sweetheart, you can give yourself credit for that." He turned and strode down the stairs, diving into the pool.

Chris felt like dropping over the balcony. In five minutes, she had gone from confusion, amusement, elation, anger, and finally regret. She couldn't watch his angry strokes anymore or think about the expression on his face when he'd raced up the stairs to help her. With her face turned away from the pool, she flew down the stairs and out toward the grounds beyond. Time alone was what she needed. Desperately.

She could see the faraway wall that surrounded the property. That's where she wanted to be, far away. Maybe she'd climb up and sit on top of that wall. She kept walking, her arms swinging wildly with each step. After several minutes, her steam ran out and she stopped and looked around. Orange trees dotted the lawn, their tiny white blossoms wavering in the breeze. She inhaled their fragrance, remembering a tiny bottle of orange blossom perfume she'd bought on a family vacation to Florida many years ago. It had come in a half shell with a silk blossom, and she'd worn the perfume all year to remember sunny days and white powder beaches.

Just when solitude soaked up her anger and frustration with Jamie, two arms wrapped around her and pulled her into an embrace.

She started to scream and had to pull back the sound at the sight of Mick from the corner of her eye.

"Why haven't you called me?" He nuzzled her shoulder and mumbled, "You know how I get when you don't call."

She pulled away from him, leaving him staring at her in starry wonderment.

"Hallie, for God's sake, don't push me away, not after what you did to me at the hospital."

The spark of wildness in his eyes gave her the willies. She looked toward the house, gauging screaming distance. Too far away.

Stay calm, in control. "I didn't do anything to you at the hospital."

He gave the sky an agonized look, and his voice went a pitch higher. "Didn't do anything?" And louder. "Didn't do anything? You chose him over me." Then he looked back at her. "You chose to stay with that bastard rather than let me take care of you."

He moved toward her, and she backed up until prickly branches jabbed her. "Mick, he's my husband. It wouldn't look right if I—"

He laughed bitterly. "When have you cared how anything looked? All I wanted to do was take care of you, darling, just like I've always wanted to do." He touched her cheek, and she tried to keep from shrinking away from him. "I was so happy you were alive, pulled from the dredges of death, and then you crushed me. Like a bug." In demonstration, he placed two fingers on either side of a leaf and squashed a little black beetle that was crawling on it. She flinched at the crunching sound.

"I—I'm sorry."

He smiled in a patronizing way. "Then give me a hug. I've missed you."

She moved slowly toward him, and he nearly fractured her with his powerful arms.

"You feel so *good*." He leaned his head away to look at her while still encasing her in his arms. Then he reached up and started fiddling with her hair. "You are so beautiful. Being with you makes me feel like a giant. No one thought I could make someone like you my wife, but I proved them wrong. They thought I was a loser, but you're going to be my wife. And we're going to be rich!"

He squeezed her hard again, and she gasped for breath. She felt like poor Bugs Bunny in the grip of the big dog with the dopey voice who wants his own bunny rabbit. *I'm gonna love her, and squeeze her and...*

"Hallie, why aren't you talking to me?" he asked suddenly, holding her away.

"Because I can't breathe!" She shook herself loose.

He looked at her, cocking his head to an angle. "I didn't mean to hurt you. You know I would never hurt you on purpose." Then his smile returned. "Is your memory returning?"

She grabbed at the excuse. "No. That's why I'm staying here until it returns enough for me to move on with my life."

"You don't have to remember how much you love me. Come with me, and you'll feel it all over again."

Panic pressed in around her. "I can't."

Once again, his hands gripped her shoulders. All the gooeyness hardened, and his gaze drilled into hers. "You remember where you put the Manderlay, don't you? You wouldn't forget anything as important as that."

Her head spun at how fast his mood changed. "I don't know what you're talking about."

"The Manderlay, the alexandrite! Dammit, why wouldn't you tell me where you hid it? You always played games like that, so secretive and coy." His eyes narrowed. "Maybe you weren't playing at all. Maybe you faked this whole stroke thing to blow me off and keep the Manderlay to yourself. Tell me you wouldn't do that." His fingers were digging into her flesh.

"Ask the doctor to see my X-rays if you don't believe me."

His face relaxed a bit, but his voice sounded hard. "I've already seen them. Hallie, come with me now. There is nothing here for you. You know how much I love you—"

"I'm not Hallie!" she screamed, pushing away his arms. Then she stopped, realizing what she'd just said. He stared at her, his dark brown eyes shining like onyx.

Then he smiled and moved toward her again. "I love our games, but I'm not in the mood for baron/baroness or whatever persona you're playing now."

She bit her lip, trying to keep another outburst at bay. "Give me time to remember everything. I'll remember where the Manderlay is, and I'll tell you."

Again, his mood swung full tilt, and he grinned and hugged her tightly again. "When we're living in France, I'll make mad love to you every day at precisely noon."

She pulled away, trying to keep the panic from her voice. "I have to go now. They're expecting me back."

His expression sobered. "I'll be watching you. And waiting. You're mine. Whatever Jamie DiBarto has in mind by playing devoted husband, remember what I did to that other guy who tried to steal you away from me."

"What did you do to him?"

He raised an eyebrow. "He just got out of the hospital a week ago. Why don't you ask him?"

She ran then, as fast as she could toward the house that now looked like a safe haven rather than a cold fortress. In her mind, Mick's hands reached out and pulled her back, but she didn't dare turn around to see if he pursued.

CHAPTER 4

Jamie stood near the back door with his arms crossed over his chest. He knew the smug grin on his face belied the frostiness in his blue eyes. Hallie's gaze flicked toward him, then back at the door she headed toward. Was she going to walk right by him without even a hint of guilt on her features? She looked flushed and winded.

His light tone of voice came out forced despite his effort. "I thought we were beyond the point of sneaking around to see him. He could have picked you up at the end of the drive in broad daylight. Or maybe sneaking around was part of the allure."

Hallie clenched her hands, but he could see that they trembled. "I was *not* sneaking around. I didn't invite him here." Her voice sounded close to hysteria, but she kept it under control with tight lips.

"So, you just happened to run into him in our yard? One of those, 'I was in the neighborhood' things, maybe? In the neighborhood miles from his home, after scaling a cement wall..."

"Jamie, stop." She pressed her fingers to her temples. "I know you won't believe anything I say, so I'm not going to stand here and argue with you. I need to be alone." With eyes red and watery, she ran upstairs and closed the bedroom door behind her with something close to a slam.

Jamie didn't want her to get away with it. Actually, he was quite pleased with the fact that he managed to find out when she was sneaking around with Mick. She used to become enraged, deny it until faced with the indisputable facts. This time she was different—rattled almost. Her hands had trembled, but he couldn't stop himself once he'd started. Each cold word pushed her further away from him. But something made him madder than catching her with Mick from his vantage point on the balcony. He turned and slammed his fist against the wall. It still hurt, damn her. Damn himself, too.

Theresa appeared from around the corner, a questioning look on her face. "What was that noise?"

She knew his manner of composing himself and hiding his emotions, but he tried anyway. "Nothing. Nothing important, anyway."

"James Angelo DiBarto, don't lie to your mother."

He hated when she addressed him by his full name. It made him feel like a little boy caught lying about sneaking out of the house with his brother again. Miguel had enjoyed getting him into trouble; probably to make up for feeling as if Jamie was the favored son.

"I don't want to talk about it. Does that suit you better?"

Theresa placed her hands on ample hips. "It's that wife of yours, isn't it? Jamie, for the life of me I don't understand why—okay, I do know why you brought her here, so much like your father I could tie you to a stake. Duty, honor, and you don't see what she's doing to you, been doing to you for years."

He took a deep breath, not wanting to get into this conversation again. "She's only been a wench for the last year of our marriage. The first two were fine." He shook his head, flinging the thought like a dog shakes water from its fur. "I couldn't dump her into Mick's care when she didn't remember him. Now that she does—"

"Ah, she was sneaking around again, wasn't she?"

Jamie regretted the words the instant they had left his mouth. "She doesn't have to sneak around anymore. In any case, I'm not going to kick her out of this house when I brought her here to recuperate. I've given her a chance to leave without any bad feelings, and for some reason, she chooses to stay. In two weeks, she'll be out of here and out of our lives forever, so just drop whatever it is you're going to lecture me about and be polite until then." Then he added with a smile, "Please."

Theresa touched his arm. "You're too nice to her. She doesn't deserve it." Her expression grew alarmed. "You're not thinking of giving her a second chance, are you?"

"Of course not."

Her features relaxed. "And what about this Renee woman? Miguel tells me she's head over heels in love with you. Which, frankly, is quite obvious by the number of times she's called since you've been here."

He twisted his mouth in thought. "I don't know. Right now, she's just a friend. Maybe when my life is back in order, I'll explore the possibilities."

Theresa's face glowed. "I think you should. You'll bring her here to meet me soon?"

Her happiness at his step back into life touched him. He leaned down to plant a kiss on her soft cheek. "When the situation warrants it."

He watched his mother return to her mahogany roll-top desk from which she continued management of his late father's investments. His shrewd investments gave them a life his salary as a vineyard worker could never have done, in California or back in Italy when Jamie was a boy. Armed with a thousand dollars and an uncanny feel for the stock market, his father had made them comfortably wealthy by the time Jamie was thirteen. Then he kept going, kept taking risks, and making more money.

More than their growing wealth and position, Jamie remembered the tension that grew between his parents. The arguments he'd overheard when Theresa tried to drag his father away from that same desk stacked with company profiles. She called it an obsession with money; he called it taking care of his family.

His mother had been happy with what they had in the early days—long days of work that made supper an occasion for togetherness. The money wasn't worth his alienation from the family. Later his father made concessions, and they approached being the close-knit family they had been before. Then he died of a heart attack.

Jamie hadn't inherited that instinct for investing, although his brother, Miguel, had touches of it from time to time. His own lack of talent for the market didn't bother Jamie. He had seen what it did to his family, and ultimately to his father after years of taking risks and worrying about the consequences. He had decided he didn't want to put his own family through that. He needn't have worried. Hallie's claim to want children someday had turned into excuses and finally flat-out refusals to ever make herself fat and ugly.

That didn't matter now. He and Hallie were over, *finito*. Then he realized he had been walking upstairs. What brought him back to present was the sound of her crying. Actually, it was more like bawling. He walked to her door, not because of a need to comfort her, he assured himself. More out of curiosity. Never had he heard her cry as she was now. Not that pretentious crying she summoned to get her way or get out of trouble. This was out and out sobbing her guts out crying. He strained to hear the words she gasped out between sobs.

"I-I w-want to g-go home! I w-want my mom. And d-dad. And Phoenix, T-tubby, and Shelby."

Jamie frowned. She had never displayed a need for her parents. Especially her dad, who was virtually non-existent. And who the heck were Tubby and Shelby? And why did she want to go to Phoenix? It sounded as though someone else were in there and not Hallie.

Then something triggered inside his mind. Her mother. Damn. She had called that morning while Hallie was still asleep. He glanced at his watch. And was coming to pick her up in an hour. He had meant to tell her when he saw her up on the balcony, but the conversation had taken a turn for the worse, and he'd forgotten. The same reason he'd forgotten again when she returned from her rendezvous with Mick. He certainly didn't want her mother to find Hallie bawling, or even looking as if she had been. Velvet would rant and rave about his neglect, and he'd have to tell her where to shove her phony motherly concern.

He was going to have to bust in on her crying session. When he knocked on the door, her crying stopped.

"Go 'way." a muffled voice called out.

He pushed the door open a few inches. She was sitting on the bed with her knees drawn up, her face buried in the pillow sandwiched between. Something about her posture reminded him of a little girl lost in despair. She didn't look up at him. He leaned against the doorframe, trying to look more at ease than he felt.

"Surely what I said didn't upset you that much."

"Go away!" her muffled voice said again. "You would never understand."

He walked closer and wrapped his arm around one of the posts on the bed—the bed they used to share on their visits to Los Almeda.

"Do you want to talk about it?"

She lifted a red tear-stained face. "No. Your duties as my husband are fulfilled. You're dismissed."

"I see." Now he was curious. Did Mick dump her? "I didn't want to interrupt you, but I forgot to tell you that your mother called this morning. She's going to pick you up in about an hour. You'll be staying with her for dinner."

He wasn't expecting the panicked look that emerged on Hallie's face. She wiped away the tears and looked at him in an almost pleading way.

"Just me?"

It took him a minute to figure out what she was getting at. "Yes, just you. Did your mother ever include me in?"

"I don't know," she answered, and he could almost believe she didn't.

"Hallie, your mother and I have a patent disregard for each other. In any case, there's no need for me to accompany you. Maybe you should invite Mick."

He had succeeded in keeping his tone light, but she still shot him an angry look.

He held out a hand in defense. "Listen, you're the one who spent two weeks out of every two months visiting Joya in L.A. and playing single. You're the one who planned to fly away to France with Mick, and you're the one who instigated our divorce, which was the smartest thing you ever did. All I'm suggesting is that since he is the one you chose to spend your life with, or at least 'til boredom do you part, he should be the one to accompany you to your mother's for dinner."

She looked pitiful, staring up at him with a parade of feelings crossing her features. Anger, frustration, and something else he couldn't pinpoint. He moved toward the door.

"Hallie, I know you feel in limbo now. Soon you're going to remember how your life was, and why you did the things you did. I can't help you with that because I didn't know you the last year we were married. I don't know why you did what you did." He couldn't keep the sigh from his voice. "All I know is that it's been a long year, and I want it over." Then he turned and closed the door behind him.

***

Chris sat there long after Jamie left, remembering the look on his face. Hallie had hurt her husband deeply. It sounded as if her affair with Mick had been the final straw. Yet, though he said he wanted it to be over, there lingered a trace of pain and regret in those frosty blue eyes. He had loved Hallie, and she had loved him too, if Chris had read their expressions right on the wedding video. What had torn them apart?

How embarrassing, Jamie hearing her sobbing. Then he had the nerve to come in to assure himself that something he said hadn't upset her. She smiled, but it vanished as quickly as it had come. He hadn't cared what she was crying about, just wanted to tell her the terrible news about her mother coming. Not that she would have confided in him anyway, with the Sharp Rehabilitation Center lurking in the corner of her mind. Still, it would have been nice if he had tried to console her, even just a little.

Pulling herself up, she lumbered to the bathroom and leaned on the long marble vanity. It was strange to see that beautiful face marred with red tear tracks and puffy eyes. When she didn't have physical proof in front of her, she imagined looking like her old self.

After splashing cold water on her face, she looked up and put on a resolve that didn't feel as solid as it appeared. "I am Hallie now," she whispered to the mirror. "Hi, I'm Hallie DiBarto. This is who I am now, not Chris Copestakes. This is my life."

She envisioned herself like a butterfly emerging from the cocoon, previously a fuzzy brown worm. Hallie walked away from the mirror, feeling the tiniest bit more in control of her life.

That feeling of control slipped through her fingers as Jamie rapped on the bedroom door. A tightening sensation clutched her insides when he opened the door partway and peered inside.

"Your mother's here. She's waiting for you in the living room."

Hallie tried to quell the urge to beg him to accompany her. Jamie in and of himself wasn't particularly comforting. Still, the thought of having him with her somehow made her feel better, and the knowledge that it wasn't going to happen left her spirit overcast.

She slowly rose from the bed and moved toward the door, finding it difficult to maneuver in the suffocating blue jeans she'd found. His eyes glanced downward before looking at her face.

"It's strange to see you without all your makeup on," he said, though she couldn't tell how he meant it.

"Oh. I just didn't feel like going through the routine. Actually, she hadn't yet done the routine, and wearing a lot of makeup wasn't the norm for her. Something else to learn.

As she followed Jamie down the stairway, a small hope harbored in her heart that he was indeed planning to go with her. When he reached the ground floor, however, he turned.

"*Ciao*. Have fun." Then he disappeared around the back of the staircase and into the confines of the house.

"Yeah, thanks a lot," she muttered, though she knew he couldn't hear her.

"Hallie, honey!" Velvet yelled when she opened the door to the living room. Then Velvet disdainfully looked around, planting her hands on her wide hips. "That damn butler always makes me feel like some kinda lowlife every time I come here. He escorts me into this room and closes the door behind him like I might escape." Then her face brightened again, helped by the vivid red lipstick and scarlet rouge. "You're looking good, honey, really good. How do you feel?"

Hallie shrugged. "All right, I guess."

"Good. Let's get out of here before they accuse me of stealing something."

Velvet steered her out of the room by her arm, then

pointedly ignored Solomon as he opened the front door for them. Hallie smiled at him, but his face remained stern. She decided then that she would make up for the old Hallie's misdeeds toward the man.

The pink paint on the Thunderbird was dirty, looking like the color of vomit. Velvet strutted to it as one would to a chauffeur-driven limousine. Hallie tugged on the loose door handle, and Velvet said, "You got to open it from the inside. Here, I'll get it." When she leaned over to pull the handle, Hallie thought the woman's chest was going to pop right out of her flowery blouse.

Once they reached the end of the driveway, Velvet turned to her with a sigh. "You really don't remember me, do you?"

The question took Hallie by surprise, and all she could do was shake her head. The hand Velvet placed on Hallie's thigh reminded her of a hooker's, with long red talons and glittery rings that only boasted illusionary diamonds and worn-out gold.

"I might as well tell you, hon. We never did get along too good." Velvet laughed uneasily. "I always thought it was because we were too much alike." She shook her head. "But you never bought that. Maybe we can make a fresh start on things. You know, be like a real mother and daughter."

Hallie could only smile weakly, and that made Velvet grin more, then pull out onto the highway. Hallie could never picture this woman as her mother, never ever. Her real mother *looked* like a mother. And acted like one. She wore her curly brown hair short and ladylike, dressed in casual, domestic clothing and never let any of her girls leave the house without making peace with them. In Janet's eyes, there wasn't room for dissension in the ranks, and never did a harsh word fly without being immediately followed by an apology.

"Are you feeling all right, hon?" Velvet's sandpapery voice sheared into her thoughts.

Hallie replaced her homesick frown with a smile. "I'm fine. Just trying to remember things, that's all."

Every time she thought about her past life, that intangible, disturbing feeling crept in to shadow her memories. She wondered what Alan was doing now, and if he missed her. In some ways he reminded her of Jamie, with his brooding ways and mood swings. Jamie, however, seemed to have more reason behind his.

"*Aaaaahhhh!*" Hallie's thoughts were smashed as she looked up to see a truck cutting a wide turn toward their car. The scream had escaped her lips before she could hold it back, and Velvet slammed on the brakes and looked at her as if she were mad.

With her hand to her chest, she said, "My goodness, girl! You nearly scared the living daylights out of me. That truck had plenty of room."

Hallie started shaking, and her face felt cold and clammy. She didn't know what had triggered her overreaction, but memories of her nightmare bridges flashed in her mind, leaving the same trail of fear they left through the night.

"I guess it just looked closer. I'm sorry."

Velvet glanced over at her before pulling back onto the highway. She seemed to drive with special care after that. Hallie stared out the window for a while, concentrating on the scenery and not her trembling hands. Once she was calm again, she studied the clutter on the floor of the car for clues about the woman she would now call mother. Two combs and a brush, Snickers wrappers, a discarded tube of lipstick. Not much to go on.

They headed north of Escondido, then west toward the Pacific. The sun glistened across a cloudless sky, and Hallie vaguely thought of Jamie's eyes. Blue like a sunlit sky. Cold as snow. Velvet turned up the radio and bounced around like a teenager to a rap song. At that moment, Hallie felt older than her mother. At least inside.

They slowly cruised by bikini shops, sidewalk surfboard sales, and beachside bars. Velvet turned down the radio, slipped on purple-rimmed sunglasses and turned to Hallie.

"Does it bring anything back?"

Hallie looked around, pretending an effort to dislodge memories. In fact, it was completely foreign to her. Surfboards attached to car rooftops, sun-bleached blondes in sandals, groups of teenagers leaning against souped-up cars. It was small town, but nothing like Maven, Colorado. Hallie shook her head when she realized Velvet was waiting for an answer.

"I thought I'd take you around to some of your old haunts, you know, try to jar some memories. Hey, how about Kent and Steve? Do they stir anything up?"

Hallie ignored Velvet's wiggling eyebrows and waved back at two incredibly beachy looking guys. They looked as if they had walked right out of *Beverly Hills 90210*. Velvet cruised by them without stopping, thank God.

"Did I go out with one of them?" Hallie asked.

Velvet snorted. "You went out with both of them. At the same time! Deny it all you want, hon, but you're just like your mama. It was two years before they talked to each other after that."

Hallie frowned. "Did sh—I break up their friend-ship?"

Velvet laughed in that harsh way of hers. "Friend-ship? Hah! They're brothers! Their father told me later that when he came over to talk to you about what you were doing to his sons, you came on to him, too! You'll have to tell me whether that was true or not when you start remembering. I always thought he was making it up, but I wouldn't put it past you."

Hallie tried to laugh it off, but her image of the former Hallie was becoming less and less amusing. Velvet parked behind a line of cars by the side of the road where it snaked alongside the ocean. Hallie followed her mother's lead and stepped out of the car. Huge brown, beige, and orange boulders led down to a beach covered with smoother, miniature versions. The sand was an odd shade of light brown, looking scorched in some places. Foamy waves stretched for about twenty yards out before turning deep blue. A bearded man and his wife threw a Frisbee into the water for their spotted dog to retrieve.

"You used to practically *live* out here. Here and Win-dansea Beach. I knew you were sneaking out at mid-night to watch those boys surf, but what could I do? If I would've said something to you, you probably would've gone out more just to defy me. You'd go there after school and spend all weekend there, too. And speaking of, let's head over to your high school."

Hallie studied the brick building, pretending once again to conjure memories that weren't there. It seemed as though the old Hallie's life had been more of a teenage soap opera than years of study and decision about life choices. If Chris had been a little too studious and serious, Hallie had been the exact opposite. And now those years of taking night courses at the community college were wasted. She had the knowledge, but the credits were on a dead girl's records.

As if reading her thoughts, Velvet said, "You took a couple of college courses, but you said you couldn't decide what you wanted to do and quit. Joya had you convinced all you needed to do was marry a rich guy and you'd be set. Not that I didn't agree and want that for you too, but..."

"Ha—I loved Jamie," Hallie stated simply.

Again, that harsh laugh. "Yeah, maybe you loved his body and looks." Then Velvet grew serious. "But I don't think you ever really knew how to love someone. It's my fault. And your father's, the good-for-nothing crumb bag. He sure wasn't there for us."

Hallie looked out the window, unable to respond. Maybe what she had seen in the wedding video was pure infatuation on Hallie's part. Maybe Jamie's too. She laughed under her breath. What did she know about love? That kind of love, anyway? She had been in love twice. But she was never sure she had actually been loved back. Hallie smiled when they passed a planetarium. She had definite memories about a place like that.

"Do you remember something, Hallie?" Velvet asked hopefully, leaning over and looking at what Hallie had been smiling at.

Hallie hadn't realized that she had openly smiled at the memory, but now had to go along with it. "Yes, actually. Something vague about watching laser light shows set to music." In her old life, she had spent many summer midnights watching shows with her friends.

Velvet had already pulled into the parking lot, and within a minute they were walking around the plant beds that surrounded the large round building. "Can you remember anything else?"

Hallie had to be careful. She remembered a lot, but not of this life. A board announced laser shows on Friday and Saturday nights at 10:30 and midnight. Longing of family and friends filled her and made her feel more distant to the woman standing beside her.

"You went to these shows?" Velvet pointed a long red fingernail at the board. "I don't remember you ever going to something like this. Not that you told me everything you did, but you always told me about neat things."

Hallie shrugged. "I probably only went once or twice. Let's go."

They drove deep into a middle-class neighborhood. Kids with skateboards raced others with rollerblades. The houses were small, lawns mildly cluttered but manicured.

"That's where Joya lived when you two were kids," Velvet pointed out. Two driveways down she pulled into one of the dumpiest houses on the street. An empty taxicab was parked just off the weedy front yard. A brown cat was curled up on the front porch in between two dead potted plants. A dead spider plant hung from a brittle macramé hanger. Hallie followed Velvet up to the front door.

"Surely this will bring some inkling of a memory back," Velvet said with a prodding tone. "You spent most of your life here."

"No, I'm afraid not."

Velvet sighed aloud, then her distraught expression changed to one a little girl might have just before she shares a secret. "I want you to meet Hank," she said in a whisper just before opening the front door. "He doesn't have a lot of money right now, but he's hard-working and he's got ideas, big ideas. That's his taxi out there."

The smell of cat pee nearly knocked Hallie to the red sculptured carpet. Sitting in a worn brown recliner sat a balding man in his late forties, wearing only blue polka-dot boxer shorts and an undershirt. Velvet seemed oblivious to the odor, swaying her hips all the way to the man and bending down for a kiss. Hallie left the door open, hoping fresh air would help.

"Hank, get your hands out of there!" Velvet said with a girlish giggle. "Didn't I tell you I was bringing my Hallie over for dinner? Look at you sitting there in your underwear!"

With feigned shame, Hank dropped his newspaper over his midsection and straightened the recliner to shake her hand. Hallie reluctantly held her hand out to him.

"Velvet," he said in a leering manner. "You didn't tell me you had such a knockout for a daughter."

Velvet stiffened, then she sprawled out seductively on his lap. "But I'm prettier, ain't I?" she asked him, nuzzling his bristly cheek.

"Yeah, sure you are," he said but kept staring at Hallie.

Hallie turned toward the open door but found it closed. The air quickly became stuffy and rancid. Something furry brushed by her, and she jumped away.

"Oh, that's just Charisma," Velvet said. "He won't

hurt you."

Hallie had to fight the urge to flee the premises. She glanced at the greasy kitchen clock shaped like a mushroom. Four. She hoped they ate dinner early. In fact, she prayed that they did. Suddenly the mansion in Los Almeda didn't seem so cold and bleak. It was paradise.

For over an hour, Velvet plied Hallie with photo album after photo album. Pictures of an adorable little blond girl on the beach, in the backyard with Joya making mud pies. Pictures of a stunning teenager with guy after guy, on surfboards, going to high school dances. Velvet hadn't changed much in all those years, but the man on her arm changed with just about every photo. If the old Hallie had been a run-around, she'd had her mother to learn from.

When a timer went off in the kitchen, Velvet said something about checking on dinner. When she stood, her skin stuck to the imitation leather furniture and she yelped like a dog. Hank, who had been immersed in a beer and game show, now turned his attention to them.

"You got a big red mark on those fat thighs of yours," he said to Velvet without the least bit of humor.

"And you're going to have a big red mark on those fat lips of yours, too," Velvet said in the same manner.

Hallie wondered if life had always been this way for the woman whose place she'd taken. It was a sad thought, and she said a silent thank you to God for giving her such wonderful parents. Most importantly, her sisters were still enclosed in the warm embrace of home. She envied them, and found herself fighting back tears.

"I made your favorite dishes," Velvet was saying.

"Mm," Hallie answered, coming back. She looked over at the dishes on the table. Tuna casserole, canned green beans, and potato salad from the supermarket deli. The smell of warm tuna fish filled her stomach with tumbling nausea. "I don't feel so well all of a sudden. I think I'll just sit in the living room until my stomach settles down."

"But tuna's your favorite dish." Velvet pouted. "Don't tell me your taste buds have forgotten, too."

Hallie kept moving away from the smell, her eyes searching out a door that might lead to the bathroom. She ended up walking outside and taking in huge gulps of cool salty air. An intimate understanding of what made Hallie the way she was began filling her.

Poor Hallie. No wonder you were so messed up.

CHAPTER 5

The mansion on the hill looked homier to Hallie than it probably looked to anyone else when Velvet's Thunderbird pulled into the circular driveway. Velvet turned and placed a cold hand on her arm.

"Hon, if you need anything at all, you just let me know."

The mood had been strained ever since dinner, and their drive back to Los Almeda had been peacefully silent. Hallie was willing to make amends, as long as she never had to endure such an evening again.

"Sure. Thanks for the memories." She touched Velvet's hand and got out of the car. "Thanks for everything. I'll call." Then she turned toward the front doors, not sure she would call Velvet again. Would it seem strange to sever ties with her mother? Probably not. And what about Joya and whoever else occupied a place in Hallie's old life? She didn't know. Jamie, now he was another issue. He obviously intended for them to sever ties in just over a week. For some reason, the thought gave her a sad twinge, one she attributed to the way she had always felt when anyone's marriage fell apart.

She went upstairs and watched the videos again, trying to concentrate on studying Hallie and not Jamie. She tried to imitate her walk and the way she spoke. In listening to background conversations, she latched onto a phrase the old Hallie used a lot: "Completely excellent!" She tried to say it the way Hallie used to, in the breathy way Marilyn Monroe spoke.

Then she walked to the bedroom, subconsciously stepping over the place where her dogs would have been sleeping. When she was out on her own, she would get another Sheltie. Later, that decision lulled her into sleep with a smile on her face, only to be replaced by a contorted expression as she fought to control a car being pushed off a bridge by a semi.

***

Find his heart.

Those words called Hallie to wakefulness, as they did every morning. This time she latched on instead of letting them slip away with morning's light. But the meaning was never within her grasp, and she thought it might be Alan's heart they referred to. With the words came a feeling of warmth and light. With the thought of Alan, however, came the nagging feeling of something not right, something not remembered.

After snooping through Hallie's purse, she now knew that the body she had taken over was twenty-seven, four years older than she actually was. She had a driver's license and credit cards. With those, she wanted to drive into town and buy some clothes she could feel a little more normal in. A little more covered in.

As she was coming down the stairs, Jamie met her

halfway. They both stopped, and he forced a smile she knew wasn't really there.

She gave him one that was. "Good morning, Jamie."

"You've got a phone call. Joya."

He said the words with such distaste, she wondered just what had passed between those two.

"You really hate her, don't you?" Hallie asked.

He looked at her with the oddest expression. "Yes, I do. And someday you'll remember why."

"Why don't you tell me now?"

"Your *friend* is waiting on the phone."

She followed him into the great room. After pointing to a phone near the couch, he walked through the French doors outside. From the cotton shirt and shorts he wore, she guessed he was heading down to do his laps in the pool.

"Hello."

"Hallie, it's Joya. How are you feeling, sweetie?"

"Much better, thanks."

"Good! You're coming with me today. We're going to Body Rhythms."

"What's that, a night club?"

Joya's laugh sounded raucous over the phone. "No, silly, the health club."

"Mm, I don't know."

"You don't have to know. You just have to come. It'll be good for you. Who knows, it might scare up some memories."

"Well, okay. I wanted to go into San Diego today anyway. Where is this place?"

Joya gave her easy directions, and they made plans to meet there at two. Now all Hallie needed was transportation. She glanced uneasily toward the doors leading out to the terrace. Asking Jamie would be less daunting than asking Theresa.

Before she stood, a picture caught her eye. She walked over to it, and her heart skipped a beat. It was a professional photo of Jamie on a shiny black motorcycle, his long muscular legs stretched out in front of him as he leaned back with crossed arms. It had been taken at night, on a sidewalk in front of a bar boasting a pink neon sign reading: *Harley's*.

Another blown-up photo showed a close-up of Jamie resting his arms on a rock down by the beach. His blond hair was lit golden by the rays of the setting sun, and his eyes blazed a wanton blue. She stared at him for several minutes, enjoying the stir of feelings it produced inside her. Finally, she moved on to a framed cover of the fashion magazine, *Men at Work*. Jamie in an Armani suit above the heading, *The Dash of Design*. Yes, he did look dashing. Model material. Hallie wondered if he still did it.

Other pictures were obviously family outings. One was of four people dwarfed by huge redwood trees. The brass plate on the frame read: *Muir Woods National Monument*. She studied the people in the picture. Jamie's father was a tall man with a large build. The man to his right was a younger version, and neither looked anything like Jamie. His brother had warm good looks, brown curly hair and brown eyes. More like a teddy bear. She instantly liked him. Jamie had taken the sculptured, finer lines of his mother.

She finally pulled herself away from the photos and walked outside and down the stairs leading to the pool. When she spotted Jamie, she stopped. He was stretching, wearing nothing but his suit and bronzed skin. His thighs and calves tensed with each movement, and the muscles of his arms and back rippled beneath his skin. She imagined running her hand through his thick blond hair down to the few inches that tapered past his shoulder. She expelled a deep breath to clear away the fuzzies building inside her stomach.

"Hello," she called from a safe distance.

He started, obviously disturbed from deep thoughts. "What's up?"

She swallowed. "I hate to disturb you, but—"

"You always disturb me, Hallie." He tempered that with a shallow smile.

Back at ya. "I'd like to go into San Diego this afternoon. Should I call a cab?"

He cocked his eyebrows, smile still in place. "Why don't you take your car?"

"I don't know where it is."

He started walking off, waving for her to follow him. They went around the house to a three-car garage. One of the doors was open, and he led her through to the last bay—to where the red Porsche sat. She stared at it while he went to a cabinet and pulled out a set of keys. The video played through her mind, Jamie leading her out blindfolded, Hallie's reaction when she saw it there with the big ribbon.

"What's wrong?" Jamie's voice cut into her thoughts. "You're going to be all right to drive, aren't you?"

She pulled her gaze from the car. "Yes, I'll be fine. I remember how to drive."

He tossed her the keys as he walked past her. "Have fun in Insane Diego. Are you coming back here to get ready? I don't want Mick coming here to pick you up, except at the end of the driveway."

Hallie looked at him in confusion. "Get ready for what? Why in the world would Mick come here to pick me up?"

Jamie had the decency to look a bit embarrassed. "I went into our room to get another bathing suit and saw the tickets for the opera. I just want to make it clear that I don't—"

"I didn't buy those tickets for Mick. I bought them to take you."

His crooked smile took on a sarcastic twist. "Come on, who are you trying to fool? You know I hate the opera."

She really wanted to believe that her former self had bought those tickets for Jamie and not Mick. She certainly wasn't taking Mick. Going to the opera with Jamie might be a way for her to smooth things over and make peace. If Hallie had loved the opera, then she would try to as well. Besides, she had never been to one before.

"You might like this one." She struggled to remember which one the tickets were for.

"Yes, it might be relevant at that. Interesting that you would choose *Taming of the Shrew*. Any particular reason for that?"

"Never mind that. Just go one last time. For old time's sake."

"There are several things I would not do with you for old time's sake, and that is one of them."

Mm, she could imagine what at least one of the others might be.

"I might hate it now, too."

"You won't." He touched his fingertip to her collar bone. "Inside the fog, you are still the same Hallie."

She wrapped her fingers around his finger, making his right eyebrow twitch. "You don't know who I am inside here." She squeezed his finger, giving him a look that would have never worked with Chris's face.

He shook his head but surprised her by saying, "All right."

"Really?"

"I'll appreciate the irony of watching it with you. Especially knowing it will be the last time."

His reminder of their divorce doused her excitement. She hated that word and hated the fact that he was so happy about it.

"I'll find something to wear in San Diego," she said.

It took her five minutes to figure out how the car worked. She drove with particular care, not because it was an expensive car, but because it was special. Jamie had picked this car out for the woman he had once loved. She caressed the leather steering wheel, remembering again the video. Hallie had been a fool for risking what she had with Jamie, especially for some creep like Mick. And now *she* was paying the price for it.

***

Hallie pulled up in front of the high-tech health club and reluctantly allowed the young valet to park her car. Music pounded throughout the large room crammed with chrome work-out machines and mirrors that made the place seem infinite. Two muscle-bound men walked by, murmuring a hello as their eyes roamed down her shiny green workout outfit. She had spent two hours in the mall looking for clothes that were more suited to her old tastes and body. Well, perhaps a little more daring.

"Hal-lie! Over here!" Joya's voice called out over the music. She was in full makeup, wearing a deep purple one-piece outfit that was made to camouflage bulges and accentuate her large chest. "Come on, I'll walk you to the locker room so you can put your stuff away."

When they returned, Hallie followed Joya to a pair of stationary bikes. Twenty minutes in, Joya's eyes were getting more of a workout than her pedaling legs, checking out every guy who passed by. Then she turned to Hallie. "You know, I can't get used to you not wearing makeup. And perfume. It's too weird."

As Chris, she had worn little makeup. As Hallie, she would have to wear more of it. "I didn't have time this morning."

Joya's mouth dropped open. "I can't believe I'm hearing that *you* didn't have time to make yourself up. The world used to wait for Hallie to get ready."

Hallie shrugged. "Guess I've changed. Joya, can I ask you something? Why does Jamie dislike you so much?"

Joya laughed. "That obvious, huh?"

Hallie flushed, embarrassed at having been so blunt. Her curiosity was getting the best of her manners. "Well, not obvious, but I can tell. Sort of. So, what happened?"

Joya smirked. "He never liked me. I didn't meet him until right before you two got married. After the wedding, I didn't see much of you. Then, after you'd been married about a year, you started flying back to California a lot, staying with me. He figured I was a bad influence on you because you got pretty wild after that. Oh, and there was something else. The three of us went out juking one night, and you and I got trashed. I suggested that you, Jamie, and I have a *ménage a trois*. I have to

92

admit, I was curious about how Jamie would be in bed. You said it sounded like fun too, but he exploded. He was so disgusted that you could share him, he dragged you right out of there." She shrugged. "His loss."

Hallie tried to keep from showing the shock on her face. "You mean that Ha—I would have let Jamie go to bed with you? I wouldn't have minded?"

She laughed loudly. "Minded? You would have been watching!"

Hallie shuddered. She couldn't imagine offering up the man she loved to her best friend. Or anyone.

Joya flipped her hand. "Aw, I don't think you'd do something like that if you were sober. But it sure was fun when we did it with Tony."

Hallie's eyebrows went up, and she half-whispered, "Tony? You mean you and me with some guy?"

Joya licked her lips. "Uh hmm. Too bad you don't remember. That guy was in ecstasy." She looked at Hallie's expression. "You and I didn't do anything together! We just took turns doing him. It was fun."

Hallie picked up the pace of her pedaling, deciding to change the subject. "Did I like the opera?"

Joya shrugged. "You told me you did, but I think you just wanted to seem uppity and socially correct."

"I'm going tonight. With Jamie."

Joya raised an eyebrow. "Really? Now that's surprising."

"Because he hates the opera?"

"That and because you two aren't exactly the wonderful little couple anymore. Aren't you still getting a divorce?"

"Well, I guess. In any case, he's leaving soon. I told him I bought the opera tickets for him."

That raucous laugh sounded again. "You're such a liar! At least that hasn't changed. You were planning to surprise Mick with them. It's his favorite opera, you told me."

"I convinced Jamie, well, I don't think I actually convinced him, but I talked him into going. I wasn't sure who I had planned to take, but I don't want to go with Mick."

Joya crossed her arms over her chest and looked at Hallie with interest, pedaling all the while. "What's going on between you and Mick anyway?"

"He scares me."

Joya sputtered. "It's about time you saw what a slime he is."

"You know?"

"Yes, and I tried to tell you five hundred times?" She placed a perfectly manicured hand against her chest. "As your best friend, I did tell you. Did you listen? Absolutely not."

"Why did sh—I keep seeing him then?"

Joya became serious. "I think you were afraid of him, but you wouldn't admit it. Maybe he threatened to do something if you left him. Do you remember anything about him? About your relationship?"

Hallie shook her head, wrapping her arms around herself as a chill washed over her. "No, but I'm learning fast. He snuck up on me when I was walking around the estate. It was as if he was watching for me. Waiting. And he asked me about something called the Manderlay. Do you know anything about that?"

"The gem that was stolen from Dave Wainthorpe's home? Why would he ask you about that?"

"I don't know. Who's Dave Wainthorpe?"

UNTIL I DIE AGAIN

"He's a friend of Jamie's. In fact, you two had dinner at his house the night before the robbery. Good thing it didn't happen while you were all there."

They moved over to the stair machines next to the free weight area. Joya walked to the one nearest the benches and seductively twisted around to give the men nearby a view of her behind. Once settled onto their machines, Joya whispered to Hallie, "The one in the pink shirt's mine. I think his name is Chad. Last time we saw them here, they invited us out on their boat for an afternoon cruise. Why don't I see if he and his friend in the yellow are up for"—she wiggled her eyebrows—"a little fun."

Hallie's looked at the hulking, grunting, sweaty men Joya referred to. She wasn't ready, nor did she want to be ready, to have a little fun with them. Bulky muscles had never turned her on. She was more into physiques like Jamie's, impressive without being unnatural.

"No, I don't think so. Joya, we're both married women. Didn't that matter to us?"

Joya smiled. "Not so much."

***

Jamie slipped into the bedroom Hallie was using and pulled his tuxedo out of the armoire. Steam rolled down the hallway that led to the large glass-enclosed shower. She had been in there forever, and he wanted to get his tux out so Solomon could press it. Why did he agree to go to the opera with her anyway? She had given him that look, that pleading puppy-eyed look he'd never seen before. He would have to be careful about that. This was the last time she was getting her way.

An hour later, he knocked on her door. "Hallie, we'd

better get going." He had thought she'd get caught up in something while she was in the city with Joya and not come home until late. Or at least until it was too late to go to this damned opera. But she had surprised him by returning with plenty of time to spare.

"I'm coming!"

She opened the door. They both stared at each other, then cleared their throats and looked in the other direction.

He glanced back uneasily at her, trying to put casualness in the gesture. "You look nice." And he meant it. She wore a stunning calf-length dress that brought out that new deepness in her blue eyes. Her dress didn't reveal most of her cleavage, in fact, didn't reveal any skin at all. The collar went right up to her neck, finished off with an amber brooch. Her hair tumbled in big curls over her shoulders, not in that wild frenzy she usually sent it in. Her makeup was light and natural, not overdone. Elegant was not a word he would have ever used in describing Hallie, but she was it now. She looked uneasy, and he realized he'd been scrutinizing her.

"You look nice, too," she said. "Sorry I took so long. Let's go."

In the garage, Hallie walked to the passenger side of the car, and Jamie opened the door for her. The setting sun created a warm, peaceful feeling in the car. He glanced over at her and found her looking out the window and fidgeting. It seemed as if a stranger sat beside him. She looked like his wife. And she smelled like her, too much perfume smothering the air. He couldn't quite pinpoint the feeling, but she didn't *feel* like Hallie anymore.

He turned up the stereo, changing the satellite radio

to the hard rock one. How deep that change had gone was something Mick could figure out. And that was strange, too. Why wasn't she with him now? Jamie had figuratively opened the door for her to go live with the jerk, but she had stayed. These opera tickets, too. He knew she had not bought these tickets with him in mind, yet she didn't want to take Mick. In fact, she had used her wiles to coerce him to go with her. He shifted in the seat, his thoughts making him feel uncomfortable.

Dinner didn't go much further to settle his nerves. Oh, the service was impeccable, as usual, the food delightful. The conversation was polite, and that was not usual. And there were a few surprises, too.

"You never liked salmon," he remarked after she had ordered. "You always said it was too fishy tasting."

She frowned. "Oh. Guess I'll order the steak then. Medium?"

"Medium rare."

The waiter gave them an odd look, but Jamie didn't bother to explain.

She ordered an iced tea instead of a glass of wine. After he said something about that, she added wine to her order, then ended up drinking the tea anyway. She put pepper on everything but never once used the salt. He looked across at her as she scooped the last bit of potato out of the skin.

"I don't think I've ever seen you eat this much. Ever." He tried to make his remark sound light, but she wrinkled her forehead.

"Oh. I guess I'm just extra hungry, that's all."

He smiled. "I'm not trying to be derogatory, Hallie. I like to see a woman eat and not pick at her food and complain about her weight like you used to do."

Her eyebrows formed a frown. "Do I have a weight problem?"

"You used to when you were younger. Before I met you. I never see you eat much, and you're always complaining about dieting."

She pushed her empty plate away. "Guess I'll pass on dessert then."

He glanced at his watch. "We'd better get going anyway."

As they waited for the attendant to retrieve the Porsche, Hallie asked, "Did I go to the health club a lot?"

His right eye involuntarily narrowed at her. "Every time we came to Los Almeda you went with Joya."

"Did I like going?"

He looked away. "Apparently. You spent five or six hours in San Diego every time you went." He didn't feel like getting into what she really liked about the club. Damn, why did it still bother him? He couldn't wait for the evening to end. Or their marriage.

When they walked up to the San Diego Opera, Hallie looked around at everything as if she were seeing it for the first time. He found himself smiling at the sparkle in her eyes as she watched beautifully dressed people flitting by. It reminded him of the first time he'd taken her to an opera, because she wanted to see what it was like. Back then everything awed and delighted her. After a while, she got used to it.

They were escorted to their seats, and Hallie sat up straight and looked around the theater, taking in every detail. Then she concentrated on her program. When the lights went down, she leaned forward and watched intently. Was her face glowing?

"This is completely excellent!" she said in her old way.

Ah, thank you for that. It reminded him that her façade, whether intentional or not, would soon fade away to reveal the woman he knew so well. He was glad she'd refreshed his memory.

CHAPTER 6

The opera had been underway for twenty minutes. Everyone was watching and enjoying the show. The sound was clear, the view excellent, the seats comfortable. And Hallie was bored out of her mind. She glanced at Jamie, who was staring off in a direction other than the stage. Now she realized the sacrifice he had made in coming here with her. Every time the tenor hit a high note, she cringed. The droning, unintelligible singing was ripping right into her nerves. She looked around incredulously. Were these people actually enjoying this? Or were they pretending as Hallie had done for so long?

Her thoughts wandered. She wasn't sure if her efforts at putting makeup on had been successful or not, the way he'd studied her with an inscrutable expression. That was probably good because Jamie excelled in keeping his thoughts from his face. And showing them when he wanted to—usually when it was disdain he felt for her. She had seen none of that, nor impatience at her taking so long. She had put makeup on the way Hallie had in her videos—and hated it. Stripping it all off again and washing her face, she applied just a light touch instead.

And that god-awful perfume. The blue bottle, Sexual Infinity, had smelled good when she'd sniffed the nozzle. The first time she pressed the pump, it just dribbled out. Hallie must have had trouble with it before; the top had been pried off to replace the sprayer. When she pressed it again, the perfume doused her. Even after trying to wash that off, she still reeked of it.

Hallie was taking shape in her mind, through the videos, her friends, and mostly her husband. She glanced at Jamie again, admiring his profile. When he started to turn toward her, she averted her gaze, pretending to enjoy the show. Then she realized something: she didn't want to pretend anymore. Sure, she would have to pretend to be Hallie, because she was Hallie. But she didn't have to pretend to like wine and opera, to hate salmon.

She made a mental list of the woman whose place she had taken. She was a cheat. A flirt. Selfish. Thoughtless. By God, the woman was a slut. She glanced down. *I don't even know where this body has been.* She had some ideas, and she didn't like them. Her gaze moved to Jamie again. Hallie had made love to him. The thought made her curious about their lovemaking. Had it been passionate? Fulfilling? Those thoughts tickled through her.

Jamie looked over, catching her staring at him. She was glad the darkness kept her blush a secret. But her smile, now that was hard to miss. It didn't look like the pleasant smiles on the other people's faces. No, she was sure hers was frisky.

He leaned over. "What are you grinning about? I don't see anything funny."

His whisper tickled her ear, sending a shiver down her neck. She nodded toward a man she'd spotted earlier. "What do you think? A toupee? Or a bush?"

The man's dark thick hair abruptly stopped two-thirds down and turned into thin graying hair.

Jamie grinned. "That's the most entertaining thing I've seen yet."

Hallie giggled. "What about that couple over there?" Three rows ahead and to the right a young man's black hair stuck up in points all around his head. His companion's head looked more like a six o'clock shadow, her scalp showing through the tiny hairs struggling to grow back.

He looked at her with a surprised smile, then took a lock of her hair in his hand and whispered, "You'd look great in that hairstyle." He glanced around. "Anyone got any scissors?"

She laughed and pulled away. "No! Don't touch my hair."

The people sitting near them turned to give them looks meant to hush. Hallie didn't care. She leaned over and quietly said, "Only if you get your ears pierced and wear earrings like his."

He looked at the punkish man she'd indicated, with three-inch handcuff earrings dangling from both ears and a spike through his eyebrow.

"In one ear or both?"

"Both."

"Hmm." He looked at her hair again. "It'd be worth it. I'll find an ear-piercing shop; you find a hairdresser. Or a hair undresser, as the case would be."

As if they were both imagining the other without hair or with funky earrings, they started laughing. Several people turned and *shhhhd* them. He laughed when she stuck her tongue out at the back of their heads.

He whispered, "Darn, they might never let us in here again."

She turned to respond and found her nose touching his. Their gazes locked and their smiles faded. Something unraveled inside, freeing her heart to jump around. And words sang to her from a distance, sweet, melodious words.

Find his heart.

The impact of what those words meant sent her backward, and she stared into the darkness around her while trying to catch her breath. When she looked at Jamie, he seemed stunned, too. And a little annoyed with himself. He stared at the stage, and she knew darn well he wasn't interested in anything up there.

"I know you hate this stuff as much as I do, so don't pretend that you're all of a sudden enjoying it," she said.

He looked at her, causing her heart to increase its rhythm. "I need an intermission. Let's get out of here."

Taking her hand, he pulled her from the seat and headed toward the exit doors. The grumps mumbled their wishes that their departure be permanent. When they reached the fresh air outside, their laughter resounded through the parking lot. He clamped his arm around her shoulder and steered her toward the car. She was almost disappointed when they reached the Porsche and he removed his arm to open the door for her. After getting in, he turned to her.

"I think that's the most fun I've ever had at one of those things." Then he looked ahead, and an uneasiness passed over his features.

"What's wrong?" she asked, desperately wanting the

mood to continue.

"I'm not used to having fun with you anymore, Hallie. It seems strange." He backed the car up and pulled to the exit.

"So? What's wrong with having fun with me?"

He looked at her for the longest time. "There's been so much between us."

She ventured to reach out and touch the hand resting on the gear shifter. "Can't we forget the past?"

His laugh held no humor. "That's easy for you to say. You *have* forgotten the past. I can't do that, even if I wanted to."

He pulled onto the highway, heading in the direction of home. The last threads of their light mood slipped away, but she grasped at one.

"Let's go to Oceanview."

He looked at her as if she were crazy. "Don't tell me you have a sudden urge to visit your mother."

"God, no. I have another idea." She grinned provocatively, hoping to pique his curiosity.

"And what might that be?"

"Come on, and you'll find out."

"I don't know if I like your surprises. Let's just go back home."

She leaned toward him, needing to close the gap between them, at least physically. "Please, Jamie. I don't want tonight to end yet."

Instead of winning him over with her pleading and honesty, he moved away. "Hallie, this is too weird. You're too different. I don't know how to act around you anymore or what to expect. We've gone along all this time being unhappy and making each other miserable. Then, just when I accept losing you as a wife, you nearly die. No, you do die. Then, when I'm ready to let you go completely, you come back. I was happy about that, I really was. And I figured, back to square three, where we were from before your stroke. But you can't be predictable, no, we go to square fifty-six, wherever that is." He dug his fingers through his hair in frustration, and all she could think about was running her own fingers through it, too.

"Jamie, I don't know what to tell you. I'm a different person now."

He glanced at her with narrowed eyes. "I'm not so sure about that either. You're different, but I'm not sure how different and for how long."

She looked at him intently. "Forever."

His fingers tightened on the steering wheel. "I'll be happy if we can part friends. That's all I want from you, is peace. Maybe that's what's different now. Maybe we can do that."

She slumped in her seat, pushed into silence by the finality of his words.

Find his heart.

The words filtered through the closed atmosphere of the car, filtered through her very being. She crossed her arms. *He doesn't have one!* But even as she thought it, she knew it wasn't true. She glanced at him, then away. Total eclipse of the heart.

It was too hard. Easier to just walk away like she'd planned. Maybe go back to Maven. But the thought of leaving Jamie left an ache in her heart. *Damn, why couldn't I have just left right away?* But she already knew the answer. Jamie was the reason she was there. To find his heart, to bring him alive again.

She leaned back, feeling tense all over. It was hard

enough to win the love of a man who'd been hurt; it was impossible when that man thought you were the one who had hurt him. She, a woman who had had two relationships, both of which hadn't gone very well, and now she had a marriage to save. How in Heaven's name was she going to do that?

Hallie looked up to see a sign that read: *TO LOS ALM-EDA, ESCONDIDO.* They had passed the road going east. They were going to Oceanview. She smiled. She was on a mission from God. That was all she needed to know for now.

She wasn't going to do or say anything that would change his mind during the rest of the ride. They pulled into the town that only looked familiar from the night before.

"Okay, where to?"

"To a department store."

"A store? Are we going shopping?"

"No. Just humor me. There, that one will do."

He pulled into the parking lot. She knew they looked ridiculous, Jamie in his white tuxedo shirt and black pants, she in her blue dress. A few people actually said hello to her, but she brushed by them with a casual wave. She didn't have time to renew *old* friendships. Well, except for one.

"What are we buying here?" asked that exception.

"Pillows," she stated simply, knowing he would still be confused.

They picked up two pillows and headed to the front register. A few minutes later, they loaded them into the trunk.

Jamie asked again, "Okay, what are you up to? Don't tell me you plan to make out on the beach, because I'm not—"

She placed a finger over his lips, not wanting him to spoil the mood. "Just humor me. Please."

"Yeah, yeah," he muttered and walked around to open her door.

She directed him to the planetarium. They still had a few minutes. She tugged his arm to hurry him up, rushing him past the sign announcing the laser light show. Thankfully the show hadn't started yet, because she wasn't familiar with the layout of this planetarium. She knew every inch of the one near Maven.

"We're seeing the planets tonight, eh?" Jamie said as he let her lead him into the dim room.

"You'll see."

Rows of seats curved around one side of the small room, and in front of them was a half-circle area on the floor. She threw the pillows down there and carefully, with her dress pulled up, sat on the carpet.

He looked at her, then up at the rows of empty seats. "You're kidding, right?"

She shook her head, a big grin on her face. For the first time, she felt at home. Grabbing his hand, she yanked him down beside her.

"Prop your pillow up on this little ledge like this," she instructed. "It gives you a headrest."

He arranged his pillow, then stretched out on his back. As soon as he got comfortable next to her, the lights went out and a voice spoke to them on the loud-speaker.

"Hello, ladies and gentlemen. Welcome to the Oceanview Planetarium. Tonight, we're going retro, featuring the classic rock bands Journey and Boston. I see that a few of you have been here before and know that the best seats are on the floor in front. Enjoy the show!"

Jamie turned to her and whispered, "You've obviously been here before."

"Um, yeah. When I lived here, I came all the time."

Don't Stop Believin' was the first song, and the red laser beam appeared in the darkness and spelled out JOURNEY above them. Then little squares of blue, green and red filled the sky, moving around in unison with the music. But nothing was more amazing than Jamie's face as he watched in complete fascination. So enthralled was he that he didn't notice her watching him for the entire song and into the next one.

She leaned over and whispered, "Well? Do you like it?"

He nodded, still watching above, and his hair tickled her nose. His cologne was a mixture of musk and masculinity. She closed her eyes and inhaled. When she opened them, she found him staring at her, the blue and green lights playing off his skin.

She instinctively moved back. She was sure, even in the reflection of lights, that he could see the glow of her blush.

He looked back at the laser show. "It's like Spirograph come to life."

His arms were above his head, stretching the white material of his shirt tight against his muscles. She forced herself to look up, commanded herself to keep watching the show. Everything brought back warm, wonderful memories of her former life. The smell of the room, the rustle of people as they moved in their seats or slipped down to the floor to join them. But getting lost in the music had never felt like this before, not with Jamie lying beside her. It surrounded her, wrapped itself around her like a hand wrapping around hers, fingers tightening around her own.

She jerked out of her trance and realized that it wasn't just the music. Jamie *had* taken her hand into his. She didn't dare look at him, didn't move. All she could do was concentrate on the tingling feeling that felt like a thousand bubbles moving up her arm, straight to her stomach. She swallowed hard, trying to dispel the sudden dryness in her throat. It was a full five songs later before she realized she'd had her eyes closed.

She had laid on the floor of a planetarium before, next to a man. And he had taken her hand and held it. But it didn't feel like this. Jamie's hand tensed then loosened, so subtly that if she hadn't been concentrating, the movement would have slipped by unnoticed. The power of his touch, the significance of the gesture. And the effect of the purely physical aspect of it. She was lost in it all, wanting to touch him more, afraid to move for fear he might pull away.

When the last song finished, he stood and stretched before she could see his face. Her hand still felt warm and moist, but the cold air started to chill it. Only giving her his profile, he reached down and offered his hand again, this time to help her to her feet. As soon as she got her balance, he let go and started moving toward the door.

Three younger women looked at Jamie with appreciative glances, and speculative glances at her. They managed to situate themselves between him and Hallie, and he held the door open for them to walk through. The three smiled sweetly and thanked him, but Jamie was watching her, waiting for her to walk through the door. In those blue eyes of his, she couldn't read a thing. Not one emotion seeped to the surface, not one clue to his thoughts and feelings.

He was quiet on the drive back to Los Almeda, and she spent the entire trip weighing whether silence was good or bad. He could, on one hand, be thinking about their future ... rethinking his feelings about her. That thought made her soar inside. But she had to take the alternative into consideration, too. Perhaps he was chastising himself for letting the music and different surroundings woo him into an unguarded mood.

The house loomed large and eerie in the clear night, the blue moonlight reflecting off the gray paint. By the time they had parked the car and let the garage door slide noiselessly closed, she was a bundle of tension. He walked a few inches ahead, his face hidden with the distance.

Maybe it was the tension exploding inside her. Maybe it was the full moon. She didn't know exactly what possessed her, but she took one of the pillows she carried and slammed it into the back of his head. The complete surprise on his face, coupled with the sight of disheveled hair sticking straight up made her start giggling helplessly. She doubled over, leaving herself defenseless when he grabbed the pillow and whipped her across the backside with it.

She let out a scream and giggle, then rushed him with the other pillow. He put his arm up in defense, and she flung the pillow across his stomach. He narrowed his eyes and tilted his head in challenge, then started for her. Her laughter, combined with delight at having altered his mood, kept her in a fit of laughter, but she managed to dodge him.

"You're just a little wench tonight, aren't you?" he said after missing her.

"No, I'm just trying to have fun!" she yelled from a safe distance. "Don't you ever have fun, Jamie DiBarto?"

He crossed his arms. "Not with you."

She bit her lip, laughter dying in her throat. How right he was. She tucked her pillow under her arm and headed toward the front doors—and was caught completely off guard when the pillow came crashing against the back of her head. Before she had a chance to retaliate, or even turn around, he had slipped an arm around her shoulders and pulled her against his hard body.

"I'm sorry," he whispered beside her ear. His breath felt soft and warm against her neck, but still she shivered. "I didn't mean that. We did have fun once."

She turned around in his embrace, and he moved backward. "We could have fun again, Jamie."

He laughed softly, running his finger down her jaw line and tucking a strand of hair behind her ear. "I bet we could. But I don't want that anymore."

"You think I'm talking about sex, don't you? A romp in the hay. A sweaty, heavy breathing session in bed, a dance between the sheets." She shook her head. She *wasn't* talking about that, was she? No, no. "Fun, like we had tonight. Yes, even the opera part. Walks on the beach, skiing, shuffleboard, anything."

"Only if you wear that dress."

"Only if you wear that tuxedo."

They stood in silence for a moment, a comforting aura settling around them. An orchestra of crickets started a stirring harmony nearby. He reached out and took her chin in his fingers.

"Shuffleboard? I'd like to see you play shuffleboard."

"Name the time and the place, honey, and I'll be there."

"In that dress?"

"Or out of it. Uh, I mean, in something different."

This time he stepped closer, and she had the urge to step back. My, but her Freudian slips were going to get her into trouble yet. Jamie's fingers trailed down her throat and chest over the shiny fabric.

"Now that's an interesting picture, you playing shuffleboard in the nude. I'll bet even you haven't done that."

She tilted her face up to his, feeling a strange tightness swirling in her middle. "You'd win that bet. Of course, you'd have to play in the buff, too."

He clucked his tongue. "Too bad we don't have a shuffleboard court on the grounds. I'd take you up on that offer."

"I made some other offers, too."

He looked up thoughtfully, scratching his chin. "Oh, yes, a romp in the hay, or a sweaty, heavy breathing session in bed."

"No, I believe those were walks on the beach and skiing. That other stuff comes later." But that wasn't what her body was saying, darn it.

With a swoop, his fingers twirled her hair up and held it pinned on top of her head. Her heart started beating faster, wondering if he would dare kiss her, hoping he would.

"I'm almost tempted to take you up on at least two of those offers, but I would hate myself in the morning, and I'd probably hate you, too." He kissed her lightly on the nose. "Let's just leave it as it is."

He turned and dug in his pocket for the keys. She stood behind him and resisted the urge to run her fingers through that soft-looking hair, pull him back and tell him he was wrong. And ask him exactly which offers he was tempted to take her up on.

He opened the door and let her walk in first. It was past midnight, but she still wasn't ready for the night to end. She had built a few steps over that great big chasm between them and was aching to close more of the distance.

"Goodnight, Hallie," his soft voice called through the dark hallway. He took the stairs two at a time until he reached the top, closing the door firmly behind him.

"Goodnight," she called to the emptiness. Then she slowly walked up the stairs and into the room she inhabited. The bags of clothes she had bought that afternoon were stacked against the wall by the dresser.

She stood in front of the bathroom mirror, brushing her long hair, thinking. A stranger looked back at her, a beautiful stranger who moved as she did. When she closed her eyes, she still saw the girl with unruly curly-Q hair, brown eyes, and a figure no man would drool over. Especially not a man like Jamie. But she never would have hurt him like his wife had.

The sound of soft footsteps brought her attention to the hallway. It looked quiet. Jamie's door was still closed. She couldn't explain it, but his room felt empty. Curious, she stepped into the hallway and slipped down the stairs. There wasn't a sound anywhere in the house, save for a faint ticking of a clock.

She crept through the family room to the French doors that lined the terrace. The door was unlocked, and she opened it and slipped through to the terrace that overlooked the pool. There, she found him, swimming through the shimmering blue water. Jamie, fighting his demons in churning water. She hoped they would win and overpower that stone wall he had erected around his heart.

She had been wrong that day he had run up to this very terrace to see if she was all right. Wrong when she had yelled that he didn't have a heart. He did, and she had felt it that night in the dark, surrounded by laser beams and love songs. Oh, how she wanted to tell him the truth, that she wasn't Hallie at all, or anything like her. He would never believe her, of course. He would send her to the Sharp Rehabilitation Center where they would electrocute Chris from her soul. Would Jamie tell the orderlies to keep Mick away again?

She shivered at the thought of the man who scared her so much. Never before had she seen such intensity in a man's eyes. Except maybe in Jamie's, but that was a different kind of intensity. His was a determination to keep himself clear and far from her. Mick's was a fierce desire to hold her close and crush her. His threat also floated back to her in the cool breeze. *Remember what I did to that other guy who thought he could steal you away!*

She imagined Mick appearing out of the shadows and dropping some electrical appliance into the pool. Or maybe jumping in, taking Jamie by surprise and drowning him. This time the shiver that shook her was violent.

She watched the shadows, now seeing them move and shift like a man's shadow would. Fearing for Jamie's safety, she remained watching over him. Not until he lifted himself, exhausted, from the pool did she back up toward the doors and slip inside. Then she waited in her room until she heard him walk up the stairs, his breathing heavy. Only then did she fall back on her pillow and close her eyes, willing sleep to take her away.

***

Jamie took a hot shower, then sat down in the upstairs living room, knowing sleep was miles away. He turned on the television, but his thoughts were far from the images on the screen. Two things bothered him about that evening. Actually three, and the last one bothered him immensely.

First, Hallie had said that she'd gone to the planetarium when she lived in Oceanview. On the way out, he'd noticed a brass dedication plaque citing a date of two years earlier. One year past the time she had lived there. He saw no reason for her to lie about it. His frown deepened. Unless she had gone there with Mick, or whoever else caught her fancy. But why did she take him there? And why did she remember that place when she'd forgotten most everything else about her past?

The second thing that bothered him was the distinct feeling that he was being watched while he was in the pool. His state of mind had been far from normal, but the feeling of another presence was strong. Even with the full moon, there were enough trees and shrubs for someone to hide behind. The word paranoia came to mind.

The third thing, the one that bothered him most, was that he'd actually had a good time. Dinner was strange, what with her choosing things she never liked before. The opera was, well, better than he thought it would be. But the laser show, that was something special.

He could have kicked himself for holding her hand. Worse yet, he'd wanted to kiss her out front, her standing there talking about romps in the hay and nude shuffleboard. God, he could have stripped that dress off right there. She was toying with him again.

He reached for the remote control and turned on the DVD player. The miscellaneous disc was still in. Hallie, gorgeous, uninhibited. A flirt. An empty shell looking for a good time and someone to support her. He hit the stop button and turned everything off before heading to bed. When he looked at her bedroom door, he stopped for a moment.

The woman in that room was not the same Hallie he'd seen on that DVD. In fact, if he didn't know better, he'd guess someone else had taken over her body, maybe an alien. But the change was temporary, and he knew it. Her health was fine, her memory returning slowly. The time to say goodbye would come sooner than he thought.

CHAPTER 7

Hallie woke with a start, clenching sheets and screaming out Alan's name. She remembered a bizarre image of Alan peeling his face off like a mask, revealing some horrible monster beneath. And suddenly she had become very small in front of him, feeling afraid and angry at the same time, powerless to act on either one. The monster had begged her for mercy, taking her hand gently in his.

She shook off the icky feelings surrounding the dream and hoped Jamie hadn't heard her call another man's name. She was already in enough trouble as it was.

A hot shower only slightly dispelled the strange feeling her nightmare had left behind. Watching the drops of water slide down the white marble, her thoughts were still on Alan. Dark, handsome. Yet the way she had felt about him didn't begin to reach the heights her feelings for Jamie took her. It was infatuation, she knew that now. She couldn't possibly have loved Alan and then fallen for Jamie, even under these strange circumstances. Jamie had to be an infatuation, because she couldn't feel that strongly about him after knowing him for just a few days.

Both men were a challenge, distant and deep. But while Alan made her think of a dark cave full of mystery and danger, Jamie reminded her of a towering mountain beckoning her to climb its steep, stony incline to reach for the sun.

She brushed her wet hair out and let it hang in loose curls over her shoulders. The blue jeans she'd bought at the mall were looser than Hallie's old selection, and the blue shirt covered her chest, yet still managed to show just a bit of her flat stomach. She could live with that, she thought with a nod, and turned to go downstairs.

"Where is Jamie this morning?" she asked Elena.

"He's out by the pool. With a guest."

"Thank you," Hallie said before turning away. A friend? A woman perhaps? The thought actually created a little pain somewhere near her stomach. She was relieved to find him sitting in a lounger by the pool talking to another man. She made her way down the concrete stairs that led to the deck, and Jamie glanced her way, looking surprised to find her there.

The other man stood with a smile and extended his hand to her. Ah, someone who knew Jamie, yet was still friendly toward her. He was tall, with a stocky build, blond hair and blue eyes. She took his hand.

"Hallie, it's good to see you doing so well! Beautiful and vibrant as ever."

Jamie stepped in, to her relief. "Hallie, this is Dave Wainthorpe. Do you remember him?"

She shook her head. "No, but it's very nice to meet you." She smiled sheepishly. "Again."

Dave's expression took on a look of surprise, and he turned to Jamie. "You're right. She has changed. You mean I can't antagonize her anymore by being nice?"

Jamie laughed, then looked at Hallie. "What he means is, you used to be pretty hostile toward Dave, for no apparent reason. But no matter what you did or said, he always came off friendly and courteous. The way he usually is. And that used to piss you off to no end. Most women fall over their feet for a chance to spend time with Dave, and you were the exact opposite."

"Oh. Sorry about that. I'm different now."

"Until she gets her full memory back," Jamie added as he leaned back in his chair.

She ignored his jibe and sat down on Dave's non-verbal request.

"So, you're feeling good?" Dave asked, turning to face her.

"Yes, thank you. Back—" She stopped herself from saying back to her old self, remembering Jamie's reaction the last time she said it. Instead she finished, "to one hundred percent healthy."

"That's great," Dave said.

"Yes, it was quite a miracle," Jamie said, and she couldn't tell whether he was being sarcastic or not. "One minute she's deep in a coma, the next she's awake and perfectly normal. Except for not remembering a lot of people and acting strange."

Dave crinkled his eyebrows. "Strange?" He gave Hallie a sidelong glance with an exaggerated lift of an eyebrow.

"Well, not strange in any particular way. Just not like her old self."

Dave laughed genuinely. "Her old self was strange." Turning to her, he said, "I hope you stay the way you are."

"I will. I don't remember being any other way."

"She'll go back to the way she was. I guarantee it." Jamie was looking at her in that stern way of his.

She stiffened. "How do you know? You're not a doctor." She was guessing on that one. Actually, she had no idea what he did.

"No, but I've been married to you for three years, and I know you."

She sat up straight. "Well, you don't know me now."

"Whoa," Dave said, hands up. "I didn't come here to talk about your problems. I came to talk about mine." He smiled, and she saw Jamie's expression soften.

"Sorry, Dave. Go on."

Glad for the respite, she leaned forward with interest, eager to hear about someone else's problems for a change.

"You probably don't remember, Hallie, but right before your collapse, I had a very valuable gem stolen from my home. It was called the Manderlay, an oval cut alexandrite. It originally came from the Ural Mountains in Takovaya."

"Alexandrite?" Hallie asked. "I've never heard of that."

"It's quite rare. What makes it so special is the fact that it changes colors. In artificial light it's red. In natural light it's green. And twenty-seven carats of it makes the effect spectacular. Besides being an architect, I happen to be an amateur gemologist, and searched for the Manderlay for ten years. The man who owned it lived in Saudi Arabia, and with all the problems over there, found himself in need of some cash flow. The Manderlay was a bargain at fifteen million dollars."

Hallie couldn't keep in the inhalation of surprise. She couldn't imagine spending fifteen million dollars on anything, especially on one stone. "Did you buy it for your wife?"

He laughed, glancing at Jamie. "No, no. I'm not crazy enough to be married, and especially not to spend that kind of money on a woman. I bought it to, well, to show it off. Mostly to enjoy looking at it, but I have to admit I liked showing it off a little. I had a thick Lucite case made, and it was protected by an alarm system that utilized laser beams. I'd had it for about two months when someone broke in, disabled the alarm, and made off with it."

Her look of shock went deeper than just hearing Dave's story. She remembered something: Mick asking where the gem was. Where she'd hidden it. And didn't Joya say that she and Jamie had dinner there the night before? Holy crap, Hallie and Mick had stolen Dave's gem.

"She really doesn't remember," Dave observed by the expression on her face. "This all happened about two months ago. On your last trip here."

She composed herself. "You must have been upset."

"Upset? I was heartbroken. Then, to top it off, the insurance company just informed me that they're not going to pay off until they're absolutely sure someone broke in and stole it. They think I masterminded the theft to get the insurance money. Hell, I'd rather have the Manderlay than the money. I can replace the money, but I can't replace that stone."

"You know," Jamie said, removing his legs from the empty chair across from him. "I'd like to take a look at the crime scene, so to speak. The last time I was there the police wouldn't let me in until they were done with the investigation. By then I had to get back home."

Dave shrugged, making the wisps of blond curls on his chest play hide and seek beneath the collar of his shirt. "Why not? Maybe you'll see something I didn't."

Hallie swallowed, hoping that they wouldn't. She needed time to figure this out.

***

Dave's house was not more or less impressive than Theresa's, but it was vastly different. Ultra-modern was obviously his thing, from the odd shapes of his lawn ornaments and statues to the strange angles of his house.

They walked through a circular archway before they reached double doors that matched the arch in shape, painted in vibrant blue. Dave punched in an alarm code, then walked in the house without using a key. Hallie could see how easy it was for her former self to gain entrance. The combination was 16372. Sixteen for her sister Bernice's age; three for her Shelties; and seventy-two, for the year her first car was made, a Camaro.

Gleaming white carpet, black furniture, and lots of shiny brass made the house seem more like a furniture showroom than a home. An elaborate entertainment system took up one whole wall, its glass shelves arranged with an assortment of crystals in natural form. The large television in the middle looked like a square eye.

The carpet squished beneath her feet, attempting to swallow them up as she quickly walked toward tile and refuge. Beyond the six sliding glass doors, an hourglass-shaped pool shimmered in the morning sun, surrounded by a maroon deck.

Nestled perfectly in a square nook, lit from above by a single halogen bulb, was a brass pedestal. The empty stand looked pitiful beneath the glare of the light. Sealed over the base was a Lucite case with a round hole cut into the side, large enough for a fist to fit into. She glanced down at her tensing hand. Yep, it would fit all right.

"This is where it was," Dave said with a sigh. "Whoever did it disarmed the laser beams with this panel and was then able to cut through the case to get to the gem." He pointed to another alarm keypad. Hallie had probably looked over his shoulder there, too, and memorized the combination. Dave had no reason to distrust his friend. Or his friend's wife. Too bad.

"You're too trusting," Jamie said, as if reading her thoughts. "How many times have you punched in those numbers in front of Hallie and me without making us turn away?"

"But that's the two of you. My mother, a friend or two. It's a natural instinct to turn away when someone punches in their password or alarm code. I've seen you do it. Everybody does."

Jamie narrowed his eyes. "Maybe not everybody. It looks like an inside job."

"The cops checked friends, acquaintances, workers. My cleaning lady checked out, then quit in disgust for being a suspect." He put his hand on his chest. "As if I had pointed a finger at her. I felt bad that they even asked where you were that night."

Jamie shrugged. "They can't write off anyone. I didn't take it personally. I was sound asleep when it happened, didn't even wake up until noon."

Hallie wondered how thorough their investigation

into Jamie and his wife had been. He had been asleep, but obviously Hallie hadn't. Maybe she'd drugged him so he wouldn't wake and miss her.

"You look deep in thought, Hallie," Dave asked. "Any ideas?"

"Mm? No, just wondering. The police don't have your combinations, do they?"

"No. The alarm monitoring company does, but they checked out, too. It's baffling."

Hallie couldn't relax once she knew the truth. Even through a mildly enjoyable lunch of fajitas at Dave's, even with Jamie being somewhat pleasant toward her, she was tense far beyond the comfort level.

The emerging realizations were burying her in quicksand. If she was caught, she could go to prison for a crime she didn't commit. Would a jury believe her story? Doubtful. The best case would be that they would rule her insane and put her in an asylum. Jamie would hate her, Joya probably would, too. Everyone would, except Mick. The thought made her cringe.

After lunch, she bid Dave good luck with finding the thief as sincerely as Jamie did. When they reached the end of Dave's driveway, Jamie made the Porsche a convertible with the push of a button. Fresh air and sunshine spilled in, washing away the pounding worry of being a convict. The wind blew his blond hair around, and the sun lit it with a golden aura. She held her hair back in a ponytail with her hand.

He pointed to the glove box. "You used to keep hair bands in there."

She smiled at his thoughtfulness as she pulled a red band out and tied up her hair. "Thanks."

He nodded but kept his eyes on the road, the wall

between them as impenetrable as if it were solid. She crossed her arms over her chest and scooted down in her seat, allowing herself a few minutes of pouting. Obviously, his stubbornness had won over the demons that led him to hold her hand in the planetarium.

She took a deep breath of salty air, then looked at him. "This would be a great day to go to the beach."

"I'm sure it is."

The hoped-for invitation didn't come forth, nor did any other words. Undaunted, she said, "Wouldn't it be nice to take a long walk down the beach?"

"You've got a car, bathing suits at the house. Go."

She pursed her lips in frustration. He was treating her like a spoiled brat who wanted her way. She ventured further. "Actually, I was thinking that maybe you could come with me." She brightened the last few words, hoping to inject more optimism than she felt.

He gave her a stern look, adding to her feeling of being a child. "I've got business to take care of today. And don't use that look you got me to the opera with. It won't work anymore."

"The opera wasn't that bad. Okay," she added when she saw his surprised look. "The opera itself was yucky, but we didn't stay for the whole thing. Don't tell me that you didn't enjoy the laser show."

"It was fine."

She was more disappointed by the sight of Theresa's driveway looming just ahead. Little time left with him before he escaped from her.

"Can I come with you?"

"Oh, no. I never get anything done when you're with me, between you talking to your friends and buying stuff."

"Jamie, I don't remember any of my friends. And I won't buy one thing, I promise." That wasn't a problem because she had never been much of a shopper.

They sat in silence as he pulled up in front of the house. She hoped he was considering her promise. And her company. His calm expression belied his next words.

"You know, Hallie, you should call Mick. After all, you wanted to leave me for him. He must mean something to you. You need to explore that."

He got out of the car and closed the door, heading toward the separate garage. She leaned on her knee and called after him, "I don't want to see Mick! I want to be with you."

He turned back. "I don't believe that."

She felt the frustration seep into her voice, choking it. "Why? Why don't you believe me?"

"Because," he said with that smug smile of his, "he was the one you remembered in the hospital. Not me or anyone else, but you knew him."

In her attempt to pretend to be Hallie and remember, she had sabotaged herself. "I didn't remember him!" she called in a last-ditch effort. "I only guessed who he was after hearing you talk about him!"

If he heard, he pretended not to and kept walking. A few minutes later, a black Cadillac sped past and down the driveway. She was so angry, so sad, that even Theresa's presence, standing in front of the double doors, couldn't upset her anymore. But her comment, as Hallie walked past her, did.

"Why don't you go back where you belong?"

Hallie paused, then turned to meet the short woman's blazing blue eyes. She saw love there, and protection for her son. For his heart. Hallie could no longer be angry at the woman. "I wish I could. But where I belong is too far away." She glanced toward Colorado. "Much too far away." Then she continued walking up the stairs.

Hallie reminded herself that Theresa's hatred toward Jamie's wife was justified. But it was also directed at the wrong woman. No one would understand that, however. She barely did herself.

Remembering Joya's strange last name, Mellondorf, she got her phone number from information and gave her a call. Once the maid got her friend on the line, Joya squealed with delight.

"Hal-lie! I'm so glad you called, sweetie. Is everything all right?"

"It's fine. I have some questions I think you can answer. What are you doing this afternoon?"

"I have unchangeable plans to lie out at the beach all day and get positively brown. You, my dear, can join me. It's been forever since we've laid out and drank margaritas together. Why don't you come pick me up?"

"Sounds fine. Where do you live? And, Joya, give me directions like you would for an out-of-town guest."

Joya detailed directions complete with landmarks and assorted memories to go along with them, like, "That was the place we used to hang out for Sunday afternoon happy hours."

When Hallie found a bathing suit and cover, she slipped down the stairs and out the front door, trying to avoid Theresa. An afternoon with Joya wouldn't be as nice as one with Jamie, but it was definitely preferable to one with his mother.

Joya lived in La Jolla; Hallie smiled at how similar

the two names sounded. Knowing Joya, that's probably why she lived there. Straight ahead was Soledad Mountain and the white cross perched atop it. The Mellondorf Residence sat on top of a hill overlooking the ocean, like Theresa's, only closer. Much more pretentious this place was, with its austere white columns flanking the huge double door entrance, its white shutters and Rolls Royce parked out front. Hallie's best friend had done quite well for herself. She was not impressed.

Before she got to the stairs leading up to the entrance, Joya appeared around the far corner of the house. After an air kiss, Joya said, "Hi, sweetie! Come on back with me so I can say bye to Stan."

Rap music pounded through the air, and Joya rolled her hips and shook her shoulders to the beat. The backyard was filled with huge, stately trees, flower beds, and spongy green grass. Hallie followed her up to the white deck surrounding the pool. White statues were randomly situated throughout the yard. Joya was still several yards from the long back porch when she waved at the man who sat in a lounge chair.

"He has to stay out of the sun since he's had skin cancer."

Hallie waved to him, and Stan hesitantly waved back before returning to the newspaper he held. "Does he not like me?" she asked.

She shrugged. "Ah, he doesn't particularly like us hanging around together. Something about us getting into trouble. He's not my father, and he doesn't tell me who to hang around with. Besides, his friends are all old farts."

Hallie glanced back at him. "Well, he *is* a bit older,

Joya."

She flipped her hand in his direction. "So? It's all in the mind. You know what he's listening to up there in those headphones? Classical music. Phooey." Then she waved again. "Bye, pumpkinpuss! Be back in a while."

"Pumpkinpuss?" Hallie repeated, but Joya didn't comment.

When they walked to Hallie's car, Joya pointed down toward the ocean. "See that string of palms down there? That's where we're going."

A few minutes later they pulled into the parking lot with the palm trees. The beige sand beach was huge, dotted with slick, shiny bodies. It curved around as it turned into cliffs. Hallie followed Joya down the sidewalk until they ran out of cement. She felt the soft sand between her toes, avoiding the clumps of seaweed washed ashore. Joya settled her chair into the sand, situated her towel and sat down with a flourish. Hallie flung her towel over the unsettled chair and flopped down.

In a matter of seconds, Joya was covered in tanning oil and barely anything else. She tossed Hallie the bottle of coconut-smelling oil. "Whoo, this is great!" She turned and poured two glasses of yellow liquid from the large thermos into two cups and handed one to her. Hallie watched Joya lick some of the salt off the rim before taking a deep drink and followed suit.

"I am so ready to go out dancing." Joya's chair was nearly tipping over with her movements. "Let's go out Saturday. It's been too long. Even when you flew here several weeks ago, you were too serious to go dancing. Let's have some fun!"

"Well, wasn't I leaving my husband then? I would

think such a decision would make one somber."

Joya shrugged to the beat of the music. "What's to be somber about? Happens all the time."

Hallie looked up at the sky, wondering how she was ever going to extract one serious conversation out of this woman.

Once oiled up and settled in her lounger, Hallie turned to Joya. "Tell me about Mick."

Her friend looked up suddenly, as if someone had splashed cold water on her. "You're asking the wrong person if you're thinking of getting back with that one."

"No, nothing like that. I want to know more about him. Remember when I told you that he snuck up on me in the yard? He also, well, I guess you couldn't call it anything else but a threat. He threatened Jamie, saying that if he thought he could get me back he would end up in the hospital like the last guy."

When Joya nodded, chills went up Hallie's spine. So, he hadn't been bluffing.

"It wasn't quite as bad as he made it sound. There was some guy at the health club that was sweet on you. You went out for a drink after a workout, and Mick caught you. The next night someone jumped him and broke his jaw. You can imagine who that someone was, although no one could prove it." Joya laughed. "That guy didn't come near you after that! I'm sure Mick had a few choice words for him."

"Joya, it's not funny. Is this Mick some kind of maniac?"

"I always thought so. He's obsessed with you. That's the best word I can think of. At first you loved it, being the attention hog that you are. After a while he wouldn't even let you go out with me. It drove him nuts when you were with Jamie. Can you imagine? Your own husband, and Mick was insanely jealous. Last month you finally admitted you were afraid of him. I think you were always a little afraid of him; you just didn't see it. You thought it was some dangerous allure thing. I couldn't figure it out."

Even the former Hallie was drawn to the dark and dangerous type. "And I was leaving Jamie for him? And moving to France? That's more than just allure."

Joya wrinkled her face. "That was kinda strange. You played around on Jamie, but you, well, you loved him. Several months ago, you were worried that he was going to ask for a divorce. That's when I knew you did love him. I think most of your problems were that you wanted to live here, near the action. He didn't. You grew bored. You'd visit me and just explode. Then you met Mick, and everything changed. I don't think you wanted to leave Jamie. I think Mick pressured you into the decision. Somehow."

Hallie picked up a dead leaf and began ripping it into shreds. "You think he could be dangerous?"

"Maybe. I say dump him now. You can stay with us here. Hell, we've got plenty of room. At least until you're ready to get a place of your own and figure out what you want."

The margarita's soothing effect made Hallie feel looser. She turned to Joya. "I already know what I want."

"What's that?"

"Jamie." Joya's surprised expression made Hallie smile. "You just said I still loved him."

"Well, yes, I know. But you asked the man for a divorce. And he conceded. I just figured it was over."

"I'm in love with him." Saying the words aloud seemed strange, yet she knew they were true. Deep beyond his icy façade was a warm, passionate man. Heaven had sent her there for a reason.

"Not that I can blame you, hon. He's gorgeous." She glanced surreptitiously back toward the direction of her house. "And he's young, damn you. Sexy and rich, too. No, I can't blame you at all." For the first time, Joya looked self-piteous.

"It's not the money. Joya, why did Ha—I marry Jamie, anyway? Was it for the money?"

Joya was fiddling with her gold anklet. "Yes. But it was everything, really. You fell in love with the whole package." She lifted her big brown eyes to Hallie's. "I was so jealous of you. I always was, and then you married the most wonderful guy in the world. I tried to outdo you. And maybe Stanford has more money than Jamie, but that's all he has, money."

"I'm sorry you're not happy."

Joya looked at the sand. "We've been like sisters. But I let jealousy get in the way. Hallie, please don't hate me."

"For what? Because you tried to outdo me? I don't care about that."

"No, because I knew you missed going out and partying, and I used that to get you to go out and party with me. Because I was unhappy and bored, I wanted you to be, too. I helped convince you that you were."

Hallie didn't quite know how to take Joya's confession. If it weren't for her interference, Hallie might have been in a happy marriage when Chris took over her body. Things would have been so much easier.

Find his heart.

Those words reminded her that if that were so, she may not have been given a second chance. Her second chance was Jamie's second chance.

She leaned over and took Joya's hand in hers. "I forgive you. Maybe it worked out for the best anyway."

Joya looked unsure about Hallie's forgiveness, but she leaned over and hugged her anyway. "Thank you. You're too sweet. You know, I don't think I would have admitted that to you if you had been, well, like you were before. But now you seem so different."

Hallie smiled. "I guess when you're that close to Heaven, you come back different."

Joya pinched her cheek. "You came back an angel."

***

As soon as Hallie dropped Joya back off at her mansion, her thoughts rotated back to that afternoon. She had a problem. Somewhere in her possession, or in a place that could be tied to her, sat a fifteen-million-dollar gem that belonged to Dave. Someone would eventually find that gem. Maybe Jamie, maybe Theresa or Solomon. Hallie would go to federal prison with women murderers and embezzlers.

She'd heard how those prisons could be. The woman released from prison would be yet another Hallie, tortured and defeated. The real Hallie would be better off.

She had to get the Manderlay back to Dave. First, she had to find it. Dave had said it was the size of his thumb. It could be anywhere! Where would a woman like Hallie have hidden something so precious?

Those tickets to France, Hallie and Mick's getaway she presumed, were dated a week earlier. When Hallie had left Jamie, it was to leave with Mick. That meant that the gem was either in the stuff she'd packed or hidden somewhere nearby. Maybe in Joya's house, where Hallie had run to first? Maybe at Theresa's house, where they had been staying when the gem was first stolen? She would start with the suitcases and the house.

Back at the house, Hallie looked at the bedroom through detective's eyes. Where would a woman like the former Hallie hide a gem?

She dumped what was left in the suitcases out on the bed and examined each item. Then she went through the dresser drawers where she had put away the clothing in the suitcases. She searched through the makeup case and the leather bag of toiletries. The bag of jewelry was next, and she looked for a disguised gem set in a ring or pendant.

She walked out onto the balcony and checked in and under the potted plants, even jabbing her fingers in the dirt. She walked back in the room and let out a long sigh. If she had to check the rest of the house, a daunting task, she'd have to do it at night with a flashlight. Then Joya's house, and she didn't look forward to trying to explain why she wanted to search her home. The former Hallie could have hidden that gem anywhere.

She dropped down on the bed. *Think like a thief instead of a detective.* What was important to the former Hallie? The Porsche. She went down to the garage and looked in every space she could find, including the engine compartment. Next, she thought, heading back to the bedroom.

Clothes. They were important to the materialistic woman. She pulled every piece of clothing out and laid them on the bed as she looked. On her hands and knees, she searched in the armoire, sticking her fingers in the far reaches of the dark, hoping not to find a dead bug. She was searching so desperately that the armoire was knocking against the wall.

"What are you doing in there?" a male voice asked.

Hallie jumped, but not as far as her heart did. She backed out of the closet and stood to face a bewildered Jamie. His gaze took in the clothes on the bed and the general disarray.

"I knocked, and when no one answered, I thought you were out. Are you packing to leave?"

She couldn't find any emotion on his features to indicate whether the prospect made him happy or not. She wished she could just tell him yes and get him out of there, but that wasn't right.

"No, I'm just looking for something. It's not a big deal. What did you want?"

"What are you looking for?" He gestured toward the mess. "It must be pretty important."

"No, not really. It's um, an earring. I can't find the match."

"Let me see what the one you have looks like; maybe I've seen it around."

She froze. Why was he being so damn obliging? "I gave it to Joya so she could look for it over at her place. I'm sure I'll find it in here. What did you need?"

He looked at her for a minute before walking to the closet. "I just wanted to get my running shoes." When he emerged a second later, he asked, "Have you checked in there yet? Maybe it came off while you were undressing?"

"Good idea," she said, walking toward the bedroom door. "I'll check there next. See ya."

He gave her another odd look, obviously getting the

hint that she wanted him out. She hated to do it, but it was necessary. Just as he stepped out into the hall, he turned around.

"Oh, Hallie. Whatever perfume you wore to the opera, don't wear it again. That stuff was awful."

She grabbed the bottle from the lineup. "This stuff? Well, the nozzle's broken anyway." She dropped it into the tiny trash can where it made a *kerchink* sound.

"That's where it belongs. Well, good luck on your mission."

Her eyes widened. "My mission?"

"Yeah, finding your earring. I hope you find it before you have this room turned completely upside down."

"I'm sure I will. Bye, Jamie."

When he finally closed the door, she started putting the clothing back in the armoire. The five remaining bottles of perfume caught her eye, looking strange with the gap between them where Sexual Infinity had been. She pushed them together.

Why had the former Hallie brought *six* bottles of perfume with her? With all the money she was going to have, she could buy a million more authentic French perfumes. She must really like these, especially the one Jamie despised. After all, she had tried to fix the one in the trash can, actually taking the time to pry the top off…

Her train of thought came to a screeching halt. She picked the blue perfume bottle out of the trash can. The scent was becoming stronger. The metal around the rim was wrinkled where it had been crimped back to the glass bottle, and drops of perfume leaked out— because the top had been removed.

She shook the bottle. *Kerchink!* She walked over to

the window and held it up to the light. The glass was dark, but very faintly she could see the outline of something not quite round inside. *The Manderlay!*

She found some nail clippers in the bathroom and started prying at the metal. Within a few minutes she had the top off and the liquid down the drain. After a few shakes, the Manderlay dropped out on the towel she had laid out.

She washed it off and studied the red gem. Just to make absolutely, positively sure, she walked outside. It turned green. Sitting in the palm of her hand was a fifteen-million-dollar stone. Her fingers closed over it. Now she had to get it back to Dave. Yeah, right. No problem.

***

"Hallie, I must admit I was quite surprised to hear from you yesterday. Especially when you asked me out for lunch."

She could tell by Dave's body language across the table that he was still a little leery about her.

"I thought lunch would be, well, neutral. I have to admit I have ulterior motives."

With his arms on the table, he leaned closer. "I care a great deal about Jamie and would never do anything to hurt him."

He thought she was going to come on to him! And no wonder, with Hallie's reputation.

"I care about Jamie, too, very much. I know that I've hurt him in the past, and I want to do everything possible to make that hurt go away. That's why I asked you to keep our lunch a secret. I don't want him to get the wrong idea about you and me."

"Neither do I. We've been friends for a long time, and I would never let anyone, especially a woman, destroy that." *Especially you*, she could hear the unspoken words.

"Good, we're in agreement on that. Your friendship with him is actually why I wanted to talk to you. The only Jamie I know is the bitter, angry one. I realize that I am the one who made him that way. What I am trying to figure out is if there's a chance...if he's the type..." Dave was watching her struggle with a hint of amusement on his face. "Why are you smiling?"

"You want him back, don't you?"

She sat back in her chair. "Is it that obvious?"

"Clear as an *F* diamond. Just watching you yesterday, the way you were looking at him, the way his words affected you. So, what you're asking me is, do I think there's a chance he'll forgive you? And want to get back together?"

"Yes, that's what I was trying to ask you."

"Why me?"

"Well, his mother wouldn't give me a scrap of compassion if I was a begging poodle. I don't know any other friends of his, and you seem like a good guy."

He took a sip of white wine. "Can I be honest with you?" She nodded. "I'm not sure I want you and Jamie together again."

She couldn't keep the hurt from creeping into her features. "Because I hurt him."

"You were, and I emphasize *were*, a real ... well, you weren't a nice person. I'd hate to see him get emotionally mugged again."

She stared into her water glass. "I really made a mess of things for myself, didn't I?"

He reached over and touched her chin. "The important thing is you're trying to make up for it."

"I want this to work. It sounds crazy, I know, after all this time."

"Jamie gives his all to the things, and people, he cares about. He expects that back. He's stubborn, and that's good sometimes. He won't give up easily. But, when he does give up, it's usually permanent. Forgiveness isn't one of his strong suits."

"But he's capable of it, isn't he?"

"Oh, I can remember a time or two. He's capable if he wants to forgive. You have to convince him that he does. Remember, you can't replace what you've taken from him. You'll have to work on building it back again, bit by bit."

She sat up straight in her chair. "I can be just as stubborn as he is. And I want this to work more than he doesn't want it to work."

He laughed. "Well, if anything, it'll make a great story."

Their lunch went from serious to lighthearted to outright fun. Dave told her about incidents from high school and college. He had her in gales of laughter on the telling of the swim meet when Jamie dove in and his bathing suit slid down his legs. He managed to get his suit up and finish in second place. His nickname for the rest of the season was *Buns* DiBarto.

"I wish I'd known Jamie then. I think we would have gotten along great." Back when she was plain old Chris with no ego hang-ups.

Dave glanced at his watch, then tossed his napkin on the table. "Hallie, I never thought I'd say this to you, but I wish you luck."

"Thanks for having lunch with me. I feel as if I know Jamie so much better now. And most importantly, thank you for your encouragement. It means more to me than you'll ever know."

He waved just before disappearing through the door. Hallie had achieved the two goals she'd set out to reach during this lunch. And she'd figured out what she was going to do about the gem. She had learned more about Jamie, and she'd won Dave's confidence. Now she was going to break into his house as Hallie had done not long ago. This time, she would be replacing the Manderlay. And it wasn't going to be any easier than stealing it had probably been.

***

Two-thirty in the morning. Hallie would have liked to think her internal alarm was precise, but the truth was, she hadn't gone to sleep since putting her head on the pillow at eleven. Nevertheless, she was up, wide-eyed and ready to become a thief. *Of sorts.*

"This one should go down in the history books," she mumbled as she flicked on the light over the dressing table. "A reverse theft."

She opened a drawer and pulled out the gloves of royal blue and the pot of eyeliner. A black ski cap, culled from the winter clothes section in the closet, joined the gloves. She was already wearing black jeans and a navy jersey.

She dipped her pinky finger in the trickle of water from the faucet and rubbed it in the black eyeliner. A smear on her cheeks, nose, chin, and forehead, and damn her shaking fingers! Not that she was trying to be precise, but the waves made her look even stranger, like a demented warrior. The thin smear over her lips turned into a grotesque parody of a smile.

"Damn!" She gave herself a chastising look in the mirror, imagining Jamie coming into find her dressed like a refugee from a campy bank robbery movie.

"Sleep-dressing," she imagined telling the shocked Jamie. "Ah, my new mud mask, that's it."

After a quick glance into the darkened bedroom, just for her blood pressure's sake, she continued putting the finishing touches to cover all that pale, reflective skin. Then she slipped on the cap and the gloves, the only ones she could find besides bulky knit ones. They went up to her elbow and matched a gown hanging in the closet. Without much remorse, she took them off and cut them to normal length with a pair of tiny scissors before putting them on again. Another check in the mirror with a pose fit for *Vogue*.

"Mama sure taught her daughter how to put on the nines," she said with a grin, her teeth glowing white against her darkened skin.

Getting out of the house wasn't so bad, but getting over to Dave's without the Porsche engine waking one and all was the trickier part. Luckily, she had the foresight to run into a little car trouble halfway down the drive the night before, and had insisted on leaving it there until the morning. Those darn foreign engines.

Once at Dave's house, her heart really started doing the can-can. She crept across the lawn, hoping the lack of walls didn't mean the presence of sophisticated sensors. By the time she reached the front entrance, flanked by ominous-looking bushes, those worries were replaced by new ones: getting in. Of course, she knew the combination: 16372. She punched in the numbers, holding her breath. Sixteen for Bernice; three for her shelties; and seventy-two for the Camaro. The click signaled success, and she turned the knob.

For a moment she waited, listening for barking dogs, the sound of a television, of an ant crossing the windowsill. Her heart started beating to the rhythmic *tick, tick, tick* of the clock that had nearly made her jump a second before. Beyond that, the house was quiet.

She stepped inside, careful to leave the door cracked for a quick escape. A soft light beneath the black leather couch in the living room gave the room a surreal look. She patted her pocket for the twentieth time since leaving Theresa's house, making sure the Manderlay was still nestled there. Then she made her way toward the square nook just past the living room. Thankfully the light was out.

Her fingers closed against the leftover cloth from her blue gloves, pulling out the precious package. As she released the Manderlay, it slipped from her grasp and jumped two feet away over the marble and onto the thick carpet. She cringed, waiting to hear the noise that would bust her. Or make her break-in futile by cracking the stone. Neither happened, and she dropped down where she'd heard its soft thud.

The white carpet looked scarcely lighter than black in the darkness, and she finally removed her gloves and scanned the floor with her bare fingers. The smooth surface caught the attention of her left hand, and she snatched it up and stood. Regaining her orientation, she stepped carefully back onto the marble and toward the nook.

Standing in front of the case, she rubbed the gem clean of her prints, then held it between her black lips for a second as she slipped her gloves back on. No more mistakes, she told herself, and reached into the hole to place the Manderlay back on its brass stand.

She blinked in the sudden light, and black lights pooled in front of her until her eyes adjusted. Panic set in quickly as she turned around. Dave was standing five feet away, wearing a blue velvet robe and holding a black gun at head level. She dropped the stone, hearing the shatter of the mirror below the stand, hoping the gem hadn't broken.

His gaze flickered momentarily to the case, then back at her. His hand was shaking, and for some insane reason, she thought he looked terribly incongruent holding a gun. It didn't fit him. Now didn't seem the time to mention it to him.

The only words that found their way out of her frozen lips were, "Don't shoot, please!"

His eyebrows raised as his eyes narrowed at her. But she didn't linger there as she slowly removed her hand from the case and backed toward the wall a foot behind her, hands raised as she'd seen on cop shows. His finger flexed as he moved closer, matching her step for step, an investigative expression on his face.

"Hallie?" Incredulity dripped from his words.

Only then did she realize what she must look like, covered in black, wearing her ski cap and shiny dress gloves. She bowed her head, hoping for that hole to open beneath her and take her away to a better hell.

"Yeah, it's me."

He still held the gun as he inched forward. "Why are you trying to steal the Manderlay? You know it's already been stolen."

She felt a laugh roil her insides but held it at bay

knowing it would come out sounding close to hysterical. "I wasn't trying to steal it; I'm replacing it."

It took a second for realization to dawn on Dave's confused features. He tossed the gun aside, and she cringed.

He waved away her obvious concern that it would discharge. "It's a water gun."

She pulled the Manderlay, still in one piece, from the case and handed it to him. He cradled it in his palm, as if making sure it was really there. Then he looked up at her.

"You? You were the one who stole it?"

"Well, as near as I can figure. If I were the kind of person before who could steal someone's gem, I'm the kind of person now who has to return it. But I didn't want you to know it was me." She glanced down at herself. "I did think of other ways, such as mailing it to you, or leaving it on your doorstep. This wasn't the easiest, but it seemed the most effective. At the time."

"How did you get—you saw the combination, didn't you?"

"Both times, probably. You're too trusting, Dave."

His lips twisted into something like a smile. "Yeah, I know. But I never figured..." He looked at her getup again. "Does Jamie know anything about this?"

"No! He had nothing to do with it. I think the man I was ... involved with took a liking to your gemstone and pressured me into stealing it. He's been asking me where I hid it since I got out of the hospital. Last night I found it."

"Who is this guy?" At her cautious expression, he added, "Do I know him?"

"I doubt it. His name is Mick. Mick Gentry."

Dave thought about it for a moment. "No, I don't know him. That's a relief, anyway. Knowing one of the thieves is bad enough."

Hallie slipped the cap off, letting her hair tumble free from the furnace of wool. She took off the gloves and tucked them in her pocket. Sweat popped out all over, and she wondered if she could possibly be dreaming this absurd situation.

Dave tucked the alexandrite in his robe pocket, obviously now intent to deal with the thief. "I think I'd better call—"

"No, please don't call the cops. I know I was a bad person before, but even you admitted that I've changed. Don't make me pay for a crime I didn't c—I don't remember committing. I'm pretty sure I wouldn't have pulled anything like this if Mick hadn't been forcing me to."

"I was going to say, maybe I should call Jamie."

"Oh, God, that's even worse. Well, not quite as bad, but close enough. Isn't there some way we could work this out?" She looked around, desperate for an idea. "I could clean your house! Yes, I could be your indentured servant for, I don't know, some period of time. You did say your cleaning lady quit, didn't you? There you go. You keep quiet, and I'll keep your house clean."

He laughed. "Taking a risk by breaking into my house to return the gem you stole, now that takes a dash of crazy to pull off. Then bribing me with *housework* to keep quiet...insanity."

She gave him a weak smile. "I can even do windows."

His laughter turned into guffaws, until he finally gathered his composure. "I have to admit, I have no idea what to do about you."

"Dave, what I told you at lunch was the truth. I want to make a new start of it, put my past behind me. I'm asking you for a second chance." A third chance, really.

"What about this guy who wants my Manderlay?"

"I don't know how I'm going to handle him."

"I could tell the police he did it."

"No! He'd mention my involvement. I might still get arrested."

His eyes narrowed. "I could tell the police that someone called and set up a rendezvous. I gave the thief a million dollars and got my gem back."

"No, then Mick will think I double-crossed him. This guy is a real wacko."

He looked at her. "You know, you could have taken this and sold it. Or even worse, just tossed it in the ocean."

"No, I couldn't have. It wasn't mine, and I had no right to keep it. I'm just sorry it happened to begin with." She looked at him hopefully. "So, when do I start work?"

His eyes widened. "You think I'm going to trust you in my house?"

"I brought the Manderlay back, didn't I?"

He shook his head. "How would you explain to Jamie that you're cleaning my house? It's nearly a full-time job."

"I don't know. I wasn't exactly planning on getting caught. But I'll think of something."

"Forget it. Besides, I've already hired someone."

She bit her lower lip. "Does that mean you're going to —"

He pulled the gem out of his pocket. "Get out of here, little thief, before I sic Inspector Clouseau on you."

She took a step toward the door and smiled, relief flooding her. "I hope you and the Manderlay will be very happy together."

When she walked out into the early morning air, her heart was racing at the speed of light. Still, she felt a thousand pounds lighter. Now she was ready for her next mission, her real one: *Buns* DiBarto.

CHAPTER 8

W hen Hallie returned home from an after-noon of driving around, the house was dark and quiet. The aroma of food lingered, and she followed her hungry nose to its source. Jamie was sitting in the great room, his legs stretched out on an ottoman, a plate of fried chicken on his lap. He looked up as soon as he saw her walk in.

"Hi," he said, only the faintest trace of friendliness in his blue eyes. "You look nice. Going out?"

She walked into the room, her feet sinking into the plush brown carpet. "Trying to get rid of me?"

"Maybe." He let the word sink in for a moment before adding, "No, you look nice, that's all. I just figured you were going out."

She sat down in the easy chair at a right angle from his. "Well, thanks for the compliment. I think. And no, I'm not going out. No formal dinner tonight?"

"No, Mom's at some charity thing tonight." He held his plate out to her. "The fare tonight is chicken from around the corner. Want some?"

"Sure." She plucked a piece from the plate and started munching, fully aware that he'd thought she would shun his offer and leave. She had no intention of doing that.

"Dave called this morning."

Her heart stopped. She looked at Jamie's expression, searching for suspicion, anger. He appeared calm.

"And what did he have to say?" Her voice sounded strained, despite her effort.

"He got his alexandrite back."

"Oh." She fiddled with the fabric on the chair. "Does he know who took it?"

"No. He figures the thief panicked and decided to give it back. Probably couldn't fence it. He found it in a paper sack on his doorstep. He hadn't even called the police yet. Said he wanted me to know first."

Hallie let out the breath she'd been holding. "That's wonderful! I'm really happy for him." *Okay, Dave. I got the hint. You can be trusted.*

When she finished her piece of chicken and declined another, he handed her a little packet that contained a wet napkin. Afterward, he walked through an opening to what she guessed was the kitchen. She almost expected him not to return.

He did come back, and she let her gaze trail down his gray striped shirt and black pants before meeting his eyes. She tried to dismiss the growing pace of her heartbeat. He looked at her as if he were considering something. His gaze flickered down to her left hand, and she saw an almost imperceptible narrowing of his eyes. She knew, of course, that he was looking at her wedding ring. *Her* wedding ring. It sounded so strange.

"I'm going down to Captain Morgan's for a drink. It's a little place on the bay, kind of tropical and laid back."

She looked at him, anticipation growing inside her,

along with confusion. Was he asking her to go with him, or just telling her where he was going? Without her. She smiled. "Sounds nice."

He nodded, but she could tell his thoughts were on something else. "So, what did you do today?"

"Drove around some, checked with the community college to see about taking some classes."

"Really? Why this sudden urge to learn?"

It's what I've always done, she wanted to say. "I have to do something with my life."

"Oh. I figured you'd gone down to the beach. Your nose is a little red."

"I went to the beach with Joya yesterday. I had some questions."

"About what?"

"Us."

"Why didn't you ask me?"

She stood. "Because you won't talk to me."

She expected a denial, or to hear again the reason why it didn't matter. Instead, he said, "Let's go," and walked right past her.

She watched that broad back and cute butt of his walk through the doorway, and she wanted to remain right there and make him come back to cordially invite her to accompany him. Then she realized that was probably as cordial as he was going to get, and she walked after him. Slowly.

***

Jamie had been looking forward to a pleasant night out at his favorite haunt. Why, then, had he invited his wife? Really, he had wanted to ask Hallie why she was interested in going back to college, why she was asking

Joya, of all people, about their marriage, and why she had made herself available to spend the evening with him instead of Mick. Even more, he wanted to know why he had invited her to join him.

Captain Morgan's was a fun place, hopping just about every night of the week. Cantina music flowed into the parking lot, and palm fronds surrounded the entrance. After requesting the outside area, the hostess directed them to a table near the water. The air was warm and breezy, the colored lights reflecting off the calm water, and Hallie looked more beautiful than he had ever seen her.

Jamie shook his head. Had he actually thought that? But as he looked at her, he could only reaffirm the thought. She was taking in every detail of the restaurant with a child's awe, smiling at the little statues of grinning pirates, at the Macaw perched on a nearby tree whistling and making remarks. Everything. He had to quickly wipe the smile off his face when her gaze came to rest on him.

"This place is so *kewl*. I love it!"

"This place is so *what*?" He had never heard her draw out the word like that before.

"*Kewl*. Cool. Neat."

He noticed that she refrained from using her old *completely excellent* phrase. "It just sounded different, that's all."

"Oh. Well, I am different."

She gave him such an endearing smile, he had to turn away for a minute to gather his wits. Yes, she was different. He couldn't deny that. But he was also sure that her old ways would return. She had lost her memory, not her personality. The miracle of her recovery could not include the miracle of a change in who she was. He couldn't get that lucky.

"What are you thinking about?" Her soft voice poked into his thoughts.

He glanced up at the approaching waitress. "That it's time for a margarita. Want one?"

"Sure."

They ordered, and within a few minutes two huge golden margaritas were delivered to their table. He watched her run her tongue over the salty rim before taking a sip, remembering kisses from long ago, when that tongue had tickled his mouth and other places.

"Whoa, that must be one good margarita."

He realized he'd sucked down half of the drink in one pull. "Damn straight."

She took another sip. "I'm not used to drinking. Uh, anymore. I feel a little high." She leaned forward on the table, already looking relaxed from the drink. "You know what Joya said yesterday?"

"I can't imagine."

She ignored his jibe and continued, looking right into his eyes. "She apologized for interfering in our marriage. She felt responsible for luring me into going out with her all the time. Joya was jealous of what we had."

"She actually said that?"

Her expression brightened. "Yes, she did. It gave me a better perspective of what had happened before. With us."

He shifted uncomfortably. "Good. Maybe you'll be better for it in your next marriage."

Her soft expression crumpled, and she took a long sip of her drink, avoiding his eyes. *I'm sorry, Hallie, but you're getting too close.* She settled back in her chair, putting distance between them.

During their second round of margaritas, their conversation stayed on safe subjects, far away from marriage and other sore areas. Her blue eyes were taking on a bedroom look, lazy with drink. Drinking had always had a strange effect on Hallie. In the early days, she became sexier, amorous. More recently she had become argumentative and usually picked a fight and stalked off. Maybe to become amorous with someone else. Now she looked more like she had back when he'd first fallen in love with her. Sexy, yet innocent at the same time. Quite a feat, but she pulled it off somehow.

Suddenly her eyes focused in on something behind him, and she stood. He turned around, expecting to see some old boyfriend or lover. What he saw was an old man. And a dog.

"A Sheltie!" She raced off to the docks beside the restaurant.

He guessed that she must be talking about the Shetland Sheepdog and not the man. He followed, curious about this sudden interest in dogs she now seemed to have.

When he caught up to her, she was kneeling and hugging the dog. The old man holding the leash was grinning with pride.

"She's three years old, and her name's Marisa. After my boat." A gnarled finger pointed at a sailboat.

"Oh, she's so beautiful. I used to have three of them, and I miss them so much."

If Jamie didn't know better, he would have thought she was in love with that dog. She caressed and hugged her, looking at Marisa's face and smiling. Her long fingers disappeared in the thick brown and white coat, and the dog happily accepted the attention.

Hallie looked up at the man, seemingly unaware of Jamie's presence. "And she's so good with people. Mine would have shied away, at least at first."

The old man laughed. "She doesn't take to just anybody. She must sense something good about you, miss."

When she finally looked up to see Jamie standing there next to her, she seemed to take hold of her senses. Her eyes glistened. Was she getting misty? Over a dog?

She stood up and artfully wiped them away. "Thank you for letting me pet her."

"I'm sure Marisa enjoyed it as much as you did."

Hallie looked at him, seriousness in her eyes. "No, I don't think so."

They walked back to the table in silence. He was completely perplexed by her reaction to the dog. She had never been much of an animal person, even to the cats her mother owned. Now she was crying over one.

"I didn't realize you had dogs when you were young."

"Oh. Well, it was a long time ago. I really miss them."

"I can see that."

She smiled, but the trace of tears in her eyelashes reflected the glow of the candle between them. He wanted to take her hand and comfort her, but it seemed like a ludicrous thing to do. She was getting much too upset over a memory of three dogs she had never mentioned to him before. One more thing to add to the mystery of the new Hallie.

***

After three golden margaritas, Hallie was feeling *whee-hoo-hoo.* That was how she and her friends used to refer to the state of feeling buzzed but not drunk. Remembering the phrase from her high school days made her smile. Since those weekend nights at Hallmont's Pass, however, her drinking had been limited. And the former Hallie's immunity to liquor, from her party days, must have worn off in the last few weeks.

"Let's go for a walk," she said, wanting to get up and move around.

Jamie paid the bill, and she felt like a bum. "I should get a job so I can pay my own way."

He looked at her in that strange way again. "You, get a job? You're kidding, right?"

She tried her best to look indignant. "No, of course not. You think I haven't worked before? I can do accounting, sales, and I can even tell you exactly why that green stuff grows in your fish tank."

"You've had way too much to drink. Let's go."

They stood, but she made her way to the walkway that led down to the docks where she had seen the Sheltie. Jamie followed, and she slowed so he could catch up. The air was clearing her mind a bit, but it wasn't doing a thing for the feelings that marched inside when she looked at him walking beside her.

"Hallie..."

She turned and moved in front of him, causing him to stop lest he walk right into her. "Hmm." One of the tall lights shone down near them, casting a warm glow all around.

He was looking at her in the oddest way. The tickle of margaritas made her grin sleepily, though she wasn't the least bit tired. She looked at his lips, poised to say something. Her eyes moved slowly back up to meet his, and her smile faded. *You are my husband, Jamie. Why can't you treat me like your wife?* She wanted to say that and more, but the words wouldn't come.

He looked at her, through her, his blue eyes imploring hers. "Don't," he said, his voice deep and throaty.

Her own voice sounded far away. "Don't do what?"

"Don't look at me like you want me to kiss you."

"I can't help it. I do."

The thin wall of ice in his eyes collapsed then, and he pulled her hard against him. His voice sounded muffled in her hair, and she felt his warm breath against her neck.

"Don't do this to me, Hallie. I can't go through it again."

She stayed in his embrace for a moment, lost in the feel of his body against hers, his arms around her. Her heart ached for all that he had gone through, and for all that she wanted to do to heal those wounds.

"Jamie, can't you forget the past? Can't you please forgive what I've done?"

His hand went to his heart. "Girl, you don't know what you did to me last time. The past is lost to you, but for me, the pain is still fresh. Only in the last few months have I been able to lock my heart away from you. Now you think you can come barging in and reclaim it? No, not now or ever."

She was losing him. Through her tears she could see his soul moving farther and farther away from her reach. But he was still there, right in front of her physically. She tried to swallow back the tears, but it became harder when she reached out to touch him.

"Jamie, when I ... when I died in the hospital. I came back for you. You are the reason I'm alive."

"Hallie, don't." He pushed her hand away, backing up.

She pulled him closer again. "You don't believe me, do you?"

"About coming back for me? No. Why would you come out of your coma for me when you didn't even love me?"

"You don't know what happened to me while I was in that coma. You don't know, and I doubt I could ever explain it to you. I was on my way to Heaven, Jamie, and I asked for another chance for love. God gave me that chance, and He gave me you. I woke up, and you were there in my room, like an angel. I am certainly not perfect, but you won't find another woman on all this earth or beyond who is more determined to make you see the power of love. If you really look, you'd know in your heart that I am a different woman now. You think I've just lost my memory and these changes are temporary. But you're wrong, and if you knew how wrong you were, you'd hold me in your arms and never let me go."

He just stared at her for a moment, as if absorbing her words. Then, very slowly, he began to clap, increasing the pace as he went. "Bravo! You've got the part, Hallie. You always were a hell of an actress."

She fisted her hands, feeling ever so like pummeling that noble nose of his. "Damn, you. I spill my guts, and you applaud?"

"That's right."

Fury bubbled in her blood, mingled with the bitter taste of humiliation. Walk away? Slap him? *Nah, go for broke*, she thought, and leaned over and kissed him. He was clearly too shocked to respond; for a moment he just stood there while she kissed and kissed again, slowly and fully. Other than her lips, she did not touch him, did not pull him closer. His lips softened, forming to hers without actually participating in the kiss. She felt a trill in her heart, a tiny triumph that increased when he reached up to touch her chin. His grip tightened before he moved her chin away a few inches.

He studied her with mingled expressions of curiosity and anger. "You are something else, Hallie."

Someone else, Jamie! Someone else. "Yes, I am."

"I liked it better when you'd pout and stomp off."

She reached up and touched the hand that still held her chin. "I bet you did."

His eyes clouded with something she couldn't identify: a memory, perhaps, or temptation as he dropped his gaze to her lips. He let go of her chin and trailed a finger down the expanse of her throat. She swallowed, feeling the warmth from his fingertips spread to her entire upper region. He stopped at her collarbone, and that cloudiness in his eyes cleared to brittleness.

"Invest your feminine wiles in someone who will pay off with better odds."

He turned around and walked toward the car. All she could do was watch him disappear into the darkness. And nothing had ever hurt so badly. Not when her first boyfriend, Greg, had left for college in Texas, not when he had returned the following summer with his new fiancée. Not when Alan had moved away from her every time she tried to get closer or tried to know him better. Nothing left the empty ache Jamie did when he walked away. What hurt even more was the fact that he thought *she* had inflicted those wounds on his heart.

His words still echoed in her heart. The way he'd called her *girl*, the raw hurt she had heard in that one word. She wrapped her arms around herself, wishing they were his arms instead. It took her a few minutes before she could pull herself from that spot and head for the car. Where he waited for her. And where, for the ride home, not another word was said.

***

Hallie woke up early the next morning and headed to the pool. Jamie had not fought his demons in a midnight swim, so she guessed he would be out there for his regular morning workout. Her heart started racing when she heard splashing as she stepped out onto the terrace. She flew down the stairs, glad for the chance to catch her breath before he saw her there.

He rose up against the wall, flinging water out of his hair. The turbulent glacial waters of the night before were replaced by the peaceful calm of early morning sky. She stretched out by the edge of the pool, letting herself get the tiniest bit hopeful about what had happened between them last night.

"Good morning," she said cheerily.

"Hallie, I need to talk to you."

"I'm right here."

"I'm going back to Caterina."

Her heart dropped. "Who's *Caterina*?"

She detected the slightest smile in his face, quickly replaced by the serious look again. "Caterina's not a who, it's a what. It's where w—I live. Where we used to live. It's the resort my brother and I own. It takes up about half of the Isle of Constantine, just east of Jamaica."

She couldn't keep the surprise from her face. "That's home? An island?"

"Not really home for you. You were never happy there. I should have seen that a lot sooner than I did."

"I thought home, whenever it was mentioned, was someplace near here, maybe somewhere else in California. Never would I have imagined an island." She laughed, trying to cover her embarrassment. "I thought it was some woman."

He wasn't laughing. "You need to decide where you want to go. I'll help you pack and move there. Of course, you're welcome to stay here if you want, but I figured we could find you an apartment of your own. I'll buy it for you as part of the divorce settlement. You have the checkbook; use it until we get the accounts rearranged. What's wrong?"

The weight of what he was saying finally sunk in. This was it. He was leaving.

"I can't believe you're leaving. Now."

"Hallie, come on. You're fine, perfectly healthy. You don't need me anymore. I'll help you get settled in a new life. We both need to move on."

"I don't want you to buy me an apartment. Just leave if that's what you want to do. Leave."

"Where are you going to go?"

"What do you care? Your husbandly duty is done. I don't want anything from you. I'll take care of myself."

"What are you going to do for money?"

She crossed her arms over her chest. "Well, I might have to use a little of your money to get started. But I'll pay every penny of it back."

"Fine."

She calmed her panic at losing him, and the tenuous link to someone she cared about in this new life. The former Hallie had inured him against dramatics. "I want to come with you."

"To Santa Caterina?"

"Yes. Take me with you."

He was already shaking his head. "It won't work, and you know it. You can take care of the divorce proceedings and send the paperwork to me."

She let out a shaky breath. "What did you tell me when I first asked you for a divorce? You said you stayed for a lot of reasons that didn't matter, then you agreed it was for the best. What was your argument before you gave in?"

He pulled himself out of the pool, standing on the edge. "It doesn't matter anymore. You were the one who wanted the divorce. I want it, too. Let's end this marriage better than we handled the middle of it. Peacefully, amicably." Water sluiced down his body, glistening in the sunlight. Damn him for looking like a shining demigod when she wanted to throttle him.

She stood up to face him. "You don't want a divorce, Jamie DiBarto, and you know it. You didn't want it then. Why would you want it now?"

He leaned closer to her, and she could smell mint toothpaste. "Because it's over. It has been over for a long time, but no one bothered to tell me. Now I can see that, and I'm ready to bury the horse."

She gritted her teeth. "The horse *isn't* dead yet!"

"Yes, it is." He started walking toward the house.

"You're a liar!" she yelled at his back.

He turned around and walked back to stand in front of her, his eyes blazing a brilliant blue. "*You* have a lot of room to talk about lying." He emphasized each word with a tap on her chest with his forefinger, nudging her just enough to send her backward into the pool with a scream.

She surged to the surface. "Jamie DiBarto, you're a

skunk!"

"And like a skunk, the farther away from you, the better, right? Right." He grabbed a towel and headed up the stairway. "We'll talk more when you've cooled off."

She pulled herself out of the water and onto the deck. He had likened their marriage to a horse. *A dead horse!* She glanced upward. *Hallie, if I ever get my hands on you...*

She pulled herself up and headed inside. The way she saw it, she had two options. She was going to employ one of them now.

Jamie answered warily when she knocked on his bedroom door. The sight of his suitcase made her heartbeat quicken.

"Hallie, I don't want to argue."

She smiled. "I didn't come here to argue. I don't want you to leave on the aftermath of an argument."

His expression softened. "I don't either. I'm sorry."

She stepped forward, looking right up into his eyes. His shoulders tensed a little when she placed her hands on them. They were wide and firm, and she had an errant thought about how nice he must be to dance with.

"I'm sorry, too. For everything. Will you try to forgive me? Someday?"

He nodded. "I'll try."

"Will you do me two favors?"

"Maybe."

"First, when you think about me, and I hope you will, try to remember me the way I am now, not the way I was before."

"That's a tall order, but I'll try. And the other favor?"

"Give me a goodbye kiss."

The convincing she thought would be necessary

wasn't. He leaned down without hesitation and kissed her on the lips, lingering with a gentle touch. She was instantly lost. Dizziness, pulsing heartbeat, the works. When he moved back, she had to pull herself together. The thought of never feeling like that again haunted her already.

She forced a smile. "We should have done that more often." She turned to leave.

"Hallie?"

She stopped but didn't fully turn back to face him. "Yes." It came out as a whisper.

"Take care of yourself."

"Yeah, sure. You, too."

***

The next morning, Hallie watched from the balcony as Jamie and Theresa drove off in the Cadillac to the airport. And she smiled. Because she could tell that he still loved Hallie, as much as it made him angry to realize that. Oh yes, she was making him realize it.

Was it the *new* Hallie he was weakening to, or just his old desires for the first one? She pushed the question aside, not willing to deal with it just yet. She was going to bring his icy heart to life again. How could she lose? She was on a mission from God. If that mission took her to some island resort to teach the man a lesson in love, then she would consider it her duty. She was about to employ option number two.

She headed downstairs and out to the garage after locating the nearest travel agency. When she started to open the Porsche's car door, a hand stopped her. But the voice chilled her more.

"Hallie, where are you going?"

She turned but already knew who would be standing there. Mick. *Does he know what I've done?*

"It's none of your business."

His grip tightened, and she wondered if Solomon was within hearing distance.

"It is my business, Hallie. You are my business, my life. Why haven't you called me?"

"I—I haven't felt well," she lied.

"Well enough to go to health clubs, go to the beach and to operas, but not well enough to call me. Is that it?"

He'd been spying on her. The thought shivered through her. "What have you been doing, spying on me? Mick, you're hurting me. Let go."

He smiled, his eyes glittery. "I love it when you say my name. Say it again."

She glared at him. "Mick, let me go!"

He didn't loosen his grip. "You don't realize how much you mean to me. How I long to hold you, caress you."

When his grip turned into a caress, she pulled back. "Go away!"

His eyes became slits of dark anger. "Hallie, you know how crazy I get when I don't see you. When I think you're seeing someone else."

"I'm a married woman. Can't you understand that?"

His brown eyes blazed with anger. "No, I can't. What I do understand is that you made a commitment to me. And what I understand perfectly is that you're a woman who has in her possession a *very* expensive gemstone, and that I have someone waiting to buy it so that we can be *very* rich together. I didn't come up with this idea just for you to enjoy the money with that man you call your husband."

He obviously hadn't heard yet that Dave had his gem back. Lucky for her. "Mick, please understand something. I don't want it. I don't want the money. I just want you to leave me alone."

He smiled again, reaching out a hand to touch her shoulder. "You're afraid of getting caught, aren't you? We talked about all that, sweetheart. If you think they're on to us, we'll get Jazz to put on some of that Hollywood makeup of his and disguise us. No one will ever realize who we are. I've got phony passports ready to go if necessary. But darling, we have to get going right away. Now."

She moved away from him, agitation creeping into her voice. "Stop calling me darling. Leave me alone, or I'll scream for help."

His upper lip twitched, causing his mustache to flicker. "You're planning to stay with him, aren't you? I saw you the other night, watching him swim. You were standing there watching him ... wanting him."

Her eyes widened as she realized her paranoid visions of Mick lurking in the shadows had been true. He had been watching her a great deal. Her hand tightened on the car door handle, but she knew she couldn't move fast enough to get in the car and lock it before he moved in on her.

"He's my husband," she stated without emotion. "If I look at him with wanting, it's my business."

He moved closer, pulling her hair back at the same time as he crushed her against his body. "It is my business, you bitch! *You* are my business because you belong to me." Then his mouth began kissing down her cheek. "I've held your body next to mine, naked and sweaty in the moonlight. I've made love to you a thousand times. How can you turn your back on me like this?"

She cringed and tried to push him and his words away. "Can't you see that I'm a different person now, not the Hallie you used to know? I don't know that Hallie, and I don't know you. All I know is that I'm married, and I'm in love with my husband. I don't care about the gem or the money it will bring, I just want to try to get my life together."

The sound of a lawnmower was moving closer. He took her chin in his hand and squeezed hard. "Don't you understand? You don't have a choice. You will be mine, Hallie. And I will do anything to get you and the Manderlay back."

He left her then, a shaking blob of fright and anger. She slipped into the car and locked the doors, pulling out and speeding down the driveway. All she wanted to do was get out of there ... and get to Jamie.

The travel agent found a lovely resort for Hallie to relax and chase away her tensions. It was called Santa Caterina, located on the Isle of Constantine. Caterina was a sprawling resort that catered to its guests, and had a reputation for cleanliness, friendliness, and a profound lack of stuffiness. Of course, it had one other valuable asset that the agent failed to point out: its enigmatic and debonair owner, James DiBarto.

Returning to Theresa's home washed away the warm, sunny feeling that had befallen her since her decision to go to Caterina. The mansion lacked the interesting feel it had when she knew Jamie was there. Still, one more night, and she was flying to the kind of place she'd only seen in magazines and travel brochures.

Hallie carefully scanned the area surrounding the

garage, looking for signs of the maniac. Everything seemed quiet, and soon she forgot about Mick and thought of that night she and Jamie had gone to the laser show. They had walked along this very route, from the garage to the front doors, and she had hit him with a pillow. He must think her some kind of *schizo*, changing from a selfish, uncontrolled woman with her hand in the nookie jar to a woman who liked to lie on floors and watch laser shows, who remembered nothing of her shady past, and who would try just about anything to save her destroyed marriage. A marriage she herself had taken an ax to. She could understand his reluctance to include her in his life again. She would overcome it.

When she opened the front door, she felt like an outsider, someone who didn't belong. After all, Jamie was the only reason she was here, and now he was gone. Left was a bitter mother-in-law and an angry servant. She longed to have Theresa's friendship and motherly advice, but that wouldn't happen for a long time. If ever.

Hallie packed up the suitcase with her new clothes, then tidied the room up. It was still about an hour before dinner time, and almost twenty-four hours before her plane left. She headed downstairs to find something to snack on.

When she passed the family room, a voice called out, "Hello!"

Hallie peeked her head in and found Theresa stretched out on the brown couch. When she hesitated, Theresa waved her in. "Are you looking for something to eat?"

Hallie gave her a small smile. "Well, yes. I was just going to see what I could fix."

Theresa gave her the friendliest smile she had ever seen. "Don't worry yourself." She tilted her head toward the kitchen. "Elena! Fix Hallie something nice for dinner. Maybe some chicken parmigiana."

"Thank you." She wasn't sure how to interpret this new side of her mother-in-law. Had she finally made Theresa see how different she was from the former Hallie? "I'm glad I got to see you before I leave. I wanted to thank you for letting me stay here."

Theresa sat up and clasped her hands together. "You're leaving? When?"

"Tomorrow evening."

"I hope Jamie made it clear that you are welcome to stay here longer if you wish."

"He did. That is very kind of both of you, but it won't be necessary. I've already made my plans."

"So, where are you off to? France, maybe?"

Hallie's heart quickened. To tell the truth or not? Always the truth. "I'm going to Caterina."

Theresa's eyes frosted over, and she leaned her elbow on the armrest. She looked as relaxed as a cat. "Now that's interesting. To pick up your things, no doubt. You left in quite a hurry last time."

Hallie's hands clenched in her lap, and she flattened them out against her thighs. "I'm planning to stay there. For a while."

Under Theresa's scrutinizing eyes, Hallie shrank, but she refused to be intimidated by the little spitfire who had loved Jamie longer than any other woman in the world. They were both on the same side, but her mother-in-law would never see it that way. Silence hung around them like fog, and when Hallie decided to get up and leave, Theresa finally spoke.

"What is it that you want, Hallie? It's certainly not my son, that's been apparent for some time. Is it money? What would make you leave him and never return?"

Hallie swallowed audibly, and the blood drained from her face. "Are you bribing me to leave Jamie?"

"Yes. Divorce my son, ask for nothing from him, and I'll give you five hundred thousand dollars cash and a condominium we own in San Diego. If the divorce goes to court, your ugly past will gain you little sympathy from the judge, you know."

Hallie tried not to flinch at the number she was offering. Still, she couldn't help respect the woman reclined opposite her. "You must love your son very much, Mrs. DiBarto."

"I do. I want him to be happy again. You are incapable of providing that," she said, grinding in the words. Then her expression softened. "He loves you." She drew the words out reluctantly, like a sigh. "I still see the fire in his eyes that burned for you long ago. It's clouded with pain, hurt. Anger. But it's there, and I hate it. And I hate you for putting it there. A man shouldn't love a woman that much. Especially a woman like you. He loves with abandon, always has. You." Her lips turned up. "You love for what it brings you. Then you get bored and go on to other things. And people."

Hallie swallowed hard, finding her throat parched. How could she defend herself when she had been an awful person? But she had one thing to go on. She had seen the videos.

"I didn't marry Jamie for what he could give me. I married him because I was in love with him. You can't deny that you didn't see love in my eyes."

The woman looked only a bit disconcerted. "What was doesn't matter. Can you tell me that you're in love with him now?"

"Yes, I can. I am very much in love with your son."

That threw her off, but Hallie tried to keep the satisfaction from showing. Could the woman see the glow of love that burned in her eyes? It was there, if only a tiny flame now. But it held promise of growth, and the more time she spent with Jamie the closer she grew to him.

Finally, Theresa rose to her feet. "Don't lie to me. I have seen you in action, Hallie Parker. And a woman who acts like that with another man does not love her husband. I know that. Jamie knows that. I want you out of his life, and I'm prepared to pay you for it. Tell me, do you even see how you have made him suffer?"

Damn, the woman had her. "Yes, I do."

"Well, at least you're being honest now. Don't make him suffer further by dragging your misdeeds through court. You think about my offer. And I suggest you not take it to Jamie, for I'll deny ever bringing it up. And who do you think he'll believe, after all you've done to him?"

Hallie tightened her lips, holding back words of defense. It wasn't fair to take the blame for sins she didn't commit. But things would change. She lived here now.

"I won't go to Jamie with your offer. Nor will I accept it. I'm his wife, not his girlfriend, so when you address me, call me by my real name, Hallie DiBarto."

Theresa flinched but held her determined expression. "You'd be better off with the money. You've already lost him."

Panic tightened Hallie's throat. "What do you mean?"

Theresa smiled, obviously feeling as if she had gained a foothold on victory. "Why do you think he turns away from you? Why do you think he refused to let you return to Caterina with him? He's in love with someone else."

Panic gripped Hallie, now moving down to her heart. "But you said you saw love in his eyes."

"Maybe so, but you'll never be able to overcome the past. Renee works at Caterina, and though I've not met her yet, I hear she is beautiful, sweet, and very much in love with Jamie. With her, he has the chance you never gave him. If you really love him, you'll let him go."

Hallie couldn't hide the disappointment she felt. With their past, how could she compete with someone who worked with him, who promised a better future? Someone with whom he was already in love? Theresa's expression was free of smugness when she walked over and placed her cool hand on Hallie's arm.

"I'm offering you enough money to start over. Take it and go. You have nothing to lose."

Thoughts rampaged through her mind, giving up Jamie, him with another woman, Theresa's offer. Had he been running away from her when he'd left for Caterina, or running to Renee?

Hallie stood. "You're wrong. I have a lot to lose."

She walked up the stairs, grabbed her suitcase, and left. She had so wanted to win over her scornful mother-in-law, but Hallie-of-the-past had made that impossible. Hallie-of-the-present hadn't helped the situation either. But she wasn't going to take a payoff to leave her husband. She had a lot of bad actions to make up for, many ridges to smooth over and hurts to soothe. If she couldn't win back Jamie's heart, then she would walk away and leave him to heal alone. Or to heal with Renee. Without taking any payoffs. No amount of money was worth giving up that chance.

She threw the suitcase into the car, pulled out of the garage, and drove off into the sunset.

CHAPTER 9

From the window of the airplane, the isle of Constantine looked like an emerald set in the middle of a huge sparkling aquarium. Hallie pressed her forehead against the plastic window, her heart beating a staccato. Jamie was down there somewhere. And he didn't want her company. The excited voices from the other ten passengers filled the plane, but their talk of island adventures seemed far away from her own thoughts. Peace. Jamie had said he wanted peace with her, so maybe he wouldn't have her thrown off the island.

The early morning sun glinted off the water and made her squint, reminding her of how tired she should be. A long flight to Miami, Florida, then the flight to Montego Bay, yet another layover in that tiny airport before the flight taking her to Constantine. She should be tired, but she wasn't. Every fiber was buzzing, crackling with electricity. If only she knew Jamie better, then she could guess his reaction when he saw her.

The plane landed on a small strip with only one jarring bump. She was the last one off the plane, gathering her courage as well as her carry-on. The rest of her luggage, the flight attendant announced, would be delivered to the lobby where a porter would take it to her room. Only she didn't have a room. Caterina was booked. The travel agent had warned Hallie against showing up without a reservation, advising her to wait the extra two weeks before a room opened up. Hallie booked the flight anyway. California or Constantine, she had no place to stay.

Warm, moist wind embraced her when she stepped outside the plane. An orange golf cart sped her to the lobby a short distance away. A steel-drum band played in the open-air bar next to the reservation desk. Two native women in flowery dresses approached the newly arriving guests with glasses of fruit punch and welcomes.

"Ah, Mrs. D," one said to her with a large, white smile. "It is nice to see you back."

"Thank you," Hallie said, a little disconcerted. Since *she* had never been there before, she hadn't thought about anyone knowing her, anyone except Jamie. She had even considered checking in with the registration desk to see if there were any cancelations. How silly. She was the owner's wife, and these people knew her well. Her heart dropped a few inches. They knew the old Hallie, and probably felt as warm toward her as anyone else who liked Jamie did. They put on a good show, anyway.

"Any liquor in those, Ruby?" Hallie asked, reading the woman's nametag.

"No, ma'am. These here drinks be for everyone, including the wee ones." Ruby placed a plump hand on Hallie's shoulder. "You had a long flight, poor t'ing. But you look good, after what happened to you. Go see

Juicy. He fix you right up."

"Who's Juicy?"

Ruby laughed, deep and hearty. "Oh yeah, I heard you lost your memory a little. He be the big bartender man 'round here. I think he work down by the pool today."

"Okay, thanks. Uh, do you know where Jamie is?"

Ruby's black brows drew together, and she put her hands on her wide hips. "You mean dat man not even show up to meet his wife after she be in the hospital an' everyt'ing?" Her eyes searched the foliage and walkways around the lobby.

"Well, actually, he doesn't know I'm coming." Hallie left it at that, not wanting to explain further.

"Oh. Hm." She shrugged. "I never know where dat man be. If he be somewhere two minutes before, he not 'dere now. I can go find him if you like?"

"No, no that's all right. I'll find him."

"Do you have luggage, Mrs. D? I'll have Bailey take it to the house."

"Yes, this and that piece sitting over there. Thanks, Ruby."

"No problem. Now you go see Juicy."

With that, Ruby was off to help the other woman with the rest of the guests. Hallie soaked in the music, fresh air, and warm atmosphere. So, Jamie had chosen paradise for home, she thought with a smile. It was relaxed, friendly. No wonder the old Hallie had upset his ways so much.

She followed a winding path past crisp white bungalows and foliage that made her mind reel with its beauty and fragrances. The sound of children splashing in the water led her to a huge pool that sparkled like diamonds in the sunshine. On one side was a rocky waterfall, and on the other was the bar, catering to swimmers as well as those on dry land. In between those two, the pool became narrow enough to allow a wooden bridge to cross over.

She searched the area for Jamie before stepping out into the open. She wanted their reunion to be, well, perfect. And private. It wouldn't be long before someone mentioned her presence to him, so it would have to be soon. Hopefully after she had a drink to calm her jumbled nerves.

"Hello, Mrs. D!" a voice called as soon as she neared the chickee hut with palm fronds for a roof. "'Tis good to see you, lady, truly it is!"

She slid into one of the swinging chairs and smiled at Juicy. He was short, in his mid-fifties with a sprinkling of white curly hair on his dark-skinned head. His one gold tooth made his smile all that much more dazzling. He took her in with a curious smile.

"It is?"

He nodded, his light brown eyes wide and sparkling. "The bossman," he whispered, "him be downright ornery since he came back without you."

She grinned. "You think he...missed me?"

"Yah, I *tink* so. You got to stay 'round here more often."

"Well, maybe I will, Juicy. Maybe I will."

Unless Jamie booted her out on her behind. As much as she wanted to believe that he missed her, she didn't want to be lured into a false sense of security. After all, he had refused to let her come with him to Caterina in the first place.

Juicy studied her, and she felt transparent. Then he leaned forward and whispered, "Dat thing dat happened in your brain. It changed you."

Her eyes widened. "What do you mean?"

"Everybody has an aura around them," he explained, illustrating with his hands. "Yours was blue before, cool and sad, all tangled up. No, you couldn't see it with the eye, but some can feel it. Now, Mrs. D, yours be pink, warm and friendly."

She sat under his scrutiny, wondering if he would accuse her of being someone else. An imposter. But he touched her hand. "Welcome to Caterina."

When he turned away to fix a drink for someone who had been waiting on the pool side, she exhaled the long breath she had been holding. How could he tell? Most importantly, would he tell anyone? Jamie would throw them both off the island at such a preposterous idea. Or send them both to the Sharp Rehabilitation Center.

A few minutes later, Juicy placed a pink frozen drink in front of her. "This be a very special drink your husband make up."

She sipped through the straw, holding the sweet mixture in her mouth for a moment before swallowing. "This is delicious. What is it?"

Juicy smiled in a soft way. "It be called Hallie's Comet."

She flushed, but her grin held. "He made this up for me?"

Juicy leaned forward and pointed at her. "Yes, for you. Pink like your aura. Exact same color."

She took another sip. "But Hallie's aura...my aura was blue before."

He smiled again, with a knowing light in his eyes. "For you, Mrs. D. He made it for *you*."

Wow. What Juicy was implying ... She felt like spilling the entire story to him, of her death and rebirth as Hallie. Oh, to share her thoughts and problems with someone. But even with his strange revelations, could she trust him?

Juicy stopped wiping down the bar. "Mr. D might be down in the courtyard by the garden." He pointed. "Down that way for a few minutes, 'den to the right." He looked at her expectantly.

She slid out of the swing and looked in the direction he had pointed. "Thanks for the directions."

He shrugged. "Didn't want you to get lost, Mrs. D."

She ambled down the white pathway that snaked amongst the flora and fauna, wondering if she didn't already feel more at home here than the former Hallie ever had. If only Jamie would accept her into his heart again. Finding him alone was crucial. Maybe then she would have a chance to convince him to let her stay.

***

"What is your problem, man?"

Jamie looked up from the paperwork and met his brother's eyes. Despite the harshness of the question, he saw concern in their brown depths.

"I don't want to talk about it."

Miguel splayed his big hand on his chest, feigning a hurt look. "I cannot believe that you won't confide in me. But that's okay because I already know what it is. Or rather, *who* it is. Only one person could get to you like this."

"Hallie ... I didn't know *you* were coming here?" a female voice said a few yards away.

Miguel lifted an eyebrow, but Jamie walked over to where the rose bushes left a clear pathway to the pool.

There stood the woman who had haunted his dreams every hour of the previous two nights. Annoyingly, his heart lurched at the sight of her. In annoyance, of course.

Looking uncomfortable under Renee's glare, Hallie looked to him for help. She reminded him of a lost little girl. Then she straightened and met each of their eyes, ending with Renee's.

Lifting her chin, Hallie answered, "I'm here to see my *husband*," accenting the last word in a possessive way.

"Excuse us for a minute." Jamie took Hallie's hand and led her far away to the courtyard. He kept walking, getting far enough away so that no one could overhear them. The extra time gave him a chance to organize his thoughts. At present, several emotions ran through him, including anger, frustration, and one he refused to name, much less acknowledge. When they reached a secluded area, he stopped and turned her around to face him.

"Hallie..."

"Was that Renee?"

She interrupted his thought-out tirade, throwing him off. "Yes, why? Don't tell me you remember her of all people?"

"Your mother was kind enough to fill me in on your blossoming romance."

"My mother—" Her arms were crossed over her chest, her lips pursed. He couldn't believe it; she was jealous. "Hallie, can we discuss the issue at hand?"

"I think this is the issue at hand. She's the reason you didn't want me here, isn't she?"

"I didn't want you here because our marriage is over. Because you hate it here. Which brings me to the question I had intended to ask you before you started in. What are you doing here?"

"You're my husband, and I belong here with you."

He couldn't help the sarcastic laughter that bellowed from some bitter well inside him. "I only wish you had felt that way before. You were back in California for a third of our marriage."

She held her arms rigid at her sides. "That was before, this is now."

"Now is too late. Hallie, go back home."

"This is my home."

She was acting as stubborn as ever, although this time it was aimed in a completely new direction. Well, he would teach her. He'd let her stay. Soon enough she'd remember why she didn't like Caterina. She would become bored and restless and go back to California. Maybe he could help speed that up.

He raised his arms in surrender. "Fine, you can stay at the house until a bungalow becomes available. Do you know where it is?"

"No. They took my luggage there, but I came right here."

He started walking away. "Follow me."

Fate did not want him to get on with his life. It was throwing Hallie at him at a time when he was finally ready to let her go. He could only hope she would see that their marriage was dead and could never be revived.

He knew she must be exhausted from her long trip, and her eyes, fiery with determination earlier, were showing signs of weariness. Even so, throughout their long walk to the house, she stopped several times to smell a rose, admire a gardenia bush in full bloom, and run her fingers through the soft feathery leaves of a Poinciana tree. The gardens had never affected her before.

"There it is," he said when they reached the house. Her lack of response made him turn to see if she was still back there. She was standing several yards back, staring at the house with wonder. "Do you remember it?"

"No, but it's wonderful."

He tried to imagine how it must appear through eyes that had not seen it before. With its simple white beauty, gardens flanking the entrance and inviting front porch, it did present an impressive sight.

"Go on in. The door isn't locked. I'd say make yourself at home, but I'd rather you didn't."

He watched her walk slowly up to the front doors, then disappear inside. She was a mystery. He had loved her so much once, but that love was gone. Or was it?

It is.

He turned and walked back down the pathway. It most definitely damned was.

***

The first rays of sunshine beckoned Jamie from a light sleep. He turned over to see if he had dreamed about Hallie showing up at Caterina. It hadn't been a dream. She was there, her blond hair in a tumble, the sheet barely covering her breasts. He leaned up on one arm and studied her. She told him she wanted a second chance. Then she'd been disconcerted about sharing the only bed in the house, shocked to discover she slept in the nude, and embarrassed about getting undressed in front of him.

She hadn't resorted at all to her teasing ways of getting what she wanted. And if what she wanted was him, why? What had made her change her mind? The doctor had said the stroke robbed her memory, but it wouldn't change her personality. So, what had happened to her?

Under closed eyelids, her eyes twitched in REM sleep, and he wondered what she was dreaming about. He had not slept much at all; thoughts of the stranger sleeping naked beside him dominated his night. The gremlin that made him wake with morning wood turned his thoughts toward sweet awakenings many months ago, when he had kissed her awake and started the day off making love to her. Things had been so different then, so...

Dreamy thoughts were shattered as Hallie's scream of anguish pierced the quiet morning air.

CHAPTER 10

Hallie bolted upright, perspiring and desperately searching the room for some reality to clutch. When Jamie touched her arm, she jerked away, then realizing who it was, doubled over and buried her face in the sheets.

He put his arm across her bare back and leaned down by her ear. "Hallie, what's wrong? Does your head hurt? Talk to me." His words shot out at her.

She shook her head, then slowly sat up again. When she glanced down and saw her bare breasts, she snatched the sheets and covered herself.

"It was a nightmare," she said between deep breaths. Her face was pale, her eyes widened.

His hand was still on the smooth warm skin of her back, lending unspoken support. He let out his own deep breath, a sigh of relief. "God, I thought you were dying."

He studied her eyes, and she blinked to clear away the trace of fear.

She leaned forward, her gaze piercing his. "I'm not going to die again, Jamie. Not for a long time."

"I'm glad you're so confident. Do you want to talk

about it? The nightmare, I mean. Sometimes it helps."

She looked off into nothingness, as if trying to conjure the image again, then shook her head. "I just want to forget about it."

He slipped from the bed, put on a bathing suit, and pushed open the slider. The pool was right off the bedroom, down two steps, so she could see it from her place in bed. Reflections of the blue sky and clouds scattered as he plunged into the pool.

Hallie stayed in bed with the sheets wrapped tightly around her, listening to the sound of quiet splashing. The nightmare's cold grip left its chilled marks on her soul. Now she understood something that had puzzled her: her terrified reaction when that semi had pulled into her lane. In her dream, she drove across one of those awful bridges and a truck smashed into her. But it was no accident. The driver had purposely pushed her to the side of the bridge, then careened into her car to ensure that she dropped off the edge and into the ravine.

She shivered again. Maybe her original bridge nightmare was simply adding events from her imagination. Maybe...her eyes closed, and the truck smashed into her thoughts. They snapped open again. Not her imagination. She was seeing the end of her life as Chris Copestakes.

She leaned forward and rested her chin on her knees, pulling her fingers through her hair in rapid strokes. Why did someone who didn't even know her want to kill her? Or did he know her? She tried to bring the nightmare back, seeing the truck jerk into her car, shove her off the bridge. The driver could have been drunk, but the action seemed deliberate. Perhaps a random act of violence then. That kind of thing happened all the time, though never in small-town Maven. Had the police found this reckless murderer?

Kneading her temples, she pushed those thoughts from her mind and tried to think of something else. Like the sight of Jamie's bare tight buttocks as he had walked to the dresser and slipped on a bathing suit. No, not those thoughts! What else? Like exploring the island.

Jamie slipped effortlessly through the blue water, his strokes even and calm. He was not fighting demons, just taking his usual morning swim. She climbed out of bed, grabbed some clothes, and headed to the bathroom. Her naked reflection caught her eye, and she stopped. She hadn't actually studied the body she now occupied. It felt like, well, almost like looking at someone else's naked body.

Her breasts were large, but they didn't sag. Her stomach was almost flat, though her hips were a bit wide. And her thighs were a bit too large. She should be in that pool swimming with Jamie. But that was his private time, and she didn't want to intrude. She would find another way to tone up. It was something she'd never had to worry about before.

She ran her hands down her sides, feeling the swell of her breasts and the ridges of her rib bones, then across her stomach and over her pelvic bones that jutted out ever so slightly. Her body now.

The sound of the sliding-glass door opening made her jump, and she slipped around the corner into the room where the toilet was. The shower started. She slipped on a T-shirt and short overalls. Steam billowed over the glass door that was fogged up...but not so much that she couldn't see his tan silhouette as he washed his hair. Lord have mercy.

No, really. Have mercy!

She was putting on socks and sneakers when Jamie appeared at the long counter, a beige towel snug around his waist. He glanced at her before smoothing shaving cream over his chin and cheeks.

"Is that new?" he said between lips stretched to one side as he started to shave.

She stood and took a few steps toward him. "What? My outfit? Yes, do you like it?"

He glanced at her again, and she had to stifle a giggle. He looked like a sexy Santa Claus with his foamy beard and mustache.

"Yeah, I do. I've never seen you wear anything like that before."

"Thanks."

He went back to shaving, and the movement of his muscles fascinated her. His back was wide and tan, and she felt an urge to trail her finger down the crevice of his spine and capture the droplets of water there. The towel hugged buttocks that almost looked as intriguing clothed as they did naked. The backs of his calves were finely shaped, strong and...

"What are your plans for the day?"

His voice broke her out of her reverie. She instantly blushed, wondering if he had caught her staring at him.

"Oh, I thought I'd explore the island, check out Caterina."

"Mm," he said with a nod. "That's something you've never done before."

"What did I do around here?"

"You sat around the pool and complained."

"That was all I did? All day?"

"Sometimes you drank at the bar, talked with the guests."

"Speaking of the bar, I had a Hallie's Comet when I arrived. What a sweet thought."

"*Foolish* is the word. But," he said, stretching to diminish the words, "I was in love, I had just bought Caterina, and I thought I had the world by the tail feathers. The only thing that could have made me happier then was to have my father there to see it."

"Did I ever meet your father?"

"No, he passed away a year before we met. My father taught me to go after my dreams with every ounce of spirit I had. And I did. Unfortunately, it took all the money he left to buy this place."

"Why did you buy Caterina? I mean, it's not every man who dreams of buying part of an island." But then again, Jamie wasn't just any man.

"When I was fourteen, my father had good luck in the stock market and took us for a month-long vacation at a resort on Grand Cayman Island. I was ruined for any other kind of life. Caterina was owned by a recluse, and when he died, the estate put the place on the market. Miguel and I invested our inheritances and turned it into a resort."

He washed off the last of the lather, and she turned away just as he untied his towel and caught it before it hit the floor. The man had no shame.

When he emerged from the closet, he was wearing baggy white pants and a black shirt with a crew neck. "I've got to go over some figures with the accountant this morning. Have fun in the jungle."

Hallie thought it was a good time to ask. "Jamie? I'm

a pretty good number cruncher. Is there room for someone else in the accounting department?"

He looked at her as if she had just asked where she could go skydiving. Finally, he shrugged. "I'll ask Renee if she needs any help."

Her face went red at the name, half-angry, half-embarrassed at her outburst the morning before. *Wouldn't want your mistress and your wife working side by side, now would we?* an unwelcome voice said. "No, that's all right. Maybe I can find something else to do around here."

"Okay. See you later."

"When?" she asked, trying to keep the eagerness from her voice.

"Tonight, most likely."

He left, and she tried to stave off the feelings of worry and loneliness. He was meeting Renee that morning. Would that woman put her hands on his body, feel him inside her? The thought made Hallie's mind roar with rage, but she kept her feelings in check. Jamie didn't realize it yet, and neither did Renee, but the game had a new opponent. What she knew about seduction could be written on a grain of sand, but she was going to learn the craft quickly. Her marriage depended on it.

***

Miguel hung up with the travel agent, dumped a bunch of papers in his drawer, and headed over to the café for lunch. As he rounded the rose garden, the sight of Hallie stopped him short. She was standing absolutely still, her shoulders stiff, staring at Jamie and Renee laughing together at a side table. A starry-eyed Renee laughing with Jamie was nothing new to Miguel, though he wasn't immune to his feelings because of the fact. No, it still hurt to see her ogling his brother.

He quietly walked up beside Hallie. "They're discussing business."

She jumped, turning to face him. An array of expressions crossed her face, relief and embarrassment being two he could identify. "You're Miguel, aren't you?"

"The one and only," he stated without a smile.

"It doesn't look like business," she said. "So, she's the accountant around here."

"Yep. She must have some good news for him."

"She's in love with him."

He was surprised to hear her words spoken so definitely, but not without a trace of jealousy. Her eyes never left the couple at the table.

"Yes, she is."

Hallie tore her gaze away and implored him visually for the truth. "Does he...is he in love with her?"

For Jamie, he wanted to tell her yes, that Hallie should give up and go home. For himself, he wanted to tell her that Jamie wasn't, and that she should try to win him back. He settled with the truth.

"He would be," he said, then was surprised to hear her finish his thoughts.

"If I wasn't here."

"Maybe. It's not as if he's in the wrong, entertaining the thought. Not after what you've put him through."

She flinched, then returned her gaze to Jamie. Jealousy was not something Miguel had ever seen in Hallie, but she controlled it well. In her dark blue eyes, he saw an aching desire. It would benefit him if she and Jamie got back together. Maybe Renee would stop following him around like a puppy and look at Miguel as more than a shoulder to cry on. None of that would be worth it if Jamie got tromped on by Hallie again. Yes, he definitely had to get Hallie out of the picture. He could do the martyr thing.

"Hallie, don't you think it's time Jamie had a chance at happiness?"

"Absolutely."

"Without you, without the past to haunt him. Renee's a great gal, smart, sexy. You've got the past to overcome, she's new territory. You haven't a chance."

She turned to him, her eyes blazing. "You don't know me, or my chances with my husband. I won't have you shoving me out the door with a tally-ho. I know you love your brother, Miguel, and I understand what you're doing. But there are things that go far beyond what you know, so leave it alone."

Whoa. He'd never seen her feistiness and determination aimed at saving her marriage. He also knew blood ran thicker than a gold wedding ring. "It's too late, that's all I'm telling you. Save yourself the hurt and humiliation and go back to California. You have no right to be here, and you know it."

She had been kneading the leaves of a nearby plant throughout their conversation. Her muscles tensed, and she twisted a branch at his final words. Instead of pulling the branch, she yanked the whole plant out of the ground. She handed it to him, roots, dirt and all, and stalked away.

***

Hallie had paced the living room until six o'clock when Jamie called from the office. He had to cover a wedding reception for the sick catering manager, he'd said, and wouldn't be home until late. She played several different scenarios of him and Renee dancing with the wedding party and doing honeymoon-type things until eleven, when she thought she would explode. The Tropical Room wasn't hard to find; all she had to do was follow the music. Twenty people still danced and partied, but she could find no sign of Jamie. The groom said he had left half an hour ago.

Hallie went back home to that quiet house again. The masochistic images continued playing in her mind. The former Hallie may not have had the right to be possessive, but she was trying to hold the tattered shreds of her marriage together, and she didn't need some *hussy* trying to steal him away right under her nose.

Jealous insanity was only another pace of the room away when she settled into the bed with a book and tried to read. Her eyes kept drifting to the doorway every time she heard a faint noise. When she finally heard the front door open, her fears and anger returned full force—and seemed to be fully justified.

Jamie's hair was disheveled, his eyes bloodshot. He squinted in the soft light of the bedroom, staring at her with a wobbly head for a full minute before saying a word.

"Hi, there. Waiting up for me?"

The book went flying, and with slow reflexes he barely escaped a nasty knock from Dean Koontz. His confused expression made her even more furious.

"Where have you been, James DiBarto?" She would have used his middle name, for the full effect, if she'd known it.

He cocked his head back in surprise. "Whoa. Now

you're beginning to sound like my mother when I was twelve." He squinted at her covered form under the sheets, her bare shoulders above them. "You certainly don't look like my mother." He sauntered toward the bathroom.

He didn't see it coming this time, and the pillow nailed him in the back of his head. Safer than a book. He turned around with an injured look. "What was that for?"

She crossed her arms over her chest. "You didn't answer my question."

He wagged a finger at her. "Listen, young lady, I have been coming and going in this house for a year without any interrogation on your part."

She frowned, but the hurt inside kept her expression hard. "You left the Tropical two hours ago. I just want to know where you were until now. You've been drinking and you look like you've been screwing every floozy in the place...or maybe just one."

As she had been talking, he walked toward her, his face inscrutable. He fell across the bed, pinning her legs, and roared with laughter.

She stared at him in disbelief. "What the hell is so funny?"

"*Shhh!*" he mumbled between gales of laughter, pressing a finger over her lips. "*Hill*, not *hell*."

"What?"

"We don't cuss around here. When Miguel and I were kids, we used other words to get around the"—he raised his eyebrows—"real cuss words. So you see, you should have said, 'What the *hill* is so funny?'"

Her shoulders drooped, but he continued to laugh. "Jamie, go to *hill*."

That started another gale of laughter. With his arm, he rolled her back on the bed and leaned over her, smiling. The sweet smell of rum pervaded the small space between them.

"You really think I was out *fugging* all the women on the island, eh?"

"*Fugging*? Oh, I see. Actually, there was only one I was really worried about."

He sort of half-snorted and half-laughed, then dropped his head down on her chest, which she only vaguely hoped was still covered. After a moment, he lifted his head and looked at her. He looked so much like a little boy, happy and silly. Silly drunk, that was.

"You're funny," he stated.

"I'm glad I'm so amusing." Something inside her was glad. That's what made her so mad that morning, her inability to make Jamie laugh the way Renee had. Hallie had done a better job, and she hadn't even tried. Still, she couldn't ignore the fact that he hadn't answered her question yet. Or the way his weight heated her body.

"You are amusing, Hallie. I've never seen you like this before."

"I've never seen me like this before either."

"I was with Miguel." He rolled off her to lie on his back.

She leaned up on her elbow, looking down at him. "Really?" The grin spread across her face.

"Yeah, really. I didn't know you cared." He crossed his arms over his chest in an imitation of her earlier stance. "And I certainly didn't expect to come home and find you all huffy. I'll never forget the way you looked."

"I just hope you'll only have this one incident to commit to memory. If this is what you went through with Ha—me before, I'm so sorry. I can't imagine going through this more than one time. Jamie? Are you listening to me?"

She looked at his serene expression and realized he was asleep. Rather than try to shift him lengthwise, she put his pillow under his head, moved her pillow beside it, and curled up next to him. For the first time in what felt like forever, she fell asleep with a smile.

***

The next morning, Jamie stared out his office window at the sparkling water of the sea and the couples who walked along the beach holding hands. What he saw was Hallie with her arms crossed over her sheet-swathed chest demanding to know where he had been. He smiled, marveling at the turn in tables between them. If one thing had remained the same throughout her ordeal, it was his inability to figure her out.

"Jamie?"

Half expecting to see Hallie, he found Renee standing at the door. "Hey. Come in."

She strode across the colorful woven rugs thrown across the wood floors to perch on his desk a few inches away. He leaned back in his chair, to get a better look at her as well as put some distance between them. She was an attractive woman with her short brown hair blown away from her wide round face. Her brown eyes were set far apart, and her lips were full and large, usually exposing her two front teeth.

"Are you busy?"

He shrugged. "Always busy, but it never gets done. What's up?"

"Do you remember that night a few months ago

when I told you how I felt about you? I said you were too good for Hallie, that you deserved better. You told me you found me attractive, too." She faltered.

He wished he could make this conversation easier on her, but he didn't know where she was headed.

"Yes, I remember."

"We both agreed that an affair was out of the question, but that perhaps, if things didn't work out with your marriage we could…give it a try."

He remembered that conversation being a little more general than that, but he waited for her point. He wondered if she was trying to tell him that she was interested in someone else. The thought didn't bother him. She leaned down until her face was only an inch away.

"Jamie, I love you. I want you. I know you said you didn't feel the same way about me then, but I know you do. You're just too damn noble to admit it. You can't still love your wife, not after all she's put you through. We've been good friends for a long time, and I think it's natural to move that friendship into a relationship. As soon as a bungalow is free, why don't you get her off your couch and let me move in?"

She closed her eyes and pressed her lips to his. For a moment, he responded to the feel of her lips. A memory of Hallie's goodbye kiss flashed into his mind.

He moved back. "She's not sleeping on the couch."

Renee straightened. "You're not sleeping on the couch, I hope. You should…" Her momentary anger slipped away and left a hurt expression behind. "You're sharing a bed?"

He leaned back in his chair and pressed his fingers together. "She's my wife."

"Don't you understand that she doesn't deserve that position?"

"I'm not saying she deserves it or not. All I'm saying is that she *is* my wife, and I've got some things to figure out."

Renee leaned her hands on the desk in front of him. "Figure what out?" Her expression lightened. "You pity her, don't you? Because of the stroke. She's going to be the same person when her memory returns. Why should you feel obligated to take care of her? Her lover, Mick, should be the one by her side."

His mouth tightened. "Miguel talks too much."

She cocked her head. "Only because he knows how much I love you. And I do love you, Jamie DiBarto. I don't intend to lose you to some pity case."

With that, she turned and left.

He liked Renee, but he was far from being in love with her. She had built a dream from their friendly chats, a dream he wasn't sure he could ever fulfill, even when Hallie did return to her old ways. Still, he might have fun trying when the time came. Until then, Hallie had confused the *hill* out of him, and he couldn't do a thing until he figured that all out.

***

It was three days before Jamie was able to spend an evening at home. Hallie had made him promise that morning that he would be home for dinner. When he'd asked if she wanted him to bring anything from the restaurant, she just smiled and said no. Since they didn't have access to TV dinners, he couldn't imagine what she had in mind. The woman couldn't even make Jell-O set.

When he opened the door, the aroma of fresh garlic, chicken, and other spices greeted him. He crept around the corner to the kitchen. The view was splendid, with Hallie bent over searching in one of the lower cabinets for something. The denim sundress she wore clung nicely to her derriere, and her legs were tan and shapely. She stuck her finger in her mouth as she looked through another cabinet.

Gone were all the sexy, slinky clothes she used to wear. She wore casual, cute outfits that fit her well, but not too tightly. Strangely enough, she looked sexier than ever. He dismissed the observation and stepped into the kitchen.

"Can I help?"

She jumped at the sound of his voice, then smiled. "Aww, I wanted to have dinner ready by the time you got home, but I forgot how long this takes to make."

He peered into a pot of boiling fettuccine, then tasted a bit of the creamy sauce in another pan. "What are you making?"

"Chicken Carbonara."

This is not what he expected. Hallie's cooking expertise stopped at grilled cheese sandwiches. She hated to cook and hardly ever did. This was an all-out affair, with breaded chunks of chicken sautéing on the griddle, crumbled bacon sitting on a plate, and not a cookbook in sight.

"You actually made all this? By yourself?"

She turned and spread her hands. "Doesn't it look like it?" Breadcrumbs clung to her long hair and beads of sweat dotted her forehead. She turned and looked in another cabinet, then made a triumphant sound. "Found it." She pulled out a colander and put it in the sink.

Hallie positively glowed, even covered with crumbs in a kitchen that looked like a culinary monsoon had swept through it. It was an image he wanted to preserve for later.

"Why are you looking at me like that?" she asked with a smile.

"I've never seen you cook before."

"Why does that not surprise me?" This she mumbled. She turned and dumped the pot of noodles into the colander. "Mom used to tell me what a great wife I'd make. 'A woman today who actually likes to cook is a rarity,' she'd say."

"Your *mother* said you'd make a great wife?"

Hallie's expression grew serious for a moment, then she looked away and continued to rinse the noodles. "Once. It was a long time ago."

They ate dinner civilly, like any normal married couple. Crazy thought. The radio picked up a reggae station from nearby Jamaica. She told him about the purple orchids she'd found in the deep secluded part of the island, and about her morning swims in the sea.

"There are these weeds that shrink when you touch them. Juicy said the natives use them to find their way back through the jungle. They know they're retracing their steps when they see the shrunken weeds. Isn't that neat?"

Picturing Hallie looking at weeds was not an easy thing to do. He helped her clear the table.

"Guess what I've got for dessert," she said.

"Flaming Alaska?" he guessed, and wouldn't be surprised if she said yes.

"No, silly. Mangos." She opened the refrigerator and

produced a bowl of four peeled, orange mangos.

"I thought they were out of season."

"They are, but I spotted these babies way up near the top of a tree."

"Who'd you con to get them down for you?"

"I got them myself. And what a view from the top of the tree! You should check it out. You can see the whole island."

His mouth dropped open. "You climbed a mango tree?"

"I could see the airstrip and the village of Contigua —"

He put his hands out to halt her. "Let me get this straight. You." He pointed to her. "Climbed to the top of a tree?"

She nodded, looking exasperated by his disbelief. "Yes, I climbed to the top of a tree. Chicken Carbonara calls for something light afterward, and Ruby said you liked mangos. The kitchen didn't have any more, so when I spotted these, I climbed up to get them. Now will you listen about the view?"

She continued telling him about the clear water and the school of dolphin twenty yards from the beach. He scratched his head and was at a total loss to picture his wife, the prissy, complaining Hallie, climbing a tree to get mangos for dessert because he liked them.

He headed toward the door. "I need to take a walk."

"Want some company?" she asked with a bright smile.

"No, thanks. I need to be alone."

Her smile faded. "Are you going to see Miguel?"

"Maybe."

"Renee?"

"No."

"Can you tell me why you're leaving?"

"No."

He stepped out into the garden-scented air and walked down to the beach to sort images from his present and past. Figuring out Hallie was like doing one of those damned two-sided puzzles.

***

As she waded into the sea two mornings later, Hallie thought how silly it was, them swimming every morning and not together. He had rejected her invitation to swim with her and had not proffered the same invite to her.

Since their special dinner, designed to bring them closer together, he had made a point to politely avoid her. When he *was* around, he watched her every move. She didn't know which was more disconcerting.

Her tired legs carried her to the shoreline, and she plopped down on the wet sand and let the waves wash over her feet. She was as tan as she used to be, and she loved her life on the island where she could explore to her heart's content. The only thing missing from her life was her husband. He was fighting her...and winning.

Renee was hanging around Jamie more and more, constantly carrying around some paper or another to show him as an excuse. It seemed as if every time Hallie saw him, that woman was walking right next to him. She dug her feet into the sand and kicked a huge chunk into an oncoming wave.

"Nice kick," a feminine voice remarked. Hallie looked up to see Renee standing there, as though her thoughts had summoned her. "Can I join you?"

"Sure." Hallie resolved then that she would not be rude, no matter what. God, give her strength.

Renee set her clipboard aside, and in her prim shorts and button-down shirt, sat down on the wet sand next to her. "I haven't had a chance to talk to you in the week that you've been back." Renee laughed artificially. "It's been so busy, what with some of our employees on vacation and such. How are you feeling?"

Hallie turned to her. "Great, thanks for asking." There was a fine line between rudeness and frankness. "But somehow, I don't think we were bosom buddies before my stroke, and I can't help but wonder why you're really here."

Renee swallowed loudly, forcing a smile. "Well, if you're nothing else, you're blunt."

"I like to get to the point when I feel I'm being sugarcoated."

"Actually, Jamie is the one I'm good friends with. I'm worried about him."

"Worried about him or my being here with him?"

Renee smiled again. "Both. I care a lot about Jamie. We're, well ... you know."

"No, I don't. Why don't you elaborate?"

"We're...close."

Close to what? Making love? Marriage? She wanted to ask but kept her cool. "I see. And?"

"Before your stroke, you asked him for a divorce. Now, all of a sudden, you want him back. I wonder if you're staying here because you feel you have no other place to go."

"I'm here because I want to be here. With my *husband*."

Renee let out a huff of breath. "Jamie and I love each

other, although I'm sure he's too noble to tell you. He won't send you away, but as soon as a bungalow comes available, he's going to move you out. And move me in. I'm telling you this so you can save face by leaving now. I know how hard that kind of thing can be on a woman."

Hallie stood, forcing Renee to stand as well. "How very kind of you to think of the wife's feelings as you try to steal her husband."

Renee turned and walked away. Hallie was too incensed to even laugh about the wet blotch on her behind. Then she dropped down to the sand and wrapped her hands across her shoulders. Yes, Jamie had told her that as soon as a bungalow became available that he would move her into it. Was that why he so politely tolerated her presence?

No, she wouldn't let that happen. Even if Jamie did have feelings for that woman, she knew he had feelings for her, too. What was the saying? Desperate situations require desperate actions? She knew what she had to do, and it had to happen tonight. She was going to seduce her husband.

CHAPTER 11

Hallie fiddled with the lace-up front on one of the former Hallie's red dresses. Through the lace, she could see skin clear down to her navel. The hemline stopped only a few inches below her buttocks. Perfect for a seduction.

She pulled up her hair, letting a few strands hang down around her face. For the first time in a week and a half, she put on makeup, though only a smidgen. Even her confident image in the mirror couldn't hide the fact that her hands were shaking. She walked out onto the lanai and talked to the only friend besides Juicy that she had on the island.

"Greenpeace, how am I going to seduce a man who doesn't want to be seduced?"

The green lizard sat where he usually did, on a white post near the pool, his legs stretched back behind him. He offered no advice, only quiet consolation.

"I've only made love to one man in my life, and that was right out of high school. I'd never made love to Alan. Something just didn't feel right when he touched me. I'll bet the real Hallie was wild in bed."

She remembered her times with Greg many years before. She had not been wild. More like stumbling, awkward and unsure of herself. Just like she felt then. Insecurity washed over her like a sudden thunderstorm, prickling her with the electricity of doubt.

She walked back inside, subconsciously pulling down the hem. The steaks were on the grill, the candles lit, and the baked potatoes in the oven. She could only hope that this dinner would bring him closer instead of pushing him away.

Jamie walked in, took one look at the candlelit table in the formal dining room, and walked straight to the bedroom. She raised an eyebrow. *Hmm*, maybe it was working already.

When he emerged, he wore baggy black pants. "I wasn't in the mood for anything elaborate," he said, his expression soft.

"I just made steaks and twice-baked potatoes."

"And mangos?"

"No mangos. I couldn't find any more."

Dinner was quiet, giving her nothing more to think about other than her planned seduction. After dinner, she followed Jamie into the family room. He flipped on a light and settled into an easy chair with a magazine.

She sat on the couch directly across from him. "Jamie, can we talk?"

He lifted his gaze. "About what?"

"I don't know, anything."

He laid the magazine down. "Okay, why does a stroke turn someone into a cover hog?"

Her eyes widened. "What?"

"You were a neat sleeper before, but now every night I have to tug the sheets from around you. You also try to take over the whole bed. I find you sprawled on my side most of the time."

This was not the kind of conversation she had planned on, although talking about beds was a start. She certainly couldn't tell him she was used to having the whole bed to herself.

She shrugged. "Maybe I like to sleep next to you."

"You never did before. You said you need space."

"I don't want to argue with you about sheets and bed territory." She walked over and sat on the floor beside him. "Can I ask you something? How long has it been since we...made love?"

"Are we talking sex or actual lovemaking?"

"The last time we really made love."

He looked up as he thought, calculating. "About a year and a half ago."

"How about the last time we had sex?"

"Six months ago. It was more like a drunken booty call on both our parts."

She chewed her bottom lip. Unless he was bedding Renee, she had libido on her side. The more she thought about Renee's words, the more they niggled at her.

"Have you made love, or had sex, with anyone else?"

He looked at her, and she wondered if he was weighing whether to tell her the truth. "No. Why are we talking about this?"

"Because I wanted to know." Warily she lifted her hand and traced a line down his arm. "I'm glad."

"I didn't abstain for you, Hallie. I did it for me. Revenge is no reason to sleep with someone."

"I couldn't agree with you more."

Her hand trailed down his fingers and dropped to his leg. From there they teased to his inner thigh. She hoped he couldn't see her trembling.

"What are you doing?"

"Isn't it kind of obvious?"

She got up and, with both hands still moving along his leg, leaned over him.

His gaze flickered away. "I wish you wouldn't."

She summoned her huskiest voice. "Do you really?"

"Yes."

He sounded convincing, but he didn't move away. She saw physical evidence that at least his body was interested and trailed her hands dangerously close. It had been so long since she had touched a man, and the thought sent pine-needle prickles down her spine.

She bent down and lifted his shirt to bare his hard stomach. Her hands trailed up over his chest beneath his shirt while she flicked her tongue against his neck between kisses. To finally feel the softness of his skin and the firmness of his muscles made her tingle.

For several seconds his body tensed, as though he were fighting any reaction he was having. Then he released a harsh breath. His hands were suddenly in her hair, moving slowly through her curls. When she thought he might snatch her head up to stop her, a soft groan escaped from deep within his chest, causing her heart to pound harder.

Scrunching her eyes shut, she unsnapped the first button of his pants, then the next. When she started unzipping his pants, he pulled her up as he stood. With his fingers tangled in her hair, he yanked her against him. His mouth crushed hers in a brutal kiss. They fell back on the sofa, but not for a moment did their mouths part. When his tongue pushed into her mouth, the groan she heard emanated from somewhere in her soul. She pulled him closer, inviting him to crush her with his weight.

Hallie was aware of every muscle and contour of his body as it pressed against hers. She felt his heat, his hands sliding down her arms. Her own heat rose and threatened to explode. He nipped her jaw line and down the sensitive skin of her neck, bringing her closer to the brink. She dragged her fingers up his back and through his soft hair. The fire threatened to consume her, the flames licking closer and closer. But this wasn't what she wanted from him. Passion, yes. But more than passion; she wanted his soul.

"Jamie," she whispered between breaths. "Make love to me. Really make love to me."

He stopped and blinked, as though coming out of a trance. Still hovering over her, he took her chin firmly in his hand. "If you were anyone else but my wife, maybe I could pretend it was making love. I can't pretend that with you."

Tears filled her eyes, but she quickly blinked them away. "Why not?"

He got to his feet and buttoned his pants while adjusting his erection. "Because making love means giving you a part of myself that I don't want to give you anymore. I don't even know if it exists."

"But it does, Jamie. Doesn't what happened here prove that?"

He glanced to where she'd indicated with a nod. "Getting a guy who hasn't had sex in six months hard is no great feat. Especially when you're dressed like that." He touched the hem of her skirt. "That's why you started touching me, asking how long it's been. You were using lust to get to me, nothing new there."

Dammit, she'd messed up again. "Okay, maybe I did

use sex to get you to come closer to me. But it wasn't about lust."

"You always had lust and love confused. Maybe I did, too. Now I see the difference, and I don't want lust anymore. Or love. Not with you."

He grabbed his magazine and walked outside, taking a seat on the lanai beneath a light. She watched him from the slider, fighting back tears of anger and rejection. Was it lust she had been feeling? She certainly was no expert on romantic love. No, she wanted to prove that she loved him. And, she realized with a slight smile, Jamie wasn't nearly as unaffected as he seemed to be. That was, unless he could read upside down.

***

Miguel sat at a solitary table in the courtyard where he and Jamie usually had their business meetings. He twirled his pencil, ducking when he tossed it up in the air and it came down point first.

"You ought to be a comedian, Miguel." Jamie laughed as he joined his brother. "You missed your calling."

Miguel studied Jamie for a moment, then glanced at his watch. With a raised eyebrow, and not a trace of humor, he said, "You're fifteen minutes late, and you have a silly grin on your face. Since you're always on time, dare I guess that you and your lovely wife made amends this morning?"

Jamie dropped down into the white wicker chair. "Dare I say that it's none of your business?"

Miguel raised his hands. "Hey, just concerned for you, little brother."

Jamie knew that, and yet he'd felt defensive. He shook his head, remembering her seduction last night.

If she had placed a gun to his head, he wouldn't have been more surprised. Hallie was usually not the one to initiate lovemaking. The few times she had, her approach was verbal. Never had she wanted to make love anywhere but in bed. He wasn't going to mention how she'd worn old sweats to bed, how she looked sexy in them despite her intentions. "Do you know she talks to lizards?"

Miguel's eyes widened. "The green anoles we have all over the place?"

"Yep. Caught her having an animated conversation with one that hangs around the lanai. She'd freak every time one got in the house, called them creepy little things."

Miguel crossed large hairy arms together and leaned back in his chair. "Did your amorous morning have anything to do with you wanting to soothe her after her conversation with Renee?"

"What conversation?"

"She didn't tell you?"

Jamie shook his head, his curiosity now piqued. Oh, brother. Hallie could get dramatic. "What did Hallie say to her?"

Miguel leaned forward, rubbing his beard. "She didn't tell you? Wow."

"Tell me what?"

"It wasn't what Hallie said to Renee, but what Renee said to Hallie. Now, don't get mad at Renee. You know how she feels about you, and sometimes she doesn't think things through. Promise you won't tell her I told you. She confided in me, but I figured Hallie had told you."

"I promise already. Spill."

"Well." Miguel leaned back and got comfortable, enjoying as he had always keeping Jamie in suspense. "Renee told Hallie that she and you were, well, she didn't come right out and say lovers. More like *close.* Then she told her that once a bungalow became available, you were going to move Hallie out and Renee in. Oh, and something about you and Renee loving each other."

Jamie dropped his head down on his hands.

"Remember, you promised you wouldn't tell Renee I told you, no matter how mad you are. You—"

Miguel stopped when Jamie lifted his head and let the laughter on his face burst out.

"So that explains it," Jamie said between gales of laughter.

"Explains what? What's so funny?"

Jamie shook his head, getting his laughter under control. "From what I gathered, Mom told Hallie that Renee and I were an item. Now *Renee* tells her we're an item."

Miguel looked sheepishly down at his hands. "I kinda told her she didn't have a chance against Renee, considering the water under your bridge. I didn't want that witch with a capital B to get back under your skin."

Jamie leaned back, a grin still on his face. "And what did she say to that?"

"Well, it was kinda weird. She said I didn't know her or her chances with her husband, and she wouldn't have me shoving her out the door. With a *tally-ho*, no less. She told me there are things I don't understand, so I should leave it alone. She was downright feisty. Now will you tell me what's so darn funny?"

"Well, my wife comes out of a coma remembering

nothing about her life, determined to save a marriage that she doesn't even recall, and everyone has told her that I'm in love with a woman I haven't even kissed. And still, she stays."

"Do you think she's brain-damaged?"

"She's less neurotic now than she ever was. Okay, there are some weird things, like the lizard. Back in California, she got weepy when she saw a Sheltie, saying how she missed her three dogs. I called her mother and asked; she's never had a dog. She's suddenly into nature. She spends hours exploring the uncultivated areas of Caterina and comes back glowing. She even cooks now. She made the most amazing dinner ... from memory."

Miguel raised his eyebrow again. "Cooks? Hallie? The Hallie we know, cooks?"

"She's not the Hallie we knew. I just don't know how long it'll be until she returns to her old self." Jamie rolled a piece of paper from his notepad into a ball as another oddity clicked. "From *memory*. She made a complex dinner from *memory*. She forgets everything in her life but remembers how to make Chicken Carbonara."

"Woman's an enigma. I'd say she's faking the whole lost memory thing to get back in your good graces, but she's acting completely different. Wish I knew what it meant. The one thing I've got to say is that the lady is determined to win back your heart, whatever her motives."

Maybe not after last night. Jamie stared at the rose bushes, remembering her hurt expression as she went for her walk that morning. She'd said she had to figure something out. Suddenly the thought of her giving up on him tightened his chest. He didn't want her to leave just yet. He had things to figure out himself.

"Well, let's get started on the budget plan..." Miguel stopped when Jamie stood up.

"It'll have to wait. I need to find Hallie."

***

Jamie followed her trail in the direction she had left from the house, using the shrinking weeds she'd told him about. He stepped over a rotted palm tree trunk and walked through a thicket of Australian pines. Less than an hour later, her cute derriere faced him as she leaned over a large rock. She was framed by the huge trunk of a wild fig tree, which looked like a magnificent gray elephant stretching its front legs up before her. All around, curtains of vines climbed up surrounding trees and made everything feel private and secluded.

She stayed motionless for so long, he wondered if there was something wrong. He started walking toward her, feeling half-worried and half-silly for following her. She cupped her hands over something behind the rock and slowly lifted it to her face. His shoe broke a twig, and she turned with a start. Instead of anger or question on her face, he saw awe in her blue eyes. She held her cupped hands toward him. "Look inside. Can you see him?"

She parted her fingers, and he bent to look inside the darkness. A tiny brown eye peered back, and he moved away. First, she was talking to lizards, now she was capturing critters in her hands.

"What is it?"

She parted her fingers more to reveal the tiniest monkey he had ever seen. It was only five inches in length, with a striped tail just as long. Its brown eyes almost looked human as they darted from him to her and all around.

"It's a Tangoo Island monkey. They're very rare and only live on some of the Caribbean islands. Juicy told me about them."

She let out a small yelp as it leaped from her hands toward her head. She looked at Jamie, her eyes filled with the wonder of a little girl.

He couldn't keep the stupid grin from his face. Her gaze followed his to the side, but what he was looking at was beyond her range of vision. The monkey was holding onto strands of her hair. Its heart pumped like an engine, its hands curled around a lock of blond hair as if it were a lifeline.

"We've got to have a talk about your hairpieces, Hallie."

She grinned. "He's on my hair, isn't he?"

He moved closer to retrieve the monkey, but on the way decided to kiss her instead. More tender than the night before, without the senseless physical lust, he touched his lips to hers. She kissed back tentatively, her eyes filled with question.

His hands trailed around her back, and he closed his eyes and kissed her again, this time letting his tongue tickle along her lips. He heard her sigh, then her mouth opened in invitation. Her hands slipped around his neck, and he pulled her close against him, feeling her curves and remembering how perfectly their bodies fit together. He explored her mouth, the faint taste of toothpaste combining with her sweetness.

He tasted her again and again, exploring, moving against her. She, who had never liked French kissing, moved her tongue through his mouth like a woman tasting chocolate after a long diet. His hands moved up and cupped her face, his thumbs caressing the softness of her cheeks.

A shrill chattering noise jarred his attention from her, and he looked up to the monkey still clutching her hair. His fingers had been pressed against its tail, and once released, the monkey clambered on top of Hallie's head.

He reached out and took the monkey from its perch, holding it out to her. She was looking at Jamie, oblivious for a moment to the monkey in front of her. Finally, she held out a finger, and the monkey jumped onto her hand. She touched its back, and Jamie ran his fingers down its striped tail. The light brown fur was coarse at the outer edges, but soft underneath. Their fingers touched and, as if exchanging static electricity, pulled away.

"What are you going to name him?" Jamie asked, desperately trying to break up the tension that crackled around them.

"Name him? I can't keep him; he belongs in the wild." She kept her gaze carefully away from his, making it hard to read her expression.

"If you want him, make him your own."

Her gaze lifted to his. "What are we talking about here?"

He couldn't help but smile, wondering himself exactly what he'd meant. "The monkey, of course. What else would I be talking about?"

"I can't imagine," she said, averting her gaze again. She stroked the monkey's fur, deep in thought. "If I show him my love, and he leaves anyway, I'll let him go. I won't cage him in or try to tempt him into staying with me. He has to want to be with me."

"What are *you* talking about?"

"The monkey." She didn't look at him, though he could see her expression was more serious than a monkey warranted.

"I heard you had a little chat with Renee yesterday."

She looked at him then. "She told you?"

"No, she told Miguel, and he felt obligated to let me know. Is that what prompted...last night?"

Her blue eyes blazed at him. "I don't want to talk about last night. It was dumb, and it'll never happen again."

They stood in silence for a moment, her stroking the monkey, him watching the creature and feeling envious. If she cared, as she said she did, then she would ask if what Renee had said was true. He realized that he had also led her to believe they had something between them by not denying it earlier. Four people had let her think he was having an affair with Renee. Would she ask?

She turned to him. "Dammit, Jamie, do you intend to stick me in a bungalow so you can move her in? Do you love her?"

His heart swelled, giving another indication that it was still there, pulling itself back together a shard at a time. If he told her that he loved Renee, Hallie might give up and leave. Or she might not.

"No, I don't love her."

She crossed her arms, her bottom lip pushed out. "And you've never made love to her?"

"No."

"Have you ever kissed her?"

"Yes." When he saw the disappointment on her face,

he felt obliged to add, "On the cheek."

Hallie's eyes softened, and she looked at the monkey before returning her gaze to him. "How about George?"

"No, I've never kissed him either. Who's George?"

She giggled, and held up the monkey. "How about George for his name?"

He wanted to kiss her again, wanted to feel her body against his. But there was a part of him that wanted to say something, anything, to push her away. What were her motives? Love, after all this time? Security? Or temporary insanity? He nodded toward the resort. "I have to get back to work."

Her smile dissolved. "Sure. George and I will just keep exploring."

He turned and headed back to civilization, to where the orchids' heady perfume and solitude didn't make him want to do rash things.

CHAPTER 12

H allie was being scrutinized, and she didn't like it one bit. It was enough that Jamie sometimes looked at her as if she were an alien, but now Miguel and Renee sat at the table watching her with curious glances.

It was the first time in two days since their kiss in the jungle that Jamie had been around, and it was in the company of his brother and the woman who wanted Jamie for herself. She had made that abundantly clear since Hallie had arrived at BooNooNoos, the open-aired restaurant.

Hallie did her best to ignore all three and immerse herself in the atmosphere of "Jamaican Night." Every week, Caterina threw a big party complete with a reggae band, unlimited rum punch, and an endless buffet. Hallie had sampled the red beans, jerk pork, and fried plantains, but her appetite was far from ravenous.

She was also playing the watching game, inconspicuously studying her competition, comparing Renee's body and the body she inhabited. Renee wore a puckered mini-dress in a leopard print. She was much shorter than Hallie, and a bit heavier. Hallie's morning swims at the beach had done much to tone and strengthen her body. Now in one of the former Hallie's sexy sundresses, she was glad she had done the work.

"Excuse me." Jamie included everyone at the table in his sweeping glance. "The Newtons head out tomorrow, and I want to say goodbye."

When Hallie tore her gaze away from Jamie's white pants and flowered shirt, she saw that Renee had not been so prudent. Raw desire filled her eyes and made her run her tongue subconsciously over her full lips. Hallie's gaze moved to Miguel, watching Renee with an ache visible on his expression before he banked it. *Ah hah*. He was in love with Renee.

Despite his hostility toward her, Hallie had a whole new respect for him. It was obviously in his best interest to get her and Jamie together. Yet he had tried to get Hallie to give up on Jamie, because he didn't want to see his brother hurt again.

Miguel's eyes shifted to meet hers, and she heard herself say, "Thank you," before she could think twice.

"For what?"

"Uh, taking care of Jamie."

Renee moved her punch glass clumsily aside. "Why don't you thank me? I take care of Jamie, too." Renee leaned forward, almost in Hallie's face. "You think you can pretend to forget the past and everyone else will, too. But you're wrong, honey. Wrong."

"I am not pretending. And I really don't care what you think. As far as I'm concerned, you're a lying, conniving"—she glanced at Miguel—"*birch*." She saw the twitch of a smile he couldn't hide.

"A what? What did you call me?"

Renee stood, but Hallie remained seated.

"Go to *hill*, Renee."

As anger exploded on Renee's expression, she leaned toward Hallie.

"What's going on here?"

Jamie's voice halted Renee, and she turned to him with a smile. "Just girl talk," she said sweetly.

Jamie glanced at Miguel, whose smirk was threatening to give way to complete laughter. He just shook his head. Jamie's gaze then fell to Hallie, and she shrugged.

"She was telling me what hair color she uses."

Jamie looked at them both with suspicion.

Renee narrowed her eyes at Hallie, then stood and leaned close to Jamie. "Dance with me. I love this song."

He glanced at Hallie, then back to Renee. "I've got to check on the entertainment in a minute."

She pulled at his arms. "Okay, let's dance for a minute."

He followed her to the dance floor in front of the band. Hallie turned away, determined not to let them see her watching.

"*Birch*. I love it."

Hallie looked with surprise at Miguel. "I would have rather called her something else, but I like your way of substituting other words for the crasser ones."

His eyes sparkled, giving him a youthful look despite his ruggedness. "Actually, the word we use is witch with a capital *B*. You had every right to put her in her place. I think she's feeling more and more threatened by you."

"Good. She's missing out on something special by being blinded by Jamie."

Miguel stared at her for a moment, possibly trying to figure out what she meant. Then the fire man came out and dazzled the audience with his skills. He stuck flaming sticks into his mouth, juggled them, and ran them along his skin. Two other men clad in colorful pants brought out a limbo stick. The fire man set it aflame, and everyone cheered when he did the limbo seven times under increasingly lower heights.

"Now it be everyone else's turn to limbo," he said, looking around with startling white eyes.

"No!" was everyone's animated response.

"You all be chickens, mon?"

The audience booed him.

He shrugged. "Okay, how 'bout I kill the fire. Then you come limbo with me?"

Some yelled yes, some no. In the end, a line of about forty people formed to try their hand at limbo. Hallie and Miguel got separated from their group. Caught up in the mood, she danced to the beat as she waited her turn.

"Why did you thank me for taking care of Jamie?" he asked from behind her.

"I realized that when you asked me to leave, you were giving away your hope for getting Renee to let Jamie go."

He cocked his head away from her. "You know? How I feel about Renee?"

"I can tell. No, you're not as obvious as Renee is. It was a noble thing to do."

"So, you're thanking me for telling you to leave?"

"Well, sort of. For the reason you did it."

He shook his head, a wry grin on his face. "Jamie's right. You *are* different."

Renee got out on her second try, Miguel on his fourth. The line dwindled down as the limbo stick lowered. Before long, she and Jamie were reunited, standing with four other nimble people.

"Must be all the swimming we do," she said to Jamie when he walked up behind her.

"Uh hm."

She took in the strange look he was giving her and sighed. "I suppose I never did this kind of thing before either?"

"Nope. You never even liked to watch it. Something about it being silly nonsense."

She reached up and tweaked his chin. "Bet'cha I beat you."

She overestimated her confidence and bumped the stick off its holders. Jamie also knocked it off. The winner was a fourteen-year-old girl who was as skinny as the limbo stick. She got a miniature trophy.

Jamie and Hallie returned to the table laughing together, and Miguel congratulated them on a job well done.

Jamie shrugged. "You have to let the guests win, but we put in a good showing."

Oops! I was having so much fun, I didn't realize the owners aren't supposed to win. Good thing I messed up.

Renee stood and wavered. Her face was shiny red as she looked from Miguel to Jamie. "I can't believe you two! You're treating her like she's some sort of...of... angel. Have you forgotten what she's done? She's putting on this act of innocence, and you're buying it!" She focused on Jamie. "And you. How can you forgive a woman who came on to your own brother?" She dropped back into her chair, glaring at all of them.

Hallie's heart tightened.

Jamie looked at her, then at Miguel. "Is it true?"

Miguel shot Renee a look that would have surely burned a hole right through her, then looked at Jamie.

"It was more like flirting. It was no big deal, nothing happened. I babbled it to Renee once and made her promise not to say anything."

Jamie turned to Hallie, and she swallowed audibly. "When?"

"About a year ago," Miguel said.

"You slug in a ditch. Why didn't you tell me? I had a right to know. Not *her*." He pointed at Renee. "Me."

"I didn't see the need to tell you. She was drunk, in one of her unhappy moods. I turned her down, and it never happened again."

Jamie turned narrowed eyes to Hallie, and she shrunk under his wintry glare.

"My own brother?"

"Jamie," she said softly, although Miguel and Renee were still within earshot. "The Hallie you married, the one who flirted with Miguel, is dead. Gone. I'm different now." She turned to Miguel. "Have I flirted with you since?"

"No," Jamie said harshly, "but you were out there dancing with him in the line. You can't get me to screw you, so you're trying out my brother again."

His words bit into her like the teeth of a shark. She had been accused of coming onto Miguel, and now everyone at the table knew she had tried to make love to Jamie and failed. Her heart twisted inside her, but nothing could keep her hand from slapping Jamie's cheek.

"You had no right to say that," she whispered hoarsely.

She turned and walked calmly out of the restaurant, holding back tears until she was walking alone on the softly lit pathway. *Damn Renee and damn Jamie, too. Damn them all!* She found herself heading toward the little bar Juicy manned, but it was dark. Laughter from several people in the bubbly cauldron of the hot tub made her feel like an inkblot in the colorful night. She climbed into one of the swinging chairs and laid her head down on the tile surface of the bar, trying to remember a kiss that felt years away.

***

After a day of holing himself up in his office, and not going home the night of the BooNooNoos disaster, Jamie stretched and glanced out the window. The setting sun made the cloudless sky look like orange juice. A warm salty breeze beckoned him to abandon his computer and free his mind of numbers.

He passed several couples, young and old, sitting together on the white chaise lounges with their arms wrapped around each other. Ah, the romance of Caterina. He harnessed his thoughts lest they roam to people he had no desire to think about.

Too late. His fists clenched in unleashed anger at Hallie. She had come onto his own brother. Jamie didn't doubt that Miguel had turned her down. He also understood why he had never told Jamie about it. But the past was irrelevant, at least for Hallie. The embarrassed, blank look on her face indicated that she had no memory of the incident.

The outgoing tide left the beach a wide sloping expanse of smooth sand. He passed the bulk of Caterina and where his own house peered out through the greenery to the solitude beyond. He stared out over a sea that was as calm as a lake. Three seagulls splashed down in the water, and he watched them bob and search for food.

When arms slipped around his waist, Jamie knew instantly that they didn't belong to Hallie. A head rested against his back with a sigh.

"Jamie, can you forgive me for what I did?"

He turned to find Renee's soulful brown eyes staring up at him, filled with regret.

"What exactly were you trying to prove?"

She took hold of his hands and moved closer. "I had too much to drink and my judgment was off. I had no intention of blurting that out, believe me. But I sat there watching her, looking so innocent and comfortable after all she's done to you. I hate her, and you should, too."

"Renee..."

Her voice became breathy. "Jamie, I love you. Never would I hurt or betray you. Let me show you how a real woman loves her man."

She leaned up and touched her lips to his, slipping her arms around him again. From libido so recently awakened, he felt a low-voltage surge of desire. He wanted to hurt Hallie the way she'd hurt him. He pulled Renee up against him and kissed her back. She moaned and ran her tongue over his lips, asking for entrance.

He closed his eyes and swallowed hard. Renee's mouth didn't fit over his right, her tongue probing at his lips didn't tantalize him like—he shook the comparison from his mind and pulled her closer, feeling her soft curves. She didn't fit against him like Hallie did, her body didn't meld with his and turn him into jelly inside. And worse yet, his words about revenge not being a good reason for sleeping with someone came back to haunt him.

He finished the kiss gently, turning it into small kisses before moving away. Renee, not realizing that it was over, ran her hands over his chest and down his sides.

"God, you're beautiful. Come back to my place. Stay with me tonight."

He realized that sometimes being subtle wasn't enough.

"I can't."

"Jamie, don't. Don't stop this. You can't tell me you won't make love to me because you're married. Your marriage is over."

He reached out and touched her chin. "No, it's not."

"Okay, not on paper, but you can't still love her, Jamie." Renee stamped her foot in the sand, sending it flying everywhere. "Not after all she's done, you can't still be in love with her!"

He took a deep breath because he was admitting this to himself for the first time. "I'm not sure how I feel about her. Since she came back from the coma, she's a different woman. I need to find out if she's going to stay that way or return to her old self. I can't walk away from her, not now."

Renee leaned her head against his chest in defeat. "Dammit, you're too good for her." She looked up at him. "And if you think I'm going to give up on you, you've got one more thing coming."

"Renee, don't interfere,"

"I won't, and I don't think I'll have to. You'll see who the better woman is, and I'll be waiting."

He started walking back to the resort. "Don't do

that."

She stepped up beside him. "I want to."

How easy it would be to start over with Renee, with no past to nip at his heels. How easy if only she made him feel like Hallie did. Damn the woman, he was more intrigued with her now than in the beginning. He needed to talk to her.

***

"Damn you, Jamie, damn you twice over."

Hallie watched Jamie and Renee finally part from a kiss that seemed to go on forever. After an intimate discussion, they walked back down the beach together. *Probably back to her place!* Hallie smacked the water, ignoring the sting on her palm. She wanted to scream, but the breeze might carry her voice to them, and she would not have Renee know she had watched them.

Hallie had lost. The evidence glared her in the face in the form of two tiny people walking down the beach together. A small consolation that they weren't holding hands. Small because Hallie was pretty sure she knew where he'd spent last night. The sting in her heart felt like a jellyfish had a hold on it. She told herself that the salty tears slipping down over her cheeks were seawater.

When Jamie and Renee were a dot in the distance, Hallie waded toward the shore and threw a towel over her shoulders. She didn't want to go back home yet. Saying goodbye to the island, to Greenpeace and George and the house where she felt so comfortable... saying goodbye to the dream would be hell.

She kept walking south, eventually coming upon a large outcropping of black rocks that reached about twenty yards into the sea. She picked her way across the rocks and settled on a shelf at the far edge where she watched the last rays of orange turn gray.

Absorbed in thoughts of self-pity and her future, time drifted as fast as the puffy white clouds. A tiny sliver of moon perched above the far side of the island, and night clouds masked the stars. When she turned to climb down from the rocks, her heart stopped for a moment.

She could see nothing of the sharp rocks and crevices that led the way back to the soundness of the beach. The rocks could have been transformed into a huge black pit to capture unwary souls. Sparks of light flashed in the water. Phosphorescence, Jamie had told her when she'd remarked on it once. Unfortunately, not light enough.

She turned to the water in front of her and considered jumping down and swimming to shore. The sound of darkness lapping against rocks gave no clue as to what lay just beneath the surface. She imagined jumping down onto a cluster of rocks below, lying there cut and broken for days.

She shivered, staring into the bleakness that must be the island. In the distance, gray smoke drifted up toward the clouds to meld and blend. Dots of light twinkled behind the movement of palm fronds in the breeze. She wasn't sure if she imagined the note of music that danced from the distance every now and then, or the sound of a voice that floated on the wind. She stared into the gloom. Yes, it was a sound.

"Help! Is anyone there? I'm stuck out here!"

At first, she heard nothing and felt the despair settle into her bones. Then she heard a voice.

"Hallie?"

No, not Jamie. Anyone but Jamie. She could stay there and not answer, let him think he'd imagined the cry for help. Humiliation or a night spent on the hard rock with only a towel for a pillow?

"No," she said in a low voice. "I'm some woman you don't know."

"Hallie, I know it's you. What are you doing out there?"

She took a quick breath, returning to her normal voice. "I can't find my way back."

She heard him wading toward her through water that looked like motor oil. Picturing again the rocks hidden below the surface, she worried that he might lose his footing and hit his head on a rock. Would she be able to find him without killing herself in the process?

"Be careful," she said, trying to make her voice seem less concerned than she felt.

"I know these rocks like I know every inch of Caterina. Here, take my hand. If you jump down right in front of me, you won't hit anything."

With her back to him, she lowered herself off the side of the rock as far as she could before letting go.

His hands gripped her sides when he caught her just before her feet felt the sandy bottom.

"I presume you know your way back as well?"

"Of course. Grab onto the belt loops of my jeans and follow me."

She wanted to wrap her arms around him. She wanted to slug him. Instead, she slipped her fingers through his loops and followed in his footsteps. Her thighs brushed against the back of his legs. The splish-splash of wavelets echoed softly against the rocks to their right.

She breathed in the scent of his spicy cologne, then wondered if he'd put it on for Renee. Or after Renee, to hide the scent of sex. Her anger blended in with the blackness and made the warm night air seem hot and prickly.

The height of the water lowered and the feel of shells beneath her bare feet told her they were nearing the shore. That's when she yanked the loop back and moved out of the way while Jamie fell backward into the water.

"What the—" *Splash!*

Before he could even sputter, she started kicking water at him, sending spray after spray into his face.

"You son of a bitch! How could you sleep with that ... that witch with a capital *B*? If you want to carry on like that, just tell me to g—*aah!*"

Her feet were pulled out from under her, and she could do nothing to keep from falling backward into the water. She hit the water with a loud *smack* but got up punching.

"Hey, hey!" Jamie grabbed her fist and held her arms away from his chest. "Have you lost your mind?"

No, I've lost my heart, dammit! Adrenaline sailed through her body. She could barely see his silhouette. Their heavy breathing and dripping water were the only sounds for a moment. She wriggled to free her arms, but he held them fast.

"Now will you tell me what that was all about? I expected nothing more than a quick thank you for saving you a night out there on the ledge, but your gratitude is overwhelming me."

"Sure, you saved me from a night out here just so you

can kick me out tomorrow and move that slutpuppy in."

He laughed, and that infuriated her even more. Another wriggle of her arms proved fruitless.

"I presume you're talking about Renee when you say —what was it that you said? *Slutpuppy*?" He yanked her closer, holding her arms behind his back. "Renee isn't a *slutpuppy*."

He was defending her. Figured. Hallie again tried to break free from his grip, but he only pulled her closer against his chest.

"The heck she isn't. I saw who kissed who. And who kissed back."

"You saw us on the beach?"

After being caught in the act, he could act so calm? That ignited her anger even more.

"Yes, I was out here swimming, so don't you dare deny kissing her."

"I won't deny it; I did kiss her. But before you drown me, let me clarify what you saw. You saw a kiss like this."

He leaned down and placed his lips against hers for a long moment. She wanted to move away, wanted so badly to turn her head away. Her lips wouldn't cooperate. Obviously not every fiber of her body was mad at him. After a moment, he removed his lips, and dammit, she didn't want him to.

"Now," he continued in his diplomatic tone of voice. "What you *thought* you saw was this."

Again, he pulled her closer and started kissing her, but this time his tongue parted her all-too-willing lips and roamed wildly through her mouth, leaving a salty trail. His fingers moved through her wet hair, and she suppressed a pleasurable sound. She dredged up her anger again, and it wasn't easy to do with most of her body sagging into his arms. When he pulled back, he still held her arms.

"Are you straight now on what you saw? I can go over the two again if you'd like."

She pushed him away, feeling the heat on her cheeks overpower the warmth still lingering on her lips.

"It sure looked like the second kind of kiss from here."

Jamie looked back, as if judging the distance. "You were quite far away, so I can see how you'd get the two confused. I definitely need to go over the two again."

She tried to hold him back, but her hands didn't act like the stiff barriers she wanted them to. Instead, they became pinned against his chest. He pulled her tight against him, his wet body molding against hers. His lips captured hers but held stationary.

"Not very exciting, was it?" he said when it was over.

Exciting enough, she thought derisively. Before she could remark on what that kiss might do to someone like Renee, he shifted her so that her hands were freed. Of their own will, they slipped to rest on his back.

"Now pay close attention, Hallie. I don't want there to be any misunderstanding about this. If I'd *wanted* to kiss Renee back, it would have gone something like this."

Gathering her face in his strong fingers, he angled her mouth up and slightly off-center before closing the distance between her trembling lips and his. He started slowly, kissing again and again before slipping that wild tongue into her much-too-willing mouth. His fingers tightened against her cheeks, and her own hands pressed harder against him in response. She couldn't breathe but decided that some things were more important than sustaining life functions. Her heart thundered as anger ebbed to be replaced by something more dangerous.

She pulled the fury back, kissing him fiercely and hoping he felt as devastated as she did. For several long, long minutes he gave and demanded ever more. When he stopped, his breath came deeper. He still held her face in his grasp, looming nose to nose with her for several seconds before moving away.

His voice sounded so irritatingly normal when he asked, "Have it straight now?"

Did it not affect him at all? He could kiss her so that the phosphorescence sparking at her feet seemed dull compared to the way she felt inside, and he could act so bloody normal. He was playing with her.

"Does Renee?"

He laughed again, but the softness was gone from his voice. "You're a fine one to toss accusations."

"I'll say whatever I want to. We're playing on new ground, Jamie. I have not kissed one single man, besides you, since I got here. I mean…since I came out of the coma. You go ahead and judge me on my past and justify your actions, if that makes you feel better."

She tore away from him and down the beach toward the glitter of lights in the distance. Jealousy, betrayal, and anger raged through her as the mental picture of Jamie and Renee kissing played viciously in her mind over and over. She wrapped her arms around herself as she turned and followed the tiny lights that led the way down the path.

By the time she reached the house, her anger had

waned to confusion. She came to a stop in the sandy path and soft glow of lights. The mental picture faded to black, and she felt again his arms pulling her close, his lips kissing hers. Jamie had kissed her four times. She had been so befuddled by jealousy and desire that she'd missed the point. Was he saying that he had not kissed Renee the way he kissed her the second and fourth time? *If I had wanted to kiss Renee*, he had said, and kissed her silly. Had he *wanted* to kiss her? Maybe Hallie had no right to doubt him, but Chris sure did. Her fingers moved to her lips, still burning from his kisses. She wondered if he would come home tonight. No, she hoped he would come home tonight.

CHAPTER 13

J amie hadn't gone home that night or the next. Their encounter in the darkness nagged at him. The taste of her lips, the feel of her wet body against his...her anger over his and Renee's kiss. This was a whole new, or should he say, yet another new side to Hallie since her stroke. Most of the time she had been too wrapped up in herself and her problems to give much notice to the attention women paid him. Not that she ever had to worry. Now, she was obsessed with Renee and his alleged attraction to her. He smiled. No one could wow him more than his wife could.

Two nights away from Hallie had left him wanting. To his chagrin, he had missed her, had missed waking up to study her in the morning. He was scheduled to take out a couple of regulars on a small charter fishing boat that afternoon. One of them had called in hungover and canceled.

Inviting Hallie would be a step toward peace, and it would be safe. No serious talks, no chance for desire to take hold. He sent an employee to give her a message and was surprised to find her at the docks twelve minutes later. Wearing one of his cotton shirts for a cover-up and her hair in a ponytail, she looked like a teenager.

"How are you doing?" he asked after taking her bag.

She took a shallow breath. "I'm okay. George keeps me company."

"And the lizard?"

"The …" She smiled in an embarrassed way. "You know about Greenpeace?"

"I saw you talking to him one morning."

"Oh. Well, I'll talk to just about anything when I'm lonely. I started talking to the couch last night."

"I'll only worry if you heard it answer."

"Not yet."

Forty-five minutes later the boat neared the reef where the water went from twelve to sixty feet deep, and where schools of wahoo and yellowfin tuna regularly hung out.

He watched Hallie lean over the edge of the boat more than the fish finder, but he'd been there so many times he was sure the fish were nearby. In the crystal-clear water, they weren't hard to find with the naked eye. His gaze followed hers to the twelve round boulder shapes beneath the water. Then he realized they were moving. *Stingrays.*

"Kewl!" she said in that odd way of hers.

Before he could tell her what they were, she grabbed some cut bait, stepped up on the side of the boat and dove into the water—right toward the stingrays.

"Watch the boat, John," he called to one of the men aboard as he stripped his shirt and dove in after her. What could she be thinking?

When he reached her several yards away, one of the rays was already upon her, and three more were heading her way. Ready to fight them off, he lifted his arm to pull her behind him. She turned to him with a glow he had not seen since their kiss a week before.

"Isn't this great?"

"What in God's name are you doing out here?"

She took his hand in hers and shoved a piece of fish into it, pressing it closed again. "Here, feed a stingray."

He lifted his hand out of the water and looked at the fish as if it could explain her bizarre behavior. "You are loony tunes, Hallie."

"I am not!" She took a deep breath and continued. "Here, let me show you how to feed them. Keep your fist clenched until the ray is close, then flatten it out so it can take the food." As if in answer to his stupefied expression, she explained, "They don't have teeth; they use their mouths to find the food and suck it in. Watch."

He watched as she held her fist out, and a ray three feet in diameter glided like a great bird through the water toward her. The mass of it nearly obliterated her entire body.

"It feels so weird!" she said with a giggle. "Okay, now it's your turn." She nodded toward another large ray heading over to investigate.

"What about their stingers?"

"They won't sting unless they feel threatened."

"Well, I'm certainly not going to threaten them. Not one unkind word."

She giggled. As she instructed, he flattened his palm and the velvety underside of the ray glided over his bare shoulder and down his arm as the mouth gently sucked in its search for food. When it found the morsel, his palm was pulled up, then released as the ray took the food and drifted away. He smiled, and she handed him another piece of fish.

He fed another one, then let his hand glide across the slimier top surface of the ray.

"Is it okay to touch them?"

"Yes, as long as you do it with your bare hand. Anything else will damage their delicate coating and let in bacteria."

He looked at her. "How do you know all this?"

Her expression turned blank for a moment, then she smiled. "I took courses at the community college, remember? One was marine biology, and we went on a trip to SeaWorld to do some research. They had stingrays there."

"I knew you took some courses, but I didn't know it went beyond English and a class on music appreciation."

"Guess there are a few things you didn't know about me." She turned back to the rays.

"You got that right."

"Hey, can we feed the rays, too?" John asked.

Hallie said, "Sure. Just be gentle and bring lots of food."

Fishing bait was sacrificed for a free meal for the stingrays. Everyone had the most fun they ever had, and John suggested regular trips if the stingrays remained in the area.

Jamie sank into deep thought as he headed the boat back to Caterina. It had been the most amazing day in his life, with the rays and with Hallie. Anger was forgotten as they discovered an incredible and mysterious creature together. Now she sat on the seat behind him, her head resting sleepily against his back. And he was more confused than ever about this stranger in his wife's body.

***

The heat and excitement of the day made Hallie fall instantly to sleep that night. She hardly had time to hope that the dreams would leave her alone. It didn't matter whether she hoped or not; they always came.

In the distortion of dreams, Alan rolled out from beneath a car and stood to face her, his black eyebrows knitted together over vivid green eyes. He looked anxious, but his words were muffled. She felt as though he had plunged a knife into her heart. He reached forward and clutched her shirt, crushing her against his chest.

"Please, Chris, give me a chance."

The familiar sequence began: the bridge, her racing heart, the black semi rising like a demon behind her, then beside her. All she could see were elf shoes before she was shoved off the side and into the ravine below.

"Nooooooooo!"

She jerked up in bed, clutching the sheets and searching the dark for shards of reality. As always, her hand reached down to find comfort in her dogs, but found it in the form of Jamie's arms pulling her close.

"It's okay, it's okay. It was just a nightmare."

She shivered uncontrollably, remembering Alan, remembering elf shoes. Trying to forget everything except the warm solid body holding her.

"Hallie, what monster is chasing you?"

She shook her head. "It's not a monster, it's a bridge. I'm falling off a bridge."

"All this for a bridge? Why are you having these nightmares? Why now?"

"I think they're trying to tell me something. But I'm

not sure what." False identity. Murder. What did the elf shoes mean? All these questions, and not one could she share with Jamie.

"Maybe you should see a doctor or psychiatrist."

"No! I don't need a doctor."

"It might help."

"They'll go away, I'm sure." Actually, she wasn't so sure. And now she would be up the rest of the night, wondering why Alan was asking for a chance.

***

That evening, Hallie walked along the stretch of beach, leaving the guests who were walking the sunset far behind. Crouching, she set her Hallie's Comet down and traced a heart in the wet, packed sand. Inside she put a C and a J, then changed the C to an H.

She stood again, and felt a little lightheaded from the fruity drink. Grinning at her silly artwork, feeling giddy and restless, she hiked her skirt up and ran farther down the beach. She had never felt so sexy and confident, with her sleeves off her shoulders, her flowered skirt showing off long, tan legs. She giggled as a large wave rushed up, swirling around her ankles.

She was about to head back when she saw the large outcropping of black rocks where she had been stranded. She walked over, wondering what creatures lived in the tiny caves and tide pools. Then her eyes rested on a creature she definitely had not expected to find there: Jamie.

On the same rock where she had found solace, he was leaning back with eyes closed. She picked her way toward him, stifling a scream when she nearly slipped and fell into the water once. The waves pulled her back toward shore like a mother keeping her child from danger. Alternately, they would push her impishly toward her destination.

When she neared him, she realized he was asleep. And naked, from the clothing lying nearby. His blond hair looked golden in the sunlight, and the waves washed gently over long muscular legs. She could do nothing but stare at him for the longest time. Vulnerable in his sleep and nudity, yet strong and virile. His skin was tan and glistening, his cheeks pink from the sun.

She couldn't ignore the feelings that coursed through her veins, fierier than the sunset, more intense than the whole ocean surrounding them. She moved closer, ignoring the pain of the rough rocks beneath her bare feet. Her next step was onto a patch of mossy green fibers, and before she could even sigh from the relief of stepping on something soft for a change, her foot slipped, and she tumbled into the water.

When she came to the surface, she expected Jamie to be staring down, annoyed at her intrusion. Instead, he remained sleeping, her splash covered by the constant sound of waves assaulting the nearby rocks. Swimming to where his rock reached over the water, she was disappointed to find no foothold to help her climb to where he sat. Except for his feet. But of course, if she used his feet and legs to pull herself up, he would wake. Picturing the sight of his muscular body, taut stomach, and gorgeous face above, maybe that wasn't such a bad thing after all.

She ran her fingers up and down his legs, as far up as the swell of the sea would allow her to reach. He instantly woke and leaned over the edge of the rock.

She grinned up at him. "Didn't think they had mermaids down here, did you?"

He blinked sleepily. "Didn't think they had mermaids anywhere. Especially ones with legs. And nice legs at that."

Her heart warmed. Perhaps he didn't mind her intrusion.

"Can I join you?"

He glanced downward. "I'm not wearing anything."

"So?"

"I didn't want you to be surprised."

"I already knew you were naked."

He raised an eyebrow. "Oh, yeah?"

She grinned mischievously. "I don't mind if you don't."

He reached down and pulled her up without so much as a grunt to show exertion. They stood facing each other, and he pushed her wet hair away from her eyes. Her skirt clung to her legs, hardly moved by the breeze that touched her wet skin.

"I always come here to think." He glanced down. "And get a little extra sun. I thought I was the only one who knew about this place until a few nights ago. How did you know I was out here?"

"I didn't. I was out walking. Thinking."

The orange rays of the sun reflected in his vivid blue eyes as they stared at her. The dreaminess had not yet left them.

"What were you thinking about?" he asked.

"You. And there you were."

She wished she could read the many things that passed through his mind and shone in his eyes. Then he closed them and pulled her close, and she moved her hands around his waist. She held back the sound of pleasure, closing her eyes and savoring the feel of his sun-warmed body against hers.

Her heart pounded harder than the waves around them, her blood ran hotter than the rays of the sun that caressed them. Jamie held her face, tilting her chin up as he started kissing slowly across her jaw line. His lips crushed hers in a kiss of power and desire unleashed at last. His hands caressed her shoulders and down her back while his tongue drew a response in her soul akin to wildfire.

She caressed the slick skin of his back, gliding downward. She could now physically appreciate the round tight buttocks she had visually savored for so long. He groaned as her fingers snaked around to the front of his thighs, grazing the softer skin of what was pressed firmly against her.

His kisses became furious, sucking away her breath and every trepidation. He slid her peasant blouse over her head, letting it fall to the rocks below. Her arms remained lifted as his fingertips grazed her breasts. He stopped to look at her for a second, taking a deep breath.

"I forgot how beautiful you are."

With hardly enough time for her to catch her breath, he pulled her close again and kissed a trail of fire across her shoulders. His hair tickled against her cheek, silky as it twined around her fingers. Electric eels slithered beneath her skin, and her entire body crackled. He was tender, he was fierce. And oh, he was good. His tongue trailing across her tender skin made her gasp for air as she drowned in bliss.

When he reached her waist, he slid her skirt down to

her ankles, helping her to step out of the wet mass. But he didn't stand again right away. Instead, he lingered below to nibble at the pale skin at her pelvis, to lick the utterly sensitive skin behind her knees, and make her realize how many erogenous zones there were on a human body.

With every sound of pleasure she uttered, his pace increased, his intensity heightened. By the time he rose to take her into his arms, his fingers had found sweet success in a spot that drove her deliciously, crazily mad. It had never felt like this before, and she was sure it could never feel this way again, shattering, splitting into a thousand pieces of light.

Hallie bent over his shoulder, taking his salty skin between her teeth and biting down as pleasure washed over her to the sounds of the surf.

"P-please...Jamie!" she cried out, but he continued until she howled like a wolf.

Only then did he swoop her into his arms and lower her to the cool, smooth surface of the rock, using her skirt as a pillow for her head. She marveled at how he could be so breathless, when it was she who was receiving such divine pleasure. His face was flushed red, his eyes intensely blue as they stared into hers.

"It's not fair to want a woman as much as I want you," he said hoarsely.

But they didn't talk about life's fairness. She wanted to crawl beneath his skin and immerse herself in him. She would love him just as fiercely, and she was going to show him then just how much that was.

He was mid-kiss when he gasped as she slid her fingers around his erection. His breath hitched in quick succession as she stroked and fondled down the length of him. She teased the tip to her own wetness, watching the muscles of his arms flex as he kept his balance over her. Taking her by surprise, he plunged down over her mouth at the same time as he plunged into her.

Her own breath hitched this time, and then a feeling of completeness—and complete ecstasy. He murmured her name in between solid, smooth strokes that took her to the top of that mountain she had long ago associated with Jamie, up, up to touch the sun where it exploded.

When she realized that the crashing sound around them was the waves and not her head, she ventured to open her eyes and make sure what had happened a short time ago had not been a dream. Not a dream the silky flesh her hand caressed, the strong body that held her tight against a chest that rose and fell in deep breaths. Reality lay in the blue eyes that studied her as she came to life again under his touch. And in the way he came to life again under hers.

Sometime later, he put on his jean shorts and slipped his shirt on her, putting much more thought than necessary into buttoning her up.

"What are you thinking about?" she ventured. Did she really want to know?

When the last button was inserted, he stood back and appraised her. "It covers everything." He draped her wet clothes over his arm, holding his other hand out for her.

She took it, wrapping her fingers around his and holding on tight. He helped her across the rocks to the sand beyond and didn't let go as they continued down the beach in silence.

She stopped, pulling him up in front of her. "What's

wrong?"

He thought for a moment before answering in a soft voice. "A long time ago..." He shook his head. "It seems like forever, but it was only a year ago. When we made love, I lost myself in you completely. I'd never had that with anyone else. It was like absolute, complete abandon, becoming only a part of you. Does that make sense?"

She nodded but didn't say anything for fear he would stop talking.

"After a short while, all that was gone. When our marriage started falling apart, making love became merely sex, and then even that became non-existent. I made myself forget about how it once was, that it probably wouldn't be like that with anyone else. I succeeded."

He looked down for a moment, and she let out the breath she didn't realize she had been holding.

"Since your collapse, you've been so different. I've wanted you again, but I don't want to get close to you. You took me off guard just now, but I'm glad. It gave me the chance to see if I could lose myself again."

He paused, and she waited the agonizing seconds to hear whether it had been the same. After all, she was a different woman, even if she did have the former Hallie's body. Finally, she couldn't stand it any longer.

"Did you? Lose yourself?"

He looked at her with such seriousness, and her heart dropped. It couldn't be the same.

"More than before. And, Hallie, it scares the hell out of me."

He resumed walking back to the house. He didn't say another word, but that her hand was still tucked in his was a good sign.

Her heart swelled at his words: *More than before.* She looked over at him, his gaze out at sea. *I lost myself, too, Jamie. I feel the same fear you do. I'm not going to let it hold me back from loving you. I hope you won't either.*

CHAPTER 14

"Who's Alan?"

Hallie's eyes widened at Jamie's question, asked so casually as soon as she woke up. His expression was blank, carefully controlled.

"Alan?"

Jamie was stretched out beside her, his head propped up by his hand. The white sheet was twisted around his waist, making him look more modest than he actually was. All she wanted to do was crawl up next to him and wish away the question he'd just asked. And the reason he knew Alan's name at all.

"You screamed his name in your sleep."

She licked her lips and swallowed harder than she had intended. "I don't remember doing that."

"You were asleep."

"I mean, I don't remember having a dream about an Alan. I don't know any Alans." She touched his cheek. "Are you sure I wasn't screaming your name?"

"Yes."

His blue eyes looked frosty, his mouth a thin line. Her heart dropped a few inches. How could she tell him about Alan? Surely, she wasn't having a sexual dream about him. She hadn't even slept with the guy. Thank goodness. She remembered the dream where Alan pleaded, "Please…" It made her shiver.

Jamie suddenly yanked her close and kissed her fiercely. Gone was the gentleness. Was he testing her? When he rolled her onto her back and crouched over her, she saw no love or trust in his eyes. Only anger. She placed her palms against his hard chest and held him at bay.

"No, Jamie."

He leaned down as close as her hands would allow. "What's wrong?"

"Not this way."

He seemed to struggle internally for a moment, then moved away. His voice took on the flat tone that pinched her heart. "Because of your dream?" he asked.

"No, because of your reaction to it. Don't use sex to make a point."

"Is that all it is to you? Sex?"

She tried to hide the smallest smile that threatened to creep in at the wrong time. "Was it more to you?"

"What was it to you, Hallie?"

"We did not have sex; we made love. You've been holding back. You still don't trust me."

"No."

His blatant admission prickled her, and she crossed her arms in front of her. "I don't want to make love with you until you're sure."

He narrowed his eyes at her. "How can I be sure when you're calling out some guy's name in your sleep?"

She leaned close to his face. "Because you have to trust *me*. Not the woman you married, but *me*. Until you're able to give all of yourself and not just the parts that don't carry a risk, I don't want to make love with you."

She yanked the sheets away and, covering herself, walked into the bathroom.

He flopped onto his back and muttered, "Cover hog."

***

Well, at least Jamie had taken her up on one offer. She spent the day in his office logging a mountain of paid bills into the computer. He had made himself scarce all day, making repairs on a few of the bungalows down by the beach. She turned off the PC, feeling good for pulling her weight. Would Jamie be home, or would he make himself scarce until bedtime like the last two nights?

The fragrance of orchids mixed with the woodsy cologne of someone recently in the area. The sound of a squawking parrot clashed with the soft calypso music. The eastern sky was a violet-blue, long abandoned by the sun. She followed the lighted path until it became sand and led the way home. The house was dark, causing her heart to falter. Another evening alone wondering where Jamie was.

She was greeted by a seductive beat as music drifted through the darkened rooms. She stepped through the walkway that led to the bedroom. Her heartbeat quickened when she saw the flicker of candlelight against the far wall. But the bedroom was empty.

She walked quietly into the bathroom and turned the corner. She opened her mouth to say something, but all she could do was smile. Twenty candles flickered around the huge marble tub, where Jamie sat

—in a tubful of green M&M's! A bottle of champagne sat in a wooden bucket of ice, and next to that two glasses filled with more green M&M's.

He grinned, then grabbed one of the glasses and held it up. "Get the hint?"

She bit her bottom lip and walked toward the tub. Her gaze swept from the champagne glasses to the hundreds of green M&M's that covered everything but his head, chest, and knees. She wanted to laugh; she wanted to cry. But most of all, she wanted to get into that tub with him.

She slipped out of her clothes and walked up to the tub. He pulled her in, and she fell into his lap. Before she could say anything, he gave her an M&M kiss. Then he leaned forward and popped the top off the champagne.

"Where in the world did you come up..." She merely looked at the tub.

"They say if you want to let someone know you trust them and want them without a shadow of a doubt, you give them green M&M's. Or maybe it's for making them horny. I don't know, but I figured, either way, you'd get the idea."

"Oh, Jamie..."

He kissed the words right out of her mouth. Then he handed her a glass with enough M&M's in it to make the champagne green.

Clink! "Here's to you and me and the green monster." He growled into her neck, then took a swig of champagne. She drank and accidentally swallowed an M&M, barely containing the cough that threatened to erupt. She straddled his waist, and he leaned her backward and kissed down her neck, collarbone, and then her breasts.

"You know we're going to be all green after this," she said.

"Yeah, like finger painting." He demonstrated by rubbing a champagne moistened candy into a smile face on her chest. "But just think how much fun we'll have trying to wash the color off each other later.

"Mm, you're right." She glanced wickedly down, then started kissing down the middle of his chest, down his stomach to the fine hairline pointing south. She lifted her glass in toast again, then dribbled it down his stomach. Leaning to lick it off, she said, "Here's to the green monster."

Hallie woke a few hours later on the bed, intertwined with Jamie's warm body. The candles had died down while they napped. She didn't need light to know that he had a green smudge across his cheek and a lot of other places. They had scrubbed most of it off in the shower, but she'd put more on him afterward.

"Are you hungry?" His voice startled her.

"How did you know I was awake?"

"I just knew. I'm starved."

"Me, too. We could eat some of those M&M's in the tub."

"Nah. Let's grab a bite at BooNooNoos."

She rolled over and yawned. "If I have the energy to drag myself to the closet."

Fifteen minutes later, they sat at a table next to a trellis crawling with purple bougainvillea. The waiter came over and greeted them.

"Lobster pizza, please," Jamie said.

Hallie looked at him. "Lobster pizza?" She tried to imagine such a thing.

"Save room for dessert," the waiter told them. "We

have chocolate cake covered with M&M's, an M&M sundae, or M&M cookies."

She felt her cheeks warm. When the waiter left, she nudged Jamie.

He reached over and grabbed a bowl sitting on the table, holding it out for her. "Want an M&M?"

She glanced into the bowl. "I don't see any green ones in there."

He looked. "Hmm, you're right. I wonder what happened to them."

"Do you mean to tell me..."

"How do you think I got all those green ones? I had an emergency shipment of M&M's flown to the island yesterday and spent all day sorting out the green ones. Now we have thousands of red, orange and brown ones left, so I gave them to the chef and told him to be creative."

She was laughing so hard that she thought her stomach might explode. "Jamie, you're crazy!"

He took her hand and placed it against his lips. "You've made me a fool for love again. I hope you accept the consequences."

Her smile faded, and she met his eyes. Did that mean he loved her? Her heart jumped around inside, and the touch of his lips against her palm made her toes curl.

"Here are your drinks," the waiter said, breaking into their moment before she'd mustered the guts to tell Jamie she loved him. "Two Hallie's Comets. Mrs. D, you have a phone call. You can take it up by the waiter's station."

She glanced at Jamie, then back at the waiter. "Are you sure it's for me?"

"He said Hallie Parker, but I assumed it was you.

You're the only Hallie around."

She shrugged. "Maybe it's Velvet's—I mean, my mother's boyfriend."

"I hope everything's all right."

She walked to the phone and picked it up.

"Hello?" She waited. "This is Hallie."

The silence made her quiver and feel cold even as a warm breeze floated by. She hung up, then confirmed with the waiter that she had the right phone. Jamie watched her with concern as she walked back to the table.

"What's wrong?"

"There wasn't anybody there. Well, there was someone there, but they—he didn't say anything." Her heart tightened as she remembered Mick's warning about giving her marriage another try.

"Hallie, what's wrong? Why are you looking at me like that?"

She clenched the arms of her wicker chair. Should she tell him about Mick's threat? Surely, he wouldn't come all the way out there to bother them. It was probably a bad connection.

She brightened. "I was just trying to figure out who it might be."

Jamie's voice remained normal, with a forced lightness. "It wouldn't be Alan, would it?"

She looked him in the eye. "I told you, I don't know anyone named Alan."

"Just checking."

She tried to act normal and relaxed throughout dinner, but that cold nagging feeling continued to hold her in its grip. Her gaze kept drifting to the shadows beyond the lights, and she hoped that it was only an irrational fear, nothing else.

**

The sun brightened her outlook the next morning, chasing away the shadows.

"When I see you out here with George," Jamie said as he moved up behind her pool-side chair, "I can't help but imagine you're out here with our baby."

George chattered as he swung from one outstretched finger to another. She reached up and pulled Jamie's head down to nuzzle his cheek.

"He's a bit of a preemie, don't you think? And those eyes—he must take after your side of the family."

George's vivid brown eyes, so human-like, darted from Hallie's face to Jamie's. His tiny hands reached up to scratch his tufted ears.

Jamie crouched down at her side, his hands resting on the arm of her chair. The sunlight lit the blond hairs on his legs to golden, and her gaze trailed up past his white shorts, broad, bare chest to a face far more serious than her quip warranted. He reached up and stroked her cheek.

"Do you think we'll have more to our family than the lizard and George?"

She leaned into his hand, closing her eyes at the warmth of it against her cheek.

"Are you asking me if we'll ever have a baby?"

"Not now, not in the nearish future. Just sometime."

She leaned over and touched her lips to his, letting them linger for a few seconds. When she opened her eyes, she found him looking at her.

"I would love to have your baby, Jamie."

Curiosity filled his blue eyes. "God, how you've

changed. It's like I'm married to another woman."

She felt a twang in her heart. How she would love to tell him the truth. Yet, despite his words, what would he really think if he knew she *was* another woman? Maybe she would try somehow. She trailed a finger across the smooth-shaven skin of his chin, realizing he was testing her with the question.

"What would I have said before, if you'd asked me that?"

"You would have whined about getting fat and stretch marks, and you weren't ready to even discuss the possibility."

"Guess that's changed, too." She pulled him close. "Do you have to leave just yet?"

"I wish I didn't. Miguel's waiting for me. Remember, we promised Ruby we'd go over to Contigua and do some patchwork on her mother's house."

"Oh, right." Only once had Hallie been to the small village on the other side of the island, population three hundred. "You'll be home before dark?"

"Absolutely." He punctuated his promise with a kiss and touched the top of George's head. "Keep her company, buddy."

Jamie had only been gone five minutes when the phone rang. She hesitantly walked to the bedroom and answered it. Silence. She placed the phone carefully back in the cradle, holding back her anxiety and anger. It probably wasn't anything at all, but why did the calls cause her hands to get clammy?

***

That night the dreams came again. In her trembling hand she held a crumpled newspaper. She could only read the word, *MISSING*.

Her heart pounded as the bridge neared, and she knew what would happen if she crossed it. She knew, yet she couldn't stop. The black semi appeared like a menace in the rear-view mirror, then beside her, pushing her off the bridge.

Her hand slapped over her mouth as she lurched up in bed, staring with bulging eyes into the darkness. She gasped for breath, pressing her hand against her heart to still it before its pounding woke Jamie.

Who was missing? Everyone in her life had been present. Then, like so many other times, she reached down beside the bed for her Sheltie.

Her eyes flew open. This time there was something down there. Her fingers touched fur. She jerked her hand back, staring at the dark nothingness on the floor. Something moved down there! She reached over and turned on the light, hoping the feeling of fur was still part of her dream.

She blinked, slowly reaching down to see if what she saw was real. The fuzzy Sheltie pup watched her with dazed eyes, blinking. He sat nestled in a basket topped with a big blue ribbon.

"Jamie." She turned to see him lying on his side, his head propped up by his hand. He was smiling with anticipation. "Oh, Jamie."

She scooped up the ball of brown, white, and black fuzz and set him on the bed. Her eyes watered, and she rubbed them before turning to Jamie.

"His name is Phoenix," he said.

"How did you get this puppy here? And when?"

"Well, let's just say I have connections. And I lied about going to Contigua. I was waiting for Phoenix's plane."

"But how...why?"

"Every time you have one of those nightmares, you reach down for the floor and call for Phoenix. I wanted to give you something to touch next time."

She hugged him fiercely, nearly squashing the pup between them. "But how did you know I would have one of my nightmares tonight?"

His eyes grew serious. "Hallie, I know you have one just about every night. You try to hide them from me, though I can't imagine why."

She hid her eyes, looking down at the pup on her lap as she stroked his soft fur. His ears folded down at the tips, and his pointy cold nose made her jump when it touched her arm.

"I don't want to bother you."

Jamie sat up, turning her so that she faced him. "Bother me? Do you think that I wouldn't stay up all night just to be there when you woke from a nightmare? Don't you know that I'd jump right inside your head and fight your bridge monsters myself if I could?"

He pulled her close, so different than the way Alan jerked her toward him in his dreams. The tears flowed, but she wasn't sure why. Happiness? For a life lost? For a past that wouldn't let go? Maybe for all three.

***

"Come on, George, don't be pissy about this," Hallie pleaded into a tall breadfruit tree in the backyard the next evening. "You're not being usurped, I promise."

George refused to come down, chattering in shrill tones. Phoenix was still a little shy, standing close to Hallie's feet as he looked up into the dark place among the branches where the awful noise originated.

She gave up on George and walked back to the lanai. Jamie was swimming laps in the pool. The pool lights were the only ones on in the house, giving everything nearby an eerie glow that shimmered with the waves. She sat and dangled her legs in the water, watching Jamie's firm bare buttocks skim just under the water's surface. Like a shark, he glided underwater toward her and tickled her feet. With a flick of his head, he sent wet locks back off his face.

"*Mm mm mm*," she said with a smile. "I sure do enjoy watching you swim, *Buns* DiBarto."

His blue eyes widened. "How did you know about that?"

"What, your moonshot back in college? Oh, I have my connections."

"Tell me where you heard about that," he said, threatening to tickle her feet again.

She squirmed when his fingers grazed the bottom of her foot. "Okay, I give up! I had lunch with Dave once, and he told me. I wanted to know more about you, about my chances for getting you back." Among other things, of course.

His grin faded. "You really wanted this to work, didn't you?"

"More than anything. You said you had reasons to leave, just as you had reasons to stay. What were the reasons you stayed with...me?"

Something flickered behind his eyes for a moment, and his lips turned up in a crooked smile. "It's silly."

"I won't think it's silly."

"Well, it's probably ludicrous. It's..." He looked at her intently for a moment. "When I met you, I had a feeling, a strong, hit-you-in-the-gut feeling, that you were the woman I was put here on earth to protect and love. I stayed because that feeling never went away."

Her heart seized up. She was that woman he was put here to protect and love. She, Chris. Drops of water slid down his cheeks and nose. Her eyes were locked to his, held by a spell of the heart.

"Do you love me, Jamie?"

He pulled her down into the pool to face him. Pressing his forehead up against hers, he closed his eyes. "Yes," he whispered. Then he opened his eyes, and she fell into their depths. "I love you, Hallie, with everything that is me."

"I love you too, Jamie. I think I have always loved you somewhere deep inside me. Now that love is everywhere."

His hands encircled her face, and he kissed her, becoming more arduous. He reached behind her neck and untied the string of her bikini. And then she heard the noise. The *crack!* of someone stepping on a twig.

"What was that?" she asked, catching her breath.

He shrugged, then pulled her close again, continuing his exploratory kiss.

She squeezed his arm. "I heard something."

"We live in a jungle. We're far away from the rest of the resort, so we tend to get a few wild animals out here. You, of all people, shouldn't be afraid of a few animals."

She searched the black curtain that surrounded them, cloaking everything but the immediate proximity. Phoenix stared into the direction the sound had come from, his ears perked and responsive.

"See, even the pup heard it."

The blood drained from her face, and she scrambled for the edge of the pool to pull herself up. Jamie followed, wrapping a towel around himself. Her heart lurched when she saw him walking toward the darkness, in the direction of the breadfruit tree. George shrieked from a short distance away.

"Where are you going?"

He turned, giving her a slightly exasperated look. "I'm checking out the noise. The only times I see that expression on your face is when you wake up from those nightmares."

He continued walking across the deck.

She swallowed hard. "There have been more phone calls. Two yesterday, after you left. Three more today. Let's just go inside and lock the doors."

He shook his head. "And have you staring at the windows all night? Uh-uh. Go on inside. I'll be right back."

With her heart in her throat, she watched him disappear into the darkness. Fear paralyzed her, kept her from taking her eyes off the area he'd walked off into. She should have told him about Mick's threat. She shouldn't have let him go.

CHAPTER 15

Movement at the far corner of the lanai made Hallie reel around, her heart thumping against her ribs. She nearly fainted from relief when Jamie strode toward her, towel still intact.

"Jamie, I'm sorry I made you go out there."

"You didn't make me do anything. I told you I was here to protect and love you."

He continued to stare out at the darkness for a moment. His light expression of earlier was gone.

"What is it?"

He shrugged. "Not sure. Probably nothing, bird noises and scurrying animals. What concerns me is that they only make those sounds when they're disturbed. It could be a panther or bobcat."

Even his solid arms wrapped around her couldn't bring on the security of sleep that night. Her eyes were wide as she stared at the ceiling, listening for any sound at all. The doors were closed and locked, the curtains pulled shut.

Even when sleep did claim her, nightmares held her in their grip. Now it was Mick who clutched her in front of the body shop Alan owned. Mick who drove the semi that pushed her off the bridge. Jamie drove her car and held her hand as they plunged to their death. She woke with a scream as the rocky ravine closed in.

"It's okay, baby. It's okay." Jamie soothed her, and she clung to him.

He's alive. I'm alive.

She shivered, even in his warm embrace. "You were dying with me," she said on a gasp. "You were in the car this time."

"I'm fine." He smoothed hair from her face. "It was only a nightmare."

"It's not only a nightmare. There's something I haven't told you." He didn't stiffen this time, a good sign. "It's Mick." She rushed on before he could even begin to think she was confessing feelings about the creep. "He threatened you, Jamie. He said he'd hurt you if I stayed with you. I should have told you earlier, but I thought it was just a threat, nothing more. But now, with the spooky phone calls, the sound we heard, maybe he's here. Booked under another name, or even living in the forest." A tremor shook her body at the thought.

His arms tightened around her. "I'd forgotten all about that scum. He wouldn't come here, not after all this time. What would he do, kidnap you? Take you where? I won't let anything happen to you. I promise."

He didn't know about the gem, why Mick might be angry enough to come after her. She squeezed her eyes shut and lost herself in his words and warmth.

***

"Good morning, Maven County Public Library. This is Clarisse, can I help you?"

Hallie clutched the receiver so tight, her damp fingers threatened to pinch it right out of her grip. She could picture Clarisse at the large desk upfront, long brown hair and a pencil behind her ear.

"I hope so. I understand a good friend of mine, Chris Copestakes, was killed in a car accident about two months ago."

"Aww, yeah. It was a real tragedy. Did you go to the funeral? There were a thousand people there, and—"

"Actually," Hallie interrupted, not wanting to hear the details. "I'm from out of the country. We were friends online." She thought about how to get the info privately. There wasn't a printer in the cabana, and she couldn't very well have the woman fax it to the office. "Could you do me a big favor and send me a photocopy of the newspaper? I don't have a printer, and I'd like to read the article, and the newspaper doesn't have articles on the website."

"I know, they're so totally in the dark ages. Would you like the obituary, too? It was really nice."

Hallie choked back a sob. "Yeah, sure. Let me give you the address here, and a credit card for the copies and postage."

She'd found a couple of online articles in the larger newspapers from the surrounding cities, but very little detail.

Then she called someone from Hallie's old life.

"You want me to *what?*" Joya screeched over the line.

"Just call Mick's house for the next few days at all kinds of odd hours and see if he's there. I'm probably paranoid, but I want to find out."

"All that paradise and sex is getting to you, darling. God, how I envy you!"

Hallie smiled for the first time since Jamie left that morning. "Joya, the sex *is* paradise."

Joya groaned on the other end. "How did you do it? Find a life so wonderful, a fantastic husband, everything?"

"I guess you could say that I finally saw the *Light*."

Hallie heard a sigh on the other end of the line. "I need to see that light, too. Hallie, I'm leaving Stan, Body Rhythms, La Moustache, and everything. I'm afraid that my nine lives will run out, and the AIDS monster might get me."

"I'm glad. I think you'll be glad, too."

Joya snorted. "Glad? Well, I might be lonely, horny, and broke, but at least I'll be true to myself. That's most important, isn't it?"

"Yeah, it is. It definitely is."

***

"Hallie, why are the curtains all closed? There's a beautiful sunset tonight."

Jamie set some papers down and nuzzled her neck, chasing away the chill. Her arms were wrapped around herself, and she had been deep in thought when he had come home. Phoenix, who had been at her side, now approached Jamie for a petting. Jamie crouched down and scratched the pup's fuzzy head.

"Hey there, little guy."

She turned and moved into his embrace. "I'm glad you're home. I hate when you work late."

"I never work late now that I have something interesting to come home to," he said, his voice laced with sensuality. "The days are shorter now that fall is here. Want to take a walk on the beach and watch the sunset?"

She glanced toward the door. "Out there?"

He laughed. "Yeah, that is where the sun is setting. Come on, it'll be good for you to get out of this house for a change. You've been so..."

"Paranoid. Just say it, Jamie. I've been paranoid. Between the nightmares and the phone calls, I'm just about strung out."

He tugged at her hand, pulling her reluctant body to the door. "I would die before I let anyone hurt you."

She shivered at his words. Yes, he would die for her, she knew that. Her gaze drifted down his strong neck, wide shoulders, and capable arms. To think of that body lying still in death...this time the chill made her entire body stiffen with dread. She squeezed his hand, and he mistook the gesture for compliance.

When they walked down the lighted pathway, she noted that some of the bulbs had burned out. Or maybe someone had started loosening them, one by one. Maybe...her heart felt strangled as she remembered vivid scenes from every horror movie she had ever watched.

"Hallie," he said as they came to a stop in the sand. "How is it that you look the same as you did before the stroke, yet somehow you're more gorgeous?"

She found the place in his arms where her body fit perfectly. The warm soft breeze made her long hair tickle her waist, and made her nose itch with the saltiness of it. She looked up at him, kissing the spot just under his chin. His eyes were filled with strength, love, and awe, a compelling mixture. Especially surrounded by the glow of the setting rays.

"Sometimes I think I really did die and now I'm in

Heaven. And you're a beautiful angel come to fill my soul with happiness."

He bent down and kissed her, crushing her against his chest. She could hear his quick shallow breaths as they slowly dropped down to the sand. And then she could only hear the crashing of waves inside her body, could only feel the tidal surge lifting her up, up to the night sky, to the sun that was always there when Jamie made love to her.

Later, in the darkness, she positioned herself so that she could watch for shadows in the jungle. Little good it would do, for Mick would be two feet away by the time she could see him.

Jamie was lying on his back in the sand, her sitting at his side. He traced his finger languorously along her leg. "Tell me what I can do to ease your fears."

She looked down at him, realizing he'd been watching her staring into the darkness. She wrapped her fingers around his forearm. "Did you ask?"

He studied her, as if weighing whether to tell her the truth. "We're the only ones getting hang-ups."

"Jamie, they're not hang-ups. Someone is staying on the line, waiting."

He sat up, wrapping his arms around her shoulders. "What are you afraid of?"

The muscles in her face were freezing into a stiff frown. "Mick hasn't been home for the last five days. Joya's been checking."

"Well, he isn't staying here."

Her eyes widened. "You've checked?"

"For you. Okay, maybe for me, too. I think your imagination is kicking in because of your nightmares."

She took a deep breath. Now was the time to broach

the subject. If he accepted the first part, she would tell him the rest.

"Jamie, what would you say if I told you I was thinking about going to that bridge in my nightmares? That I think I know where it is, and I want to see why I keep dreaming about it."

He gave her an odd look. "I'd say you were crazy. Why would you want to do that?"

She sat up straight, her shoulders stiff. "Crazy enough to put me away in the Sharp Rehabilitation Center?"

"The what? Oh." His face colored. "You heard about that?"

"I overheard you and Dr. Hughes talking about it in the hospital. I'm not crazy."

"Hallie, it's one thing to chase your dreams. It's something different to chase your nightmares. They're manifestations of some dark subconscious part of your mind, probably a side effect of the coma. If you feel that strongly about it, I'm taking you to a doctor, just to have him listen to you. Maybe he can hypnotize you."

Her heart raced. *A doctor? A shrink?* And if he wanted to hypnotize her, what would she say in her trance? They'd commit her to Sharp Rehabilitation Center for sure, and she'd never find out the meaning of her nightmares. No, she couldn't let that happen. She froze, trying to keep the panic from her face.

"It was just a thought, nothing more. They'll go away. If they don't soon, then we'll talk to someone." She would never see a doctor about it, especially to be hypnotized. She hoped the article would clear up a few questions she had about the day of her death. Maybe once she knew all the answers, then they would go away.

***

"Look like you got some important mail there, Mrs. D," Juicy said with a nod toward the envelope in her hand.

Hallie sidled up to the bar and scooted into one of the swinging chairs. "How did you know?"

His brown eyes twinkled, set off by gleaming white teeth. "I could tell you I have special powers." He tapped a finger to his nearly bald head. "But in truth, I see how you clutch the envelope in your hand."

He mixed her up a Hallie's Comet and plunked it down in front of her before adding a red hibiscus flower. She pulled it out of the glass and slipped it behind her ear. Juicy mixed up a couple of drinks for poolside customers, moving with a slight bounce to the reggae music that played everywhere in Caterina. Music that now seemed a part of her soul.

She and Juicy had had many conversations over the last month and a half, but they never again talked about her aura. Every time she saw him, he smiled brightly and said, "Ello there, Mrs. D," in that singsong, knowing way of someone who shared a secret.

Although she couldn't wait to read the articles that had just come in on the plane, she needed courage. She never let go of that envelope, not once during her entire drink.

When she got up to leave, Juicy said, "Be careful, Mrs. D."

Her eyebrows drew together. "Why did you say that?'

He leaned forward on the bar. "I don't know why I say that. It just come out of my lips."

She hesitated. "Do you chase away evil spirits,

Juicy?"

He shook his head. "Oh, no, ma'am! I stay far, far away from dem. And you should, too."

Her heart felt like a thickened lump inside her. "What if they come after you?"

Juicy's brown eyes grew darker. "Den I say, run from dem, sweet. Run as fast as you can."

She found her pace brisk as she walked down the beach to the rock where she and Jamie made love the first time. Now she could find her way across the rocks, even in the dark. The afternoon sun made her squint as she ripped open the envelope. The lump inside her grew larger, pressing against her ribs. Looking at her face, at her old face, made it hard to catch her breath.

Just as Clarisse had promised, she had sent Chris's obituary. She took a deep breath, staring out into the vast openness of the sea before shifting her gaze to the paper in front of her. Through a glaze of tears, she read her sister, Paullywog's, goodbye letter. There was also a family photo, and Hallie pressed it to her heart for a moment, squeezing her eyes shut.

Her photo was also in the article, next to a picture of the bridge with a gaping hole in the safety railings.

HOMETOWN GIRL KILLED IN CAR ACCIDENT

Maven native Chris Copestakes, 23, plunged to her death inside her car off Crystal Bridge yesterday at approximately 6:00 p.m. She died from massive injuries at the hospital shortly after arrival. The sheriff's department was unable to determine whether a malfunction or driver error caused her loss of control because of the condition of her automobile.

"Malfunction? It was a semi, not a malfunction!"

Copestakes's boyfriend, Alan Messino, was distraught over the accident. "She was acting weird before she left. I shouldn't have let her leave. I kinda thought it was PMS."

"PMS? *PMS!* He's saying that my period made me lose control of the car?" She screamed and stomped her feet on the hard, wet rock. "Why is he making it look like I lost control of the car?"

The article went on, with friends and family speculating about her state of mind. She took the pencil she had borrowed from the front desk and underlined the pertinent points. Then at the top, she wrote, MURDER?! She made the question mark into an exclamation point.

Something flashed in her brain, accompanied by a spear of pain. Something from her nightmares, maybe? Or from her lost memories? It was Alan, clutching her in his arms, alarm ringing in his eyes.

"*Please, Chris, give me a chance to explain."*

"*I am. Right now. Then I'm going to the police."*

"*No, you can't do that! Let me explain it all, and then you can do what you have to. I can prove I'm innocent."* He looked desperately around, grabbed a notepad, and scribbled down an address, along with a primitive map. "*Meet me there in exactly one hour. You'd better go now; it's going to take you that long to get there. I've got to pick something up, the proof. Then I'll be there."*

"*Why can't I come with you to get the proof?"*

"*Because...because I have to break into this guy's apartment to get it. I don't want you to be involved in that. Don't look at me like that, babe. I'm not going to run. Here, the keys* to my cars, my trailer. I'll be at that address, and I will prove to you that I'm innocent."

"Who are you really?"

"My name is Randy Vittone. Alan Messino isn't dead. He's the one behind this. Chris, he's blackmailing me. I can't go to the police, but you can. I'll show you that Alan's not dead. If you turn him in, then I'll be free, and we can get married."

The memory faded, leaving her mind clawing for more. She felt betrayal and shock. What had she found out that Alan was going to explain? What proof was he going to get her, and who was Randy Vittone?

She shuddered, remembering the dream about Alan pulling off a mask. Then he'd revealed himself to be someone else. She tucked both articles into the mangled envelope and sat staring at nothing for a long time, wondering how much was reality, how much nightmare.

***

After hours of tossing and turning, it seemed like Hallie had only been asleep for a few minutes when she heard the noise. Her eyes flew open at the sound of the sickening thud of metal against bone. Then a muffled yelp from the pup. She looked around in the blackness, hoping the noises had been another nightmare. For a moment, she was lulled into that belief. Then Jamie groaned. She saw a shadow of something coming down on his head, heard another thud.

She jerked up in bed. God, this was no nightmare! The dark figure reaching for her was no figment of her dreams. The rough hands yanking her from the warm confines of bed, no illusion.

"Jamie!" she screamed as she was tugged away from his still form. She reached for him, but the figure pulled her away, holding her hair back so she had to look up to keep her scalp from disengaging from her head.

"You betrayed me, Hallie." Mick's voice hissed. "You gave the Manderlay back to Wainthorpe!"

"The gem doesn't belong to us. I gave it back, and he promised not to press charges. Go steal someone else's gem, but leave me out of it!"

"Look at you, slut! Sleeping naked next to him."

"He's my husband. I belong with him."

Mick's grip tightened on her wrist, her hair. She was almost doubled back now. "Self-righteous bitch! You and the Manderlay belong to *me.* Since I can't have the Manderlay, I will have you. Do you understand me? You're mine."

"Please," she whimpered. "Don't hurt him."

The wicked sneering laughter made her heart stop beating for a moment. "He's probably dead. If it makes you feel any better, I'm sure he didn't feel a thing."

"Noooo! Let me see if he's all right."

He yanked her arm around toward him, finally letting go of her hair. "Come on."

She dug in her heels, leaning all her weight backward. He let her go, and she dropped to the floor. She tried to scramble under the bed, but he grabbed her ankle and yanked her backward.

"You're coming with me. If you don't cooperate, I'll kill the dog, too."

Her sobs almost obliterated her words. "Noooo! Please let me go. Go away."

His fingernails dug down the length of her legs, harder with each word she uttered. She knew she was making him madder, but she didn't care. Nothing mattered if Jamie was dead.

No, he can't be dead. Can't be.

She reached for the bed and grabbed onto the sheets. Mick pulled her back and succeeded in freeing her death-grip. She had a handful of sheets. And a howl inside her like a banshee. He slapped her so hard, she had to run her tongue along her teeth to see if they were loose. The last thing she saw was the pup cowering in the corner and Jamie's limp form in the darkness. She struggled harder, but Mick's grip was like a steel clamp.

She wrapped the sheet around her as he dragged her through the house and down the pathway she and Jamie had so recently walked down arm in arm. Jamie, her protector and lover. When she felt something wet and sticky, she held her hand to the light. Blood. Jamie's blood.

She cried out and dropped down to her knees, but Mick dragged her along the sand toward the beach.

"I have to go back to him. He needs me."

"I need you, Hallie. But you deserted me. You gave our future back to Wainthorpe, then ran away." His voice became a growl. "And you made love to him." He leaned down to where she crawled backward to the house. "Every time you kissed him, you rammed a knife into my heart. Every time you touched him, my skin burned. But you didn't care. I told you that you couldn't toss me aside. You will pay, Hallie." His breath was coming in short gasps from his rage. He clutched her chin in his fingers, but his voice rose. "And then you'll be glad I disciplined you. You'll be glad."

She slapped his hand away and tried to get up to dash back home. He leaped at her, causing them to fall.

He crushed her with his weight and the force of gravity, knocking the breath out of her. She glanced at the house one last time before he dragged her, kicking and screaming, toward the beach.

"What are you going to do to me?" she asked as they headed toward the expanse of rocks. "You can't get off this island. They'll find you!"

He turned around and slapped her again. His brown eyes gleamed feral in the moonlight. Brown greasy locks of hair hung down in his face. Suddenly, his eyes glazed over, and he pulled her close, stroking her head.

"I'm sorry, darling. I didn't want this to happen. But you left me no choice. It's your fault, don't you see? You knew how I felt about you, how much I loved you, and you betrayed me. It'll be fine, darling. You'll see, I'm going to punish you for what you've done, and then everything will be fine."

He was psychotic. She tried to get away again, but he yanked her hair back. Damn her hair. Tears blurred everything around her, making Mick seem more distorted than he already was. She was shaking beyond control, trying to tie the sheet tighter around her. The stickiness of Jamie's blood clung to her fingers.

Click.

"Now, darling," Mick was saying through her dazed thoughts and the fear pounding through her brain. "Don't make me use this."

She stared through the blur at the knife he held poised at her chest. "Mick, don't," she heard herself utter, the strength draining from her.

He touched the blade to her chest, drawing a tiny line of blood down to where the sheet covered the top of her breasts.

"I'd rather see you dead than with another man, Hallie. Are you going to come nicely now?"

She nodded, afraid to move and drive the knife deeper into her skin. The stinging made her fingers curl. With his hand on her back, he guided her toward the beach as a gentleman would guide his date through the crowd at a party. They climbed the rocks, leaving Caterina behind and entering Contigua's dense forest. Only a thin strip of beach reflected the moonlight. And there, several yards away, sat a yellow raft.

She turned to him. "You're going to kidnap me in a raft?"

He pressed close to her, and she controlled the urge to spit in his face. The sour smell of his sweat engulfed her.

"No, my darling, I plan to take you away in that." He pointed to the sea of darkness, to the tiny light that bobbed up and down.

Her heart leaped into her throat. He was going to take her away in a boat and keep her a prisoner forever!

"Mick, you can't do this. It's not right. Somewhere deep inside you, you know that."

"Oh, but it is perfectly right. You made your choices when you gave that gem back. Come. And no tricks." He held the cold flat blade of the knife to her cheek.

She walked to the raft, which he pushed out over the wavelets and held for her. Still holding the sheet around her, she climbed in. The water, so clear and blue in the daytime, looked black and murky. Mick climbed in easily, as if he'd had lots of practice doing it.

"Row," he ordered.

She rowed. Slowly. Then she started rowing backward toward shore again. He didn't catch on until they were only a few short feet from shore after ten minutes of rowing.

"Hallie," he said with a huff of impatience. "Don't fool with me."

"Go to *hill*!" she said, trying to cling to Jamie in whatever way she could. She started rowing toward the bobbing light again.

When they neared the large silhouette of the boat, Mick stood and readied himself to grab a rope. Her eyes widened as something brushed beneath the raft, then lifted Mick's half up, knocking him off balance. In her confusion, she fell out of the raft, ready to be eaten by a shark. Her heart leaped as slick hair rose to the surface. *A blond shark!*

"Jamie," she uttered breathlessly.

Mick regained his balance on the raft, an oar in his arms. He struck Jamie in the head, pushing him down into the depths of blackness. She dove under and found his arm. He pressed it to his mouth before moving away from her. She couldn't catch her breath. She held onto the side of the raft, unable to touch bottom. The knife was lying on the bottom of the raft, just inside the rim. She reached for it while Mick was busy looking for Jamie...and plunged it into the thick rubber.

"Hallie, get in the raft!" Mick ordered, unaware of her assault. "Hallie!"

She started swimming away from the commotion Mick created when he slapped the paddle into the water. She frantically searched for any sign of Jamie. The raft was sagging fast, making it harder for Mick to hold his balance. Arms yanked the glob of yellow rubber sideways, sending Mick into the water.

Hallie swam toward the two men struggling in the

water, coming up behind Mick. Jamie pushed Mick up against the side of the boat, smashing his head into the hull. Mick made a gurgling noise before Jamie slugged him in the face. Mick sagged into the water and sank for a minute before Jamie pulled him to the surface.

"Bastard." Jamie said, holding Mick up against the hull.

"Jamie, are you all right? Please tell me you're okay."

"I'll live. Are you all right?"

"Yes," she said on a breath. "Now I am."

"Good. Can you help me get this slime to shore? I can't see anything."

Her heart lurched inside. "What do you mean?"

"Everything's black."

"Don't say you're blind."

The fear in his whisper cut through the darkness to clutch at her heart. He groped through the water to fasten his fingers around her arm. "It's probably the blood in my eyes. Scalp wounds bleed like a bitch. Help me get to shore. I'll hold onto Mick; you guide me in."

Blood ... scalp wounds. Don't panic. You need to stay calm; he needs you to stay calm.

Mick murmured and groaned all the way back in, but he didn't struggle. Jamie left him in the shallow waters and crawled up to shore.

She dropped down beside his prone body and leaned close. "Please, talk to me. Are you still blind?"

"Everything's spinning. I think I'm going to be sick.

He sat up and put his head between his knees, but didn't get sick. She pressed her cheek against his sandy back, holding him close. After a minute he turned to her with closed eyes, squinting to see her. In the moonlight, she saw dark splotches dripping down his forehead and into his eyes.

"You're right, there's blood in your eyes." She wiped it away with her fingers. "Thank God. We're going to be okay." She hoped they would be all right. If he didn't blame her for this. It was Hallie's fault, her affair with Mick, that had brought this to them. Once again, *she* would pay the price.

***

"It's your fault this happened to him," Renee said when she passed Hallie on the way out of the bedroom.

Even in the light of day, Hallie was still too shook up to be angry at the remark.

Miguel touched her arm, and the gesture caused a tear to spring to her eyes. "It's not your fault. It must have been a hell of an experience for both of you."

She glanced at Jamie lying in their bed asleep. "I don't know what I would have done if Mick had killed him. I thought I was going to die from the fear of living without him."

Miguel looked at her, his brown eyes filled with something she couldn't describe. He smiled. "Take care of him, Hallie."

"I will. You know I will."

Everyone at Caterina had heard about the incident by the next morning and came by to wish Jamie well. Mick was sitting in a four-by-four jail cell in Contigua that was mostly used for the occasional drunken native. Before Mick, that had been the most serious crime ever committed by a Contiguan, besides the occasional fight.

When the resort doctor finished his paperwork, he gave Hallie instructions, including peace and quiet, and left her alone with Jamie for the first time in hours. She sat by his bedside, watching him sleep fitfully. His eyes were swollen, and the bandages on his head were gruesome evidence of his multiple concussions. Phoenix was lying on the bed at Jamie's feet, looking guilty for not doing more than cowering.

"It wasn't your fault, puppy. And really and truly, it wasn't mine either. The only people we can blame are the *former* Hallie and Mick."

Jamie's fingers twitched, and she pulled his hand into hers. He had saved her life, and nearly died in the process. Even against the white sheets, he looked pale. Purple bruises dotted his chest and arms. She kissed her finger and pressed it gently to each bruise she could see.

"*Psst!*"

The sound came from the walkway leading to the bedroom. She spotted Juicy standing there hesitantly and waved him in.

"How he be?" Juicy whispered.

"Okay. It was a hell of a night."

His eyes were wide, his gray brows knitted with concern. "I need to talk with you, Mrs. D." He nodded his head toward the glass slider. "Out there."

She glanced at Jamie, then back. Juicy waved a hand in the direction of the bed. "He be okay. Open the curtains. You can peek in on him."

She opened the curtains, then walked outside and positioned herself so she could watch Jamie as they talked. George, hanging from the breadfruit tree, chattered when he saw her. It almost looked as if the bobbing branch he was hanging from was waving at her with its finger-like green leaves. She waved at him but stopped when she saw Juicy's concerned expression.

"What's wrong?"

He looked around, as if to make sure no one else was listening. "I have a bad feeling. Dis Mick man, he think you Hallie." Juicy thumped his head. "He still wild in love with her. There be not'ing you can do 'bout it. If he want to possess you, he will do anyt'ing."

Her heart tightened. He had already nearly done *anything*. What more could he do?

"I don't understand. He can't do anything from jail."

"Ah, right now he be in jail. Contigua not so strict wit' criminals. Not used to them, you see. Rumsoakers, all dey have to worry about. Drunkards. Mick, he be out sometime, maybe not for a while, but sometime. Then he come after you again."

Fear prickled over her skin. "What are you saying?"

"You need to tell him the trut'. 'Bout who you really be. Your lives, yours and Mr. D's, depend on you convincing dat crazy man you are not the woman he t'inks you are. You see?"

She nodded slowly, but his implications were only just sinking in. The danger wouldn't go away until she told Mick the truth. *Convinced* him of the truth. Then she realized exactly what Juicy was saying. He knew. Knew she wasn't really Hallie.

"What do I tell Jamie? I can't tell him the truth. I started to, but he wanted me to go to the Sharp Rehabilitation Center."

"Da where?"

"Insane asylum," she whispered. "Where they electrocute you into being normal. Or catatonic."

Juicy shook his head. "No, no, you don't tell Mr. D anyt'ing. Not even that you saw Mick. You convince Mick, den get him off the island."

She swallowed hard, unsuccessful at getting the lump out of her throat. "I don't want to see Mick again. He scares me."

"Mrs. D, your lives may depend on seeing him again. I got the feeling, and my feelings are always right. Right?" He gave her a knowing look.

"All right. Will you come with me? Maybe it will help convince him."

"Yes, I go wit' you. But we must go soon. Before he has time to t'ink up somet'ing else."

CHAPTER 16

J amie slept most of the day under the power of medication. Only once had he awakened, looked into Hallie's eyes, and smiled.

"Are you okay?" he asked, squeezing her hand with a death grip.

She couldn't help but laugh as she smoothed back his hair from his forehead. "Am *I* okay? Are *you* okay?"

He grimaced. "I'm really tired. But I'm all right as long as you're here with me."

His eyes drifted closed, but a trace of his smile remained. She touched her finger to his lips.

"I love you, Jamie," she whispered.

She watched his eyelids twitch and wondered how a man could look so gorgeous when he was battered and bruised.

Miguel knocked softly before stepping inside the bedroom. He walked over to the bed, studying his brother.

"He's all right," she said. "He just woke up and talked to me for a minute."

He scratched his fingers through his beard. "I sure wish they had capital punishment in Contigua. With their rules of justice, Mick will probably get a slap on the hand."

Her heart froze. "You mean they'll let him out of jail soon? He'll be able to come back here?" She glanced toward Jamie.

"They'll probably send him away, but there's no policing every beach to make sure he doesn't return." Miguel's broad chest puffed up, and his eyes were trained on Jamie. "If he comes back and I get hold of him, he's dead."

His words made her mission even more important. "Thanks for coming out, Miguel."

"Have you even left the house all day?"

"No. I've hardly gone to the bathroom."

He gestured toward the hallway. "Be my guest."

She walked in and pulled a brush through tangled hair that hadn't been combed since she'd gone to bed the night before. The mirror image reminded her of the one she'd seen more than two months ago in the hospital: pale, scared.

She returned to the bedroom. "I need to run some errands."

"Stay out as long as you want. I'll be here 'til you get back."

She couldn't take her eyes from Jamie. "I won't be long."

Twilight skies washed everything an eerie pink hue. She and Juicy rode the golf cart as far as they could before embarking through the woods to Contigua. She walked in silence, tensing her hands and glancing around at the moving shadows. The smells of smoke and pork filled the heavy air. She felt traitorous, sneaking off to see the man who had nearly killed her husband.

The village of Contigua usually shut down at dusk, but Juicy had called ahead to arrange a special visit with their most important criminal. The jailhouse was only as big as her bedroom, with rough white stucco on the outside and two glassless windows. A tin sign over the wooden door squeaked in the breeze, *JAIL* hand-painted in blue.

Miguel hadn't exaggerated about the size of Mick's cell. Smaller than a closet, it held a cot, toilet, and sink. The floor was dirty concrete. Nothing else, and literally no room to even stand and use the toilet and sink. Obviously, Mick had to use the facilities from his cot. She hoped he wouldn't demonstrate while they were there.

Mick was facing the wall when they stepped inside. With a nod, the uniformed man with an afro bowed and backed out of the room, standing just outside the door.

"Mick?" her voice croaked out, echoing against the bare brick walls.

His shoulders jumped first, then he whirled around to grasp the rough black bars. "Hallie? Hallie! You came!" Then his brown eyes took in Juicy, and his expression faltered. "Is he a lawyer?"

"No, this is a friend of mine. His name is Juicy."

Mick slipped on his thick glasses and studied the man standing beside her. "Why did you bring him?"

Juicy walked around to the tiny metal desk and pulled two folding chairs around for them to sit on.

Hallie said, "I have to talk to you, Mick."

Mick flopped down on the bed, causing a metallic shriek. He sighed, staring at her between the bars.

"I'm sorry for what I did. When I found out about your giving the Manderlay back, and coming here, I got crazy. I followed you, watched you make love to that man, watched you enjoy it…" He turned away, removed his glasses, and ran the back of his dirty hand across his eyes. "I got crazy," he whispered. Then he turned to meet her eyes again. "*You* made me crazy."

She leaned forward, but still outside reaching distance from the bars. "*I* didn't make you crazy. *Hallie* did."

Mick stared at her for a moment. "That's what I said."

"Not exactly. You are in love, obsessed, with Hallie. She is the woman you met at La Moustache with Joya, the one who stole the gem, the one you've been seeing up until her brain hemorrhage. That woman was Hallie, and *she* died."

He laughed oddly, rubbing his fingers into his forehead. "But you came back."

"That's right. *I* came back, but I am not Hallie."

"This is crazy. You're punishing me, aren't you? For what I did last night."

"No, I'm not punishing you. Not that I don't want to strangle you for what you did to Jamie. No, I should have told you this long before, but I had no idea it would escalate to this."

"I know you're different. You don't have to tell me you've changed."

She took a deep breath, aware that Juicy was leaning toward her, listening intently.

"Mick, what I'm telling you is that I am a different person, absolutely, completely different. I never was Hallie. I'm Chris Copestakes. I was born in a small town in Colorado where I lived until I was twenty-three. Then I had a car accident and died."

Mick's face went pale, but he didn't say a word.

"When I asked God for a second chance, I woke up in Hallie's body." She gestured to herself. "This isn't Hallie, it's me in her body. Do you understand?"

Mick shook his head. "That's crazy. Why are you telling me this?"

"Because you need to understand why I don't love you. And why you don't love me. Not who I am now, anyway. The woman you love is dead, Mick. Dead. My name is Chris, and I am alive. In Hallie's body."

Juicy spoke up. "She be a different person. Her aura is different, pink instead of blue. You can't change your aura. When she come to the island, I knew she not be Mrs. D anymore."

Mick's gaze drifted back to Hallie. "Then why are you with Jamie?"

"Because as Chris, I fell in love with him."

Mick leaned back and crossed his arms. "If you're really someone else, prove it."

She pulled out the torn envelope and handed him the two articles. "I ordered them from the library in my hometown."

After reading them, Mick looked up. "This doesn't prove anything."

"It's all I have. But I can tell you everything you could ever want to know about Colorado. My dad taught me how to ski when I was six, in Telluride. My sister Bernice never picked up the skiing thing, but my sister Charlene competes nationally. My third sister, Paula, never cared to try. I wore nothing but jeans my whole life, except on Sunday when we went to church. I climbed every tree within a half-mile circumference of our house. I was five-foot-four with kinky brown hair and no chest. Would I make this stuff up?"

Mick's expression was uncertain, his eyes fixed on her. "And Jamie knows. About you being this *Chris* person?" His fingers were white where they clutched the iron bars.

"No. There's no need to tell him."

"And what if I tell him his wife is either a wacko or another woman in Hallie's body? What would he say?"

"He'd think you were the crazy one. I only told you because I thought you should know about Hallie." Her heart was tightening, but she fought to keep a calm expression on her face. "Do you think I'm a wacko?"

"I don't know. Whatever you are, whoever you are, you're not the Hallie I knew. She wouldn't have given the Manderlay back, and she wouldn't have made me come get her." He lifted his arm to show the fingernail marks, then tilted his head to show gouges on his neck. "She was too afraid to fight me like this."

"You tried to kill my husband," she stated with a flat voice.

"I just wanted him out of the way until I could get you back to your senses and find out why you double betrayed me." He bowed his head to show her a glob of dried blood. "I'd say we're about even."

"The hell we are. He's..." She stopped herself, not wanting Mick to know that Jamie was defenseless in bed. "He got it a lot worse than you did."

"But he's alive?"

"Yes. If you come back again, both he and his brother will kill you if I don't do it first."

Mick leaned his head against the bars, his eyes closed. "Hallie?"

"No, Chris."

"Chris, if what you say is true...if Hallie died, do you

think she got a second chance?"

"Not in my old body, she didn't. Maybe in someone else's."

He raised weary eyes to hers. "How can I find out?"

"You can't. She'll have to find you." *If she wants to, and I doubt that.*

"My trial is tomorrow. What kind of trials do they have around here?"

Juicy said, "It be in Ralph's house. Mr. D will sign papers, then you, him, and Mrs. D assemble in his living room and proceed to tell your stories. He decides which story he like better and give his ruling."

Hallie saw something alight in Mick's eyes. "So, I will see Master DiBarto tomorrow then?"

Juicy's voice became deep and harsh. "Dis time you see him face to face. In the daylight, not sneaking up on him like a coward."

Mick winced but didn't respond.

She stood. "I have to get back home. Come on, Juicy."

"Goodbye, *Chris.*"

Mick's words sent shivers down her spine and throughout her whole body. Those words, spoken carefully, deliberately. Why did they bring back her nightmare? She left the jailhouse, Juicy at her side.

"Do you think he'll tell Jamie what I told him?"

Even in the dark as they picked their way back to the golf cart, she could tell he was shaking his head.

"Hard to say. Da man be a kook. His aura be dark, all crazy."

"You got that right. Oh, God, I can just see this whole story coming out at the trial. Do I deny it, or admit it to Jamie? No, I can't tell him. I can't risk Jamie thinking that I've lost my mind. And what if he tells Jamie that I stole Dave's gem? He might hate me for that. Juicy, what will they do with Mick if he's found guilty, which he'll most assuredly be?"

Juicy shrugged. "Well, dey already decide to keep his boat and give to da fishermen. Dey might keep him in jail for a long time."

Her heart leaped. "Here? They'd keep him here?"

"Where else?"

"I can't keep worrying that he might somehow tell Jamie what I just told him. Or break out and come back to do God-knows-what. No, I've got to convince Jamie to drop the charges and send him away from Constantine. If I've convinced him of who I am, he'll probably leave us alone. Do you think I convinced him?"

Again, Juicy shrugged. "I t'ink you convince him of somet'ing, but he not sure what. Give him time, he may believe you." They reached the golf cart and climbed in, but before he started the engine, he turned to her. "Dese nightmares you tell me you have every night, do you t'ink dey are trying to tell you somet'ing?"

"No, they're just..." She turned to him. "Yes, but I don't know what. That's how I realized that a truck ran me off the bridge. I keep seeing the accident, just like I'm there again. And I get flashes of other things, too."

All she could see were the whites of his eyes in the darkness, looking straight at her. "What other t'ings?"

"Like a newspaper article, but I can't read the words other than the word *MISSING*. And my boyfriend begging me to give him a chance, but I don't know for what. Alan telling me that his name is Randy Vittone, that Alan is alive and he's blackmailing him into doing something. He was going to get proof, and I was meeting him somewhere. He wanted me to go to the police after I had this proof, but the truck ran me off the road before I got there. I don't know. Maybe I am crazy."

Juicy leaned over and pulled her closer. She rested her head on his shoulder and let the tensions of the past weeks seep out in a long sigh.

"What are you going to do?" he asked.

"I don't know. My life here with Jamie is wonderful, but these nightmares won't go away. How can I go on with my new life when my old one won't leave me alone? Or rather, my death won't leave me alone."

He lifted her chin so that her eyes met his. "Do you think somet'ing is tellin' you to go back home and find out what happened? Maybe the nightmares go away, and you can live in peace."

She listened to the night sounds, the rustle of leaves and screeching calls of a bird. In the warm breeze a chill climbed from her feet and slowly traveled up to her scalp.

"I can't leave Jamie."

"Dat be your decision. Maybe the dreams will go away."

She knew they wouldn't. Somehow, she knew.

***

Hallie thrashed in her sleeplessness for two hours before dropping off. But sleep would offer no comfort, no escape. The images crashed into her mind, one after the other with alarming clarity. Mick held her in a grip. "Goodbye, Chris," his voice said in an odd lilt. Then he turned into Alan, still holding her. "Goodbye, Chris. Drive carefully." She held a newspaper clipping in her hand, and all she could read in the crumpled letters was the word *MISSING*, and her heart felt as if someone had ripped it out of her chest. When the familiar scenario started with her car reaching the bridge, the dream changed again.

Jamie was standing there, reading the newspaper article, crumpling it up in his hand and throwing it at her. "What you're telling me is crazy. I knew you weren't right; I knew all along that something just wasn't right. Dr. Hughes warned me to keep an eye on you. After a couple of shock treatments, you'll be fine." He patted her shoulder, a phony smile on his face. "Just fine."

She sat up with a jerk, trying to catch her breath. Then she glanced toward Jamie, wondering if he had noticed. He was deep asleep, probably with help from the pain killers.

Missing. Who was missing? Not Alan, because he had been there. Randy Vittone? Alan's words came to her again. *My name is Randy Vittone.* She clutched her head, feeling the ache of the many questions that haunted her.

"Jamie," she whispered. "Don't hate me."

***

"You want me to do *what*?"

Jamie sat up straight before getting dizzy and setting his head back against the pillow. His mind was still foggy. He was sure he'd heard Hallie wrong.

Her voice was small, quiet. "I said, I want you to drop the charges against Mick. Will you listen to me while I explain?"

He crossed his arms, anger bubbling inside him. The terror of finding that his wife had been dragged from their bed was still too fresh in his mind to think of anything other than murdering the son of a bitch. It had only been two nights before.

"Okay, explain. Don't tell me that you're just a forgiving person, and I won't even hear anything like you don't want him hurt."

Her blond hair fell about her face as she leaned toward him, blue eyes pleading. She nervously licked her lips, lips he'd rather kiss than hear these words from.

"No, it's nothing like that. I want to strangle him myself." Her hand felt warm as her fingers encircled his arm. "Jamie, if he's found guilty, they'll keep him in prison for a year or more."

"So?"

"They'll keep him *here*. He'll be right over there all that time. That jail cell isn't made to hold anyone indefinitely. What if he breaks out? What if he comes after us again?"

He softened as he heard her plea. Not for Mick's comfort but for their safety.

"What are you suggesting?"

"That you drop the charges only if he's immediately sent back to the States. Neither one of us will talk to him or even see him. He'll be escorted directly from the cell to the airfield and flown away."

"What if he comes back?"

"He won't."

"How can you be so sure?"

She was avoiding his gaze. Besides the trace of desperation, he saw guilt. He moved his arm out of her grasp.

"Hallie, did you go see him?"

Her chin twitched, but she didn't answer. He threw her hand off the bed and pushed her away.

"Damn you, Hallie."

She wrapped her arms around herself and stood. In blue jeans with her hair in a ponytail and no makeup, she looked like a teenager who'd been caught sneaking out.

"I didn't see him on a social visit. I had to convince him that I wasn't the woman he thought I was. That I'm different now."

"Did you go alone?"

"Juicy went with me."

His eyes widened. "Juicy, the bartender?"

"He's a friend of mine. He was my only friend for a while."

He felt a twinge of guilt. Wait a dammed minute. She was the guilty one. "Hallie, leave me alone." There was such fear in her eyes, he felt compelled to add, "I need some time alone."

"Don't hate me, please. I just want him gone from our lives. He won't be gone if he's right there, a short walk away."

"Leave."

She dropped her head and left without giving him another look. He stiffly got out of bed and stretched. His muscles were still too sore for his morning swim. The doctor had said no activity for a couple of days, but one more day in bed and he'd go nuts. Phoenix was lying by his side of the bed, and Jamie got a major head rush when he leaned down to pet him. The throbbing pain in his head increased its tempo.

Even though he wasn't supposed to, he took a shower, then got dressed. Hallie was sitting by the pool, throwing peanuts to George, who was hanging on one of the skinny branches of the calabash tree. They had developed the game some time ago, taking turns tossing peanuts and dried fruit bits to the upside-down monkey. This time she was flinging them a little too hard, and George was missing most of them and not too happy about it.

When Phoenix wandered over to where she was sitting, she instantly looked up at Jamie. Her eyes took in his clothes, but she didn't say anything. Her expression was hesitant, full of that sadness he had seen in the days after her release from the hospital.

"Make the arrangements," he said.

She stood. "For Mick, you mean?"

"Take care of everything without seeing him, do you understand?"

"I will." She studied him. "Are you … all right with this?"

"My head hurts too much to figure out how I feel about it."

"Where are you going?"

"To work. I'll see you later tonight."

He left her standing there with a bag of peanuts in her hand, staring after him.

***

Hallie had gone to the office, too, but had been careful not to run into Jamie. Her relief from avoiding the trial had not erased the feelings of guilt for getting Mick off easy, no matter how valid her reasons. When she couldn't stand it anymore, she'd gone to Jamie's office and found it dark. Worry sent her running home to see if he was there.

She found him lying on a chaise lounge by the pool. His blond hair was plastered to his head from a recent swim, although wisps of it broke free as they dried in the sunshine. She stood there for the longest time, staring at him. The ache in her heart that had started out as a dull thud now had a tearing-of-flesh feeling.

Jamie, how I love you. Please don't hate me.

Everything around her looked different through eyes that might not see them for a while. George sat in a tree nearby, picking at a bigs green breadfruit; the palm trees danced in the wind; and the late afternoon sun made everything feel warm and hopeful. Not the way she felt at all.

She walked over and knelt down by Jamie. He woke with a start, blinking at her through the sunlight behind her. He reached out and roughly pulled her toward him, kissing her.

"Never," he murmured into her hair when he held her close. "Never see him again, Hallie. Or talk to him."

She couldn't talk for fear that tears would start gushing out. She could only shake her head. After a moment, he pulled her face back for another long kiss, his hands yanking off her shirt. In one swift movement, she was the one lying on the lounge, and he hovered over her.

"Jamie," she said between kisses. She didn't want to make love with him, not before she had to tell him she was leaving.

"*Shhh*," he ordered, kissing her into silence.

Feeling his tongue moving with hers and his body pressed against hers, she realized how much she wanted this, the bliss before the storm. He slipped out of his bathing suit, then slid her skirt and panties down. She felt his strength inside her, his tongue dominating her mouth. Her legs moved up to encircle his waist, and her arms slipped around his neck.

She trailed her fingernails down his back, gritting

back words and tears as he moved inside her. He gave her no mercy, no space to breathe, no tenderness—just raw passion. They both gasped for breath, not willing to wait for it to catch up to them.

Her body convulsed, sending her rocketing to some other place where pain and decisions were nonexistent. Oh, how she wanted to stay there, touching the sun, feeling engulfed in heat. His shudder yanked her back to reality, and he pulled her closer for a tighter hold. They remained there for a few minutes before he moved away to look at her.

"Why are you crying? Did I hurt you?"

She only then became aware of the tears streaming down her face. To stave off the torrent, she shook her head.

"What's the matter?"

Not now, she couldn't tell him now. She took in short breaths, trying to regain control.

"I'm sorry, Jamie," was all she could manage.

"No, I'm sorry. Let's put it behind us."

She nodded in agreement, blinking to keep the tears back. She studied him, subconsciously memorizing every detail, every nuance of him. His dark blond eyelashes captured the sunlight, casting tiny shadows on the tops of his cheeks. Tiny beads of sweat accumulated on his forehead, and she reached up to wipe them away with her finger. His blue eyes studied her, unable to hide the uncertainty.

Her fingers trailed down his neck to mingle with the soft fuzz on his chest that was only visible close-up. She closed her eyes and memorized each ridge on his chest and stomach, the feel of his belly button.

"I love you, Jamie," she said, finding her voice uncooperative. She wanted to say it again and again, to make him understand and believe that he was her life, her soul. Everything.

"Then why are you crying?"

"Not now." She looked away, but he held her chin and moved it back so that she faced him again.

"What not now?"

"Jamie, please," she whimpered.

He moved away from her, but his eyes never left hers. "It's Mick, isn't it?"

"God, no." She bent her head and rubbed away her tears. "It has nothing to do with him."

Jamie stood up and put on his bathing suit. Towering above her, she couldn't see his face with the sun blinding her from behind.

"*What* has nothing to do with Mick?"

She started crying again, the sound of sobs and the blinding of tears that blocked out everything around her and left her feeling alone and scared. She couldn't see him, but she knew he stood there watching her.

"What's going on, Hallie?" His voice had that flat tone again. It dulled her senses, making her able to look at him.

"I h...have to leave, but it's nothing to do with Mick or you."

He whirled around and walked inside, leaving her talking to the empty air. She jumped up and followed, finding him holding his head with one hand and leaning against the wall with the other. Her heart leaped into her throat.

"Jamie, are you all right?"

His eyes were filled with anger and disbelief. "Why?"

She took a deep breath. "I can't explain because

you'll send me away to the Sharp Rehabilitation Center. I won't have you thinking I'm crazy."

"You'd rather me think you're heartless."

"You know that's not true. I'll be back soon, I promise."

He leaned into her face. "No, you won't."

"But I will."

"You walk out that door without any explanation, and I don't want you back."

Her eyes widened. "Jamie, you don't mean that."

"I mean every word of it." He turned too quickly, then grimaced. His hand moved up over his heart. "Hallie, don't do this to me."

Her tears started anew. "I'm not doing it to *you*. I'm doing it to *me*. I don't want to leave. Before I can live in peace, I have to find something out."

"Find out what?" His eyes glared at her, and his body was stiff.

She looked at him, weighing how much to tell him. Telling him something was better than leaving him completely in the dark. "What happened on that bridge."

His eyebrows furrowed. "The one you keep dreaming about?"

She nodded. "There's a reason it haunts me every night. I have to put the pieces together. And don't start talking about seeing a doctor. This isn't something any doctor can figure out. Only I can."

"Hallie, this is—"

"Don't say *crazy*. Don't. It's not crazy to me. Something happened when I was in a coma. Something put these images in my head. I have to find out why. It's as important as the feeling that I'd come back for you."

She knew he was thinking that her brain had been injured, by the tightening of his mouth, his expression of both worry and anger. "So, you're going to, what, go searching all the bridges in the country until you find the one in your nightmares?"

She didn't want him to know where she'd be going. "Something like that."

"Then I'll come with you."

"No, I have to do this alone. I feel strongly about that; it must be…just me."

He turned away from her. "Mick's flying out tonight. Why don't you see if you can fly out with him?"

"It's not Mick. Please trust me." She moved up behind him and tentatively touched his back. "I know it's a big thing to ask, but I'm asking anyway. Trust me."

He turned around, and the pain in his eyes made her heart break. "I can't. I can't give you that."

Her voice was a whisper. "I have to go. I don't want to lose you, but I have to go. When I'm finished, I want to come back."

He closed his eyes and shook his head. "No."

"Jamie?" She reached out for him, but he moved away.

He grabbed some clothes and, without even a glance in her direction, walked out the door. Or rather his blurry figure did, through her tears. Now that the damage was done, she couldn't change her mind. Everything she had worked so hard to achieve had disappeared through that door. She let herself think of the soft blond hair she would never run her fingers through again, the eyes that would never look at her with love, arms that would never hold her again after a nightmare.

She shook herself from the fit of self-pity. She had to get rid of these nightmares, find out the truths behind them. Then she would return and, maybe, just maybe, Jamie would forgive her. But she had to face another possibility: maybe he wouldn't.

***

"This is how you take care of my brother?"

Hallie turned at the sound of Miguel's cynical voice. She bowed her head, not wanting to face him. The lobby was filling with new arrivals, ready for an exciting first day at Caterina. A handful sat soberly waiting for the golf cart to take them back to reality. None were as sad to leave as she was.

She finally summoned the courage to meet his eyes. "I told him I'd be back."

Miguel leaned against a post, his large arms crossed over his chest. "From where?"

"I can't tell you."

His eyes softened. "Hallie, don't do this to him. He loves you, more than he's ever loved anyone before."

The tears were at the ready, giving everything a surreal, wavery look. "I have to go. Miguel, I love Jamie more than anything in the world, but I can't be completely happy until I resolve something from my past. It's not a man; I'm not in love with anyone else." She saw the cart pull up. "I have to go. Goodbye, Miguel. Tell Jamie I'm sorry and that I love him."

"You tell him."

"He was the one who left last night. He was the one who didn't answer when I knocked on your door this morning. Please, tell him for me."

He reached out and touched her arm. "He means it,

Hallie. He doesn't want you back if you leave. Don't you realize that you've run out of second chances?"

Her lip trembled. "I have to go." She turned and ran to the cart, throwing her bag in back and ordering the driver to get her out of there, fast.

CHAPTER 17

J amie started drinking at four o'clock, in blatant disregard for the doctor's instructions to avoid alcohol while taking the pain killers. Juicy was giving him particularly pitiful looks, and he guessed that everyone knew Hallie had left him.

"Your wife, she love you very much," Juicy said softly. "She be back as soon as she can."

Jamie lifted his head and narrowed his eyes. "What do you know about where she's going? You're her friend —did she tell you?"

"I don't know where she go, jus' dat it be hard for her to leave."

Renee sidled up to the bar and took the seat next to him. "Hi, stranger."

"Go 'way," he slurred, angry at his own susceptibility to liquor. He needed both arms braced on the counter just to keep himself upright.

"Absolutely not. In fact, I'm taking you home. You don't want the guests to see the owner like this."

She took his arm and pulled him away from the stool. He knew she was right. Her arm was linked with his as she guided him down the pathway that led home.

When he was faced with the cozy exterior, lighted and welcoming, he stopped. So many nights he saw this scene and couldn't wait to get inside and be with Hallie.

"I don't want to go home," he stated.

"Fine, come home with me, then."

He turned unsteadily, and she caught his arm to keep his balance.

"Jamie, how did you get so drunk? I've never seen you like this."

He fished in his pocket for the bottle of capsules from the resort's pharmacy and held them up to her.

"Geez, you know better than that!"

The smell of gardenias made him feel nauseated, and he sped up the pace.

"I guess you know about..."

"Yes," she interrupted. "I know."

"Bitch," he slurred.

"Yes, I know."

She fumbled with the keys at the door to her bungalow. He stepped inside without any invitation and looked around at the ruffles, lace, and pink gingham.

"I didn't know you were a closet fru-fru."

"What's a fru-fru?" she asked, coming up behind him.

"One of those women who likes this kinda stuff." He made a vague wave.

"What's wrong with fru-fru?"

He shrugged. "Nothing, I guess. Just didn't expect it from you."

She turned off the light, pitching them into sudden darkness. "I'm going to turn on a softer light." She moved up behind him and slid her arms around his waist. "Jamie, I—"

He threw her down on the couch and lunged on top of her. His lips mashed down on hers, and she groaned. His hands trailed down smooth cool skin, and she reached down to unbutton his shirt. When she had him bare-chested, he tried unsuccessfully to unbutton her shirt, then ripped it apart.

"Jamie," she said.

"*Shh.*"

The skin his hands roamed over was softer, spongier, not taut like—he wouldn't think of her.

Renee had her hands on his belt, tugging at it. He shoved his tongue into her mouth, and her hands fell to the side. After a moment, she started working at his belt again. She was making little whimpering noises. He stopped kissing her, then forced himself to start again. She unzipped his pants, but before she could start pushing them down, he rolled away from her.

When he turned on the light, it revealed a startled expression on her flushed face. It had a sobering effect on him. She sat up and moved next to him, her brown eyes wide in confusion. When she reached up and touched his hair, he couldn't stop the involuntary reaction of moving away. She dropped her hand.

His voice sounded thick. "I'm...sorry. I can't."

"Why?"

"Because," he said, running his fingers through his hair. "In the dark, I see Hallie."

She forced a smile. "We'll leave the lights on."

He was already shaking his head. "It's more than that. I wanted you to be her."

Renee's shoulders drooped. "I can't be her, Jamie."

He reached out and touched her chin. "I know that. It would be wrong for you to try."

Her chin trembled. Tears made her eyes shiny. "She left you. Why can't you forget her?"

He sighed. "I wish I could. But God help me, I can't. I need to find out why she left. If it's for another man, I can put it to rest. But I can't let her go until I'm sure, and I'm really not sure."

Renee reached over and put her hand on his shoulder. "I'll be waiting for you."

He stood, then offered Renee his hand. Helping her to her feet, he pulled her closer. "You know, there's someone else who needs you more than I do."

She tilted her head. "Someone else? What do you mean?"

He smiled. "You really haven't noticed, have you? Someone who appreciates what a beautiful woman you are, how wonderful and kind. Someone who's a lot more deserving than I am."

Renee's eyes widened, and a smile lifted her face. "Miguel?"

Jamie nodded. "He's been in love with you for a long time. He's never admitted it to me, of course, but I can tell."

"But Miguel is my friend. He's warm, wonderful, sweet. He's..." Her eyes widened more. "Oh, I don't know."

"He's a good guy. And very patient."

"Patient, indeed." Then her expression dimmed. "But he's still mad at me for spilling the beans about Hallie the other night."

"He'll get over it. If I can forgive you, he can."

She pushed out her lower lip. "Have you forgiven me?"

"Yes. Just don't tell me anything else, okay?"

"There's nothing else." Then a thoughtful frown lit her face. "*Miguel.* I'm not sure I could feel that way about him."

"You could try."

"I could. I love him as a friend, but I'm just not sure." She grinned. "I told him I was going to seduce that woman right out of your head. He's going to think..."

"Not if you go over there now."

She smoothed her hair and put her shirt back on. "I think I'd better change into another shirt," she said when she found no buttons to insert.

"Sorry about that."

"It's going to be hard getting over you, you know."

Jamie shook his head. "Nah. I predict by the end of this evening you'll have forgotten all about me."

She walked over and leaned up to kiss him on the cheek. "Don't count on it. You're a hard man to forget."

"You'll have other things on your mind. Have an eventful evening. And describe the look on his face when you show up." But he already knew what Miguel would look like. He could imagine it well enough.

Renee changed her shirt, then walked with him to the door. She stopped and looked up. "You'll be all right?"

"Something tells me I will."

She sighed, biting her lip. "I'm never going to forget that kiss, Jamie."

He raised an eyebrow. "I wish you would."

The door closed behind them, and she walked slowly down the lighted pathway. He was glad for his brother. He hoped it would work out.

As for Hallie, she was dealing with something right now, but he didn't think it had anything to do with a man. It was something she couldn't share with him, something more than bridge nightmares, and that hurt. He was her husband, and his place was by her side, no matter what she was facing.

Hadn't he closed the door himself by suggesting she see a doctor about her dreams and paranoia? Her paranoia had turned out to be valid. But she also seemed abnormally afraid that he would send her to the Sharp Rehabilitation Center. He sighed, and headed in the direction of home. After all, she'd made her decision. And he'd made his. He just wasn't sure if he could stick to it.

***

Is this what it would feel like to be returned home after ten years in an alien ship? Maven was another world, a place she had dreamed about, a distant memory from someone else's life. Tucked amidst the mountains at over eight thousand feet, thoughts of palm trees and beaches seemed ludicrous.

As they had for generations, the residents of Maven were stringing up Christmas decorations from the lampposts on the very first day of December. Hallie sat in her rented SUV along Main Street, watching them … smiling and crying at the same time. Her entire life had been spent there, growing up, laughing, playing. Dying.

She wrapped the coat she'd purchased on her layover tightly around her and stepped out of the car. The red buildings held the flavor of the old west, some with white columns and wooden porches in front. It seemed so different now. Maybe because she was different. A woman who had died and been reborn, had loved and been loved.

She couldn't keep the cry from escaping her throat,

and she bowed her head into her gloved hands. So recently she had been in Jamie's arms, making love to him, knowing it could be her last time if he never forgave her for leaving.

"Miss, are you all right?"

She jerked up to see the owner of the store she was standing in front of peering anxiously at her.

"I'm fine, Mrs. Stanford."

The woman's soft brown eyes became curious, her mouth curved in a smile. "Do I know you?"

Hallie glanced at the sign. "I, uh, saw the sign. You're the owner, aren't you?"

"Yes, I am." She laughed. "You just guessed that?"

"Uh-huh."

"It's awfully cold out here. Would you like to come in for a cup of coffee?"

"No, but thank you. I've got to get going."

Hallie walked carefully across the icy sidewalk to her car. She drove down the small strip that constituted the main drag of Maven. Cheech's Pizza Parlor looked cozy and crowded, brightly lit and full of activity. If she thought she could walk in without sobbing, she would. It was strangely disappointing to see life going on without her, yet she knew it must.

Just before the road turned rural, Alan's auto shop sat at the corner, dimly lit. She slowed down, and with her pace so did the beating of her heart. He was there in the office, alone. A new black pickup truck sat out front, perched high via a lift kit. She could stop and talk to him right then. The numbness inside her warned that it wasn't a good idea. Not yet.

Curiously, the sight of his shop didn't cause a melancholy to settle over her, didn't make her heart swell.

Instead she felt colder than the snowflakes swirling around her car. Not that anyone could cause the response Jamie did. She squeezed her eyes shut. No, she would never feel that way about anyone else. But still, shouldn't she feel *something*?

She kept driving, wanting to take in everything around her—the sight of the frosty mountains rising around her, covered in misty fog, the snow-laden aspens sagging under the weight, the wooden railing encircling acres of farmland. Everywhere she looked, a memory leaped at her. Tears slid down her face, not for things lost, but for things she had, for a happy childhood and a family who loved her.

Dense branches made the stands of bare trees look as though they were going up in smoke, giving them a hazy appearance. Only when she spotted the cedar house set back from the road a short distance did she realize why she had come this way. Her heart dropped down by the brake pedal she pressed so hard in front of her parents' house.

Through the huge windows in front, she saw the fireplace's reflection dancing along the walls, an occasional movement inside. Her parents. Maybe a sister, maybe all three. *Why did I come out here? I knew it would be like this.* She wanted to walk up to the window and watch them all evening, even after they went to sleep.

The sound of a horn jarred her, and she whirled around to see a truck waiting for her to move along. She pulled into her parents' driveway, hesitating only a moment before backing up again.

Hallie headed back to town, pulling down the side street where the Maven Inn was tucked away. The inn had been resurrected from the gold rush days, with shutters and red paint specially treated to look almost as old as it really was. Home for now. She pulled out her bag, picked a clump of snow from a tree and pressed it against her eyes to help with the swelling. Hopefully the clerk would think it was just the cold that made her look as if she had been crying for days.

She handed Jake her credit card, suppressing the urge to call him by his first name. If Jamie turned her away when she returned to Caterina, maybe Maven would become her home again. As long as it wasn't really true that home was where the heart was.

***

It didn't take Hallie long to be sharply reminded of her reason for coming back to Maven. The nightmare came back with the force of the train that roared by the outskirts of town. She woke in the night, hearing the distant whistle that echoed mournfully in the distance.

She turned on the light and snuggled into the blankets more, wishing the heater in the old place worked better. Without leaving the bed, she leaned way over and pulled her suitcase from the nearby dresser. She dumped the contents out on the bed. The article and obituary had disappeared. She tried to remember if she had read them on the plane, but she couldn't recall thinking of anything but Jamie. Could she have left them at Caterina? Possibly. She took only a bit of reassurance in the fact that he would never find them in their hiding place: taped beneath the dresser in their bedroom.

At seven o'clock that morning she was sitting in the saloon-style restaurant drinking her fourth cup of coffee. Downright jittery by eight, she stepped out into a clear day with only a smear of thin clouds to interfere with the deep blue sky.

In a few minutes, she found herself staring at the auto shop again, wondering why the feeling of dread was creeping up her like a shadow. She shook it off and walked inside the cluttered waiting area that smelled of gas and stale smoke. When Alan walked out of the tiny office, she felt the blood drain from her face. It returned when she stepped forward and introduced herself.

"Hello, I'm Hallie DiBarto. I just moved into town."

His green deep-set eyes appraised her unashamedly before lazily wandering back to meet her eyes. "Yeah, I'm sure I've never seen you around here before." He smiled. "You're awfully tan for this time of year."

She glanced down at herself, trying to push away memories of beaches. "I, uh, tanning salons. I like to keep my color."

He moved a toothpick from one side of his mouth to the other with his tongue. "Won't find anything like that around here."

She shrugged. "It doesn't matter. Listen, I was just wondering if you needed anyone to do your books or office stuff."

He leaned back and stuck oil-tinged fingers into grimy jean pockets, a curious expression on his face. "As a matter of fact, I do need someone to take care of my books. How did you know?"

"Lucky guess?"

She knew he looked much better cleaned up and shaven, but she couldn't imagine what had drawn her to him so many months ago when he'd first moved to

Maven. Out of place was the thick, gold rope hanging around his neck. It was new, and as her eyes lingered on it, his hand moved to twist it around.

"When can you start?" he asked.

"Now. I need the job."

"This is only part-time."

"That's fine."

He showed her to his large cluttered desk and cleared a small place for her.

"Now don't mess with anything else around here, okay? I know where everything is, so I don't need anyone tidying up."

"I understand."

She sat at the desk where Chris had spent many hours doing his books, talking with him. As she was familiarizing herself with his system again, his presence leaning just above her made her gaze drift to him.

"What brings a sexy lady like yourself to this stinkin' place anyway?"

"Dreams," she said. "I always had a dream of living in a small town in the mountains. And I don't think this town stinks."

"You're new. Give it some time."

He lingered for a moment, as if weighing her answer. Finally, he walked out to the garage where, through the glass window, she saw him glide beneath a car. The nightmarish feeling gripped her insides, and a flash of her last conversation with Alan. *My name is Randy Vittone. What does it mean?*

When she got off work at three o'clock, she decided to find a place to live. First, she would drive by her old house. That would prove less emotional than her parents' house. Unless maybe there was a *For Sale* sign out front.

The dreaded sign was there, planted in the dead grass of the front yard. When she took a deep breath to read it, she exhaled and smiled. It said *ROOM FOR RENT*. She walked up the familiar concrete pathway, past the spot where pink honeysuckles and Indian paintbrush grew in the summer, past Phoenix's favorite shady spot.

When the door opened, Hallie saw a belly first. A slightly off-balanced Paula grinned as she leaned against the door frame. A very pregnant Paula with long light-brown fuzzy hair and blue eyes. Hallie's heart swelled, and she leaned over and touched her niece or nephew before catching herself mid-way.

"Oh, I'm sorry. I just couldn't resist."

Paula thrust her stomach out even more than Hallie thought possible. "Go ahead. Everybody does it. Are you here about the room?"

"Yes. I just moved into town, and I can already tell the Maven Inn isn't going to cut it."

Paula wobbled backward and waved her in. "I can see why. I'll show you the room, but you're going to have to bear with me. I go very slowly up these stairs. My husband usually does this, but he's out right now."

Kerry. What a goof, Hallie thought with a smile, remembering the five-seven blond electrician.

"I can find the way on my own, if that's okay. I don't want you to hurt yourself. Which room is it?"

"It's the one in the back, facing west. It has a nice view, with a bathroom of your own down the hall. I'll warn you, though, it is kind of small. And you're going to have to put up with..." She patted her belly. "The little one pretty soon."

"The end of December, right?"

"Yeah, good guess. Most people think I'm due any hour now."

Hallie walked up alone, wondering if it was such a good idea to live in her own house with her sister. She was ever so grateful to her parents for giving her house to Paula and Kerry, the two who needed it most. The room would be fine, she decided, without even opening the white door. She already knew it—her someday future nursery.

*****

Hallie had lived more than two weeks in a pseudo-life, dreaming about Jamie and a tubful of M&M's, having nightmares about bridges and death. Still, she was no closer to finding the answers about her death than when she'd first arrived in Maven. The thought of having these nightmares the rest of her life scared her almost as much as the possibility that she may have lost Jamie for nothing.

Paula brought a steaming bowl of oatmeal to the table and snapped her fingers to draw Hallie out of her thoughts.

"Did you have another one of those nightmares again?" Paula asked. "I didn't hear you scream last night."

"I'm really sorry about waking you up." She forced a laugh. "And you thought the baby was going to keep you up all night."

Paula sat down after scooping mushy brown stuff into the bowl in front of Hallie. "I don't mind really. It just scares me out of my wits until I realize someone's not murdering you. What are they about?"

Hallie looked at Paula's concerned face, and ventured, "I keep dreaming I'm driving off a bridge."

Paula's face went white, and Hallie feared she would faint and fall to the floor. *What a stupid thing to say.*

Paula was covered in goosebumps and shaking. "I can't believe you said that."

"I'm sorry. I didn't mean to—what did I do exactly?"

The sadness that crept over Paula's features made Hallie feel terribly guilty for bringing it up. But a trill of warmth shot through her, too. Her sister missed her, maybe as much as she missed Paula.

"How long have you been having those dreams?" Paula's eyes were wide and wild-looking.

"For a few months. Why?"

Paula put her hand to her heart, breathing deeply. "My—my sister died a few months ago. She drove off a bridge. I thought maybe her ghost was in the house and had possessed you. This is her house, you see. I didn't want anyone to sell it, so Kerry and I took over the payments."

"No, I don't think her ghost is around. I'm so sorry to hear about her death. Why did she drive off the bridge?"

Paula pushed her bowl of oatmeal aside. "They *said* she lost control of the car."

"But you don't believe that?" Hallie asked, trying to calm her excitement.

"No. And I think that damn boyfriend of hers..." Paula's eyes widened, and she slapped her hand over her mouth. "Sorry, you work for him. I shouldn't say anything."

"No, tell me. I owe him no loyalties. What about Alan?"

"He knows something. I'm not sure what, but he does. He tried to make it sound like she'd lost control of the car by being careless while crossing the bridge. I know—knew my sister. She always had this thing about crossing high bridges. In fact, she refused to even walk across the Royal Gorge when we were kids. Anyway, she would've been really careful going over that bridge."

"Why do you suppose he made it sound like it was her fault?" Hallie was trying hard not to sound too interested. Desperately interested.

"I don't know. But he out and out lied when the police were investigating. She called me just a little while before the accident. She sounded weird. Angry, shocked. I don't know. But she said she had to talk to me later that evening. When I ordered her to come right over, she said she had to meet Alan someplace in an hour. She..." Paula dabbed at her eyes with a wadded napkin. "She never made it to my house.

"But Alan denied she was meeting him. He said that maybe she was meeting someone else, like maybe on the sly. If he's good for anything, I think it's for lying. I know what my sister said, and she wasn't a cheater or a liar. Maybe he was just feeling guilty for sending her on the trip that ended her life. I don't know. She shouldn't have gone via Crystal Bridge anyway. There's a much safer way to get to Amberville, but it takes about a half-hour longer. I wonder why she didn't go that way."

Because she had to meet Alan to see proof of his innocence, Hallie wanted to say so badly she had to keep her finger in her mouth to stop the words. Why had Alan denied asking her to go to Amberville? Of course, he couldn't have told the authorities why she was going there.

Paula sighed hard, then used the corner of the table to push herself to her feet. "I'd better get over to Ma's. I told her I'd keep her company since she's laid up."

Hallie's heart quickened. "Laid up? Is she all right?"

Paula's mouth stretched into a frown. "She hasn't been all right since Chris died. Instead of paying attention to where she was walking, she was daydreaming and twisted her ankle. It's swollen up like a squash."

Hallie quickly wiped the forming tears from her eyes. She had glimpsed her dad in town once, and Charlene another time at the house. It was all she could do to keep herself from giving them a hug, telling them the truth about herself. She didn't think she could handle seeing her mother. Not now, not ever.

"Thanks for sharing your thoughts with me, Paullywog."

Paula stopped cold and stared with that wide-eyed expression again. "You called me Paullywog," she said softly.

"I did, I'm sorry. I had a friend in California named Paula, and I used to call her that. You remind me of her."

A tear slipped down Paula's cheek. "Chris used to call me Paullywog. She was the only one who did. Hallie, you remind me so much of her. Not the way you look, but the way you act and talk. Oh, I miss her. I miss her so much!"

Hallie slipped her arms around Paula, savoring the sisterly affection she thought she would never feel again. Her large belly pressed up against Hallie, and she longed to be part of the birth and raising of the youngster inside. She wanted Jamie, and she wanted to be Chris again, all at once.

When they parted, Paula wiped her eyes and laughed. "I got you crying, too. I'm sorry."

"It's okay," she whispered. "I lost my family, too. I

know how you feel."

Paula leaned over the white porcelain sink and splashed water on her face. "I try to be the strong one in the family. Only Kerry knows what a wreck I really am. And now you do, too."

"I'll keep it a secret." Hallie was good at that now. She leaned down and rubbed the protruding belly. "Cheer your mom up, okay? She needs it."

When Paula left, Hallie sat in silence. Through the tangle of emotions that wrapped around her, two words penetrated the wall of tears: *Goodbye, Chris.* She lifted her head, thinking of Mick sitting in jail. Did he believe her? Pressure built up around her heart, squeezing it in a grip of fear. What if he returned to Caterina? What if he attacked Jamie again, before realizing she wasn't there?

She glanced at the phone on the wall. *One call, just to make sure he's all right. I won't say anything, just listen to his voice and hang up.* She already knew that if she said a word, she'd want to tell him where she was, and then she'd have to explain why she was there. He wouldn't believe her. He'd hang up on her. Shaky fingers dialed the number, and she waited an eternity before the ringing started.

"Good mornin', Caterina," a sing-song voice said.

"J—" Hallie cleared her throat. "Jamie DiBarto's office, please."

"Just a moment, and I'll connect you up."

Her heart stampeded inside, her hands felt clammy. She squeezed her eyes shut when she heard him pick up.

"This is Jamie, how can I help you?" he asked in a voice that sounded so close.

She couldn't have said anything even if she wanted

to. Her throat was constricted, mouth dry.

"Hello, is anyone there? Hallie, is that—"

She slammed the phone down and fell in a heap on the linoleum floor, trying desperately to catch her breath. To hear his voice again, to hear him say her name. It broke her heart and filled it at the same time. She leaned her head against the cabinet, pressing her cheek against the cool surface. Would it ever be the same between them when she returned?

***

"You look depressed." Alan leaned into the doorway as soon as Hallie had arrived at work. "You okay?"

"Just a little homesick. I'll get over it."

His tall legs carried him quickly to face her across the desk piled high with papers. "Would you like to go out to dinner with me tonight? Maybe I can cheer you up. Hey, we could drive to Denver for the whole weekend, rent a limo, dance and party."

There was nothing blatantly lewd about his invitation, but for some reason it angered her. "I don't think so." When he stood back as if slapped, she added, "No one could cheer me up right now. I'd rather just be alone."

"Well, you know where to find me if you change your mind."

When he left, she realized why she was burning inside. To Hallie, it seemed like a year since she'd been killed in the accident. Chris had only been dead three and a half months, and Alan was drooling over another woman. Okay, it was her, but *he* didn't know that. She sat back and took a deep breath. Maybe she was over-reacting.

It was noon, and all the bills and paperwork were caught up. She rubbed her head, willing away the fatigue that was trying to get a foothold. Sleep had eluded her for over two weeks. To make matters worse, Jamie never left her thoughts for more than ten minutes. The longer she stayed away, the more Caterina seemed like a dream, and Jamie some fantasy man. Was he lost to her now?

When she dragged herself up from the desk, she knocked a stack of papers onto the floor. The article beneath it all looked familiar. She had read every line several times before in Caterina. It was the article about her accident. It had been ripped unceremoniously from the newspaper and left buried under three months' worth of debris.

Hallie dropped back down in the chair and started reading it again, hoping to find a clue now that she was closer to the story. From seemingly out of nowhere, a greasy hand snatched the article from her fingers.

"This should be filed away," Alan said tersely, stuffing it into the third file folder in the bottom drawer. He slammed the drawer shut and turned to face her. Instantly, the tense expression transformed into pure charm.

"I really should clean this place up. Look at the mess I've made you work in for two weeks. I promise it'll all be put away by tomorrow."

She leaned back in the chair, almost dizzy from his quick change of demeanor. Putting on her own casual mask, she asked, "Did you know her? The woman in the article?"

"Yes."

"Was she your girlfriend?"

Alan walked around to stand behind her. "We dated sometimes. You remind me of her a little. Which is weird because you don't look anything like her. You're much more beautiful."

She shivered and moved away. *Dated sometimes?* That's what he considered their relationship, eight months of seeing each other almost every day? She tried to hide her anger as she turned to face him, though her voice came out high pitched and strained.

"Were you close to her?"

His voice was smooth, soft. "I don't want to talk about her. She's dead."

Fury rose within her. "You son—"

Beep! They both jerked from the surprise noise as a van careened into the parking lot, the driver leaning on the horn. Hallie let out a sigh of relief, glad she didn't give herself away with what might seem to Alan as unaccountable hostility.

"I'll get back with you later. I've got to talk to Harry." He touched her elbow, effectively leading her out of his office. "Take the rest of the day off until I can get that office cleaned up."

As soon as he opened the van's tiny hood and stuck his head inside, she walked back to the filing cabinet. She opened the drawer and pulled out the third manila folder. The clipping about her accident had been crumpled where he had hastily jammed it in the file. There were other articles, but the sight of one made her heart stop beating for an instant. She didn't take time to read more than the word *MISSING*, but rather stuffed it into her pocket. It was the crumpled newspaper article she saw in her dreams. When she heard the door open, she knew it was too late to hide what she was doing.

"What the hell are you doing in my files?" Before he even finished his sentence, he had ripped the file from her hand, shoved it back in the drawer, and closed it, making a point of pressing in the locking button. Then he turned to her, his eyes blazing with demand for an answer.

"I, um, wanted to know more about the girl you dated. I'm sorry for snooping, Alan. I was just curious."

His teeth clenched together. "Don't be curious, Hallie. Remember what it did to the cat?"

Her eyes widened and she backed up toward the door, quickly dashing out of his office. She escaped to the restroom before he had a chance to follow her. That was not the Alan she had known. That look in his eyes was not mere irritation at one who was being nosy. He had something to hide, and that file contained the clues. But what did the article about her death have to do with it? And what about the article that made a crinkling noise in her pocket? She had to get out of there and read it.

She trembled as she leaned over the sink. Her face was pale, and she saw fear in the reflection looking back at her. What had he said about *curiosity*? And why did that statement ring an alarm bell inside her head? She composed herself and stepped outside to find Alan waiting for her.

"More threats, Mr. Messino?" she asked, trying hard to keep her voice even.

"I'm sorry. It's just that, well, I'm really funny about people going through my stuff. You understand that, don't you?"

Did your *Chris understand that, too?* she wanted to ask. She had to get out of there.

He cocked his head. "Are you all right? You look strange."

She forced herself to breathe again. "I'm fine. Just a little dizzy. Alan, it was wrong of me to nose through your file. It won't happen again."

He smiled, and she knew it was phony. His green eyes scrutinized her, trying to gauge her honesty. "No hard feelings, then?" She shook her head. "Me either. Let me take you to dinner tonight. You know, make peace."

"No, no. Thanks, but I really have a lot of running to do." Then, at his suspicious expression, she added, "How about lunch tomorrow?" She didn't know why, but she felt that she should allay his doubts.

His expression softened. "Good. Tomorrow, then."

She sucked in great gulps of cold air on the way to her car, worried that he had seen realization in her eyes. When she reached the road that led to her parents' house, she pulled off and sat in the quiet and pulled the newspaper clipping out of her pocket.

CHAPTER 18

He hated her, he loved her. Jamie couldn't get her out of his mind, no matter how hard he tried. Phoenix nearly tripped over himself to follow Jamie around the house, feeling just as confused about his mistress's absence as Jamie did. George chattered angrily in the tree, demanding Hallie's playtime. Jamie did his best to accommodate the little monkey, but just being around George reminded him of her, of the day she'd discovered him.

Her presence penetrated every corner and crevice of Caterina like never before. His special place on the rocks, the house, the office, the M&M's that still lingered in bowls on the restaurant tables. And the phone call that afternoon. He *knew* it was her, could feel her presence over the silent phone line. Why hadn't she said something, just to let him know she was all right? He had to talk to her.

He walked down the beach where the rocks formed a barrier and stretched out into the sea. Phoenix's tail brushed against his legs as he walked and sniffed, careful not to let Jamie get more than a couple of inches away. Jamie knelt down and scratched the pup's head for a few minutes, his eyes staring at nothing.

He stripped off his shirt and tucked it into the back of his jeans, letting the late afternoon sun warm his numb exterior. If he could walk away from her before, he couldn't do it now. He stretched his arms up and behind him, closing his eyes and remembering.

His eyes snapped open. *Am I going to sit here and wade through a self-constructed maze of pity until she calls or returns? Hell, I told her if she left, I didn't want her back. Pride be damned, I do want her back. I've got to let her know. She can finish whatever it is she feels she has to do, but I want her to know where her home is. Where she belongs.*

After more than an hour on the phone, he fell back on the bed. Joya didn't know where she was. Velvet didn't know. Hallie hadn't started a phone number of her own anywhere. She was gone, vanished. He stared blurry-eyed at the ceiling for a long time.

Finally, he rolled over and hung his head off the bed, letting the blood rush to his brain to help him figure this out. Where else would she have gone? She was born in California, had never lived anywhere else but Caterina, had hardly been anywhere. She hadn't charged the flight on her credit card.

A tearing noise drew his attention to the floor where Phoenix sat intently ripping a piece of paper to shreds. He offered the pup a firm *no*, and he retreated, duly chastised. Jamie had lost more receipts and notes to the dog's paper shredding habit. He picked up the soggy papers. Copies of two newspaper articles. When he idly unfolded them, the irrelevancy of the headline made him curious. He sat up and read the first one.

A woman named Chris Copestakes had been killed in a car accident in someplace called Maven, Colorado.

Some things were underlined, like the fact that her boyfriend Alan blamed her loss of control on her being upset. At the top, the word *MURDER* had been written in Hallie's handwriting. It was dated about three months earlier, at the time when she was in the hospital. In fact, the day after her stroke.

Alan. The name she'd screamed out once.

He set that one aside and unfolded the next one. He pieced the photo back together and studied the picture of Chris and her family. Kinky hair, round face, and a sweet smile. He had no idea who she was, or why her obituary was in their house. She didn't look the least bit familiar. Jamie read on:

> *It's not fair that I should have to say goodbye to my sister Chris. She was my best friend, the godmother to my baby-to-be, and a wonderful person. She could make herself one with nature, spending hours in the woods with the wild creatures she treated like family. She was going to school to learn how to protect them, and she took with her to class dreams of making our world a better place.*
>
> *When Chris cared about someone or something, she worked tirelessly to win them over, love them or take their pain away. She was always there, willing to take your burdens from you, with room left on her shoulders for your tears.*
>
> *The thing I regret most about her unfair passing is that she never got to really fall in love, never got to have a family of her own to share all the love she carried inside. Somewhere, the man who was destined to marry her is out there feeling an emptiness he can't explain, mourning a lost love he*

never found.

Those of us who felt her love will carry it with us always in our hearts. Me, Mom and Dad, Bernice, Charlene, Tubby, Phoenix, and Shelby will miss her more than life itself. She lives in us.

Paula Copestakes-Garth

He stared at the article, then read the words again. The first thing he realized was that it could have been written for Hallie...if she had died. Every word fit his wife perfectly, at least the post-stroke version of her. And the feeling of emptiness and mourning did fill him constantly. But Hallie had not died, had never been to Colorado, and did not have a sister.

Then there were the names of the dogs. Phoenix, the name she mumbled when she awoke from a nightmare and reached down to the floor. Tubby, Shelby, those names he'd heard before, too—at his mother's house when Hallie was crying to go home.

He ran his fingers through his hair, his head swimming in confusion. She must have read those names in this article. He wasn't even sure they were attached to dogs. So, she read the names and pretended they belonged to three dogs she never had. Okay, that was a good explanation. He looked at Phoenix, whose ears perked up at his glance.

"But why, why would she pretend to have three dogs? Why did she cry that night when she saw one of you guys at the dock? That was real. Say, where did you get this stuff, anyway?"

Jamie crawled down on the floor, exciting the pup who promptly retrieved a bone to play fetch with. After searching for a few minutes, Jamie found a piece of tape still clinging to the bottom of the dresser. He pulled it off and matched it to the rips on the pieces of paper. Obviously, the pup found it and thought it might be fun to pull it down and shred it.

He sat back down on the bed and stared at the article again, studying the word *MURDER.* She'd written a question mark first, then made it into an exclamation point. She had concluded that this Chris had been murdered. Except that nothing in the article hinted that she might have been murdered. Why did Hallie think that? Where did she fit in with this Chris?

His gaze went back to the article. Chris Copestakes drove off a bridge. Hallie's nightmares. They had to be connected. But how?

***

The next afternoon, Renee walked into Jamie's office and stood in the horizontal shadows the blinds cast. He was staring at a blank space on the wall with an even blanker expression.

"Hello. Is anyone in there?" she asked, knocking on air.

Jamie slowly pulled his gaze to the doorway. "What can I do for you?"

His voice sounded far away to him, as far away as his thoughts had just been. He blinked, then focused on Renee. She looked at the open door, then back at him with narrowed eyebrows.

"I'm sorry to disturb you, but I found something you should see." She stepped forward and laid the bill on his desk, pointing to a highlighted entry. "I thought it was an error and called the hotel. They said it was charged by Hallie. She wanted to pay cash, but they only take credit cards. I thought you'd want to know."

When his gaze saw the line, his heart stopped for a beat: Maven Inn, Maven, Colorado.

***

Hallie sat in the car near her parents' house. Her trembling fingers smoothed out the crinkled newspaper over her knee. She held it there to read, knowing her hands would be too jerky to hold it still.

Local Man Still Missing After Four Days

> *Alan Messino, a carpenter who has lived in the area for two years, is still missing after four days of searching. His only family, sister Marie Messino, suspects foul play. "We were very close. He wouldn't just take off like that. Yesterday I got a strange phone call, some guy mumbling that he was Alan and he had to get out of town for a while. It didn't sound like my brother." Investigators and volunteers have sent search parties out into the desert and will continue to look for Messino.*

The picture of Alan Messino was torn away, but she remembered how the man looked. Not like her Alan. Wait. She remembered. Pieces and flashes of memory from her last day as Chris filled in the holes.

She had ordered an Indian jug from a store in Southern Utah for her parents' anniversary. When she pulled the piece out of the box, several wads of newspaper fell onto the floor. The name Alan Messino caught her eye, the same name as her boyfriend.

She had been sure the name was a coincidence, but the date on the newspaper header was right around the time Alan had popped into Maven. She had wondered what he was running away from, feeling obligated to mend things between he and his sister. She decided to visit Marie, but first wanted to make sure this Alan was the same man she was dating. That town's newspaper was online, and she looked up the article.

Alan Messino was not *her* Alan. Or rather, her Alan was not Alan Messino. She had scrolled back two days to find the original article on Alan's disappearance and had nearly fallen off the chair when she read the headline next to a picture of a face she knew well. *Randy Vittone killed in fiery crash. Linked to bank robberies.* But Randy Vittone wasn't just a bank robber—he was the man Chris had been seeing for eight months!

The eerie realization had crept over her like a slimy monster from a horror flick. If Randy was living under Alan's name, and living *period*, then Alan must have taken the fiery fall for him. There had been a chance, a wee chance that the picture just looked similar to her Alan, and that Alan just happened to have the same name as the missing man's. She had to give him the benefit of the doubt before going to the police.

She had gone to Alan's shop and found him beneath a car, where she'd kicked his leg to get his attention. He'd taken the article from her, and the expression on his face told her his guilt. He *was* Randy Vittone. He had clutched her in his arms, begging for a chance to explain in the conversation she had remembered at Caterina.

"My name *is* Randy Vittone. Alan Messino isn't dead. He's the one behind this. Chris, he's blackmailing me into robbing the banks for him. I can't go to the police, but you can. Now that you know, I'll get you the proof you need, and I'll show you that Alan's not dead. If you

turn him in, then I'll be free, and we can get married."
He'd taken her hand, bowed over it. "You don't know
how hard it's been, all this time wanting you, but not
wanting to drag you into my problems. It's actually a
relief to get it out into the open."

She had wanted to believe he was an innocent pawn
in a dangerous game. Now she just wanted the truth.
Looking back, she could see the desperation in Randy's
eyes as he'd told her about Alan being alive. Alan was
dead, she knew that. Somebody had died in Randy's car.
Sitting in the car, his parting words rang in her ears:
"Goodbye, Chris. Drive carefully."

Hallie swallowed hard, and the words sank to the pit
of her stomach. The way he'd said those words, his last
words to her: "Goodbye, Chris." *Goodbye.* As in forever.

Her gaze darted around to make sure Randy wasn't
standing there outside her car. The windows were
fogged up, and everything looked eerie, white and
blank. Her fingers wrapped around the steering wheel,
helping to hold back a scream. Fear, anger, confusion.
Those feelings had been with her all along, haunting
her dreams and her life. Now she knew why. But wait.

She gained control of herself and took a deep breath.
Chris had left Randy's and headed to Amberville via the
Crystal Bridge. Presumably straight to Amberville, and
probably driving rather quickly. How had Randy pro-
cured a truck and caught up with her that fast, only
twenty-five minutes from his place? The only place
that catered to trucks that size was Sweet Alice's, and
that was at least ten minutes in the opposite direction.
It was impossible.

She drove back to Paula's in a daze. Bernice was visiting, and the two women were in the kitchen, laughing

and cutting up potatoes.

"Hi, Hallie. Have you met my sister Bernice? Hey, you all right?"

Paula stood at the foot of the stairs as Hallie walked straight to her room. "I'm fine. Just tired."

Not to mention confused, angry, lonely, dying from missing Jamie, and almost wishing she hadn't gotten that second chance. She quickly glanced up at the ceiling. *I take that back.*

***

Randy regarded her quietly when she walked in the office the next morning. She hoped he couldn't hear her heart slamming against her ribs, hoped he couldn't see the knowledge in her eyes.

"Good morning," she said softly.

"*Mm-hm,*" he answered.

He stood in the corner of the office with a clipboard in his hand, checking items off a list. She glanced at the bottom drawer in the file cabinet. She had the crumpled article in her purse and a keen desire to get it back where it belonged before he realized it was missing.

His green eyes surveyed her above the clipboard. "Hallie, you didn't take anything out of this office yesterday, did you?"

Too late. Her heart stopped, but she gained control over the fear that threatened to creep into her features. "No, why?"

"Just wondered." He smiled that phony smile again. "We're still on for lunch, aren't we?"

She returned a smile she hoped looked more genuine. "Oh, lunch. Sure, I'm planning on it." Under no circumstances could she give away her fears or suspicions. "Are we going to Alice's?"

He set the clipboard down and walked over. "Actually, I thought we'd go to my place for lunch."

She couldn't hide her discomfort at that suggestion. Especially remembering that the travel trailer he lived in sat on a rather desolate patch of land. "Uh, I don't think that's a good idea."

"Sure, it is. Besides, I already bought some fresh hamburger and rolls yesterday, a head of lettuce and tomatoes. Oh, you think I'm after a bit of afternoon delight, huh? Don't worry, I won't try anything."

He smiled and walked out of the office. It wasn't seduction she was worried about.

All morning she watched the minutes fly by, dreading each time the hand moved around the face of the clock. At noon, Randy washed his hands and sauntered into the office to fetch her. When he led her out to his new truck, she felt like the proverbial lamb.

The trailer was sloppy, but not disgustingly so. Pretty much the way it had always looked. After they ate, he put his feet up on the edge of the table and lit a cigarette.

"Where are you from?"

"California. A town called Oceanview." Her gaze darted everywhere except at Randy.

"Why did you come to Maven?"

"I told you, I'd always dreamed of living in a small town in Colorado."

His cigarette bobbed up and down between his lips as he eyed her through the smoke. "Why Maven, exactly?"

"Why all this chitchat?" she asked, perhaps too tersely. But, after all, she remembered how little of his past he had revealed to Chris.

He lifted an eyebrow. "Ah, do we have a past to hide?"

She leaned forward and met his gaze. "I don't know. Do we?"

His feet dropped from the table's edge, and he stood up. "Let's go."

Her heart jumped. "Where?"

"Uh, back to work."

He was watching her, and she assumed an easy smile that pushed her anxiety from the surface.

"Kewl. I'm ready."

Randy froze in the middle of slipping the coat over his shoulders. She bit her lip but managed to keep a casual expression on her face. After a moment of tense silence, he put the coat on and walked right up to her. She stared at him, forcing herself not to back away, even an inch.

"You know, Hallie, there's something about you. I don't know what it is, but I'm going to find out."

His voice carried a subtle threat, and his green eyes were like emeralds flashing with danger. Her courage ebbed, and she turned and walked toward the door, opening it. Then she turned back to him once she was breathing the cold icy air.

She gave him a tight smile. "You'll find out my secrets when I find out yours."

***

At quitting time, Hallie slammed the checkbook shut and leaned back in the chair with a sigh. She glanced at the bottom drawer of the file cabinet, then out the glass window to the shop. Randy was watching her. Oh, he was pretending to be working on a Jeep, but his hands were only moving enough to perpetuate the notion. Was he waiting for her attempt to put the newspaper article back?

She leaned out into the shop. "I'm taking off now."

"Sure. Have a good one."

"Thanks. Have fun with the Poker Putzes tonight."

She turned and started to leave, but he grabbed her arm just as she reached the door.

"How did you know about the poker group? And why did you call them the *Poker Putzes*?"

She shrugged. "I don't know. Those words just came out. I have no idea where they came from."

His eyes widened, and he backed up a few inches.

Until I find out what you had to do with my wreck, and until I can prove it, I might as well have some fun with you. Only Chris had called his buddies the *Poker Putzes*.

"G'night." She left him standing there gawking.

Once the cold wind whipped around her, the smile faded from her lips. She was playing with matches and she knew it. The dynamite was just around the corner. No more psyching out; she had to find some answers.

The junkyard was closed, and no wonder, with snow piled all over the cars and metal remnants. She stood in front of the gate, trying to find Chris's old GTO. The cold metal fencing bit into her bare hands as she searched. The crunched-up trunk of a white car in the back caught her eye. She shoved her hands into her coat pockets and walked nearer to get a better look. The car was obscured between two other piles of flattened cars.

"Hello!" she called, but only the sound of the wind whistling its way through car bodies howled back.

She looked for signs of a recent presence at the junkyard but saw none. The chain that held the gates together was loose, as though the person securing it was in a hurry. Hallie pulled at the bottom of the gate, stretching it away from its mate. The bottom hinge was rusted, and with a little effort, she pulled the lower portion far enough for her to crouch down and slip through.

The snow crunched beneath her boots, and she was sure that everyone in Maven could hear her. She picked her way between the piles of cars to the one on the far side and stopped short. The sight of the monstrosity squeezed the air right out of her lungs. With her arm, she shoved the snow from the hood and trunk, careful not to snag herself on the jagged metal. She stood back to survey the twisted horror.

Not one inch of her car remained unmarred. Shards of glass clung to the outer edges of the windows like thousands of broken teeth. The hood was smashed in enough to encroach on the passenger side. She inched up to the window and looked inside. The driver's door was ajar, still bent from the jaws of life apparently. The driver's seat was flattened out and pushed sideways. She almost expected to see blood, her blood, all over the seat, but there was none.

How did I even make it to the hospital?

Once the shock of the twisted metal wore off, she remembered what had led her there. She needed to find clues that a truck had hit the car. One side of the car was smashed in, flatter than the other areas. She couldn't tell where the truck had hit her, the side or back. If her nightmares weren't so vivid, she'd wonder if the semi hitting her wasn't her imagination.

Hallie stomped away from her car, not ever wanting to see it again. She wandered from pile to pile, plowing through snowdrifts. The metal creaking in the wind made her jump and look for another intruder, but she was alone. Some piles rose so high, she wondered how long it would take someone to find her if one collapsed on her. She kept walking, looking for—she halted, sucking in a cold deep breath.

The truck.

If the truck from her nightmares was black, this one was ashen gray from the torture of flames and intense heat. The paint was bubbled up in some places, non-existent in others.

The front corner was smashed in, and all along the side were dents. It had definitely been in a wreck. She walked around the other side, and her heart stopped beating for a moment when she saw the faint outline of green elf shoes beneath the crackled finish. Below that in green letters: *ELF PRODUCE. FRESH TO YOU.*

Her teeth chattered, but not from the cold. Whoever had last driven this truck was the person who murdered her. Her stomach churned. She had to tell someone. But who was going to believe her connection between the truck and Chris's car?

She would make someone figure it out, she thought, icy wind chilling her bones.

"Who the hell *are* you?"

Hallie's shoulders hunched up, and she fought the lightheaded feeling that threatened to make her faint at the sound of Randy's voice. She turned around, knowing her face was pale. He stood there, narrowed eyes filled with something akin to fear and anger. She glanced at the truck, then back at him, unsure how to play her hand. The wind picked up, howling viciously.

"I told you who I was."

He stepped closer, his own gaze flicking to the truck before zeroing in on her again. "Yeah, I know what you told me. But who are you really? Who sent you here?"

She pulled her hair out of her eyes. "No one sent me. I came here on my own."

"Because you dreamed of living in a town like this?"

"Yes."

"No. You show up at my garage and offer to do my books, *guessing* that I need help. You go snooping through my files, *taking* things from my files." He leaned closer, so close his warm breath fogged in front of her nose. "And now you're here, of all places, in the junkyard, looking at one particular car, and one particular truck."

She backed away. "I've looked at a lot of cars here. What's the big deal?"

He nodded toward the truck. "Ever seen that truck before?"

"Maybe I have, and maybe I haven't. What's your interest?"

He took another step closer. "It was stolen awhile back. The thief ran it into the side of a mountain, and it burst into flames. Maybe you know who stole it."

"You don't look like a cop to me," she said, standing tall and straight. "And you never answered my question. What's your interest in it?"

Before she could move away, he grabbed her arms. "Tell me who you are," he hissed.

"Get your hands off her," another voice said from a few feet away.

She knew that voice. Her heart jumped before she even looked to see Jamie standing there, rigid and ready to kill. *Jamie.* But ... how?

Randy's grip relaxed, but his fingers remained around her arms. "I don't know who you are, but I'm having a little fight with my girlfriend, so if you know what's good for you, you'll leave."

Jamie took a step closer. "I don't know who *you* are, but you've got your hands on my wife, and I'm not going anywhere without her."

Surprise registered on Randy's face, and with Jamie's bruises, he looked like a man who regularly tangled with others. Hallie took the opportunity to twist free and race to Jamie's side. Strong arms encircled her, but he remained facing Randy with stiff shoulders and a challenging stare. When Randy did nothing, Jamie steered her away to the front gates.

"Hallie DiBarto," Randy's voice called after them. Jamie kept walking, and she didn't look back. "We're not done yet. I will find out who you are."

She shuddered, but the security of Jamie next to her injected the courage that was now faltering inside her. They walked past her rental car to his, and before they reached it, Randy stalked to his truck, shooting her a threatening glare before jumping in and driving off.

Before she could turn back to Jamie, he wrapped his arms around her and pulled her into his warm embrace. "Before I say or ask anything, I just want to hold you."

She wanted to laugh, cry, scream. Instead, she soaked up the feeling of being with him again. It was stunning, unbelievable. It was a full minute before he finally moved back to look at her.

She ran her numb hands over his head. "You must be freezing!"

He glanced down absently. "I don't have many coats in Caterina. You're the one who's cold. Your teeth are chattering Let's get in the car."

He'd left it running, and the heat felt wonderful. But not nearly as much as seeing him did.

"How did you find me?"

His eyes widened. "You're going to ask *me* questions first?" He took a deep breath. "I found credit card charges from the Maven Inn."

"They wouldn't take cash. I couldn't believe it."

He shook his head. "You paid cash for everything so I wouldn't find you."

"It wasn't to hide my tracks. I didn't want to stick you with the charges."

He gave her an exasperated sigh, and she saw the raw pain in his eyes. "I don't care about the money."

She touched his cheek. "You thought I was hiding from you. I'm sorry. It never occurred to me that you'd try to find me, especially after you told me not to come back."

He took a deep breath. "And you weren't going to give me a chance to change my mind?"

She smiled then, biting her lower lip. "Do you think after all we've been through I would give up on you that easily? I just ... I had to take care of some things here before I could live in peace. I couldn't explain it to you because you would think I was crazy and send me away to the Sharp Rehabilitation Center."

"The bridge nightmares?" She nodded. "Well, I'm here now. Can you explain now why you left? Why I found my wife standing in a junkyard clutched in the arms of some greasy thug?"

She inhaled deeply, giving herself a moment to think. Jamie would never believe the truth. Maybe a half-truth would be easier to digest.

"A little more than three months ago a woman was run off a nearby bridge and died."

"You mean Chris."

"You know? About Chris?"

"I found the article and her obituary."

"How in the world did you find them?"

"Phoenix outed you. Remember, he has a paper fetish. He also likes to crawl under dressers and things. So, go on, what about Chris? The article never said anything about her being run off the road. Her boyfriend, *Alan*, said she lost control of the car because she was upset."

She felt the blood rush to her cheeks. "I—she was not upset. Well, she *was* upset, but she didn't lose control of the car. A truck ran her off the bridge."

"How can you be so sure? Three and a half months ago you were in California. You've never even been in Colorado."

"I, well, in a way I was. You see, I had these dreams about the accident, you know, the ones about being run off a bridge. And I knew Alan—Randy, had something, well, back then I thought he..." She dropped her head, rubbing her fingers across her temples.

When she lifted her head, her insides tightened at the penetrating look Jamie was giving her. In an exhale, she said, "I'm Chris. I know you're not going to believe me, and I don't expect you to. I just ... I can't dance around it anymore, and now that you're here..." Tears flooded her eyes, tears of relief and of sadness that when he knew the truth, he wouldn't want anything to do with her.

She waited for something, a word, an action. He just sat there and looked at her. Behind those blue eyes raced a thousand thoughts, all hidden from her. Then he reached out and touched her wet cheek with his thumb.

In a ragged whisper, he asked, "How?"

Her heart filled like a helium balloon, causing her to inhale sharply. "You believe me?" she whispered.

"I knew you were different, but I never imagined it was anything like this." He shook his head. "I don't know. I couldn't imagine anything like this. But when I read that obituary, it was you. The dogs, the way she was. And the accident, your nightmares about bridges. And that time you screamed out Alan's name. You looked like my wife, but you felt different." His fingers traced the lines of her face. "You're really someone else in there? A completely different person?"

"Yes. I'm Chris Copestakes, I was born here in Maven, I went to the community college to become a forestry technician, I had three sisters, three Shelties, and when I was twenty-three, I was murdered."

His eyes looked luminous, taking in every word, every movement. "But you came back?"

She touched the hand that was pressed against her cheek. "Do you remember that night at Captain Morgan's in California? When I told you that I had come back from death for you? That was true. On the way to Heaven, God told me I had a task, and I heard a voice say, *Find his heart*. Then I woke up in Hallie's body, and you were there in my room. I came back for you, Jamie. Because you needed a second chance, too."

She realized that the gleam in his eyes was actually a film of tears, and that made her eyes water even more. His hand slid down her arm, taking her hand and pressing it against the softness of his lips.

He squeezed his eyes closed. "Everything I said,

everything I did … I said a lot of mean things to you, I told you to leave me alone. But you stayed."

She leaned over and touched her mouth to his. "Because I loved you. I wanted you for me, not just because you were legally my husband."

"Then why did you leave me when everything was perfect?"

"Because inside me, it wasn't perfect. The nightmares kept telling me that my death wasn't an accident. I knew I wouldn't have any peace until I found out what really happened."

"And the jerk I found you with?"

"That's Randy. The man I knew as Alan Messino."

"The Alan in the article? Chris's—your boyfriend?"

"Former boyfriend."

She told him what she'd found out months earlier, filling him in on all the pieces of the puzzle except one. "I don't know how he could have stolen the semi and caught up to me by the time I reached Crystal Bridge."

Jamie pulled at a loose thread on his green sweater, deep in thought. "According to the article, Paula said you were meeting Randy, which he denied. She couldn't prove...hey, wait a minute. Where did you call her from?"

"I don't even remember calling her."

"But you stopped somewhere to call. That would give him some time."

"Yeah, but not that much time." Her eyes widened as the final piece of the memory jigsaw puzzle slid into place. "My tire went flat. I stopped and put on the spare. There was a gash in it; maybe a knife slash. He cut my tire, and that gave him the time he needed." Then the blood drained from her face. "Oh my God, Randy really did kill me. How are we going to explain all this to the police? Will they ever believe us?"

"It's going to be tricky, trying to explain how you know all this when you just moved to town. We've got to get that file from Randy's office."

She looked at Jamie. "No, you've got to go back to Caterina. Dammit, you shouldn't even be here!"

"Of course, I should. Despite whoever you are inside, you're still my wife." His eyes blazed with determination. "And because of who you are inside, I love you. I'm staying with you."

"No, Jamie, this is my problem. I don't want to drag you into it. Look what I've already done, what with Mick attacking you. This is my fight, and I've got to do it alone."

He leaned closer, his eyes narrowing. "The hell you are."

"*Hill.*"

"No, the *hell* you are. You think after what I saw earlier, and after what you just told me, that I'm going to leave you to deal with this by yourself? I think you know me better than that."

She didn't want to drag him into this. But she didn't know what she would have done if Jamie had obeyed her and left.

"Jamie—"

"Don't argue with me, woman."

"I was going to say, I love you."

He pulled her hard against him, and for an instant, she had a crazy thought that the sound of crashing glass was the sound they'd made when they came together. It wasn't. It was the crowbar that was starting to swing in through the open window again.

CHAPTER 19

Hallie felt the sting across the back of her head before Jamie shoved her down and grabbed hold of the swinging crowbar. Dizziness swarmed in her brain amidst the grunts of the two men above her battling for the crude weapon. Anger, fast and furious, raced through her. Randy had taken her life before, and now he meant to take it again—along with Jamie's.

She reached for the door handle and shoved it open, toppling Randy onto the snow-covered ground. Before he could get to his feet, she jumped out and leaped on top of him, pounding her fists into his face.

"You son of a bitch! I am not going to let you kill me again!"

His green eyes widened, registering confusion. After that, everything happened too fast. She saw Jamie in the corner of her eye, then Randy twisted around and suddenly she was pinned beneath him with a knife at her throat. The horror in Jamie's eyes matched the fear in her heart. He froze.

Randy gasped, his eyes shifting from Hallie to Jamie. "Don't come an inch nearer, or she'll be coloring the snow red."

Jamie raised his hands, but his voice remained harsh. "Put a scratch on her and die."

"You might be bigger than me, but I've got the knife." He pressed the blade harder against her throat.

She found herself memorizing every feature on Jamie's face, pressing the image into her mind to take with her to Heaven. She wanted to plead but was afraid to move for fear the blade would cut her.

Randy nudged her. "Whoever you are, get in the truck. Both of you."

She wanted Jamie to run, but she could tell by the look in his eyes he wasn't going to leave her. He walked to the truck and slid in, never once taking his eyes off her.

"The driver's side!" Randy barked in her ear, making her flinch. "Okay, you get up slowly. And no more attempts at being Superwoman, or you won't get a chance to say goodbye to your hubby, got it?"

She didn't answer, just got to her feet along with him. He shoved her along the icy ground toward the black truck. The sky started spitting half-frozen water, reminding her only then how cold she was. She slid into the cab next to Jamie, and Randy squeezed in and closed the door. The knife was still pressing against her throat.

"Start the truck and head east," Randy ordered.

Jamie complied, pulling out of the parking lot and onto the narrow road. It hurt to look at him, to feel his arm against her shoulder, and know that they would never get to explore a new life free from old hurts and deception. Her heart felt like a rubber ball, hard and tight inside. If she would have just left it alone, lived with the nightmares, this wouldn't be happening.

Randy gestured. "Turn down that road."

She knew where they were going: his trailer. It was hidden by a stand of evergreens that encircled it half-moon style. The truck struggled through the snow on a road that was never plowed except when Randy cared to do it himself.

"We're home, kids!" Randy chimed before yanking her out of the truck backward. When Jamie moved in retaliation, the knife took its former position, biting into the skin of her neck. "Watch it, hero."

Her inadvertent cry restored Jamie's calmness, though she saw the muscles in his throat straining against his skin, holding back his fury.

They stomped through the snow and flurries to the aluminum trailer like a party of mourners, Jamie in front. When he reached the dilapidated wrought-iron steps, he turned.

"You've got the key." Randy pointed to the keyring Jamie held. "Open the door."

Jamie's gaze lingered on her for a moment before turning and trying the different keys on the ring. When he found the right one, he turned the key. Her head spun at the speed in which Randy moved. Before she realized what was happening, he grabbed a broken bar from the steps and slammed Jamie in the back of the head with it. He dropped to his knees, then fell to the ground.

"Jamie!"

Randy caught her arm and jerked her backward. "Help me get him into the trailer."

"Oh, God, not again." Blood colored Jamie's blond hair.

"Lift his head and help me get him inside. Or do you

want me to drag him feet first?"

She gently lifted Jamie's head and shoulders and kicked the door open. They laid him on the worn green carpet in the living room. Randy grabbed her arm and yanked her outside into the cold again. They walked to the tiny woodshed, and her heart shuddered as she tried to remember what he kept there. Thankfully, he reached in and only grabbed a coil of rope. *What small favors I'm grateful for now.*

When they walked back in the trailer, Jamie was moaning. She leaned down and touched his face, willing his eyes to open.

"Wah, wah." Randy jerked her down a narrow hall to a bathroom the size of a kitchen cupboard. "You're killing me. Sit down, behind the toilet."

"What are you going to do with us?"

"I'm working on a plan. I wasn't exactly planning on house guests."

"If you're busy, we can always come back later."

"Smart asses die first."

She thought of escape. She could push him out of the way, rouse Jamie. No, not enough time. Besides, she was trapped, Randy between her and the doorway. She squeezed between the shower bin and toilet. Randy crouched down and secured her with the rope to the back of the toilet, running it around the porcelain base.

"Jamie! Jamie!" she screamed, hoping to wake him before Randy could reach him. It was their only chance.

Randy cinched the knot and tore out of bathroom. She couldn't even wriggle. She heard a thump, something breaking. Jamie was conscious again. Fear gripped her insides, and she struggled to get free. Then she heard the gunshot. Every muscle collapsed and left her near fainting.

"Nooooo!" The sound echoing against the walls.

Her body went cold and numb. Seconds ticked by, and she restrained herself from calling his name.

Jamie appeared around the corner, and she wanted to cry out with relief. Behind him, Randy pushed Jamie forward into the bathroom, holding a gun to his head.

"Jamie, are you all right?"

"I'm fine. Are you okay?"

She was too busy looking for gunshot wounds on his body to answer with more than a nod. When she saw the blood on his head, panic shook her. *No, he can't be shot in the head. He wouldn't be standing there, wouldn't be talking to me.*

Randy tied Jamie up between the toilet and the cabinet, a space barely suitable for a child, much less a man of Jamie's size. All the while, Randy had the gun trained at Hallie to insure Jamie's cooperation. In his eyes, she saw determination, anger, but he saw that gun pointed at her.

Randy tied the final knot. "Don't you two look cozy?"

She glared at him, her fingers flexing, aching to scratch out his eyes.

"What do you want from us? We haven't done anything to you."

Randy rested the barrel of the pistol against his chin in a thoughtful way. "No, but you were going to do something to me, weren't you? How did you know about the car and the truck? Who sent you here?"

She pressed her lips together, not wanting to satisfy his curiosity.

"You're going to die anyway. Don't you want me to know why you're here?"

Hearing those words ... "Nobody sent me here. I came on my own."

"Hallie," Jamie warned.

"I do want him to know why I came here. I know you're Randy Vittone, and that you set up Alan Messino to die in your place after you robbed some banks. I know you killed Chris Copestakes because she knew the truth."

Randy's eyes widened, and his mouth hung open until he clamped it shut. "How the hell—"

"No, Randy, it's how in Heaven I know. When you killed Chris, she went to Heaven and got a second chance. I'm Chris."

Randy blinked hard. "No. You're making this up, playing some head game because you think you can talk your way out of this."

"I don't care whether you believe it or not."

"Where did we meet?"

"Cheech's Pizza Parlor. I was with Toni and Jeff, and you joined us for a sausage and anchovy pizza. You were born in Georgia, but your parents died, and you took off and never returned. That's what you told me, anyway. I used to call your pals the Poker Putzes because Mac, Bob, and Kurt *were* putzes. The only personal thing you ever told me was that you hated rich people and wanted to be richer than them so you could rub their faces in it like they always did to you. You just never told me you were going to murder and rob your way there."

Randy leaned back against the wall. "If I thought Heaven and Hell existed, I'd almost believe you."

"You'll believe in Hell soon enough," she said.

He laughed, but his expression was still dumbstruck.

"I was born in Alabama. My mother was a hooker and my father a bum who beat me for kicks. Mom decided that hooking was better than getting hit, so she left me with dear old Dad. I took off when I was fourteen and headed to Utah. I survived by robbing little old ladies and then convenience stores. Banks were the next logical step except I panicked and shot a manager. When the cops got too close, I found someone who fit my type and let him die for me so I could get a new start."

He leaned closer to Hallie, and she shrunk away. Continuing, he said, "But that didn't work, because when I moved here, I ran out of money, and it was too tempting to pick up where I'd left off. I was good at it. So, *Chris*, would you have gone out with me if I'd told you my real-life story?"

She backed away even more, ignoring his question. Dark and dangerous, that was what had attracted her to Randy. She hadn't realized how dark and how dangerous.

Randy leaned back against the wall again. "You want to know what I'm going to do to you? I've been working this through since we left the junkyard." He smiled in a sinister way. "I can't take all the credit. I saw it on a television show. I've already turned on the gas. The police will think there was a leak, and poor Hallie happened to be over at my place when it blew. Think how much fun the town will have with that gossip." He lifted a wallet. Jamie's wallet. "Then off I go."

Her heart pounded with fear and dread, but anger fueled her mouth. "No one's going to believe that Jamie is you. They'll test the remains for DNA." The thought of it, investigators picking through their ashes, their *re-*

mains, turned her stomach.

"Honey, this place will be an incinerator. There's not going to be enough left to identify. Besides, there'll be no reason to suspect otherwise. Your car will be here, along with my truck. I already told my buddies how I got the hot chick who's working for me to come here and have lunch." His mouth twisted into a leer. "How we got it on."

"My people will track me here," Jamie said through tight lips. "They'll figure it out."

"But they're going to find your car in New Mexico. Hallie, or Chris, or whoever you are, you should have learned the first time to keep your nose out of other people's business."

"*Other people's business?* You killed me! When I came here, I only knew that my death wasn't an accident. It wasn't until later that I remembered what you had done and figured out how you did it. You think I could walk away from that?"

He looked at her, speculating. "All I can say is, next time—if there is a next time—don't come looking for me, because I'll have an eye out for you."

He walked out and closed the door, shutting them into the tiny space. She started shaking. No more talk. No more explaining, and begging wasn't going to help.

"Jamie, he wasn't lying about the gas. I can smell it!"

"*Shhh.*"

He nodded toward the door. The knob was jiggling. After a few moments, it stopped. Footsteps led outside, and the door slammed shut. The crunch of his shoes on snow sounded outside, fading.

She strained to listen. "I haven't heard his truck start. Wait, he said he was leaving it here. He's probably going to walk to the junkyard to get my car."

"Walk? In this weather?"

"I know this area. If he cuts through the woods, he can get there in no time. Then he'll be back..." She took a stuttering breath. "I'm so sorry I got you into this."

"Hush. You didn't get me into anything. It was my choice to come here."

"Are you all right? He didn't shoot you, did he?"

"No. He probably didn't want the police to find a bullet in my bones. Sorry," he said when her head drooped. "When I heard you scream, I tried to get up, but he was right there. He pulled the gun from beneath the couch cushion. When I lunged at him, he shot it over my head."

"Is your head still bleeding? I was so worried when he hit you. How many times can you take a hit on the head?"

He managed a wry smile. "It was in a new spot this time."

"You're awfully cavalier for someone about to die."

She saw a spark in his blue eyes. "Because I know we're *not* going to die."

He lifted his hands, free from their constraints. Her heart leaped into her throat. He un-wedged himself out of the tight spot and freed her. "He didn't tie the ropes that well, which may have been intentional. In any case, I don't think he suspected we'd get out quite this fast. I was working on them while he was talking."

"But why would he tie them loose enough that we could escape?"

"I'm not sure, but remember, he saw it on television once. Who knows what trick he picked up." As she reached for the door, he said, "Don't touch it!"

She froze. "Why?"

He knelt down and looked at the doorknob, then ran his fingers along the edge of the door.

"We might set off some kind of booby trap. Look, between the door and the jamb. There's something lodged there."

She studied the two rows of red bumps. "Matches. And sandpaper. Oh, God, I would have set the whole thing off if I'd opened the door."

"I don't know if it would spark, but we don't want to find out." He turned to the tiny window high above the shower. "Do you think you can squeeze through if I help?"

"Not with baby oil and a plunger. But water would do the trick."

Jamie snapped his fingers. "Good thinking. Wet matches can't ignite."

They found a cup and filled it. After three cups' worth thrown into the crack, he said, "The match tops are disintegrating."

Very, very slowly they pushed open the door. The soggy matchbook flopped to the yellowed linoleum with a soft thud.

"Jamie, it's snowing out there. I can find you a coat—"

"We don't have time. He'll be back anytime with your car."

They stepped outside, and she pulled in a lungful of air as she searched for Randy. His truck was parked where they'd left it, the engine ticking as it cooled.

She pointed. "There are his footsteps. He's definitely walking to the junkyard. If we follow his trail, he'll be driving back here by the time we get to your car."

They trudged through snow toward the thicket of

trees. The sky was white, and the flurries made everything hazy and surreal. Jamie's hand felt cold when she took it in her own. She knew he had to be freezing.

The junkyard came into view, Jamie's rental car sitting alone. Over the crunching of the snow and her breath coming fast and hard, she heard another sound. An engine!

"Get in quick!" Jamie called, but he didn't have to tell her.

When they reached the car, her SUV came up over the incline. Had Randy seen them? Why had he doubled back? She leaped in and scooted over so Jamie could jump in behind the wheel. He turned the key. The engine struggled, then died out. She watched the car get closer.

"Come on, come on." Jamie twisted the key again.

The engine whined, then rumbled to life. Just as he put it into gear, Randy slammed into the side of the car. She screamed.

Jamie jammed the gas pedal, and the car jerked forward. "Hold tight."

The SUV's headlights cut through the dimness behind them. Jamie gripped the wheel, intent on his driving.

God, can you hear me? I haven't spent enough time with Jamie yet. Please get us out of this alive! Please. She stared beyond at a sign: Crystal Bridge. Barricades blocked the way, advising of a safer, alternate route in the snow.

"Jamie, no! This is the bridge I was killed on."

"I can't turn back. He'll smash us while I'm trying to turn around."

"No, no, no," she kept chanting, knowing he wouldn't, *couldn't* turn around.

She clutched the seat with a death grip. They pushed past the barricades and onto the icy bridge. The ravine gaped on either side, ready to devour them. The tires slid for a second before gripping the road. She turned to see behind them. Headlights coming closer. Closer.

Randy pounded into the back of their car, sending them into a spin. The sound of crumpling metal echoed in her head. It was her nightmare all over again. Her death all over. She closed her eyes as the car headed toward the railing. Over. They hit a post with a thud, throwing her against the door.

"Hallie, get out of the car!"

Her eyes snapped open. They were stationary, not falling down. Her SUV was backing away. She heard the gears grind and the tires spin when Randy threw it into drive. Jamie pulled her from the car just as the SUV came smashing forward, sending Jamie's rental car careening down the bridge to rest a short distance away.

Jamie clutched her hand as they ran beside the safety railing. Randy came at them again, and she saw the wild expression on his face.

As Randy closed in, Jamie pushed her backward, where she slipped and fell. And where she watched with horror as the SUV skated across the ice right toward Jamie. The brake lights flashed, then remained steady as the car skidded onward.

At first, it seemed that Jamie was diving toward the vehicle, and she thought she must be losing her mind. Landing on the ice with his arms in front of him, Jamie slid between the tires. The SUV drove over him and broke through the safety railing. But the car didn't fly off the edge. Instead, it teetered over the ravine, precariously balanced between life and death. The front wheels spun in mid-air. Somewhere under that car was Jamie.

She struggled to her feet. Through the thin fog on the windows, Randy slowly turned and glared at her. Then he grabbed for something on the seat. The gun, aimed at her.

The window shattered. She dropped. The car lurched forward as the bullet cut through the air beside her. In slow motion, the SUV rolled off the bridge.

She didn't want to look, but her eyes betrayed her. Randy's expression through the shattered opening of glass was terror. His guttural scream pierced the air as the SUV fell from view. Through the foggy air, the sound of compressed metal seemed far away; inside her, it was all too close.

"Jamieeeeee!" she screamed through tears and terror and grief and made her way over to him.

He was lying between the slushy tire tracks. She dropped down beside him, taking him in as he sat up. No sign of anything crushed or broken.

He patted himself. "It feels like I'm all right. I wasn't sure how that was going to work."

She threw herself into his arms, holding him tight. "I thought you'd gone crazy." Then she pushed him back. "What were you doing?"

"When I saw him bearing down on us, I knew he wouldn't be able to stop once he hit us. So, I waited until the last minute, pushed you away, and dropped down flat. It looked as though there was enough clearance beneath the car. I figured, if I did get run over, it'd be better than getting hit and pushed over the side. And you'd be safe."

"Jamie, you're crazy. I put you in danger and you save

my life by risking your own."

He drew her close again and kissed her frozen nose. "You're worth it. But before I could even rejoice in being in one piece, I saw the gun aimed at you." He got to his feet, then pulled her up, smoothing the hair away from her wet face. "I pushed up on the bumper with my feet." His face paled as he looked at the edge. "I sent him over."

"It was the only way. He was over the edge in more ways than one."

The wind shook the broken railing, making it appear to wave her closer. She took a step toward it.

Jamie tightened his hold on her hand. "Don't look."

"I have to. I have to be sure."

The wind cut through them like a thousand icicles. They stood, arms wrapped around each other, and looked down. Her car had gone over near the shallower edge. The SUV had fallen in the middle of the ravine, where it was deep and rocky. Pieces of it were scattered in the snow, chrome and glass and metal. The bulk of it was a mass of twisted metal, hardly recognizable as a vehicle.

"It's awful," she said, her voice barely audible.

"Now he can't haunt your dreams anymore."

She snuggled closer to Jamie, only nodding in agreement.

"Thank you for coming," she whispered.

"I wasn't going to lose you again, Hallie." He kissed the top of her head. "We have to figure out what we're going to tell the police."

She nodded, then looked up at him. "I want them to know who he is, what he did." She reached into her pocket and pulled out the crinkled newspaper article.

"I have the proof. I just have to come up with the story that explains how Hallie DiBarto figured it out."

"We'll figure it out. First we need to get off this bridge."

***

The car pulled hard to the left, but Jamie managed to steer it with one arm. The other was around Hallie's shoulders, holding her close. He moved only to turn the radio on, a welcome respite from the events of the last few hours. He smiled, and she lifted her head to look at him.

Bing Crosby sang *White Christmas*.

"It's Christmas Eve," she whispered.

"And it's white." He nodded to the snow falling all around. "So, this is where you grew up?"

"It seems like forever ago when I was sitting in a classroom learning the effects of acid rain and what levels the water boatman could survive as opposed to the salamander. Or seeing bunny tracks after a fresh snowfall. Or when the mountains look like they're on fire with the aspens turning in the fall. It was literally a lifetime ago."

"I'm sorry it was all taken away from you."

"In some ways it's sad." She looked at Jamie. "But in some ways, it's wonderful. I would never have met you if I hadn't died."

"I'm not glad you died, but I sure am glad you came my way."

She sat up straighter, looking around, soaking in the surroundings and music. "You know, it's funny. I don't feel like I belong here anymore. I belong with you, in Caterina."

His heart felt warm and full, and he leaned over and kissed her. "Yes, you do. Should I call you Hallie or Chris?"

"Hallie. That's who I am now."

He ran his finger down the bridge of her nose. "Yes. Yes, you are." He traced down to her soft mouth and lingered there. He knew in his heart she was someone else, but it was still incredible. "Show me where you grew up."

Her smile faded. "The last time I saw my parents' house, I felt so sad and lost."

"I'll be with you this time. I'll make sure you're not sad and lost."

She looked at him, and he saw apprehension turn to trust in her deep blue eyes. "Okay."

They followed a winding road to a wooded section with ranch houses and barns. The house she pointed to looked warm and cozy, and he tried to picture the girl he'd seen in the article living there, throwing a Frisbee to her dogs on a lazy summer day. A Christmas tree twinkled in the window. Five cars were parked outside. He got out of the car.

She got out, too. "Where are you going?"

"Just want to get a closer look." He looked around at all the white, like a winter wonderland. "I've never heard this kind of silence before. It's absolute."

She smiled. "I loved going outside when it snowed like this and listening to the silence. No one understood that. Except you."

He nodded toward the house. "Have you seen your parents yet?"

"No, I couldn't handle that. I lived with my sister, in my old house, and that was hard enough. I've seen my other two sisters, but I avoided them. My mom broke her ankle because she wasn't paying attention to where she was walking. You don't know how much I wanted to come here and tell her that her daughter isn't dead."

"Why didn't you?"

"When I came here, I promised myself I wouldn't tell anyone. The truth is too strange, crazy, bizarre. My father has a weak heart, and I'm sure my death put enough strain on him. He'd think it was a hoax and get angry and maybe have a heart attack." She stared at the house. "And maybe I'm a little afraid that they wouldn't accept me now."

The silence was broken by three exuberant Shelties racing to the edge of the fence, snarling and barking. Hallie knelt down and put her arm out. Jamie tensed, ready to pull a crazy woman out of a pack of wild dogs. When they reached her, they stopped and stretched their noses toward her while keeping their bodies as far away as possible. Shiny black noses sniffed her hand, clothes, hair. Tails started wagging, and they crowded in on her. She squealed in delight when they covered her in wet kisses and wet paws, all three climbing up on her crouched knees to get closer.

She looked at their faces and greeted each one. "Tubby, Shelby. Phoenix. I've missed you guys so much!"

"Believe me, she has."

He leaned against a fence post and watched the woman he loved, already planning to have two more Shelties flown to Caterina. So entranced was he with the scene, he didn't notice the woman approach.

"My goodness, I've never seen them act like that toward a stranger!"

Hallie hastily wiped her tears with the back of her hand and stood to greet the woman with the kind hazel eyes and curly brown hair. She was limping, and her foot was bulky beneath her rubber boot.

"Guess they know I'm a dog lover," Hallie offered.

Her mother watched the dogs clamor around Hallie's feet with a shocked expression. "No, they don't take to people that easily. I heard them barking and came out to see what the ruckus was about. This is just amazing."

If Jamie had doubted Hallie before, which he hadn't, he knew now that she was telling the truth. The tears flowed freely, and the heartache showed like a thunderstorm in her eyes.

When Mrs. Copestakes looked up and saw Hallie's tears, her expression softened. "Hon, are you all right?"

Jamie stepped in. "She recently lost her parents. You look a bit like her mother."

The woman touched Hallie's arm, causing more tears to flow. "I know how you feel. My daughter Chris was killed in a car accident a few months ago." Her own eyes began filling. "I'll never get over it, my little girl, gone." Then she laughed through her tears. "Look at us, standing here boohooing on Christmas Eve." She pulled a hanky out of her pocket and dabbed her eyes. "You two aren't from around here."

"I've been renting a room from your daughter Paula."

"Oh, yes, I've heard about you. Hallie, right?"

She nodded, her jaw tight from her attempt to keep her emotions from her face, he guessed.

The woman smiled. "She thinks a lot of you. We're all inside now, pretending to be happy. It's pretty pitiful if you ask me. Why don't you come in for hot cocoa and Christmas songs? We can be pitiful together. I'm sure Paula would love to see you." She sighed. "Being with family is what the holiday is about. As crazy as it sounds, I've felt my daughter's presence lately." She looked up at the flurries coming down. "We'll toast to our loved ones, both here and gone."

Jamie glanced at Hallie and saw the subtle shake of her head. He turned back to Mrs. Copestakes. "We'd love to. Thank you for asking."

Hallie shot him a chastising look. "We probably should—"

He squeezed her hand. "We have time." Time to talk to the police, to sort through the tangle of truth and lies. No one would be going across that bridge anytime soon, and Randy was no doubt dead. "Let's make a toast to family, both lost and found."

With Hallie's hand gripped in his, he followed her mother to the house. The Copestakes family was about to get the most amazing Christmas present. He had already gotten his.

Thank you so much for reading *Until I Die Again*. If you enjoyed it, please consider telling your friends and posting a review on Amazon.com, BookBub.com, and/or Goodreads.com.

Find links to more stories in the Love & Light collection and other series by Tina at www.WrittenMusings.com/TinaWainscott or www.TinaWainscott.com.

SNEAK PEEK

The carat diamond on her wedding set sparkled as Hallie DiBarto ran her fingers across the black velvet surface of the sofa. Not the appropriate distraction to avoid her husband Jamie's eyes, she realized, and shifted her vision to her silk stockings. She deserved the bitterness those blue depths radiated at her. But if she didn't go through with this, who knew what Mick would do to her. Or to Jamie.

"I want a divorce," she said softly, her words absent of emotion. She would have to put more meaning into them to convince him. If only her migraine would subside enough for her to summon her acting skills.

As it turned out, she didn't need to.

"Absolutely," he told her.

That word sent a chilled rush to her bones in spite of the warm California sun pouring through the windows.

Her voice quivered. "Just like that?"

Jamie sighed, running a hand through his blond hair in frustration. It was a gesture she had seen many times, had *caused* many times, if she was honest with herself.

"What do you want me to do, Hallie, drop down on my knees and beg you to stay, to stop seeing that maniac? No, I'm done. Done with you, this marriage, and the farce it's become."

Pain shot through her skull like an iron lance. She'd had horrible headaches all her life, but this sense of fear enveloping her was new, the pain sharper. She dropped her head into her hands, and her thoughts scattered like ants on a trampled hill. Jamie's words were unintelligible, as if spoken through layers of gauze. Her body convulsed under tremors of cold, and she slid onto the tile floor, unable to stop herself from falling.

"Make it stop. Make it stop!" she cried out through a fog of pain.

The touch of Jamie's hand, tight on her arm, seemed to tingle, then disappear. She tried to move her hand, her arm. In sheer horror, she realized she could not. Black dots clouded her vision, and she heard her heartbeat slowing to nothing as the darkness closed in. She heard a whistling sound, like a faraway train. As the pain lessened, she welcomed the dark cloud of death as it took her away. Anything to make the pain go away.

CHAPTER 1

Hallie DiBarto had come back from the brink of death a changed woman. That in itself was not unusual. Coming back in a different body was.

And not just a different body, but a different life. Someone else's life. Marti, they kept calling her. Who was Marti? Hallie felt the surge of panic that enveloped her every time she realized that *she* was Marti. Before she'd had a chance to ask where Jamie was, or tell them they'd made a mistake in her identity, she realized something was terribly wrong.

She glanced down again at short fingers and stubby nails, at the body of a stranger. She took a deep breath, willing away the panic. How had she ended up in Chattaloo, Florida? In this bruised and aching body? She remembered dying as if it were years ago, remembered jagged pieces of a life in California. During her stay in the hospital, those memories melded together to form a past that did not coincide with what she'd found here.

She had never before been to Florida, been a brunette, or been short. She had never seen the tall man who helped her out of the wheelchair after they went through the hospital doors, watching her with a worried expression. The man who claimed to be her husband, Jesse.

Jesse's thick brown hair lifted in the fat breeze as they bid the doctor farewell and walked into humid sunshine. He was twenty-five years old; she'd seen his date of birth on a form. He studied her openly, and for that she could not blame him. After all, he'd been told that his wife had been assaulted, nearly raped, and hadn't spoken to anyone since the attack. She didn't know how the man with those dark green eyes would take her crazy story: that a tall, blue-eyed, blond stranger lived inside his wife's petite body. Hallie had to cling to the only truth she knew: that woman still existed.

For now, playing the part of silent trauma served her best. She looked to the cloud-riddled sky. *God, I know I've made mistakes. Okay, I was awful, hating myself and taking it out on the people closest to me. Looking back, I see how much anger I held inside me. Lord knows—okay, You know I haven't prayed often. But I guess you gave me this second chance—or is it punishment? I'm not sure yet. Give me a sign, God. Tell me what to do.*

It was not God who spoke, but Jesse.

"I don't know what's going on," he said, softer than she thought a man of his size could speak. He held out a hand to her. "But let me help you."

A sign? His hand remained in mid-air, unwavering as she contemplated. Then, very slowly, she reached a thin arm toward him. Somewhere deep inside her, down where she still existed, a small coal of warmth sparked to life as his fingers wrapped solidly around her own.

"The truck's parked over there."

She nodded, maintaining the silence that had seen her through the ordeal of being questioned by Deputy Thomas, the doctor, and Jesse. It bought her time, if nothing else. She stuck her finger in her mouth to nervously chew on a nail, but found with dismay she had none to chew; they were already clipped short. Jesse helped her climb into a dusty red pickup truck.

"Marti, if you want to talk about"—he glanced uneasily at her, then looked ahead—"what happened, I'm here. Dr. Toby said not to press you, and I won't." He reached over and grazed a spot on her cheek where she knew a violet bruise blossomed. "I want to make it better, but I don't know how. Tell me."

Give me back my body and my life! she wanted to scream out but clamped her lips shut instead. Keeping the panic from her eyes was harder than keeping her mouth shut. Could he see the confusion she saw whenever she looked in the mirror?

Jesse sighed as he turned back to the steering wheel and started the engine.

After spending most of her life nestled between the Pacific Ocean and the mountains of Southern California, the small town of Chattaloo seemed flat, boring. She picked at the lace on her jean shorts. A thin scar edged along the top of one knobby knee. How had that gotten there? She loosened the scarf Jesse had bought to hide the bruises around her neck. The sight of them had aroused a queer sense of fear in her, even though she had not suffered the attack herself.

Trying not to look overly interested, she pulled the worn-out wallet from the vinyl purse lying next to her. Not leather or alligator, but *vinyl*. Even when she was dirt poor, she at least owned leather. Maybe from the thrift store, but still. One library card and a driver's license. The brunette gave the camera a forced smile. Next to the photo read, "Marti Jeane May." Marti was twenty-three years old, four years younger than Hallie. Marti had an identity, a life, a husband. Now Hallie had those, and she didn't want them.

"Is anything missing?" Jesse asked, breaking into her thoughts.

A strangled laugh escaped, which she disguised as a sob. Only her life and identity! At his concerned look, she shook her head, keeping her silence.

The orange groves flanking the two-lane highway grew gradually into downtown Chattaloo. Tiny frame houses were snuggled under oak trees, kids raced each other on bicycles, and groups of teenagers gathered around trucks and Jeeps. Normal life, going on as if the strangest thing in the world hadn't just happened to her.

Jesse turned onto a dirt road. Distant barking materialized into one of the ugliest dogs she had ever seen, speckled, stocky, and, worse yet, large. It ran alongside the truck as they passed under a canopy of oak trees to a house in the middle of the hammock. Its tail was wagging, so that meant it wouldn't eat her ... she hoped.

The dog jumped all over Jesse when he got out of the truck, but he didn't seem to mind the grubby paws. He opened the passenger door and held out his hand, but she didn't move. The dog looked hungrily up at her, flinging its tail, heck, it's whole rear end, from side to side.

"What's wrong?" He followed her stare to the dog. "You're not afraid of ol' Bumpus, are you? You've been living with him for two weeks."

She opened her mouth to say something, then caught herself. Yes, she was afraid of ol' Bumpus. But that ugly dog was the least of her problems, she thought, trying to put him in perspective. Bumpus cocked his head, his wrinkled brow looking thoughtful as he waited for some acknowledgment. Jesse whistled, then gestured. Bumpus moved to where he pointed and sat down with a whine.

"He's just concerned about you, is all."

She took Jesse's outstretched hand and climbed down. He led her up the stone walkway to the small gray house washed pink by the dying sunlight. Bumpus followed, his tail wagging wildly as he sniffed around her ankles. She moved away, but he followed, trying to jump up in front of her.

"Bumpus, what's your problem?" Jesse turned to her. "Maybe he knows you're hurting."

Maybe he does, she thought, eyeing him. And maybe he knew she wasn't Marti.

Inside, the house looked larger than it seemed from the exterior. A ceiling fan whirred above, barely moving the wilted leaves of an ivy. Marti obviously hadn't had much of a chance to feminize the place, and a brief glance at Jesse left Hallie little doubt as to where the bride's time had been going. Probably enjoying marital bliss. He was a kicker, as she used to call the good-looking ones. In a country sort of way.

The blue plaid couch looked lumpy, but it reminded her how little sleep she had gotten last night. Jesse was watching her, perhaps thinking she might faint, cry or worse. She tried to put herself in his place.

His wife is almost raped and nearly strangled. When she wakes at the hospital, she is so traumatized, she appears not to recognize either him or the doctor. And she has not spoken a word since. He might reasonably expect her to fling herself out the nearest window.

"You look tired," he said.

Again, he held out that large strong hand of his. She only hesitated a moment before reaching out and letting him lead her someplace where she could hopefully let sleep wrap her in the comfort of familiarity. Would she dream Hallie dreams or Marti dreams? The thought was disturbing.

He led her to a room that held a king-size bed, one long dresser and not much else. She sat on the edge of the bed while he dug through a disorganized drawer and pulled out a long nightgown splattered with blue flowers. She hadn't worn a nightgown like that since she was five years old, but she wasn't in the mood to be picky.

He stood by the door, shifting from one foot to the other.

"Do you want me to sleep on the couch tonight?"

It took an effort for her jumbled mind to put together what he meant. Well, of course, if he and Marti were married, they slept in that king-size bed together. The thought of his body lying next to her was unsettling. A stranger who might hold her in his arms. He wouldn't expect anything more, not after what she'd been through. Still, she wrapped her arms around herself and nodded.

There was a strange light in his eyes, deep and protective. "If you need anything, anything at all, let me know."

But he didn't leave. "I know you're not in a talkative mood, but can I ask you something? Why haven't you asked about the baby? Even Dr. Toby expected you'd be freaked out, worried."

She could only give him a blank expression. Was there a baby in the house?

His shoulders drooped, and he stepped closer. "Don't you even remember that you're pregnant?"

She slid off the edge and fell into a heap on the dark green carpet. "P ... pregnant?" she croaked out, then realized she'd broken her silence.

Jesse pulled her to her feet and helped her back on the bed. His green eyes held a mixture of confusion and surprise. He still gripped her hands in his, kneeling in front of her.

"Thank God you can still talk." He gently touched the bruises that ringed her neck, causing an aching tingle. "Dr. Toby was worried that your vocal cords were damaged." He removed his hand and looked intently at her. "Did you really forget about the baby?"

Her stomach flip-flopped as she tried her best to compose herself. Could he tell her hands were shaking within the confines of his grasp? She took a deep breath, hoping for some divine intervention in the form of a really good reason his revelation had shocked her into talking. Damn, but this complicates matters, even more than they were!

"The past is muddled right now," she whispered in a hoarse, strange voice. Her hand slipped from his and touched her nearly flat stomach. "Are you sure?"

"I'm sure. You're only two months pregnant. Didn't Dr. Toby tell you that the baby was all right?"

She shrugged. "She might have, I don't know. My head was spinning most of the time." She covered her mouth. "Oh gawd, I'm pregnant."

"Maybe I'd better call Dr.—"

"No," she blurted out. "I ... I'll be fine. Really. Just give me some time."

"Time," he repeated with a nod. "I'll give you time. But this not remembering stuff is scary, Marti. Maybe your brain was deprived of oxygen for too long."

"My brain is fine." It was, wasn't it? She did some math problems in her head. Remembered a joke about a priest and a frog in a bar. Her first kiss in third grade, her self-absorbed mother. She shuddered. She'd sure like to forget that woman.

"Are you sure you're okay?"

He'd been watching her ruminations, no doubt. She nodded, then walked into the adjacent bathroom so he wouldn't see the panic in her eyes. Her heart sank when she saw the stranger in the mirror. She had looked at that reflection a hundred times in the last day and a half, but it was always the same. The swelling was going down, making the purple bruises look more pronounced. There was one bruise, or mark really, that was different from the others. It looked like a sideways V with two little marks below it. The skin was broken where a sharp object had dug in.

Oh, how I wish this were all a nightmare, and if I screamed, I would wake up in my bedroom with pounding heart and realize it was all over. Then I'd just be back to worrying about the obsessive, crazy Mick. But it's not a nightmare, is it? She'd pinched herself so many times red marks lined her arm.

She had to remember a life she had not participated in. Or run like hell from this place. But run where? Home to her husband, Jamie, and tell him that she had somehow gotten herself into the body of another woman, a *pregnant* woman?

She thought of Jamie, her real husband back in her real life. It had been two months since then for him, where she had lived in some abyss. She couldn't dare to hope that he missed her. And she couldn't dare blame him if he didn't.

***

Jesse flipped on the television and settled onto the couch. The room was dark except for the bluish glow from the set. Two weeks ago, he had married a woman he hardly knew because she had manipulated him into getting her pregnant.

He couldn't deny the protective instincts this attack on her aroused, but he didn't much like them. Could she have staged the whole thing to elicit sympathy from him? He shook his head. No, Marti wasn't gutsy enough to pull off something like that.

Through the night, he kept moving, twisting, sighing deeply every time he realized he wasn't asleep. It didn't take much to put him on alert, even the sound of quiet footsteps walking past him and the *snick* of the front door. Had he really heard Marti go outside alone, after what she'd been through?

Swinging to an upright position, he eyed the digital clock: 5:49. He located his jeans and slid into them as he walked toward the window. He spotted her silhouette on one of the swings that hung from the large oak tree out front.

She was slumped over, using her toe in the dirt to move slowly back and forth. He watched her for a while, trying to imagine what it would feel like to be overpowered and attacked in such a vicious way. He couldn't. What he really wanted to do was find the son of a bitch and rip him apart. His hand clenched with the need for that, the fury.

He glanced at the clock again: 6:10. He wasn't going to let her wallow in self-doubt or whatever else she was dealing with any longer. He walked out into the damp foggy morning.

"What the devil are you doing out here by yourself?"

She shrugged, staring down at the toe that kept her swing moving. He dropped down in the swing next to hers. They sat in silence as the early morning glow filtered through the oak trees. She looked at him for a few minutes, studying him. He held her gaze, wishing he could read her eyes. There was something different about her, but of course, there would be, given what she'd gone through.

"Do you believe in God?"

He narrowed his eyes. "Sure, I do. Do you?"

"I do now."

"You think it was God who helped you get away from the … creep who attacked you?"

"It's a lot more complicated than that."

He wasn't following her, but he wanted her to get out her anxieties. "Sometimes near-death experiences bring people closer to God, or give them religion when they didn't have it before."

She laughed, a strange thick sound. "I'm not talking about a near-death experience." She pressed a clenched fist against her lips. "What do you think happens to people when they die?"

"They go to Heaven. Or hell." He shrugged. "But you didn't die."

"Do you think it's really cut and dried like that? I

mean, is your only choice Heaven or hell, or is there another option?"

He crinkled his eyebrows. "Catholics believe in Purgatory, so I guess that's a possibility."

She studied him again, as if weighing whether to go on. Then she took a deep breath. "What if a person dies, but they don't go to Heaven or hell. They wake up and are alive … but it isn't their body they're in anymore."

"Marti, you're not making sense."

"Humor me. *If* that happened, what would you think had occurred?"

Something had gotten knocked loose in her brain. "It couldn't happen."

She bit her bottom lip, shaking her head. "I knew you wouldn't understand."

"Marti, what you're saying is crazy. It would be incredible, amazing."

"But God can do anything, right?"

"I guess, sure. But things like that don't happen."

"Yes, they do. Something crazy, incredible, and amazing happened to me. I don't know why, but it did." She took a deep breath, muttering what he thought was, "'Cause I sure didn't deserve it." She spoke louder and enunciated each word, as though he were slow. "I am not Marti. My name is Hallie DiBarto, I'm from California, and I'm married to a man named Jamie."

She might as well have been speaking a foreign language as far as he was concerned. It had to be delirium. Encouraged by his silence, she continued.

"Two months ago, something happened inside my brain, and I died. I think God gave me a second chance here, in this body, this life." She gestured vaguely around her.

There was no hint of craziness about her, no odd light in her eyes, but she was sure talking crazy.

"You've been through a lot. It's just the stress—"

She stood and faced him, taking the chains of his swing in her hands. "It is not stress. I know it sounds crazy, it *is* crazy." Her voice dropped to a whisper. "But it's true."

"Wait a minute, let me understand this." He ran his fingers through disheveled hair, trying to make his brain understand. "You're saying that you're someone totally different in Marti's body?" He was trying to put it together, but it sounded so ... she had the right word: crazy. "That you died and came back in Marti's body?"

"That's what I'm saying."

He stood and paced a few feet before turning to face her. She dropped into her swing again and twisted nervously, watching his reaction.

"If you're really some woman from California, then where's Marti?"

She touched the bruises around her neck. "I don't know. She must be dead."

"Nolen Rivers swore you were dead when he found you by the side of the road, but—no, it's crazy. I'm calling Dr. Toby—"

"No!" she said as loud as her hoarse voice could manage. "There's nothing she can do about it. Do you think I'd make something like this up?"

"The problem is you believe it."

She looked so fragile, sitting on the swing with desperation in her eyes. Like a battered doll. But it couldn't be true. Yet, it could explain why she didn't know she was pregnant. And why she didn't look at him with annoying adoration the way she had before the attack. He shook his head.

She stood and crossed her arms over her chest. "Well, it doesn't matter if you believe me or not, I won't be around much longer anyway."

He realized then that the woman before him was like a stranger. Those were not Marti's words. "What do you mean by that? Where are you going?"

"Probably home to California. I can't stay here. I'm married to someone else, for Pete's sake, and I don't even know you."

Those words made him smile. "You didn't know me before the attack either, doll." The endearment had slipped by.

She relaxed her tensed shoulders. "What do you mean?"

He shrugged. "I hardly knew you before we had sex. It just sorta happened, and you said you were on the pill to make your periods lighter. A month later, you were pregnant. That was two weeks ago."

She seemed to absorb that. "She tricked you into getting her pregnant?"

"*You* tricked me into getting you pregnant. At least you finally admitted it."

She let out a sound of exasperation. "I'm not admitting it. As bad as I was, I would never has used a baby to snag a guy."

"Marti, enough of this bizarre conversation. Let's go inside."

Thank you for reading this sneak peek of *Stranger in the Mirror*. Find links to it and all of Tina's novels at www.

WrittenMusings.com/
TinaWainscott or www.TinaWainscott.com.

ABOUT THE AUTHOR

I hope you enjoyed *Until I Die Again*! If you did, I'm happy to tell you that I have many other novels available for your pleasure in different subgenres of romance. I'm a *New York Times* and *USA Today* bestselling author of more than thirty novels published with St. Martin's Press, Harper Collins, Random House, Harlequin, and Written Musings.

I have always loved the combination of suspenseful chills and romantic thrills, especially with a bit of paranormal thrown in, so I decided to release my favorites in the Love & Light Collection. Although many of the stories have connections to other books in the series, all the novels are stand-alone stories—no cliffhangers!

Find the entire collection at
www.WrittenMusings.com/TinaWainscott
and www.TinaWainscott.com

Printed in Great Britain
by Amazon

17238446R00219